The Maelstrom

♦ ♦ ♦

By

David Cone

1663 Liberty Drive, Suite 200
Bloomington, Indiana 47403
(800) 839-8640
www.AuthorHouse.com

This book is a work of fiction. People, places, events, and situations are the product of the author's imagination. Any resemblence to actual persons, living or dead, or historical events, is purely coincidental.

First published by AuthorHouse 01/14/05

ISBN: 1-4208-1368-4 (sc)

Library of Congress Control Number: 2004098905

Printed in the United States of America
Bloomington, Indiana

This book is printed on acid-free paper.

To Mom and Dad,
For all they gave their children

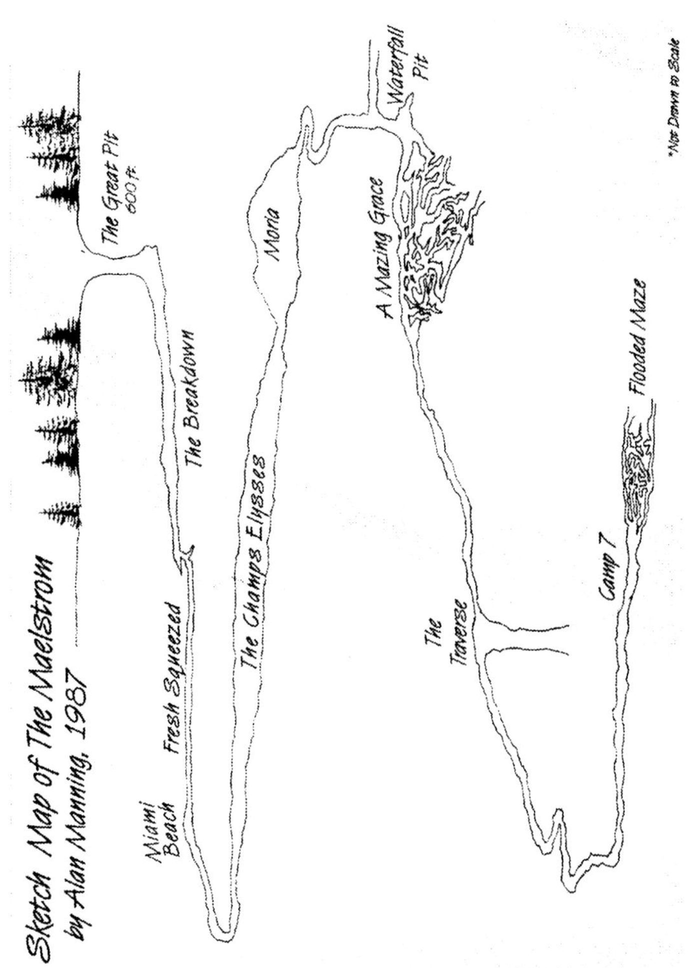
Sketch Map of The Maelstrom
by Alan Manning, 1987
The Great Pit
600 ft.
Miami
Beach
Fresh Squeezed
The Breakdown
The Champs Elysses
Moria
Waterfall
Pit
A Mazing Grace
The
Traverse
Camp 7
Flooded Maze
*Not Drawn to Scale

PROLOGUE

High on a wind-blasted glacier, a tent glows warmly while inside, alpinists tell of their experiences on the great peaks...Everest, Nanga Parbat, K-2. In the valley of Yosemite, with camp stoves roaring through the pine-scented starry night around them, climbers laugh and commiserate about their adventures on the big walls of legend...El Cap, the Moose's Tooth, the Polar Sun Spire. Around a blazing campfire deep within the Great Smoky Mountains, paddlers tell of their narrow escapes and moments of calm reflection on the great whitewater runs...Section IV, the Iron Ring of the Gaulley, the Devil's Washbowl. And in a tiny chamber, deep beneath the mountains, the rivers, and the big walls, a small group sits around a lantern and talks of the great cave systems. But when someone mentions the Maelstrom, voices trail off to silence. One person sits looking awkwardly at his hands; another traces little drawings in the sand with her finger. There are no funny stories about the Maelstrom.

It is the Everest of alpinists, the Polar Sun Spire of big wall climbers, the Iron Ring of whitewater paddlers. It is not the deepest nor the longest nor the most difficult. But it has all these qualities to a high degree, and it has a chilling, staggering list of defenses.

* * *

The water lay quiet in the tunnel's blackness. Untold eons of time had passed in dark silence without so much as a ripple to disturb the water's surface. But something was coming, sending out before it waves of fear and panic. A man's head and torso exploded through the water's mirror surface. His lungs were burning, screaming for air. Deep within the cavern, his racking gasps echoed from walls where no sound had ever been. His headlamp showed dimly across a watery surface that had never known light. Two companions were somewhere in the labyrinth of flooded passages behind him. Somehow he had lost them and by now they must be dead.

The man clambered out of the water onto a sloping beach. He had only postponed his own death. There were so many possibilities, he thought. Hypothermia? He was soaking wet and shivering. Maybe starvation. There was perhaps two days' food supply in his pack. And behind door number three, Mr. Stickley? Death by a major fall when your lamp burns out! He pulled a dirty but dry pair of coveralls from his waterproof pack and took stock of his assets...matches, candles, spare batteries, a little food.

He was trapped! The flooded passages blocked his way back to the explored parts of the cavern. It didn't matter how many air tanks he had, it was a Pacific Ocean. His only chance of survival was to find some other way out.

Very soon!

For the first time, the man inspected his surroundings. A rim of rock rose at his back and beyond that, a blue glow emanated like an alien sun setting behind a bank of clouds. He rose unsteadily and walked to the top of the rock mass, piled layer upon layer in front of him. As he reached the top, all thoughts of death and escape left him. Before him lay a vista the like of which no man had ever seen.

A room of incredible dimensions stretched far into the distance. Its vaulted ceiling was supported by countless massive columns and hung with thousands, millions of stalactites. But most incredible was the blue light that seemed to cover every formation. Curtains and flowstones seemed to shimmer with blue motion. Lit with this ethereal light, he could see formations that seemed a mile away. And centered in this cathedral of light was a lake, an inland sea whose mirror surface reflected the thousands of lights above it like a blue, starry night.

The man stowed his gear and walked forward toward the lake shore, moving carefully down a steep slope. Just to his right a large stalactite was a solid mass of light, not just laced here and there like most of the formations. He walked into its aura, and reached out tentatively.

At his touch, the stalactite seemed to flow like viscous water down his arm and quickly engulfed him in the cool, blue flame of its light. He desperately wiped at himself, dropping large masses into a quivering, glowing pile at his feet. Disgusted, he began to walk toward the lake in order to wash thoroughly. The man slipped in the blue mass, now covering himself completely and frantically wiping thick masses from his mouth and eyes.

Hours later, he sat shivering but clean near a small candle and ate two energy bars. 'Pretty funny', he remarked, 'I'm starting to glow just like all you guys.' Deep under his skin, there was indeed a faint glow, but it didn't really bother him. As he fell asleep, he began to fantasize about walking through the cavern with no lantern. He would be his own candle, his own sun and moon in this unexplored universe.

He was very weak in the morning, and all of his joints were hurting. Toes and fingers, ankles, wrists, even in his rib cage and skull. He stood to walk away from his little camp and relieve himself. The man took only two steps and fell forward. One hand flew out to break his fall, and he screamed in pain as he felt bones breaking. Not just one bone, but every little bone in his left hand and wrist. His hand was an almost shapeless mass of tissue and broken fragments. His face hit the rock, smashing a cheekbone into dozens of pieces. Flashes of pain rolled through him as muscle and sinew were torn by bone fragments.

He stood again, but his legs would not support him. He crashed to his knees, which shattered like the corpse of a fluorescent bulb. His torso buckled, there was a last shot of intense pain as the spinal column disintegrated, and the man tried to breathe once more, his heart to beat one more beat. But there was no framework to support muscles and movement. A gurgling sound rose from what had been a throat, and the man mercifully died. His face, his whole body began to lose definition, until disengaged tissue, clothing, and a watch were all that remained.

* * *

The Maelstrom is not a malevolent, sentient creature; but people have died in its grasp.

And it is about to kill again.

CHAPTER ONE
1987

Alan Manning was more than halfway down the Great Pit of the Maelstrom...and yet there was another two hundred feet to go. It was hard to get a proper perspective of the pit's true size. It would easily swallow any office building in Atlanta. But when Alan looked below him, his headlamp could only pick out the kernmantle rope that hung dangling into the black depths. Just as well, he thought. Nobody in their right mind would go into this pit if they could see all the way to the bottom.

Two hundred feet below, Drew Cisco waited for him. Not patiently, Alan supposed. His friend and fellow spelunker for the last two years, Drew was usually like a crazed horse straining at the traces. Well, he was just going to have to strain a while longer.

Alan had been on the rope for more than forty-five minutes. High time for a break! He dropped his right leg straight down and wrapped the rope around twice, moving the loops to his upper thigh and bringing his leg back to a 'sitting' position. With this added friction, he was able to free both hands and relax.

Manning spun slowly like a spider on a very long thread, his lanky arms and legs dangling in repose. As he turned, the headlamp shone on walls of a thirty foot wide tubular pit. The fine-grained, gray limestone, stained by years of falling surface water, was layered with much thinner strips of sandstone. These layers were tilted, so that they seemed to spiral downward toward the bottom of the pit, an effect that had led partially to the cavern's name. The Maelstrom of geography, swirling crosscurrents and rip tides that are part of Norwegian sailing legend, was thought to be the gateway to the interior of the Earth. Or perhaps to another world entirely. In 1987, no one knew how prophetically the Maelstrom had been named.

Alan reached awkwardly behind him and groped inside his knapsack for a pack of cheese crackers. He tried unsuccessfully to open the wrapper and finally tore it apart with his teeth. The first cracker fumbled out of the package and promptly fell two hundred feet. His headlamp off to conserve batteries, Alan spun slowly in the tenebrous space surrounding him. The twenty-five foot opening to the Great Pit shown above him like a receding spotlight, its shaft of light dispersed too soon to reach him. With no other light, the distant opening was Alan's only reference point. There was no visual hint of the bottom of the pit, or even its sides.

"Hey, Pancho!" The voice came drifting weakly from two hundred feet below. Alan smiled to himself.

"Hey, Ceesco!" Two years earlier, Drew's exploits and nerve while exploring a system in North Georgia had earned him the moniker of 'the Cisco Kid' among his spelunking friends. The exchange had become a call sign between Alan and him.

"You're not eating cheese crackers up there, are you? Not when you should be working your tired butt down that rope."

"You're giving me grief because I shared a cracker with you?"

"Share, hell! Do you know the final velocity of a cheese cracker when it hits down here? Atoms! That's what I got here. Cheese cracker atoms."

"Stop whining, Drew. I'm on my way down."

"Could you give it a little speed?"

Alan didn't dignify the request with an answer. Six hundred foot descents are no place for fast, showy abseils. An abseil (what most people think of as a 'rappel') of six hundred feet at speed could build up such heat that there was a serious risk of damage to equipment.

Alan moved down the rope on automatic pilot. Rather than the simple brake bar and carabiner or the figure eight favored by 'rappelers' on the surface, Alan used a series of bars set across a large open rectangle of metal. His single 10.5 millimeter perlon rope wound over and under these bars, giving so much friction that Alan would have to eliminate some bars in order to go fast at all. This hardware was attached to a central carabiner that was in turn the point of attachment for a seat harness and a chest harness. The two harnesses kept Alan in a sitting position relative to the rope. Of course, there wasn't enough friction to keep him from moving at all, and this meant that Alan still had to control his descent simply by moving the rope out and away from him or by bringing it in closer to him.

Above his descending hardware and its point of attachment to his harness, Alan had placed a Gibbs descender. The device slips easily down the rope until weight is applied to it. Then its rounded teeth jam tightly... so tightly that Alan didn't like to rest by putting weight on it. But if equipment failed or if he were to become unconscious, the Gibbs would hold securely. Everything Alan did...climbing, teaching, investing... had a Gibbs of some sort, something he could depend on if the main system failed.

On the other hand, Drew couldn't be bothered with back-ups. He climbed with long, dizzying lead-outs on tenuous chock placements. Drew would be down a rope while Alan was still checking out the anchors. It was an approach to high-risk activities that Alan couldn't understand, and was a sore point between two otherwise close friends.

Twenty minutes later Alan touched down at ground zero and looked above him. They had traded the spangled heavens of Earth for a dark starless canopy, in which the opening of the Great Pit, far above, showed like a single sickly star.

Alan's headlamp picked out his friend a few feet away. Drew Cisco didn't have what Alan thought of as a spelunker's build. Drew was short and stocky, and the long stretches that Alan could do so easily were difficult for him. Silhouetted by someone else's lamp, Drew Cisco reminded Alan of an ambulatory boulder. He was 'Mutt' to Alan's 'Jeff'. Where Alan had sandy hair and serious blue-gray eyes, Drew was dark-complexioned, with black hair and dark eyes that danced with mischief. He had, in fact, a boyish quality in a face that was almost always lit with an infectious grin. Whatever disadvantages his build may have given him were more than compensated by a lionesque strength, enthusiasm, and plain grit.

Alan tossed his pack and gear bag on the ground and lay down on a slab of rock. He breathed a sigh of relief and studied the scene above them.

"Why do I feel like a cockroach at the bottom of a long bathroom drain?"

Drew tossed a clutch of brake bars and carabiners at him. "Because you are a cockroach! Come on, let's make Camp 2."

"Camp 2! Camp damn 2! You crazy bastard! Do you know how far that is? I was counting on a total collapse at Camp 1!"

Alan stood up and reassembled his gear while Drew started out. "Hey! I got an idea," Alan shouted as he hurried to catch up. "Why don't we just bust ass all the way to Camp 7 and then head back out? We could save a lot of time. I mean, hell, we don't have to look at any formations or enjoy ourselves. Man, I bet we could be out of here and at a Pizza Hut by midnight."

"Okay!" Drew grumbled, "Camp 1 it is. Does everybody get as testy as you when they hit the big 3-0?"

"I'd just like to look around while we're down here, but you've got a freight train mentality going on. Remind me never to tour the Louvre with you."

"The Louvre? I could do that in twenty minutes flat." Drew turned and started to pick his way through the Breakdown, a long hall strewn with broken, jagged plates of limestone. They were piled up like jackstraws, and constantly threatened to tip or catch an ankle in a crunching grip.

The Breakdown reminded Alan of a storm-swept sea, flash frozen and placed in the Maelstrom as yet another barrier. On the surface, in the full light of day, no one would hike through such a minefield...three hundred yards of accidents waiting to happen. In some cave systems, a trail could be found in an area such as the Breakdown due to the traffic of many spelunkers. In the Maelstrom, few had the equipment or commitment to descend the Great Pit. Of those who did, their resolve often melted after only a few minutes in the Breakdown.

In front of him, Drew appeared and disappeared, rose and fell as he negotiated the crazy quilt of rock slabs. "I always get the ominous feeling these rocks just fell," Drew called back, "Like within the last six months."

Alan stopped for a moment to look at the ceiling above them, spreading his arms to keep his balance on the steep slope of a large wedge of limestone. "The accepted wisdom is that it takes about a century to produce a cubic inch of stalactite. It's only a general yardstick, but using that, I'd estimate it's been five thousand years since the Breakdown was formed. Can you imagine being in this hall when that ceiling let go? It would be incredible...the noise, the choking dust."

"The deaths!" Drew shook his head. "So these have been lying here since the Pharaohs? Time sort of stands still down here, you know? Everything's in slow motion." He jumped across a five foot gap and landed with perfect balance on another chunk of former ceiling.

"Cept you, of course! Wait up, Drew!"

When Alan caught up with him, it was only because Drew had come to an apparent dead end. The gallery ceiling sloped down more and more until finally it wasn't possible to stand upright. To the uninitiated, the gallery had come to an end. Even those who knew about the small crack hidden behind some boulders would not consider going farther. Alan had discovered the opening ten years earlier as a college student majoring in geology. The two-foot opening gave way to a vertical tunnel fifteen feet deep. It was the true portal to the Maelstrom.

While Alan repacked his gear in preparation for the ordeal ahead, Drew walked a few feet away and then returned, carrying a piece of four-inch PVC pipe with a screw-on lid. Pulling out a small, bound registry, he penciled in his own and Alan's name and checked 'Yes' under a column headed 'Going On?' On the first page of the registry was a letter written by Alan two years earlier...the first trip he and Drew had made together into the Maelstrom.

"Entry into Fresh Squeezed requires a head-first descent and two hundred yards on your stomach. You cannot turn around until you hit Miami Beach and you cannot back up the vertical shaft unassisted. One or two members of your party should remain here until the others make sure the way is clear. This may take three hours, but it is time well spent. A group of people trying to back out of Fresh Squeezed is your worst nightmare."

Drew replaced the journal and put the container back in its rocky niche. "You know, pal, if you're trying to scare people out of the Maelstrom with this, its working. No one has signed in past this point in almost a year."

"I just want people to know what they're buying into."

"You didn't have a warning letter ten years ago. Pass the food over."

Alan handed Drew a package of pilot biscuits, a tube of peanut butter, and some summer sausage. "No, no letter. As far as I know, I was the first down that shaft. That's one of the rushes when you're exploring caves...to enter a passage or a room where no human has ever been." Alan was lowering his pack into the shaft ahead of him. "You ready?"

"Yeah, but try to move things along. I don't want to stare at your size twelve Vibrams the whole way."

Alan looked back before he started into the small rift that marked the beginning of the crawlspace. "Do your English students know what a damn marathon man you are?"

"Just ask them how much material we cover in a semester," Drew grinned.

Alan had learned that the best way down the vertical tunnel was a controlled fall of sorts. His daypack, made of cordura nylon and leather, was designed for abuse. Alan repeatedly dropped it down the shaft before him. The rest of his caving gear was in a duffel bag attached to his ankle, where it became intricately involved with his feet during the descent. In only a matter of minutes, Alan had reached the beginning of the horizontal stretch and pushed his pack into the space ahead of him.

Dragging his gear bag behind him, he moved forward twenty feet and waited. With Drew's shorter arms and heavier build, it would take him longer to negotiate the shaft. Alan switched off his light and laid quietly, his head resting on his folded arms. This was part of his mental preparation for the long ordeal in front of him. He could sense the rock only a foot above his head. Almost any caver could handle the physical aspects of going through Fresh Squeezed, but many were just not mentally prepared for the experience. Alan had his own little tricks that would take his mind off morbid thoughts of shifting rocks and blocked passages. Grabbing little catnaps was one of them.

His reverie was broken by what Drew considered a cockney accent. A Monty Python freak, Alan thought. Why me, Lord?

"Aw right then, laydies and gents. I 'ope you're enjoyin' this here tour of the body 'uman. We are in roight now what you might call your small intestine. You'll find yourself makin' ever so much better progress if you just slither along. A litt'l role playin', you moight say."

"Do I have to listen to your lousy cockney again?" Alan complained

Drew ignored him. "Wait a mo', folks! What's this ahead? Looks like a bloomin' blockage of some sort. Oh, this is a bit o'luck! This here, roight in front of me, is your classic piece of..."

"Shut up, Drew!"

"Lor, as I live an' breathe, its sentient shit. I 'ave 'ardly seen a finer specimen...except for some, of course, as you might find in high political office. 'Tho we can 'ardly call them 'sentient' now can we? I'll just see if I can poke this specimen a mite and get it to move along the passage, as it were. Lor', but they can be slow."

"All right, I'm moving already." Alan switched on his light and started out as Drew's insane drivel receded.

"You'll want to stay back, lad. These sentient type shits can have a real temper, you know."

It was not crawling, for there was no room to go on hands and knees. It was not even a classic military stomach crawl, because they couldn't bring a leg up to one side and push forward. The only effective technique involved shoving the pack ahead and pulling forward using whatever purchase could be found with hands, knees, and feet. After thirty minutes, Alan's leg and back muscles were demanding some other position...any other position. But the limestone ceiling continued to stretch relentlessly forward. In some places, the men were able to turn on their sides for a few minutes of freedom.

Drew dealt with the mental challenge of the crawlspace by reciting every line he knew from 'Monty Python and the Holy Grail' or singing snatches from 'American Pie'. Of necessity, this became Alan's diversion also. But to Drew's background accompaniment, Alan enjoyed watching the panorama of fossils just inches away from his face. There was nothing large, for when the ancient sea laid down the material that would become limestone, there were no dinosaurs, no land animals, no large marine animals. But the walls and ceiling of the crawlspace were littered with the fossils of small invertebrates...bivalve mollusks, snails, and corals. Some of the better specimens had become landmarks to Alan, mileposts by which he could measure their progress through Fresh Squeezed.

Two hundred feet of physical tedium and mental exhaustion accumulated as the floor crept slowly underneath them. Now the ceiling took a sudden dip. Alan closed his eyes and sighed. Despite his many trips through Fresh Squeezed, he was never quite prepared for the Maelstrom's next defense. He removed his helmet and placed it on the floor in front of him, tilting his head sideways. The ceiling had dipped to only twelve inches, and would remain so for forty feet. The interior of the mountain now pressed down only three inches above their heads. Their arms had to remain straight in front of them, for there was little room to draw them back. Inch by inch ground into feet, the men pulling along by fingerholds on the rough floor. One foot, then two. The limestone just six inches from their faces. Ten pulls and then rest.

Alan looked down past his feet in Drew's direction. "You're mighty quiet back there, Ceesco."

"Not enough room for extra words, Pancho."

"Not much further. Then we can lift our heads for a while."

Another hour and Alan Manning spilled out of the crawlspace into a spacious room with a ten foot ceiling. The floor was covered with clean sand and spotted here and there with blocks of limestone. A small stream gathered in pools on the far side and dashed along a tunnel. After the numbing confinement of the crawlspace, the room had seemed so luxurious that Drew had dubbed it 'Miami Beach'. Alan stood up, tottered for a couple of steps, and promptly fell into the sand. Drew was spewed out a few moments later and lay spread eagled beside him.

"That was great, man! Just a lot of fun, Alan. Is there anything we left back in the Breakdown 'cause I'd like to go through that puppy again."

"We've got everything anybody would want six hundred feet underground." Alan struck a match and lit a small Gaz lantern fueled by a butane canister. The chamber was flooded with a soft light that seemed to chase away the shadowy memories of the crawlspace misery. Another Gaz canister fueled a small one burner stove on which Alan had placed a pot of water. Each of them had a thin blanket inside a nylon bivouac sack. Drew had rolled these out and was sprawled on one of them, looking up at the ceiling above them. “No stars out tonight! And I can’t hear the surf. You sure this is Miami Beach?”

“You’re confusing this with another Miami Beach, Drew.” Alan tossed a ziplock bag at him. “Have some dried fruit while the shells and cheese are cooking.”

“You’re right! There are bats here. Hardly any bats on the other Miami Beach.”

Alan leaned back against a slab of limestone. “How are Meg and the boys doing?”

“Fine! They’re visiting her folks at a real beach this weekend.”

Alan passed Drew a plate of steaming macaroni and some hard rolls. “Hard to divide your time, isn’t it?”

“Man, you get pulled in so many directions! Things I want to do, time for Meg and me, time for all of us together, time for the in-laws. Oh, and time to teach college students English Literature. It’s a real balancing act.”

“Have you taken the boys caving yet?” Alan asked as he put water on to boil for the tea.

“Scott’s too young, but Winner...”

“Winner?”

“My pet name for Winston. He’s ten and I’ve taken him in a couple of easy ones.” The two were silent for a few moments, each with their own thoughts.

“You’ve been out of that race for a while, haven’t you?” Drew finished his plate of macaroni and sopped it with another hard roll. “You know, juggling schedules and all.”

“Yup. Free as a bird. Divorce is the great liberator. Lets you go caving anytime you want.” Alan passed some aromatic Red Zinger tea over to Drew. "But you pay a lot for the freedom.

"Alimony?"

Alan sipped his tea thoughtfully. "Loneliness."

Drew turned off his lantern and climbed into a bivy sack. Alan sat cradling the cup of hot tea. "See you when the bats come in, Alan."

CHAPTER TWO

At 6:30 in the morning, the bats returned from their nocturnal foraging. Their strident squeaking awakened Alan as surely as any alarm clock. He lay in his bivvy sack, fascinated as always with the total darkness.

Eyes closed...darkness

Eyes open...same darkness

Open, closed...there was no difference. Alan passed his hand just inches over his face.

Nothing. Absolute visual deprivation. The darkness was so complete, so unyielding, that it almost seemed to be something, like air or water. A material substance that you could spoon aside or pack into a bag, lessening its effect. Except for a faint dripping from the stream at the other end of the chamber, there was also total audio deprivation. Although he had done it hundreds of times, waking up in a cave always amazed Alan.

Geology was his chosen profession, and his love of caves had led him to it. He had taken his undergraduate degree at the University of Georgia in Athens and then attended the Colorado School of Mines for his graduate studies. Only five years earlier, Alan Manning had returned to the University of Georgia to assume a teaching position in the geology department. In that time, he had gained a national reputation for his expertise in speleothems, the infinite variety of formations found in caverns.

Alan turned on his side and looked in Drew's general direction, as if he might penetrate the ink that surrounded them. Still asleep, he guessed. Maybe they wouldn't have to start out at the crack of ...what? Dawn? Drew had been awed by the beauty of the cave those first few trips that he and Alan had made together. But now he breezed past the formations and the geology, looking only for the challenges. Drew had originally been a climber, but tired of 5.13 finger-jammed laybacks. He and Alan had met at a faculty barbecue for new instructors. Drew was in his first year teaching English Literature while Alan had just been named an associate professor. They were drawn together by their mutual abhorrence of standing around with a wine glass trying to make conversation. The next weekend found them in the Maelstrom together.

Drew was a great companion, always looking at the upside of any situation. He was dependable and knowledgeable, but he attacked any activity as a personal and physical challenge. Drew had simply traded in his climbing chocks for a headlamp, but went about both in the same tireless attack mode.

Alan felt in the sand around him for a few pieces of limestone and tossed them in Drew's direction. A sleepy stretch sounded from the darkness.

"Sky's falling, Chicken Little," Drew mumbled.

"I figured I'd be the one to wake you up, just for the novelty of it."

Drew crawled out of his bivvy sack and lit his headlamp. Immediately, the seeming corporeal darkness rushed away to hide in the far reaches of the room, behind and under boulders. The light of one headlamp had transformed Miami Beach into a normal room in a normal cave.

"Okay. I'm up. If you'll excuse me, I have some business to attend." Drew removed a PVC container from his pack, not unlike the one that contained the register at the beginning of Fresh Squeezed. With toilet paper and plastic bags in hand, he disappeared behind a large limestone block. Double bagging human excrement had long been proper etiquette on high glaciated peaks like Rainier and Shasta. Without this process, such highly populated peaks would be dotted with cold-storage turds that would never decompose in the eternally frozen landscapes. By using one plastic bag as a glove and then turning it inside out, waste material could be neatly disposed. A second bag served as insurance. There was nothing much that could be done about urine, except to dig a little cat hole and hope that the filtering system of the earth would do its job.

Among true speleophiles, impact on the fragile environment of a cave system needed to be zero, if at all possible. Not only did Drew and Alan take precautions with their 'toilet', but their meals were eaten on paper plates. After use, these were torn in pieces and put into a ziplock bag. Their hot meals were in boiling bags or cooking pouches so that no pan had to be dirtied and subsequently washed.

"Pretty slack," Drew called out. "No magazines back here! You want me to leave the shitsafe out for you?"

"Yeah, thanks. I've got some breakfast laid out. I kind of figured you didn't want to take time to cook anything."

The two men sat in the light of their lantern, conserving their headlamps. Bread, cheese, dried fruit, and Tang made for a quick meal. There would be no lunch...just an occasional energy bar or a piece of hard candy. In less than twenty minutes, Alan and Drew had packed their bags and were heading out of Miami Beach. With Fresh Squeezed behind them, the men were able to tie their gear bags onto their day packs, leaving their hands free.

From Miami Beach the little stream flowed noisily through a rough-hewn corridor. It was fairly easy walking, not much different than walking along a mountain stream at night. Large columns, formed by the grafting of stalactite and stalagmite, bordered the stream in an imitation of trees. From the ceiling, large stalactites hung in massive but oddly graceful symmetry. Long tubular soda straws grew in thick clusters, so delicate that the brush of a spelunker's helmet could wipe out centuries of accumulation. But these were formations with which both men were familiar, and they tended to walk by them as they would small trees and common wildflowers in a forest. There was appreciation of the speleothems at some level, but it was a passive, almost unconscious acceptance of them.

After little more than a hundred yards, the small corridor began to pitch downward more steeply. The stream that they had been following suddenly dove into a small fissure, falling noisily into unknown depths. The gentle incline became a steeper gully with a high ceiling, forcing the men to finally climb down...what Drew would call a class 4 scramble. No ropes were needed, but hands were required for balance. The last thirty feet were vertical. It didn't take much imagination to realize that a stream had once flowed through the area, and that the vertical section had been a waterfall. When the stream was diverted, then the dry, sloping pathway resulted.

The descent required a chimney technique. Without missing a beat, Alan swung his pack and gear bag so that they hung in front of him. With his back against one wall and his legs scissored between two walls of the gully, he was able to move down the thirty foot vertical drop quickly and easily. To a casual observer, it appeared as if Alan were walking down a vertical wall. Drew would have a harder time with the chimney technique. His shorter legs would not allow him to put his back against one wall. Drew would have to do a full chimney, his feet on either wall and his body suspended half-way between them. It would take a while.

Drew reached the bottom to find Alan leaning back on his pack, munching a snack bar and making a big show of cleaning his nails.

"All right!" Drew tossed his daypack toward Alan. "Yes, in this whole forlorn sewer outlet, there is thirty feet where you aren't panting behind me like the little rat terrier you are."

"Picturesque, Drew. I never saw myself in quite that way." Alan handed Drew a water bottle. "Rat terrier, huh? Most people would have called me a 'motherfucker' or a 'shithead'. Must come with the English major...colorful language and all."

"It is, sir, a mark of respect for your intellect. I realize that you know what a rat terrier is and have a mental picture of the miserable beast. Beside that, my hockey coach at Cornell taught me a lesson or two about cussing." Drew paused. "Are you changing batteries?"

"Yeah. I want some good visibility for the rest of the day." Alan took the old lithium batteries out of his Petzoldt headlamp and marked these with a red grease pencil. In this way, he designated them as 'old, but not gone.' If they had been entirely useless, he would have carefully removed the metal jacket so that they could not be mistaken for good batteries. Alan wore a small beltpack that held spare batteries, extra bulbs, candle and matches. In his gear bag, a waterproof ammo box held the same items in addition to an old style carbide lamp. In a cave, even your backup needs a backup.

"So what did your coach tell you?"

"Well, you have to realize that the hockey season is really long." Drew took a long pull at his water bottle and sat down beside Alan. "From preseason practice to postseason games, it stretched over eight months. At the first player's meeting, he laid down the ground rules. No smoking, no drinking, and no cussing. One of the guys called him on the cussing. We could understand the smoking and drinking. 'But when you guys cuss out on the ice,' Coach Ned told us, 'you lose control. And when you lose control, you lose the game.'"

Alan stood up. "Good philosophy. So when you get mad, you use Shakespearean metaphors?"

"Nope! When I get mad I clam up."

Alan laughed and started down the passageway. "Then in two years I've never seen you mad."

For fifty feet they had to crawl on hands and knees along a level tunnel until the sound of water came from around a sharp bend. Here the stream that had disappeared earlier reappeared from an opening high above them. Rather than flowing out forcefully as a waterfall, the mineral-laden water had seeped out along a crack, creating a beautiful flowstone formation. From the fissure fifteen feet above, the calcium carbonate had formed a sloping mass of blue-white rock. Tiny ridges running across the slope gave a feeling of movement as a thin sheet of water washed over the formation. As Alan and Drew approached the flowstone, their lights picked out the angular surfaces of calcium carbonate, flashing like Christmas glitter. The thin coat of water collected at the bottom of the massive formation and flowed off into the darkness. As it did so, the stream began to form a series of small pools, each rimmed by deposited mineral material, so that the water flowed over each rim into another pool.

"Damn, Alan! Look at this." Drew shone his headlamp to the right side of the flowstone. Three or four muddy Vibram footprints marched up the formation. "Somehow 'rat terrier' doesn't seem adequate right now."

Alan sighed and opened his gear bag. He pulled out a small brush and began to scrub at the prints. "These weren't here six months ago. And you said that no one had signed the register for Fresh Squeezed in almost a year."

"So someone without much caving sense worked their way down here and didn't bother to sign in." Drew washed down the rock with water from the stream while Alan continued to scrub. "Another year and those prints would have been encased in the flowstone forever."

The flowstone marked the entrance to one of the most dramatic cavern galleries that Alan had ever experienced. For almost half a mile, a corridor stretched before them. Dramatic fluted pillars receded into the distance on either side of the gallery. Travertine curtains glowed with banded translucence. Delicate soda straws clustered on the roof by the thousands. There were massive stalactites hanging as if in defiance of gravity while beneath them their stalagmites grew in glowing mounds. By the time the stream had reached the chamber, it was forming large pools six to eight feet across, but only inches deep. The pools were terraced by their own travertine rims, so that each lay like a series of mirrors in the magnificent hallway.

From the first time he had walked among such beautiful formations ten years before, Alan had imagined the gallery as a glittering boulevard, decorated as if for a visiting monarch. To Alan the gallery became the Champs Elysees. Walking through the area was almost as easy as a stroll down the famed avenue, and they did so mainly in silence. Even Drew was reticent while in the chamber, pointing out formations and taking in the beauty around them. The two men walked as Lilliputian explorers in a vast chamber of outstanding beauty.

At the end of the Champs Elysees, Alan and Drew entered a large room whose main feature was a stalactite twenty feet long. The ceiling of the room was so high that their headlamps could barely pick it out, so that the huge formation seemed to float in mid-air. Beneath the mammoth stalactite was a mounded stalagmite large enough for five or six people to sit. The large room's other feature was a flowstone perhaps twice as large as the formation at the entrance to the Champs Elysees. It seemed to pour forth from high on the wall like a frozen Niagara of blue-white ice, glistening in the muted room as if lit by moonlight. Unlike the Champs, the floor of the room they had entered was littered with huge blocks, canted at crazy angles. They were the remains of one or two ceiling cave-ins, which predated the formation of the giant stalactite.

Alan and Drew picked their way through the fall. As usual, Alan was taking his time while Drew was moving through the room like a singed cat.

"Drew, look at this!" Drew reluctantly backtracked and peered under the large block with Alan. "See the remains of this stalactite. It could have taken an easy fifteen thousand years to form this...and then the roof went. Then another thirty thousand years for that monster to grow. This chamber is fifty thousand years old and counting, Drew!"

"I've finally thought of a good name for the room. How about Moria?"

"Which is?"

"The ancient mines of the dwarfs in *Lord of the Rings*."

"Well, we'll put it out and see if it flies."

"C'mon Alan, let's get a move on." Drew shouldered his gear bag and turned to leave the room.

"What's your big hurry to get wet?"

"I figure if I can get you to move a little bit, we could make the summit by midnight." Drew considered any goal as if it were an assault on a Himalayan peak. Despite the directional ambiguity, Drew thought of the deepest penetration in the Maelstrom as its summit.

Alan started throwing things in his pack with unnecessary roughness. "What's the matter with you, Drew? Why in hell should we run to the summit just so we can turn around again?" Alan's voice had risen and resounded about the room.

Drew's calm voice sounded in counterpoint. He seemed to whisper. "I don't think that's the end of the Maelstrom, Alan."

"It is the end. I don't care if there are galleries of gold and crystal past Camp 7. The way is blocked, Drew. As if it were solid rock."

"But it's not solid rock, Alan." Same quiet voice. It only served to frustrate Alan.

"Any goddamn analogy you like. It's an ice-covered 5.14 overhang. It's the Khumbu ice fall on a hot summer day. Those aren't routes. They're damn death traps. There's only one approach route here, Drew. And it's not taking you any further."

Alan was heading out of 'Moria' at a Drewian pace. He turned around and shouted back. "Someday! Someday you're going to break your stupid neck trying to go where you shouldn't. But I'm not going to be with you!"

For the next hour the two traveled in silence. Alan had finally slowed down so that they were walking together when they first heard the waterfall.

"Shower time," said Drew.

They both stood at the mouth of a pit boring 120 feet into the cavern. A third of the way down water gushed out of a passageway and fell the remaining eighty feet. The abseil down the pit was protected from the waterfall for much of the way by an overhanging ledge that caused the falls to shoot out into the air. There was no way, however, to avoid a wet descent through the falls itself. Alan clipped a carabiner into a pre-placed bolt, set a chock for backup, and then clipped 165 feet of Bluewater caving rope into the carabiner. Drew had already stripped to his boxers. His clothing and the rest of his gear was placed in plastic bags inside his pack.

Drew covered the first thirty feet quickly and then hung about ten feet above the plume of the falls. Alan looked down at his friend slowly spinning, the falls roaring dully and unseen from the depths of the pit. He had regretted his outburst back in Moria as soon as the words were out of his mouth.

"Are you getting cold feet down there?"

"Nope," Drew answered. "Just want to make sure you're watching my technique. It's gonna be beautiful." With that, Drew let out a long yell, went into a free abseil, and plummeted through the falls. The force of the falls swung Drew like a kid's toy and the shock of the cold water took his breath away. He stopped his descent as soon as he was under the ledge, readjusted his harness, and moved smoothly down to the bottom of the pit. Here the stream cascaded away into further depths. Where Drew stood, an area of broken rocks was almost dry, except for a mist blown back from the force of the falls. As he toweled off and put on his dry clothes, Drew could hear Alan yell. True to his form, Alan's technique was more conservative and he let himself go slowly through the falls. In a few moments, he joined Drew at the bottom of the pit. Drew took Alan's packs for him as he changed clothes. Alan, shivering badly, pulled on his dirty coveralls.

"Look, Drew. Let's compromise. Why don't we push on to Camp 4 before we spend the night? That will put you within shouting distance of Camp 7 with most of the tough stuff behind us."

"Fair enough, I guess. Does this mean I can start talking again?"

Although the stream left the wet pit through a fairly large channel, Alan knew that it was a dead end. In a surprisingly short distance, the roof lowered to the stream level and became impassable. Oddly enough, the route to Camp 7 led upwards from the pit and then leveled off. Alan considered the next hour as the most dangerous to someone who had never been in the cave before.

A maze in a cavern can sneak up on a novice spelunker. In the halved light of headlamps, a passage splits once and it seems easy to take one direction or the other. Fifty feet further and the passage breaks again and then immediately again. At times passages will intersect others so that the wanderer is turned back in the opposite direction without knowing it. In a matter of moments, in an uncomplicated maze, a spelunker can become hopelessly lost.

But the Maelstrom's maze was not merely complicated. It was an unholy nightmare of honeycombed passages, broken shafts, and dead ends. At times, three or four passages lay before Drew as he led through the labyrinth. The maze was made worse in that it was three-dimensional. Not only a pattern of right and left turns, but passages that divided into upper and lower halls. It had taken Alan three years to carefully map the passageways and finally break through to the main gallery beyond. Alan still needed a map to get through the maze, but Drew seemed to have an uncanny sixth sense. After going through the maze a few times, Drew had every turn memorized and led the way unerringly. Alan trailed behind and double-checked with his map.

"How do you do it, Drew? I'd be a goner without the map."

"Bell South!" Drew answered and held his finger to his lips. Alan remained quiet until they exited a Mazing Grace a half hour later.

"Okay, so do you want to give me a better answer?"

"How many telephone numbers do you know?"

"One, maybe. I think I can remember my home phone."

"Well, for some reason, I can remember ten or twenty. I still remember my 7th grade locker combination. There are about sixty turns in a Mazing Grace, so I keep six sets of ten directions in mind."

"Bullshit! What's the third set?"

"R-R-L-R-L-L-L-R-L-L. Of course, I have to vary the sequence when we have to go up or down or if there are multiple passages."

"You figured that out all by yourself?" Alan said dryly.

"It's a gift," Drew shrugged. " 'Course, I know it may be hard for you, what with the memory going after you reach thirty."

Alan threw a chunk of limestone at his friend and headed into the next chamber.

CHAPTER THREE

Alan took the lead as he and Drew headed out of a Mazing Grace and into a long gallery, obviously the remains of an old riverbed that had carved its way through the limestone. Although the ceiling was level and covered with stalactites, the corridor itself was 'V' shaped, typical of stream erosion. Alan was traversing an easy passage when he caught his shin on a slab of limestone and pitched forward. His headlamp went out and he lay sprawled on the rock, cursing.

Drew approached him nonchalantly. "See what I mean. You start with the foul mouth, you lose control, and first thing you know...wham! Limestone facial."

"Shut up, you troglodyte! I fell. Then I cussed." Alan fished around for a replacement bulb. He lit the lamp and shone the light around to make sure that it was working at full capacity. As the light swept the ceiling, Alan stopped its movement and grabbed Drew's arm.

"Oh, God, Drew! Look up!"

Drew directed his light upward and swept the ceiling.

"Sweet Mary! I don't believe it!" The ceiling of the passageway was thickly covered with stalactites. But the area directly above them was clean and smooth, the limestone a bright, gray-blue color. "How long ago, Alan?" Drew was looking at the pieces that littered the floor.

"A week ago, no more. Maybe a lot less!"

"What caused this? Not an earthquake."

"No. There'd be a lot more damage over a larger area. A ceiling like this gains a lot of mass as stalactites grow. It finally just lets go."

Both were inspecting the new ceiling above them. Drew pointed over to the edge of the fall area. The pieces of ceiling that had crashed to the floor had broken off and left several jagged ends, like the macerated flesh of a terrible wound.

"Alan, that doesn't look very good." Drew pointed to a large slab, covered with stalactites that appeared to be slowly peeling from the ceiling. It hung precariously, several tons held by molecular cement.

"Any time, huh?" Drew said.

"Any second, any decade. Who knows?" They picked their way over the rubble of ceiling blocks and broken stalactites while Alan continued to explain about the possibility of further cave-ins.

"If you presume the whole cavern system is producing formations at a similar rate, then you can also assume that the whole cavern system will undergo periods of instability. According to the evidence in your dwarf's mine room, the last period was about twenty-five thousand years ago. If we're entering another period, the whole cavern could conceivably reflect that instability. Of course, there are a lot of variables."

"So we could be looking at cave-ins throughout the Maelstrom?"

"Well, geologically speaking, a period of instability could last for twenty years. That would be a blink of an eye, an instant of instability, over the life of the cave."

Drew seemed uncharacteristically awed by the prospects. "A day earlier and we could have been walking this passage when the ceiling let loose. What a trip." There was a wistful tone in Drew's voice.

"Part of you would like to be there, right?"

"The same part of anyone who wants to see a tornado or a hurricane. You just don't want to be personally affected...sort of terror by proxy."

For six hours, the two men struggled through more of the Maelstrom's obstacles...clambering over house-size slabs of limestone, wading streams, and a long stretch on their hands and knees through mud and water. Finally, there was only one more hurdle between them and a good night's rest at Camp 4.

"You go across, Drew. I'll belay." Before them, a deep fissure cracked the surface of the limestone like an ugly scar. Alan had never measured its depth, never been able to haul in enough rope to abseil into the fissure. He had once dropped a flare into the darkness, but the brilliant light continued to fall until it was no longer visible. It was one of the few places in the Maelstrom that Alan had left unmapped.

He set a chock into a small, well-worn crack behind him and jammed the metal downward so that it wedged tightly. As Drew paid out the rope, Alan clipped a carabiner through the back of his harness into the chock's wire loop. The only thing worse than a climber falling is to pull the belayer in after him.

Drew began to edge his way along a sloping ledge, several inches short of a foot wide. It was slick with mud, so that firm handholds were the only way to stay on the wall. Alan paid out the rope carefully, knowing that the further Drew went across the ledge, the further he would fall before Alan's belay could stop him. But Drew eased his way across the ledge with a nonchalance that left a knot in Alan's stomach.

"Drew, for God's sakes, jam into that crack like we always do!" Drew was reaching for a small flake that would only give him the most tenuous grip with his fingertips, completely ignoring a sound and safe crack into which he could jam his whole fist. The tiny handhold... really just a nubbin, a bulge on the rock face... was out of Drew's reach. He pressed himself against the cliff, his feet angled downward on the muddy ledge. His right hand carefully released one handhold so that he was standing on the ledge unsupported, the great gulf of the pit behind him.

"Drew! Damn it, don't!"

"Not so tight on the rope, cockroach. You'll pull me off the ledge. I need slack!"

Alan gave a couple of feet of rope. Drew looked back at him over his shoulder, grinned wickedly, and lunged for the flake. For a second Alan thought that he had made it, but Drew's feet slipped out from under him suddenly. He swung in a huge arc toward the cliff face below Alan and hit with a soft thud. The force pulled Alan forward against his protection point and almost knocked the breath out of him.

Fifteen minutes of hard hauling on the rope brought Drew's bloodied, grinning face up to the edge of the cliff. Alan reached forward and grabbed a handful of dark hair.

"Now would you please go back and cross the ledge like a sane person so we can get to camp?" Alan shook Drew's head 'Yes' for him and hauled him onto the cave floor next to him.

"Sorry," Drew said as he started across the ledge for a second time. "I thought sure I had that move down right. Just need some more practice."

"Not on my time, you moron. You fall again, I'm pitching the rope in after you!"

Camp 4 was located near a wide stream that flowed through a crack in a flat layer of limestone. The ceiling was only seven feet high and was supported by several dozen columns. Camp 4 didn't seem likely to suffer from ceiling instability. Alan walked back up from the stream carrying two pots of water.

"Let's splurge a little on food tonight, Drew. I'm about to starve."

"Suits me," Drew called from his bivvy sack. "Wake me when it's ready."

"Yes, memsahib."

Alan cooked up four large servings of rice, each in its own perforated bag. Gravy was sealed in cooking pouches, and he added two cans of white meat chicken. His small lantern worked hard to light the camp, but the weight of darkness seemed to extinguish its efforts just beyond the first pillars. Alan stared off into the distance of the room and could pick out the pale forms of other, farther columns. His thoughts were accompanied by the soft sound of water bubbling in the cooking pots, the roar of his stoves, and Drew's deep breathing. The man could sleep anywhere, Alan thought, but that's a key to success in high-adventure, high-stress activity. Sleep whenever the opportunity arises.

"Hey, your highness! Wake up."

"How about one good reason?"

Alan set a bowl of chicken and rice down in front of his face. "You have a way with words, Al. So I'm getting up." Drew brought his bowl over to Alan's kitchen area and sat down, leaning back against a column.

"Man, this is really great food."

"No leftovers allowed. I don't want to pack this stuff out."

Drew laughed. "I hate to tell you this, buddy, but we're going to...one way or the other."

The two ate in silence for a while. Drew tore a baguette into pieces and handed some to Alan.

"Why did you start spelunking?" Drew asked.

Alan held up a finger while he worked on the chewy bread. "Well," he swallowed, "these aren't in any order...discovery, adventure, knowledge, and a good time."

"Thrills, challenge?"

"Sure, but not much. My thrill is in finding a new passage or a variation on a formation...seeing things for the first time. Like I said," Alan took another bite of bread, "aventure, chawenge."

"I'm always looking for a 'chawenge'," Drew said. "I look for a route that says 'you can't'. Then I kick its butt. If there's not something to overcome, I'm not interested."

"Even if it's only setting a record for getting through Fresh Squeezed?"

Drew lay back against his column and stretched. "Fresh Squeezed isn't a challenge anymore, Alan. There's no question of getting through the thing. It's just fighting the tedium. Now the freakin' idiot who went through it first...there was someone who enjoyed a challenge. Or was just stupid! At any rate, I've got to tell you I'm getting a little bored with the Maelstrom.

Alan sighed. "Damn it, Drew. You'd get bored on Annapurna."

"Yeah, sure. If I'd climbed it ten times."

"So you try to make things rougher, like all that tap dancing on the traverse this afternoon." Alan cupped his Red Zinger with both hands and inhaled the spicy aroma. "You could have plodded across that like a mountain goat. But no, Drew has to pass up perfectly good, sane handholds and stretch for little loose flakes that probably won't support him. You know, Drew, you don't always have to be pushing the envelope."

"Yeah, that's the problem." Drew paused and looked up at Alan. "I sort of do."

"Well, sort of help me finish off the dessert." Alan opened a ziplock bag with a roll of date nut bread and a wedge of cream cheese.

"You're no slackard when it comes to food." Drew slathered cheese onto a thick slice of bread.

"An army travels on its stomach, physically and mentally. If I've got a novice down here who's about to freak out over something like Fresh Squeezed or the traverse, a good meal is reassuring. It says, 'Hey, so you're a quarter mile underground. Look at this meal. You'll survive!'"

"Sometimes this pushing the envelope business is something I can't help, like drinking or doing drugs. 'Adrenaline junkie' is not such a bad description, you know." Drew headed down toward the stream to get more water.

"I've never noticed you doing things that are dangerous," Alan called after him. "Just a little crazy."

"You never saw me during my climbing days." Drew sat down and began cleaning up the supper mess. "God, it's a wonder I'm still alive. I was beginning to scare myself so I found some shlep to start me in a new sport."

"And now you're bored. That's a little scary."

Drew was quiet while he finished up his clean-up duties.

"What's on your mind, Drew?"

"I want to talk to you about Camp 7"

Alan lay down on his bivvy sack with a sigh of resignation. "Have I got a choice?"

"Sure! You could go find someone else to talk with. So tell me about your 'rock wall'."

Alan stared off into the nothingness that seemed to surround their campsite. "The first time I got to Camp 7 I figured there was nothing else the Maelstrom could have in store... not anything worse than what I had been through. When I saw the pool there I figured I would bring tanks the next time and force a passage."

"And...?"

"I had two friends with me when we entered the pool. I took one turn and then another and then one more...I should have known better! It's a maze, Drew. And I swear to you it's worse than a Mazing Grace. A flooded maze."

Alan drained his cup of tea. "We got separated in there! I had no idea where we were. Two of us were buddy breathing when we came up again at Camp 7. But we lost Roger Stickley." Alan closed his eyes while a shudder racked his long frame. "He died in there, Drew! Somewhere in those dark tunnels he took a last breath and died! It took me three years to map a Mazing Grace and I've gone far enough in that death trap at Camp 7 to know I don't want to go any farther. I don't think that you can go farther."

"I'm not questioning that. But if the Maelstrom does go on, then maybe there's another approach."

Alan got up and walked to the limit of the lantern's light, looking off into the blackness. "The Maelstrom's not known for alternate routes. It's strange that way."

"Can you picture in your mind the map you made of the Maelstrom?"

Alan sighed. "Okay. I've got it. What am I looking for?"

"What's directly under a Mazing Grace?" If he had been able to see Drew, Alan would have noticed a fire in his dark eyes.

"Camp 7...by about a hundred feet."

"The stream that flows out of the waterfall pit...we know that's a dead end."

"Yeah, go on."

"But the maze is directly above the pool at Camp 7. I think there's a shortcut, Alan. A way around that flooded maze."

Alan pulled off his boots and coveralls. "You could be right, Drew. But I'm not sure that I'm your man," Alan said as he climbed into his bivvy sack. "It's been a long day, you know?"

Drew didn't answer for a moment and made no move to turn in. "Yeah," he answered finally. "See you when the bats come in."

Alan awoke with a start. He had slept soundly and knew instinctively that it was late in the morning. "Drew," he called. "Time to get going." He lit his headlamp and checked his time. Nine a.m. The light of his lamp swept the room as Alan turned his head.

Drew was gone! He was not 'taking-a-dump' gone. He wasn't 'out-for-a-stroll' gone.

Drew and his gear were gone!

Alan couldn't believe it. To leave a caving companion with no notice or explanation. To leave at all...Alan sat down on his foam pad, trying to think things through as he gathered his gear. He was determined to think calmly before he reacted. When Alan started out, he had to choose the right direction or it could be days before he made contact with Drew again. His mind went back to the previous night's conversation. If Drew were bored with the Maelstrom, would he simply leave? Not a chance, but neither did it seem likely that Drew would press on to Camp 7.

Damn, Alan thought. He must have returned to a Mazing Grace, to 'push the envelope'. Something he had to do. Those were Drew's words. Maybe he had given Alan notice that he was going to leave. Alan just hadn't caught it. He physically shuddered. If Drew had been drawn into something by a narcotic urge for adventure... Alan started from Camp 4 at a trot, heading for the maze. There was a way to tell for sure if Drew had headed back away from Camp 7... back to a Mazing Grace.

In an hour, Alan had his answer. There, at the traverse that spanned the gaping fissure, Drew had left a safety line in place. There was no way that Drew would have gone past the traverse and stranded Alan with no safety rope. Once past the traverse,

Alan moved with a single-minded purpose. He was going to find Drew, and given that he was safe, kick his butt back to the surface.

Alan was almost halfway through the maze when he saw it. A piece of red, 5mm perlon rope had been tied off to a bolt and led into an alternate passage. Alan fairly ran along the passageway, until the ceiling lowered so that he had to crawl on hands and feet. Frantic with worry about Drew, Alan almost crawled into a deep pit where the guideline ended abruptly at yet another bolt placement. A length of kernmantle rope was clipped to the bolt, dangling into the silent darkness. Alan called several times, but the black hole only threw Drew's name back at him.

He abseiled carefully down the shaft, being careful not to dislodge any loose material. At the bottom, a small chamber held a pool at one end. There was little room for anything else.

Except for Drew.

He lay partially pinned under a mass of stalactite material. The minute Alan saw his friend, all the anger and blame melted away.

"Drew!" Alan rushed toward the motionless form. "Oh, man...no!" Drew moaned softly as Alan kneeled next to him. His eyes fluttered open. Drew moved his head so that he could focus on Alan's face.

"Sorry, Al. I know you're mad..."

"Shut up, Drew!"

Drew was not breathing easily. "Bunch of material from the lip of the pit let loose as I was heading back up." He coughed and spat some blood on the cave floor.

"Lie quiet, Drew. The first thing is to try and get this off of you."

"Alan, you can't!" Drew grabbed the sleeve of Alan's coveralls. "I'm not going anywhere."

Alan rushed to the block of carbonate material and began a frenzied effort to move it.

"Alan!" Drew's voice was weak but nonetheless commanding. "Come back here, cockroach."

"What do you need, Drew?" Alan's dirty face was streaked with tears. He knew what had to be.

"More than my legs. Something's not right inside. I..." Drew winced and looked once more at Alan. "I'll be fine right here," he coughed weakly. "Better than any skimpy six feet, right?"

"Right," Alan choked.

Drew didn't speak for a few minutes. Alan sat next to him, his head buried in his hands. When Drew spoke again, his voice was raspy and quiet. Alan lay down so that he was face to face with him.

"Found it...was coming back to tell you. Found shortcut." Alan held Drew's hand tightly. He coughed weakly, a thin trail of blood appearing at the corner of his mouth.

"So beautiful, Alan. And light, soft light." Alan was close enough to Drew's face that he could feel his labored breath.

"Tell Meg for me...you know."

"Sure, Drew."

There was total silence for a full minute.

"Hey, Pancho!" The words came from Drew as if he had thought of something else to say. But he expelled softly and his head sank. Alan put his forehead against Drew's.

"Bye, Cisco."

CHAPTER FOUR
2003

The courthouse grounds in London, Kentucky had been Joshua Lowry's haunt for so many years most people thought that he was a permanent employee. On the contrary, it had been thirty years since Josh had been employed anywhere. People knew where they could find him if they needed some sweeping done or a little rough carpentry. Josh was pretty handy, and then there were other sources of income. Not that he would panhandle right in front of the courthouse, but if he were pleasant and pitiful enough, someone would slip him a five-spot every once in a while

And he wasn't a wino. No sir, not Joshua Lowry! He'd spend that five-spot on some food or a new jacket down at the Goodwill store...or maybe salt it away in a secret place where he had almost sixty dollars. But not today, Josh reminded himself as he sat on the shaded park bench near the courthouse entrance. Today was Monday and that meant his weekly visit to that hotsy nurse at the Public Health Center, where she would give him some medicine for his...shitsofrenia, Judge Clemence had called it. Five years ago the judge had told him to get his medicine every Monday or he would have to send him away. Josh wasn't sure where away was, but he didn't like the sound of it. So he had been pretty faithful about his Monday appointments and it was true that he didn't worry as much about spies and assassins and poisoned drinking water.

Josh was about to start his long walk to the health center when Mrs. Judge Clemence crossed the street, coming toward the courthouse with two of her friends. Josh always tried very hard to be pleasant toward the city's elite. It was good to cultivate friends in high places and they needed to know that he was not some bum on the streets.

"Hello, Misrus Clemence! How's your plumbing today?"

She rolled her eyes while her two friends stifled laughter. "Oh, Joshua! Just shut up!"

Josh nodded with conviction. "Mine too!" He pulled at his butt cheeks to emphasize the point. "I bet it's something in the water!" Josh ambled off glad in the knowledge that he could carry on a conversation with wealthy, educated people. They would remember him when it came time to rake the yard or put down some mulch.

It was more than just another Monday. Today, Josh was moving into his new digs. The city had torn down the old school building that had given him shelter for so many years. It would be a long walk, but Joshua's new home was perfect. Four miles outside of town, he had found an old barn with a good tin roof. The property owner was an absentee, a friend at the courthouse had told him, and only rented out his fields or paid to have them mowed.

Josh had bought a Goodwill sleeping bag, taken a shower at the health center, and splurged at a local buffet. It was growing dusk when he neared the barn, and wisps of fog began to rise from a stream that flowed quietly just below the back side of the old building. That stream wouldn't do for drinking water. Not for Joshua Lowry! He knew the poisons that people could dump into a creek. It was the well that made this place special. It was deep...very, very deep and the water he drew from it was clear and sweet and cold.

Josh pulled a bucket of water to last him for the night, took a long drink, and settled into a dry pile of hay with his sleeping bag.

Life was good, he thought. And they can't get me here!

"You get your ass back in here, boy!" Janine yelled from the back stoop on their trailer as her fourteen-year-old started toward the woods.

"Gimme a damn reason!"

"I'll give you two! Doc says you gotta take these pills or your broke arm ain't never going to heal. And I'll tell your Dad to beat crap outta you!"

Dennis Blake kicked his baby brother's plastic tricycle across the yard and stomped up to the trailer, his dark eyes burning defiance.

"It's not my fault the thing ain't healed." He waved his arm, wrapped in a dirty cast and a dirty sling, in Janine's general direction.

"It is if you don't take your medicine. Doc says its calcium and that's what your bones need." She handed him a large pill and a paper cup of water. "Now here!"

Dennis' anger was morphing to sad bitterness. "I can't shoot hoops, I can't go swimming, I can't do shit! Larry Forster's arm never healed!"

Janine closed her eyes at the mention of the Forster boy and shook her head slowly. "Just...just gotta be patient. That's all." Dennis' brother began squalling somewhere in the depths of the trailer and she turned to go. "Be back early for supper. I stewed a chicken," she called over her shoulder. Dennis slouched down the stairs and began to walk along the creek that ultimately led to Woods Creek Lake.

It was not a nice woods to walk through. Logging had taken its toll only twenty years earlier and most of the trees were scrubby pines or small blackjack oaks. The ground was a mess of catbrier, fallen trees, and old gullies from the days when the area was clear-cut. It was, however, Dennis' shortest route to his hideout, a place to smoke a few cigarettes and get away from his smelly, noisy baby brother.

Holding on to tree limbs with one arm, Dennis let himself down the slope of a gully and then laboriously clambered up the other side. Under normal circumstances he would just take a running leap, but that's how he had broken his arm in the first place. He wanted nothing, absolutely nothing to keep his arm from healing.

The barn soon appeared through the heavy growth of the woods. He'd have maybe thirty blessed minutes to himself...look through some of the x-rated magazines his buddy had stolen, smoke a couple...

There was something wrong. Dennis could see right away that the door had swung open and the cover was off the well. There was good water in the well, and he and his Dad had often used it when they were mowing and putting up the hay bales. But they always kept it covered and they never left the door unlatched. Dennis crept carefully up to one side of the barn and looked inside through the unchinked logs. Empty, he thought, and walked around to the main door.

No one was in the barn, but they had been. A sleeping bag and two boxes were piled in one corner on a large pile of hay. Something else was there, lying close by the straw in the dim, dusty light of late afternoon. Dennis moved closer, his eyes adjusting to the semi-darkness. It was just a pile of old clothes, after all. In the half-light of evening, they looked a little like a body lying in the straw.

"Those are my things. Please leav'em be."

Dennis turned to see a figure in the open doorway of the barn, silhouetted by the setting sun. He was an older man- Dennis couldn't tell how old. He was not much taller than Dennis, unshaven, and stooped as if he carried a large rock around on his back.

"I'm not going close to your damn things," Dennis replied. "What are you doing here, anyway?"

"Name's Joshua. I been living here for a month." A terrible thought struck the old man. "You're not the owner, are you?"

"My name's Dennis. I'm only...sixteen, so no, I'm not the owner. My Dad and I mow the fields and my Dad raises some corn and stuff."

"You think he'd let me stay? I ain't got no place else and I'm not doing any harm."

Dennis lit up a smoke. Might as well play the part, he thought. Am I the owner? Sheesh! He walked around the barn, making an inspection of the structure and the condition of the hay. He faced the old man and looked thoughtful, a man making a decision. "Okay, I guess it's all right. You gotta be careful with fires and smoking, though."

Joshua beamed. "I'll do her. And can I use the well, 'cause I don't drink any wine or whiskey and colas cost way too much."

"Yeah, sure. Hey, I gotta get back or I'll get a tanning." Dennis turned back at the doorway "Look, sometimes we got some leftovers from supper. I'll bring some down once in a while."

Josh drew himself up. "I don't need charity! 'Course my arthritis has been hurting right smart lately. Somedays it's hard to walk into town." He smiled gamely and spread his hands. "I guess I'd like something once in a while...just when you can spare it."

Dennis walked back home along the dirt road that wound by Woods Creek. Longer than going through the woods, but in the dark the woods were impossible. For the first time in weeks, he hardly noticed his arm. Someone was depending on him. An old man who thought of him as an adult and who needed him. It was a new and very good feeling.

It was still September, but autumn was making an early appearance in the hills around London, Kentucky. Rain had fallen for a full day, and the accompanying wind was beginning to strip away red and yellow leaves from their twigs. The day dawned gray and quiet, but clouds were low and Erica was sure that they would burn away in a few hours. She locked the door of her lakeside cottage and started a daily run of three miles, along the edge of Woods Creek Lake, up a short trail, and then on an ancient paved road back to her house. The old highway was wet from the previous night's rain, fallen leaves plastered against the pavement.

Dr Erica Qwan was the first woman to become Chief Medical Examiner of the Laurel-Pulaski regional coroner's office. She was also the first black Chief Medical Examiner. And the first Oriental Chief Medical Examiner. "Makes me wish I'd played football in college," she wrote her mother. "Then I'd be something special!"

As Erica labored up the long hill that marked the last stretch to her house, she began to review her day's work. It had been a quiet week, and promised to be a quiet day. As of the previous afternoon, there had been one suspected heart attack and one death by vehicle. She would assign both of them so that she could continue her reorganization work and the huge task of revamping procedures

Erica relished the hot shower that took away the morning chill. Dressed for work, she stood in her small kitchen and indulged in a bagel spread thickly with vegetable cream cheese. In her business suit, or for that matter dressed for jogging, Dr. Qwan was a striking woman. She was tall and long-boned, so that you might think that she had played basketball. Her skin was a delicate cinnamon color, but Asiatic features had asserted themselves in her cheekbones and eyes. This morning, her jet hair was tied back in a ponytail. Erica's eyes matched her hair, dark and lustrous. When the Chief Medical Examiner for the Laurel-Pulaski Regional Coroner's Office (CME-LPRCO... for short!) walked into a room, people tended to notice.

Erica folded her six-foot frame into the CME's official Toyota sedan and drove nine miles into London and the county government building.

Entering briskly through the front door, she gave her usual enthusiastic greeting to the night shift. With Erica's physical size, she could have adopted a demeanor that was commanding, even a little scary. But there was a graciousness in Erica that belied her physicality.

As if her presence in the office were a cue, Alec Martin materialized in front of Erica's desk. He was a valuable member of Erica's team, and everything that Erica wasn't...punctual (Erica didn't wear a watch), procedural (Erica could write up office procedures, but couldn't follow one around the block), and organized (Erica lost her keys, her ink pen, her cell phone, on a daily basis). Dr. Qwan, however, knew her trade like few others in the profession, so people put up with her shortcomings.

"Good morning, Erica. I just wanted to update you before I left for the day."

"I can always count on that, Alec. How about a cup of coffee?"

"I've lived on coffee all night. No, thank you."

Erica searched for her coffee mug for several minutes until Alec found it on her desk. "Thanks! Okay, so what's up this morning, Dr. Martin?"

Half-glasses perched on his nose, Alec pulled a small pad out of his coat pocket. "Other than the two cases you already know about, Dr. Talbot asked if he could drop by about eleven this morning."

"Sure." There was no appointment book in evidence so Erica scribbled a note to herself. "I'll put it in the computer later. Any idea what he wants?"

"No, but while you have your scribble pad out, make sure you've got the staff barbecue down for my place next weekend. You're still coming?"

"And miss my first southern pig-picking? I'll be there!"

Alec took the pad from her. "I'll put a reminder in the computer for you."

At a quarter past eleven, Erica was swearing savagely at the vending machine that had failed to deliver its promise of a cream-filled oatmeal cake.

"Come out of there, you little sucker!" She shook the machine violently and stood back with her hands on her buttocks. Not on her hips. Hands on buttocks was her body language for really exasperated.

A portly gentleman stepped beside her. "Here. Let me help!" He gave the top of the machine a shove, rocking it back and releasing Erica's oatmeal cake.

"Thanks!" She held out a hand. "I'm Erica Qwan."

"Henry Talbot, Dr. Qwan."

"Nice to meet you, Mr. Tal...Oh! Dr. Talbot! We had an appointment!"

"We still do, I hope."

Erica hit herself gently on the head with her clipboard. "No excuses, Dr. Talbot. I just forgot! Come into my office." Erica started down the hall with Henry Talbot in tow, and then stopped. "Sorry," she muttered. "Office is this way." In the ensuing twenty-five feet of hallway, Erica dropped her clipboard, spilling its sheaf of papers; bumped into a lab table as she tried to talk with Henry Talbot and walk backwards; and managed to finish her oatmeal cake.

Erica opened her office door. "I'm sorry! You must think I'm some sort of goof!" She motioned him to a couch.

"No. Your reputation in the examining room precedes you. I've got a neuro-surgeon friend who can hardly operate a car, but in the operating room..."

"So what can I help you with?" Erica sat on the couch next to him.

"Dr. Qwan...Erica, I've been seeing more than my share of broken bones lately. Arms and legs, mostly. But the thing that's got me bothered is they're taking so long to mend. Two or three months will go by with no growth. I put them on calcium supplements; they leave my office and do all right for a while, and then its downhill again."

"Downhill?"

"We can test bone density in the field...non-invasive and everything. They see me and in a week, their bone density goes up. Two weeks later it's back down again. I was wondering if you've had any customers come through your lab lately with bone problems...thin, weak, marrow, anything."

"I'll check, of course. A lot of times, we never make those measurements."

"I can narrow things down for you. It's the second part of the mystery. All of these cases live on Woods Creek, just north of you." Dr. Talbot rose to leave. "I lost one kid, Larry Forster. The sheriff is Jack Forster's cousin and he got the coroner to sign a death certificate. No one but the family ever saw the body, so I don't know what part his broken arms played in his dying."

"Broken arms?"

"Broke one and six months later broke another one! Keep an eye out for me, Erica?"

CHAPTER FIVE

An ancient red Jeep screeched to a halt in front of The Mountain House, the place in Boone to get a hearty breakfast. A crowded parking lot at seven on a Saturday morning was testament to the restaurant's popularity.

Roy Bergdorff looked at his watch and drummed the steering wheel impatiently.

"Annie, go in and hurry them up. Hell, we've only got the weekend."

Annie threw a mock salute and walked leisurely toward the front door. She had known Roy for two years and learned not to buy into his frenetic lifestyle. Roy stewed; Annie sauntered.

The Mountain House was packed to the rafters. Waitresses bustled between cramped tables and the air was rich with the smell of coffee, bacon, and sausage. A striking blonde girl seated alone was studying Annie, and then suddenly smiled and waved her over. Annie waved back and found her way to the table.

"Hi! I'm Annie Lieberman. You must be Ellie."

"Ellie Wilkerson. Glad to finally meet you." As she stood to shake hands, Annie recognized the classic signs of a swimmer...broad shouldered, strong upper legs, hair cut short. Butterfly stroke, Annie mused.

Ellie began walking the two of them toward the door. “Ken’s in line at the cash register. I guess Roy is waiting outside?”

“Waiting! He’s probably left by now and already in the cave.” They pushed through the front door and found Roy shying rocks into a little stream.

“Ken’s on his way out,” Ellie called. “You can start the car.”

The girls climbed into the back as Ken Hardy flew out of the restaurant and jumped into the front passenger seat. “Let’s go! Three hours to Kentucky. What a friggin’ morning!”

It was, indeed, a ‘friggin’ morning in the North Carolina mountains, as only a fall day can be. Route 421 took the four students through Boone and the Appalachian State University campus, northwest toward Tennessee and Kentucky. The road wound through a narrow, alpine-like valley. Misty clouds still enveloped the higher peaks, but a brilliant blue sky had settled on most of the landscape. The autumn foliage was at its peak...fiery red and orange sugar maples amid the deep green of spruce and hemlock. Old fence rows along the highway were bordered with tall ranks of bright blue fall asters and Joe-Pye weed.

True to Ken’s schedule, they entered the outskirts of Croftin, in eastern Kentucky, three hours later. Annie leaned forward. “Roy, how about finding a gas station with something like a clean restroom.”

“Yeah, okay. We’ve got to pick up spare batteries anyway.” Roy flashed a smile in the rear view mirror and Annie gave the back of his neck a little kiss. She left her hand there, rubbing the short blonde hair that Roy kept in a military 'buzz cut'. "Convenience store at two o'clock," Annie pointed past Roy's shoulder.

She hurried into the ladies room while Roy pumped gas and Ken scoured the shelves for batteries. When Annie came out, Ellie passed her on the way in. "Pretty clean," Annie commented and did her saunter all the way out to the car. She leaned against the back fender and gave a long, audible sigh.

"What's up?" Roy said.

"I'm a mouse, that's all. Mousy hair, mousy figure, mousy muscles. Look at Ellie! Did you see the thighs on that girl?"

"Grotesque, man. You know, she swims every day. This weekend's probably the first time she's missed in months. All those muscles!" Roy turned off the pump and gave a thumbs-up to Ken, standing in line to pay at the register. "Poor Ken!"

"You're overdoing it. I could start swimming every day, or lifting weights."

Roy leaned over and kissed Annie. "I love you just the way you are." He kissed her again. "I don't care if she can crack walnuts with those butt cheeks!" They were still laughing when Ken and Ellie climbed in the Jeep. Ken pulled out some hastily scribbled directions and began to navigate while Roy drove them into the countryside north of Croftin.

"Just up ahead, Roy. There should be a one-lane bridge and then an abandoned gas station. Pull in there." Everyone piled out of the Jeep, stretching and beginning to unload their gear.

"Uh...Ken?" Ellie was strapping on a large internal frame pack. "Annie and I couldn't help but notice how you guys were poring over the directions. You've never been in this cave, have you?"

Ken shrugged. “No, but it’s not much of a cave. We’re just going in for the long rappel, spend the night, and make the ascent tomorrow. Not to worry.”

“A friend of mine at UK in Lexington told me about it,” Roy added. “There should be a trail behind the station that goes up the mountain.” Rampant undergrowth at the edge of the woods hid the path and it took them some time to find it. Further into the woods, the trail was more distinct. It rose steeply at first and then began to level off. A fresh breeze rustled the few leaves that had begun to fall and sent them skipping over outcroppings of gray limestone.

The open mouth of the cave appeared without much notice. It stretched darkly across a wooded scene full of color. The entrance was actually at the bottom of a steep bowl of limestone and scrubby cedars. Both girls sat nervously some distance from the edge of the bowl.

“Does anyone else know where we’ve decided to spend fall break?” Annie asked.

“Yeah, I told the guy who runs the rental office at the outing club.”

“What’s the name of this cave, Roy? Something dramatic like ‘Gates of Hell’ or ‘Anal Retention’?”

He thought for a few seconds. “Ah, I think Jake called it Millstream. Yeah, the Millstream cave. C’mon, let’s get set up.”

Annie looked around at the dry mountainside, decided that Millstream was a particularly dumb name, and shrugged her shoulders.

Ellie could still see Ken standing near the edge of the pit as she descended smoothly. He clasped his hands over his head in a victory sign. Ellie released the hand brake on her descender, stopping long enough to give a wave back. Once the abseil was started; once she had left the edge of the pit, Ellie was all right. Like most people, she was really uncomfortable at the beginning of an abseil, in those few moments when a person rotates from the horizontal to the vertical world. Once started down the rope, beyond the reference point of the cliff edge, there was very little feeling of height.

This was especially true in the cave, where she couldn't see Roy or Annie waiting for her at the bottom. For all her bravado, Annie seemed more nervous than Ellie. Annie had a bad time starting over the edge of the pit, concentrating on the vast gulf below her rather than on the rope and gear. She made several false starts before almost crawling past the lip of the pit. Ellie's nerves were quickly disappearing, and she was able to concentrate on her environment and on the skills that she needed to make the descent safely.

At the top, the edge of the pit was rimmed with broken and jagged limestone, here and there smoothed by water that flowed during heavy rains. Large tree roots snaked their way over the gray rock, and even longer tendrils of Virginia creeper and honeysuckle trailed over the edge. As Ellie moved down the rope, the light of her headlamp weakly defined the walls of the pit. Over eons, the limestone had eroded into fantastic vertical shafts and tubes. Rather than being a uniform gray, this limestone material had been layered with sand near the shore of a primeval sea. The resulting bands of smooth limestone and darker sand seemed to spiral down the deep shaft.

To negotiate the six hundred feet of the pit, Ken had joined four lengths of perlon rope, each 165 feet long. In twenty minutes, Ellie made her way cautiously down to the first double fisherman's knot. She took a deep breath and carefully went over the procedures in her mind. A Gibbs ascender was attached to a central carabiner that connected both chest and seat harnesses by a long nylon sling. Ken and Roy referred to this sling as a 'cow's tail'. Ellie wasn't sure that some joke was being made at her expense.

The Gibbs was such an efficient and dependable design that it had not changed much in twenty years...the Volkswagen of climbing gear. It was meant to slide up a rope freely. Its toothed cam, however, would prevent sliding back down. During the descent, the Gibbs was not actually connected to the rope, but only used when a knot had to be negotiated.

Ellie carefully attached the Gibbs to the rope about two feet above the knot. With her weight entirely on the device, Ellie was able to disengage the Kong Speleo descender. For just a moment, while she reattached the Kong below the knot, she was suspended by only the cow tail and the Gibbs, 450 feet of rock and darkness below her. Ellie exhaled, and felt it was her first breath in five minutes. She reached above the knot, pulled up to give a little slack, and disengaged the descender. Twice more in the next hour she went through the same procedure to bypass knots and was finally within speaking distance of Annie and Roy.

"Are you guys down there?" Stupid question, she thought to herself. She hadn't noticed them passing her on their way back up the rope.

"Waiting for you with open arms." Annie's voice sounded surprisingly clear.

"This is great, Roy. I'm glad we came."

"Well, there's the climb back up," Roy answered, "but we'll worry about that tomorrow."

Ellie chatted back and forth with them for the remainder of the abseil, glad to rid herself of the lonely feeling she had 300 feet higher. She touched down to high fives and hugs, and shed herself of harnesses and hardware. Roy stood with his hand on the rope and when he felt it lifted a few feet, gave it a sharp tug.

"Ken's starting down," he announced.

Annie sat next to Ellie on some large chunks of rock. "Where do we camp, Roy?"

"Well, the cave just goes in one direction. I guess we'll follow that until we find a decent place."

From a hundred feet above them, Ken could make out three headlamps aimed at him. He was going to have to say something about wasting batteries. Mainly, he was just glad that everyone was down safely and seemed to be having a good time.

"Ken, that was really unbelievable!" Ellie called out as he reached bottom. "What a trip!"

Annie looked toward the top of the pit and then around the large room. "Yeah, but it's a little creepy. I mean, look where we are!"

"Let's get a quick lunch and then find someplace to camp," Roy said as he began digging in his pack for provisions. They munched on gorp, dried fruit, and candy bars, taking in the enormity of the pit they had just descended. After a few minutes, Roy stood up and shouldered his pack. “Okay, quick lunch over! Let’s see the rest of this cave!”

An hour and a half later, the foursome arrived at the end of the large passageway, exhausted from clambering over the broken slabs that had fallen by the thousands from the ceiling. At this point, there was not much headroom, but neither were there as many slabs on the floor. Ellie found a level spot, removed as many loose rocks as possible, and stretched out on her Ensolite pad.

“I’ve never walked through anything like that,” she moaned. “It was like walking through pick-up sticks...two-ton pick-up sticks.”

“God, my shins are ruined!” Annie flopped down on the floor next to Roy.

Ken cleared his throat. “Hey, we all need to be more careful with batteries. Everyone’s got a spare set, but if we’re just sitting around, we don’t need all the headlamps burning.”

Annie got up. “I suppose I can use mine while I go behind the rocks for a minute. See you soon.”

“Go way over there!” Roy yelled after her.

Annie returned very soon, carrying a four-inch diameter PVC pipe with a screw top. She tossed it to Roy. “What do you think it is?”

Roy took the tube and began removing the lid. “Probably a register.” He extracted a spiral notebook and read through it for a minute. “Seems the cave doesn’t stop here after all. There’s a crawlspace that goes on for a way and then opens up.”

“We could check it out,” Ken said tentatively. “Do a little exploring?”

Ellie sat up. “What have you been smoking? I’m looking forward to a good night’s rest.”

“Well, we’re down here...,” Roy started to say.

"Why, Roy, you are so super observant!" Annie could cut like a razor when she wanted. "Just cause we're down here, we should do something stupid and useless. Let's see, with that rationale, we might as well learn to fly! After all, it would be a big help going back up and...," she snarled, "we're down here!"

Roy glared at his feisty girlfriend. "I was going to say that since we're down here, we might as well try it. The part where we go down headfirst is pretty short."

"Headfirst? Where's the part about being drawn and quartered?"

"Let's get that good night's sleep," Ellie said. "We'll see how everyone feels tomorrow."

In the morning, the girls were not much more enthusiastic, but finally gave in. Roy led them over to the small opening and started down without hesitation. Annie looked at the hole and bit at a fingernail.

"I don't think I can do this, Ellie."

"It's gotta be easier than the rappel we did yesterday." Both girls were standing next to each other, staring after Roy.

"Okay, here I go."

"We're right behind you."

Annie's lithe form practically fell down the fifteen feet of the shaft. "Roy, slow down! I can't see you."

"Right, right! I'm sorry," Roy yelled back from the passageway. "I just want to keep moving."

By now all four were in the crawlspace, moving as fast as they could. After twenty minutes, Ellie stopped. Ken came up behind her.

"What's the matter?"

"I...I can't go any further. It's like I can't breathe. Ken, I need to stand up or something."

"Ellie, listen to me. Just take a couple of breaths, and move forward slowly. Keep at it and we'll be out."

"Okay, okay," Ellie answered tearfully. "I'll be all right."

Up ahead, Annie was scrambling out of anger, energy, and panic. She was right at Roy's heels when he stopped.

"Keep moving! I feel like I'm breathing limestone here."

Roy was quiet for a couple of beats. "It's getting smaller. I don't know if I can get through."

"Don't even say that, Roy. No way we can back up." Annie's voice was beginning to shake with panic. She slapped the floor of the crawlspace with her hand. "Roy, move. I can't just lay here. How can this get smaller?" Her muscles were aching just to be moving...moving in any direction at all. The tension was incredible.

Roy's feet moved away from Annie's eyes by a few inches. "I've got my head sideways and can move just a little. But if it gets any smaller..."

The group could now only make progress with their hands stretched in front of them. There was no room to bring their elbows up. Roy stopped again. "I can't get through here, Annie. I'm too damn big. Back up! Shit! Back up!"

They tried squirming backward for a few feet. "Wait! We can't back up that shaft! Roy, you can get through. You're not that big!"

There was silence for a minute. Only the sound of labored breathing filled the narrow tunnel. "Okay! I'll try again!"

Ken moved up close behind Ellie and touched her ankle. “Talk to me, Ellie. Take your mind off it.”

“Damn it, I’ve got solid rock six inches from me all the way around. I want to turn over, but I can’t. I want to look back at you, but I can’t. It feels like...like a coffin.”

“No! Tell me about your kid brother. Where’s he going to school?”

“Duke, he thinks. Big dreams!”

“When we get out of this crawlspace, I’m going to plant a big wet kiss on you.”

“When we get some room, I’m going to kick your ass for taking us in here.”

“It’s opening back up a little,” Roy shouted back. “Not much, but it feels like heaven.” They resumed a frantic pace. When they collapsed into Miami Beach, Ken and Ellie fell into each other’s arms and lay in the sand. Annie was laughing and crying at the same time.

Ellie sat up. “Now we have to go back through that.”

“Yeah,” Roy answered, “but we know what to expect this time. It’ll be a piece of cake.”

“Hey, everybody. It’s 9:30 in the morning. I don’t want to dive right back into that crawlspace.” Ken was doing his best diplomatic job. “Let’s just walk down this passageway and see what’s there.”

“No more crawl spaces?”

Roy spoke up. “That’s a deal. We’ll stroll down some corridors, look at the sights, and head back here. We should be out for a late supper at a good restaurant. Let’s say we go until noon, and then turn back.”

Over the next two hours, the four friends were treated to the best a cave can offer. Long galleries of outstanding formations and beautiful pools entranced them and made the horrors of the crawlspace seem distant. In very little time, they were standing at yet another shaft. A pebble tossed into the shaft told them that this one was nothing like the entrance pit.

"More than a hundred feet," Ken guessed. "Maybe 150." Roy started to uncoil their remaining rope.

"What the hell!" Ellie protested, "It's almost noon, and we've got to get back."

Roy turned to face Ellie. "I can't explain what this has been for me, these last few hours. I think I've found a whole new world. It won't take long to get to the bottom. No knots to negotiate. Give us until one o'clock, okay?"

"We agreed to noon. You can't keep extending the deadline."

Ken had kept quiet during the exchange, but finally stepped in. "I know what he means. There's always this feeling of what's around the next bend, over the next hill. Let's go until one...another hour. If you don't feel like doing this abseil, you can wait until we get back."

Ellie gave an exasperated look at Annie. "No, we're going," she said. "But I'll tell you now that we don't feel like we've got much choice and I'm pissed about it."

Roy was right. It had not taken them long to abseil to the bottom of the pit. They had given themselves until one o'clock.

The Maelstrom had all the time in the world.

CHAPTER SIX

Ken looked up from the bottom of the shaft. "There used to be a lot more water in here. Did you see the passage we went by on the way down?"

"Yeah," Roy answered. "I'd say there was a major waterfall here at one time. Wonder what dried it up?"

Ellie slogged through a small stream. "Well, it's still dribbling enough to get me wet and now I'm getting chilled."

"Thirty-five minutes, boys," Annie said, "and I'm holding you to it. I hate to think what we've got to do to get back to the surface."

"Think it through and it's not too bad," Ken countered. Suddenly his headlamp blinked out. "Whoa! Hold on." He gave the lamp housing a couple of sharp thumps. The light came on and burned brightly. "Anyway, we go back up this rope in a flash and can practically run back to the crawlspace. I know that's nothing to look forward to, but we can go through it like scared cats. Once we're at the bottom of the pit, it's just a matter of waiting your turn."

"You make it sound like it can't take more than thirty minutes." Ellie leaned against Ken. "I think it's going to take more like thirty hours."

Ken gave Ellie a hug and lifted her off her feet. "It never seems as long going back to the barn as it does going out...that's what my Dad always said."

"Which way, Roy?" Annie folded her arms. "As if you have any more idea than I have."

Roy looked around in all directions, walking around to check out possible routes. "It looks to me like there are two choices. The old stream bed goes down and the other passage angles upward."

"Well, honey," Annie drawled in a sugary voice, "You'all make the right choice now, 'cause we ain't got time to try'em both."

"I vote for 'up'," Ellie said. "Somehow 'down' doesn't appeal."

Roy took the lead and Ken brought up the rear, the order in which they had been for the entire trip. In fifteen minutes, they had made ten intersections and the real danger of the situation was beginning to dawn on them.

"Roy! Stop, damn it!" Annie's voice had a note of desperation that Ellie had not heard before, not even in the crawlspace. "My lamp's getting dim...really dim."

"We need to start back, guys." Ellie glanced at her watch. "Jeez, my light's so bad I can barely read the time. Does anybody know what turns we've taken?"

Ken held up a piece of railroad chalk. "Not to worry. I've been leaving little breadcrumbs."

They had gone through two turns, grateful for the chalk marks, when Ken's light went out again. Rapping the lamp did no good.

"I guess we'd all better change batteries," Roy said as he opened his pack and gave some to the girls. Ken stood sullenly.

"What's the matter?" Ellie asked. "You need to change batteries."

Ken almost whispered. "I did, back in that big room."

Annie was incredulous. "And they're already dead?"

Ellie nervously fumbled the batteries into her headlamp. "Well, you'll just have to stick close to me." She turned on her headlamp, but the filament barely glowed.

"Oh, God!" Ellie whispered. "Oh, please God. No!"

"Motherfuck!" Roy shouted. "These batteries are supposed to be brand new." His own lamp lit the passageway feebly.

Ken held up his hand. "Quiet down! The one thing we can't do is panic. These batteries have probably been sitting on that convenience store shelf for two years."

Annie's own lamp was little better. She clutched it as she hypnotically watched its waning light. "If these lights go out..." Suddenly she threw herself at Roy, striking out with her fists. "We had to keep going, didn't we? Just a little further. Just a little damn further!"

"Look, we didn't know..."

"No, you didn't know shit. But you kept pushing anyway!"

"We've got to move like hell with what light we have left," Ellie said quietly. "We'll shout at each other later."

They stumbled along the dimly lit passage. Ken, following along at the rear, could see little and kept one hand on Ellie's back. Roy's light slowly dimmed to nothingness. They passed another intersection and found Ken's mark. Annie had vented her anger and now followed Roy, their hands clasped. At the next intersection Ken called a halt.

"I've got one candle and a book of matches here. I didn't want to light this until our lamps were gone. I guess that's now." A match flared, its pungent odor filling the small corridor. The candle cast a much greater glow than Annie's lamp. For a while, their spirits were raised.

"It's going to take a long time, but we can get out with this much light," Ellie said. But the mistakes were piling up, deeper and heavier than the thousand feet of rock above them. They had entered an unfamiliar cave. No one locally knew where they had gone and when they were to come out. They had changed their game plan, deciding to press farther into the unknown with inadequate equipment. Their batteries were not reliable and they had virtually no backup light.

The Maelstrom was not a 'killer' cave. It did not lie in wait like a predator in the African night. To those who were prepared, it held unparalleled beauty and excitement. But its environment was one that brooked few mistakes. Four innocent college kids had made a lot of them. They were about to make one more.

In their hurry, and in the guttering light of the candle, they passed through an intersection. Ken's white chalk mark was on their left. A small mass of white calcium carbonate was on the right. In the convolutions of a Mazing Grace, one wrong turn could mean wandering for days...or worse.

The four of them did not have even hours. Darkness was a crouching beast, held at bay by the candle's weak light. Finally the candle became too small to hold, the flame guttering feebly. Hot wax burned Roy's fingers, and he dropped their last source of light. Impenetrable and unyielding blackness rushed upon them, devouring their last reserves of will and morale. Annie's scream echoed through the myriad passageways.

"Everyone stay where you are," Ken shouted. "Don't move! All right, reach out and touch someone. Let's hope it's someone you know." Ellie actually laughed nervously. Deep in the maw of the earth, the four of them huddled on the corridor floor, taking small comfort in each other's presence.

Ken finally spoke. "I don't think we have much choice but to sit where we are and wait for rescue."

"How long?" Ellie asked, her voice trembling.

"We won't be missed until sometime tomorrow. The guy at the outing club knows that we're near Croftin."

Roy spoke, but his voice cracked a little. "They'll find my Jeep tomorrow night. They could be in here late that night or the next morning." He reached out and found Annie's shoulders, pulling her to him.

"I'm sorry, babe!"

"So let's eat a little, drink a little, and sleep a lot." Ellie felt for Ken's pack and gave everyone a half sandwich while Roy passed around a water bottle. They sat against the dank tunnel wall, each girl enfolded in her boyfriend's arms.

"We've got each other," Ellie murmured to Ken. "We'll be okay."

They slept the sleep of fear, where unconsciousness was more desirable than facing the reality of where they were. All rested fitfully, and occasionally all were awake at the same time. They talked quietly about the certainty of rescue, even if later than they expected. No one talked of any other option. The rescuers would find the Jeep, would find their abseil ropes, would find their extra gear at the opening to the crawlspace. They would find their single rope in the pit and the rescuers would find them. The four were going to have to face their stupidity and admit it publicly, but they would be safe, alive, and in the world of sunlight and open air.

More than twenty-four hours passed in total darkness. Their food was gone, and they had almost no water. For awhile, they sang snatches of old songs, played word games, told jokes and recited life histories. But the sound of their voices was almost as disturbing as the tomblike silence around them. In a darkness that never changed and in which their senses were numbed, they became quieter. Perhaps no where else on earth, except in the great ocean abysses, could four people be so alone, so cut off and insignificant. They were, in a way, submerged. Submerged beneath a thousand feet of oceanic muck frozen in place by countless eons.

Another day passed, although there was no clue to the passage of day and night except from their watches. They stretched and relieved boredom by taking short walks in pairs. Ken and Ellie would walk ten steps in one direction in the black corridor. When they returned, Roy and Annie would walk ten steps in the opposite direction. The floor of the passage was surprisingly smooth and free of obstructions. They came to know their small world as a blind person comes to know a familiar room.

The hunger pangs were bad, but not life threatening. More importantly, their energy level was dropping and they were beginning to feel the effects of dehydration. Ken noticed that it was becoming hard to swallow, and his mouth felt dry, almost dusty. He was stretched out, with Ellie lying beside him, her head on his chest. She seemed to be shivering a lot and her clothes were damp. The cave floor threatened to suck the heat from them, reducing their core temperatures as a first sign of hypothermia.

Roy and Annie were walking when suddenly Roy's voice sounded out in excitement. "Ken! Ellie! Come here. We've found something."

"No way," Ken shouted back. "You guys come here. We can't risk losing this spot." They could hear Roy and Annie moving toward them in the darkness. The sound of their footsteps became very close and Ellie felt Annie collapse beside her.

"What is it?" Ken asked.

"We decided to try fifteen steps instead of ten," Roy replied. "Five more steps was all it took."

"Hell, Roy. We decided ten paces. Changing the rules got us in this fix!" If Ken could have seen Roy he would have throttled him. "So what did you find?"

"I was feeling along the wall with Annie holding onto my shirt. My hand hit something hard, something metal."

"A bolt?"

"A bolt with a piece of Perlon rope tied to it. We went a few more steps and the rope continues along the wall."

Ken was excited, grasping at any straw. "A route marker. Someone left it as a guide."

Ellie was doubtful. "But shouldn't it go in both directions? Why does it start there?"

"We think it ends there," Annie explained. "Somebody came in as far as their rope allowed. Then they either went back or continued making marks on the wall like we did."

"So what are the pros and cons?" Ellie asked. "We've been sitting here for two days. Man, I can't believe that. But we're safe and we could be rescued any time."

"But it could be another day or more. That rope can lead us back to our pit where there's plenty of water and where we'll be found more quickly. It could lead us right into their arms."

"I don't want to make you feel like you're being forced into any more decisions." Ken took Ellie by the shoulders. "Look into my eyes." Ellie smiled. She couldn't see Ken's eyes or anything else. "You and Annie decide. We'll do whatever you say."

"Annie, what do you think?"

"If we're really careful, the rope should be all right to follow. There's a lot to be said for getting back to our last rappel and a water supply."

"She's right," Ellie said. "I don't want to sit here until we're too weak and dehydrated to do anything. Let's go for it."

Ken sighed with relief, "Good! You lead off, Roy. But not too fast and everybody stay in touch, literally." The four slowly retraced the twelve or fifteen steps it took to reach the bolt.

"I've got it," Roy called back. The four of them felt along using the small perlon rope as a handrail, another hand on the person in front of them. There was little question of their moving too fast. Lack of food and water, coupled with incipient hypothermia, was making a difficult task almost impossible. Suddenly Roy slammed into solid rock as the ceiling lowered and they were forced to begin crawling.

"What time is it?" Ken asked.

"Seven o'clock," Ellie glanced at her watch. "Tuesday morning."

"Any time now, Ellie. Just hang in there."

Roy spoke in the darkness. "I think we've got another bolt. But there seems to be another knot, too."

Suddenly Roy pitched forward. He screamed as his arms and legs found nothing but black emptiness. Annie was holding onto Roy's shirt and was pulled forward, her own scream drowning Roy's rapidly fading yell. They could not hear it, but Roy's plaintive cry ended abruptly.

Ellie grabbed at Annie's arm, but missed. Annie was more than halfway over the edge of the pit, held only by Ellie's weight on her legs. Ken grabbed for Ellie, but missed.

"Help me. I'm slipping." Annie's head and torso were suspended, her hands pushing against the smooth wall of the shaft.

"Ken! I can't hold her. Where are you?" Ellie was laying on Annie's knees and lower legs, trying to hold on to her and keep some grip on the rock floor. Ellie shouted desperately, "Ken! Ken, we're going over!"

Ken looped a leg through the perlon guide rope and wrapped both arms around Ellie's waist. Annie was crying now, desperately trying to stop her gradual movement over the edge. Ellie's weight wasn't enough.

"Ellie, reach down and grab her belt. I've got you." Ellie found Annie's waist band and pulled back as Ken fought to help. "Keep her feet under you, Ellie. Don't let her legs swing around over the edge."

"Right! I've got her. Pull us back, Ken. Pull!" Ellie's strength was ebbing fast. "Try to work your hips back over the edge, Annie. You've got to help us."

"Let's do it now!" Ken heaved back on Ellie. Annie got one hand back on the edge. Ken and Ellie were both able to pull back and bring Annie to safety. Ken held them both as Annie cried into Ellie's shoulder. She was gasping for breath. "Roy!" she sobbed. "Oh, Roy!"

"I can't believe it," Ken moaned. "So fast, so sudden."

"Is there any chance, Ken?"

Ken crawled forward and tossed a small rock toward the shaft. The silent seconds spoke volumes. Ken sighed. "Fifty meters."

Ken crawled back to the girls. He hugged Annie tightly. "We'd better follow the rope back."

"Ken?" Ellie's voice was quiet but had an amazing quality of strength. She reached out and touched him lightly.

"Yeah?"

"Mistakes are too expensive down here. We can't make any more."

CHAPTER SEVEN

"This is the office of the Dean of Students. Dean Stoddard speaking."

The caller seemed taken aback that she had contacted the dean himself. A woman's voice spoke tentatively. "Dean Stoddard, I'm sorry to bother you. This may be nothing, but I guess you know about worried parents."

"I'm often one myself. How can I help?"

"My name is Monica Wilkerson and my daughter Ellie is a junior at the school. She and some friends went on an outing Saturday. She promised to call when they returned, even if it was very late.

"Well, young folks can sometimes..."

"She's very good about keeping in touch," Mrs. Wilkerson interrupted. "She knew that I was particularly worried about this trip."

"Where did they go?"

"They went caving. In Kentucky, I think. Ellie's a cautious girl, but there are so many things that can happen and ...there was no answer at her apartment this morning."

Ben Stoddard got out a notepad. "Give me a number where you can be reached and I'll get right on this. Do you know who she was with?"

"I only know Ken Hardy... a young man she's been seeing a lot since last year."

"Try not to worry too much. And call me if you hear anything from them."

By mid-afternoon, Ben Stoddard was worried himself. In addition to Ellie and Ken, his assistant had found the name of Ken Hardy's best friend. None of them were at their lodgings or had been to class. Ben canceled his other appointments for the day and sat down with his staff to find a way to cope with the problem.

"They're probably just running late, Ben. Do you have any idea where they went?"

"Ellie Wilkerson's mother thinks Kentucky."

"Big state. Not Texas or Alaska, but big enough. And a lot could happen. Car breaks down; an accident, God forbid. Perhaps something to do with the cave itself. But most likely just running late and not thinking about people who are worried about them."

"We're going to assume a worst case scenario," Ben said as he scratched his head. "Get a description of the Bergdorff boy's car. He has to have a parking permit." Yet another cup of coffee had gone cold, and Ben winced at the taste. "I wish we could narrow this search down to something smaller than a state."

"Outing club, Ben. They're bound to have rented some equipment."

"Good! I'll check on that myself." Ben opened the door to his office and called to his secretary.

"Maggie, would you get me Chuck Hayes in the Athletic Department?"

Benjamin Stoddard was of the old school and felt strongly about the university's responsibilities. Ellie's parents, and the parents of all the students, could not be on campus. But he could be there for them. He sat down behind his desk with a fresh try on a cup of coffee just as his phone rang again. Maggie's voice, dependability itself, spoke to him.

"I've got Chuck Hayes on the phone for you, Dean."

Ben swung around and picked up his desk phone. "Afternoon, Chuck. I need to cut to the chase. We've got three missing students. They may have checked out some equipment from the outing club...caving type of equipment. The kids left last Saturday and haven't returned."

"Oh, brother! What do you want me to do?"

"Come on up here in about an hour with your student outing club president. And we need a local caver, if you can find someone."

"Spelunker, Ben. Or speleologist. And that's not a problem. My wife's brother is head of the local grotto."

"What's a grotto, other than the blue one in Greece?"

"It's a local chapter of the NSS, the National Speleological Society. But Ben, I've got a team meeting for the incoming basketball players in half an hour."

"Chuck, pretend these are your kids."

"See you in an hour."

When Dean Stoddard walked into his office later that afternoon, a small group had assembled.

He pulled a chair around to the front of his desk. "Thanks for coming, everyone."

Chuck Hayes made the introductions. "Dean, I think you know Joe Mazeppi, who heads up the outing club and runs the rental operation." Ben shook Joe's hand and then turned to meet Chuck's brother-in-law.

"And this is Roger Blanton, head of the Appalachian Grotto of the NSS." Roger extended a hand. He was short, not more than five and a half feet and lean. His sandy hair was thinning on top and had hints of gray. Ben guessed him to be just over fifty, but looked to be in great shape. He also looked as if he could squeeze through some pretty small openings.

"Joe, do you know any of these students?" Ben asked as they sat down.

Joe thought a moment. "Ellie Wilkerson is in one of my classes, but I don't really know her. Both Ken and Roy have been on the climbing scene for a long time...North Carolina Wall, Looking Glass, New River Gorge. I think Roy has a girlfriend over at Western Carolina, so I suppose that's your fourth person."

Roger Blanton broke in. "Good climbing skills don't always translate in spelunking. They got pretty good judgment?"

"Sure. They're careful about their anchors and belays. We wouldn't have rented them equipment if they didn't know what they were doing. Both of them are nice guys with good sense."

"All right," Ben said. "We've got to narrow things down if we can."

"My friend Randy rented the gear to them. He said they mentioned Croftin, Kentucky."

Roger looked up, startled. "That's not good. What equipment did they check out?"

Joe consulted a small logbook. “Two ropes, descenders, ascenders, harnesses, headlamps, helmets.”

“A couple of ropes won’t get them into too much trouble,” Roger sighed. “Enough, but not as bad as it could be.”

Dean Stoddard wrote a note and buzzed for Maggie. “So what’s the next step?”

“There’s a lot of caves in the Croftin area. I’ve been there myself several times. Some can be pretty dangerous, even for an expert. If we can find their car, we’ll have a good idea of which cave system they’ve chosen.”

“How bad could this be?” Chuck Hayes asked guardedly.

“Usually you wind up with some people who are cold, tired, hungry, and scared. Flood conditions are bad; cave-ins are almost unheard of.”

Ben stood up. “I’ve asked my secretary to contact the Highway Patrol and the local police in the Croftin area for some assistance in finding Roy Bergdorff’s Jeep. Can you help us once we’ve found the car, Roger?”

“Sure! Just give me a call. Or better yet, I’ll have an early supper with Chuck and then drop back by here.”

An hour and a half later, Roger Blanton made his way back to Dean Stoddard’s office. Although the sun was still high above the real horizon, the mountains that closed in on Appalachian State University had already cast their shadows across the campus. Lights were beginning to come on along the pathways and in the parking lots. The highest peaks were still bathed in that warm, golden light that graces an autumn evening in the high country.

The Dougherty administration building was deserted, except for the lights burning on the second floor, where Maggie was still doing telephone legwork. As he entered, Maggie waved Roger toward the dean's office. Ben's desk was littered with take-out food which he swept aside as he came around the desk at a trot.

"We got the Jeep, Roger. In fact, the county police have been watching it since Sunday afternoon. Seems they're used to cavers...ah, spelunkers who park their cars in odd places. The police like to make sure that the cars don't stay in one spot for too long. Bad sign."

"Where is the Jeep?" Roger asked as he pulled up a chair.

Ben looked at his notepad. "At an old Pure station on Bradley Falls Road."

Roger's face blanched and he sat down heavily, murmuring to himself. "Only two ropes..." He looked up. "Joe said the boys were climbers, didn't he? I guess they had their own ropes, too."

Ben sat down across from him. "What's the matter? Do you know where they are?"

"I'm sorry to tell you this, but they're in the Maelstrom, Ben. They're in the damn Maelstrom!"

"I take it the Maelstrom isn't just another cave?"

"Those kids may as well have tried to climb Mt. McKinley. They couldn't have entered the Maelstrom with just two ropes, but with four or five... Forget what I said about cold, wet, and tired. We'll just count ourselves lucky for each kid that comes out of there alive."

By eight o'clock, the local grotto in the Croftin area had assured Dean Stoddard that a rescue team was being formed. Maggie was bustling around the office, picking up coffee cups and soft drinks cans while Roger and Ben talked and waited.

"Maggie, you've been here above and beyond." Ben rose and took the trash can from her. "Now scoot, before I call your husband to help me drag you out." He gave her a brief hug and helped her into her coat.

"All right, I'm going," Maggie snorted. "But you had better call me, Ben Stoddard, if you hear a word about those kids."

"I promise, Maggie. And thanks again."

He plopped down in a chair across from Roger Blanton. "So tell me about this bad cave, Roger."

"You're familiar with the original Maelstrom?"

"Sure. It's a terrible set of cross tidal currents off the coast of Norway. There is a whirlpool effect that can trap small craft."

"Local legend and authors like Poe have glorified it," Roy said. "The thing is supposed to suck hapless sailors into its vortex, never to return. Legend says that it is the doorway to another world."

"And our Maelstrom?"

Roger sipped his coffee, holding both hands around it as if he were chilled. "It's hard to put your finger on. I've been in the Maelstrom twice. It's a long cave; it's a deep cave, and it's tough. None of which would bother any decent spelunker. But you've got to understand that most caves are riddled with different routes...side passages that open unexpectedly and lead to new areas or at least give you a shortcut around some obstacle. It's the nature of a cavern system. It's how they're made. In the Maelstrom, there's only one route...no alternatives."

Roger had leaned back in his chair and was staring at the ceiling. "It's the most amazing thing I've ever seen. You have no choice but to follow through every obstruction...crawlspaces, breakdowns, waterfalls, mazes. It goes on and on. It's almost like you were being sucked downward. There are no amusing little side trips. Anyway, for some reason, more people have died in the Maelstrom than any other single cave. Some are still there."

Ben opened a bag of chips. "Superstitious, are you?"

"No! But I know how I feel, even if it's unreasonable. I've slogged through mud holes and pits that you wouldn't believe, trying to force a passage. I'm not happy in the Maelstrom though, and I know a lot of folks who feel the same way. There's a sense of impending doom that weighs down on you more than any crawlspace. Too many ghosts, maybe."

"Have you...lost any friends in caves?"

"Not in the Maelstrom." Roger was quiet for a moment. "But I've had three friends die underground. One of them was in a chamber during a flashflood. The room filled in less than a minute, as far as we can tell. Two others went into a maze and never came out. Another spelunker found them almost a year later."

"I don't know, Roger. I've never understood the attraction of high risk sports. The level of danger is incredible and everyone just seems to accept it."

"What everyone seems to accept is the level of danger in driving home on the interstate. At least the dangers of caving or climbing are so obvious that people are really careful. Driving a car is so insidious because it seems safe."

"We've pretty much got to drive, so we accept the risk. No one has to paddle over waterfalls."

Roger leaned forward, looking intently at Ben. "Have you ever wanted to be part of the space program, Ben? To tumble weightless on a tether with the whole planet below you? To see new, unexplored worlds glide past your spacecraft... to actually walk where no human has been before you?"

Ben smiled and nodded. "As a kid, like being a fireman."

"Some of us never grow up in that regard. I still want to be an astronaut."

Roger started picking up Coke cans. "That's what a cave is, you know. A whole new world, different and untouched. People will always risk their lives to explore them, just like astronauts. You enter a cave in the same spirit as sailors came to the end of their maps. 'Here be ye dragons'."

.Roger started to put on his coat. "You may as well go home and get some sleep, Ben. It will take a little time to get a rescue team together for the Maelstrom. You don't want to send in folks who are unfamiliar with the cave. Some of the team will have to drive quite a distance."

"So it'll be morning before they go in?"

"At the very least. And it may be a day or two before they come out."

For the fourth time in two weeks, Dennis was bringing Joshua Lowry some supper...stew and some big hunks of bread. He had come to like the old man and his oversimplified view of things. His health was failing, though. Dennis wrestled with the idea of telling his folks and getting a doctor for him. If he was still in bad shape tonight, Dennis decided, he would do just that.

The autumn days were getting shorter, so that Dennis had to take the road down to the barn in the late twilight. A cold wind rushed down from the ridge tops and hit him in the back, shoving him along. Some trees were losing leaves, their bare branches stretched across the evening's cheerless, gray-blue sky. Dennis could see the barn in the distance and as he approached, could see a faint blue light coming through the chinks. Good! Joshua had a lantern going. Twice before Josh was asleep when Dennis arrived, and the barn was almost dark.

The door creaked on its old peg hinges as Dennis pulled it open.

"Josh?"

There was silence. Some rustling in the far reaches of the barn as mice scurried for cover. The bluish lantern light glowed softly from the pile of hay where Joshua slept.

"Got some stew for you, Josh! You awake?"

Dennis moved closer. Something wasn't right. And now there was an odor, like ...like potatoes when they go bad and get mushy.

The sleeping bag was in its place, nestled down in the hay. There were a lot of open food cans lying around, which surprised him. Joshua was usually neater. The pile of clothes lay near the hay, as always. It was strange, though. Almost as if the clothes had been thrown over the lantern.

A little more light would be good. Dennis reached carefully toward the clothes, but froze in mid-reach. There wasn't a lantern! There was a hand sticking from a worn shirt sleeve, and the fingers of that hand were glowing, softly pulsing with a blue light.

Dennis fell backward on his butt and quickly pushed himself further away. He stood slowly, not really wanting to come closer. But he had to look. Dennis was being drawn to the pile of clothes by a fatal curiosity. There was a mass inside the clothing...lumps of skin and flesh with no form. Finally, his eyes adjusted to the dim light, Dennis could pick out the mournful glob that had been the face of Joshua Lowry.

The boy turned and retched violently, his hands on his knees. He remained that way for a minute, and then returned to look again, to make sure he wasn't mistaken. He stood inches from the glowing heap that had been a man only three days ago. Dennis summoned all of his strength and tried to look at the mass analytically, not like some scared kid. He was intently focused on the old man's face, so focused that he did not notice the slight motion of what had been a hand. What had been inches from his feet was now creeping onto his shoe.

Some instinct made him look down to see the toe of his right boot engulfed by glowing, amorphous stubs that had been fingers. A primal scream rose from his throat and shook the quiet woods and fields along Wood's Creek. The boy stumbled wildly from the barn and ran straight into the woods that rose between the barn and home. He could see the lights of the trailer blinking warmly a half mile away. Branches and catbriers whipped across his face and arms as he careened through the undergrowth, shouting his father's name.

The edge of a deep gully surprised him, and Dennis tumbled down the slope in a painful series of somersaults. He crashed roughly against a downed pine tree, and yelled again...this time in pain. Dennis knew immediately that he had broken his other arm. His howl of anger, pain, and fear could be heard inside the trailer.

Two broken arms, he thought as he yelled into the night air. How could he write at school, how could he bathe or even go to the bathroom? Dennis lay in the bottom of the gully, crying for himself and for what had been Joshua as his father's flashlight bobbed through the woods, coming in his direction.

CHAPTER EIGHT

Hoke Smith and his younger brother Johnny were brought up in the eastern Kentucky hill country where their father grew tobacco, their grandfather brewed 'shine', and their uncle poked around in caves on weekends. Uncle Hank was absolved of being branded the family idiot only because he would bring out pieces of formations and sell them by the roadside on route 421. As long as he augmented the family income, they tolerated Hank's penchant for coming home covered in mud .

In the summer and during the fall color season, the boys would help Hank Smith at his stand, explaining to tourists how the formations came to be. In high school, Hoke began to work as a guide in the local commercial caves, while Johnny stuck to the family farm. From that point their lives diverged. Although both kept their love of caves, Johnny raised a family and was putting his kids through college. Hoke had started buying and selling gems and minerals. It was a feast or famine existence, but Hoke and his wife were able to travel the country together, gathering specimens and spelunking.

It was Hoke Smith who was traveling from Nashville to meet Johnny at the old Pure station near Croftin. As the only available spelunkers who had much experience in the Maelstrom, the local grotto had called upon them to head up the rescue effort for some college kids from North Carolina. When Hoke arrived at eight o'clock on Tuesday morning, , Johnny was standing by the old blue and white Pure sign... a valuable piece of Americana stained with rust here and there and rising now from a patch of blackberries.

Hoke's wife Marion drove their old van into the station parking lot. It had been an all night trip since Johnny's call the evening before, and Marion drove the last few hours so that Hoke could get some sleep. He climbed out the passenger side, stretched, and walked over to his brother. Both men were long and lanky. In his jeans and boots, Hoke gave the impression of being mostly legs with as little torso and head as was needed to qualify as human. Johnny wasn't showing much gray yet, but Hoke had definitely gone to salt and pepper.

"Hey Johnny!" Hoke took his brother's hand and clapped him on the shoulder. "We gonna pull some kids outta that bad hole?"

Johnny gave his brother a half-smile, as if he weren't sure he should be smiling. "Sure hope to." He turned toward the van. "How you doin', Marion?"

"Fine, John," she answered. "I'm going to drive over to your place and visit. You bring my Hoke back over there when you're finished being heroes." Marion threw Hoke a kiss and headed down the road, a cloud of dust following her.

Hoke pulled on his overalls and checked his gear. "So what do we know?"

"Four college kids, two boys and two girls, went into the cave on Saturday afternoon. Their gear is still in place. That's their Jeep over there." Johnny started walking toward the break in the brush that indicated a path up the mountainside. Both were men of few words, but Johnny made Hoke seem almost effusive. "Hoke, you're in charge of this bunch. I'm pretty rusty and I never have liked this cave very much."

"Johnny, Johnny! You know you love her. Sometimes she might irritate you a little, or drive you a little crazy. What woman doesn't? So then you don't like her for a while. But you still love her, don't you?"

Johnny finally did smile. "Nope! Hate her limestone guts."

Hoke was stretching out the pace as they went up the hillside, leaving everyone behind except Johnny. "You've just been away too long. What you need is a little intimacy with the Lady Maelstrom. C'mon, Farmer John. Let's show these youngsters how to climb a hill."

The crisp air of an October morning had not yet warmed, but the steep uphill pull did its work. By the time they had reached the Maelstrom's entrance pit, the rescuers were sweating profusely.

"Look at all the chocks on their setup," Hoke commented. "You can tell they're rock climbers. They've got our bolt setup and Alan Manning's to choose from. They must not trust us."

"Giv'em credit for being careful. They didn't know who set these bolts or whether they're still good."

Hoke shrugged his shoulders. "Whatever. What human packhorse did you use to get that thing up here?" Hoke pointed to a gasoline powered winch mounted near the entrance to the pit.

"It was brought up in two pieces...about eighty pounds each. It'll come in handy if we have to evacuate anyone." The men had set up two ropes for the descent, one attached to the winch. The ropes were six hundred foot continuous coils, eliminating the need for complicated and potentially dangerous knot bypasses. Using both ropes, the entire team of six rescuers was at the bottom of the pit in little more than an hour.

Hoke looked around at the crazy pattern of fallen rocks. "Well," he sighed, "I was sort of hoping we would find them all right here, trying to figure out how to use their ascenders."

"Or just plain forgot to bring the gear," one of the team said. "Remember those idiots in Fantastic Pit?"

"Yeah," Johnny replied. "Had all the best hardware money could buy, including full length ropes. They just forgot to bring ascenders, and not one of 'em knew how to tie a prusick knot."

"You suppose they got through the crawl space?" This from a college student at U of K and the youngest member of the rescue team.

"If you can get through the headfirst, you can make it through the whole thing, so I imagine they got at least as far as the falls." Hoke slung on his pack. "If they didn't have more rope, then they should be someplace before that. Let's move out."

The team clawed and scraped their way through the breakdown in grim silence, looking for signs of the lost students. One of the team slid down a canted piece of limestone and wedged his ankle under another slab. Despite their expertise, the rescue team arrived at the entrance to Fresh Squeezed bruised, scraped, and out of sorts.

"Damn," Hoke muttered, "I'd rather walk on bowling balls and broken glass."

Johnny looked around and immediately found two packs and began looking through the contents. "Looks like they had the right equipment to make the ascent...Kongs, Gibbs. They didn't skimp."

"Food, sleeping bags, extra batteries...wherever they went, they didn't plan on being gone for long."

Hoke took a look at the register. "Yeah, they signed in. We'll give them another point for that. They've got the time down here as seven on Sunday morning."

"Man," one of the team spoke up, "more than forty-eight hours ago. Where are they?"

"Two choices, as far as I can see," said Hoke. "If they don't have a rope, then they've had an accident somewhere in the Champs." Hoke pronounced it as most did, referring to several prize fighters. "I don't really see that, because it doesn't make sense that all of them are injured. Somebody would've come back here for help."

"What's the other choice?"

"Probably the right one. They've gone through the waterfall pit and right now they're wandering around in the maze."

"Hope they're not wandering around."

"How come, Johnny?"

"I don't think they've got a light. These spare batteries aren't worth shit."

* * *

The three of them lay huddled together in the dark passage that had become home. Ken was afraid that it might become their crypt. They had not had food since Monday morning, but more importantly they had taken no water in almost forty-eight hours. Ellie's exertions in trying to save Annie had drained her. Now she was going through bouts of violent shivering. She was still cogent, but her awareness and interest were ebbing. Ken made sure that all three of them kept closely entwined, their arms around each other. He tried to encourage some movement or exercise, but Ellie couldn't or wouldn't and Annie was terrified of walking around.

Ken finally convinced Annie to walk with him, ten steps down the passageway and away from the rope that led to the unseen pit. On the way back, Annie tripped and instinctively threw her hand against the far wall for balance. She drew her hand back immediately and tugged at Ken's shirt.

"Ken! My hand. It's wet! There's a wet place on the wall." She licked the scant moisture off of her hand.

"Can you find the spot again?"

"Hold on. Yeah, right here!"

Ken felt along Annie's arm until he found the wet area. He licked his hand and then put his tongue against the rock. "Ellie, here. It's not much, but it makes a difference." Ellie just sat on the floor. Ken bent to her and lifted her gently. "Come on, hon. You've got to try!"

"Just tired, Kenny. Tired and cold."

Ken put her hand on the rock and then brought it to her face. Ellie licked it feebly.

"Let's move our packs here," Annie said. "We need these few drops."

"All right," Ken nodded. "It's as good a place as any."

"For what?"

"Just...it's as good a place." To wait for nothing, Ken thought. Maybe forever.

Ken was beyond just worrying about Ellie. He knew that her violent shivering and seeming inability to respond was a dangerous level of hypothermia. If she stopped shivering...

* * *

The rescue team arrived at the pit where Ken's rope hung in mute testimony to their route.

"I can't understand how they could go so far," one of the crew commented. "They've got to be nuts!"

Hoke anchored a coil of rope and tossed it into the pit. "The Maelstrom sort of pulls you along. You get through Fresh Squeezed, and then it throws some pretty formations at you. You get here and figure 'What the hell, it's only a rope length. Bet there's some pretty stuff down there.' Before you know it, you're wandering through that maze like a rat in a sewer. And old Maelstrom is just laughing at you. Lots of folks never get through the maze. As soon as they realize what they're getting into, they head back looking over their shoulders like scared cats."

"If they're stranded in the maze with no light and no water," Johnny said, "we've got our work cut out for us."

The six men were at the bottom of the pit in minutes. Hoke assumed a take charge attitude that belied his casual friendliness. "All right, this is crunch time. In that maze, they could be a hundred yards from us and we'd still take two days to find them. We can't afford to do that."

"Andy, you and Steve take Manning's map and go through that maze. Run through it, but get to the other side and then head back. We've got to see if they actually got through or not." Hoke pointed a long finger at Andy. "I want you to shout 'Ellie' about four times a minute." The long finger pointed upright. "Don't, and I mean don't, shout or say anything else. If you hear a response, just keep saying 'Ellie'. Any questions so far?"

"But if they call back...".

"Watch my lips as they move, son. Don't shout anything else but 'Ellie'. If everybody starts trying to carry on a goddamn conversation in that maze, yelling out all sorts of encouragement, directions, exhortations, well...we'll just never find them. If I know that 'Ellie' is the only thing we're yelling, then anything else we hear is our lost souls."

Hoke picked up a small day pack. "Another 'don't'. If you get a response, don't leave the maze route to find them. If they find you, that's fine. When you hear a response, one of you freeze where you are; the other head back to this spot. Johnny and I will be going through passages other than the main ones, and we'll be listening for a response too. The rest of the team will stay here and act as a base."

The rescuers started up the incline that marked the entrance to a Mazing Grace, two of them hanging back at the bottom of the pit. Hoke turned at the entrance and pointed. "Remember, no one yell anything except these two. And don't you yell Rosalind or Marmaduke or any damn thing but Ellie or you won't have to climb out of the pit. I'll kick you out!"

* * *

Ken had removed Ellie's damp shirt and replaced it with his own. She lay huddled on his lap, her hands under his armpits. He had placed both packs behind him so that he didn't have to lean, bare-backed, against the rock wall. Annie was sleeping, pressed against both Ellie and Ken so that they all contributed to each other's warmth.

"Ellie." Ken shook her hard.

"What?" she murmured.

"Let's talk for awhile...get a little conversation going. What time is it, Annie?"

"It's two o'clock. Doesn't matter though, does it?"

"Yes, it does! Annie, we're going to be rescued by a bunch of nice cavers with water and food and lights. They're trying to find us right now."

Ken stroked Ellie's head. "You know I haven't seen you in two days."

"Still here," she whispered, "same face."

They lapsed into silence. Despite his assurances, Ken was beginning to doubt that Ellie could survive much longer. Tears came to his eyes as he began to think of that possibility and of Roy's death. If only they had just done what they had planned to do. If only they had stopped earlier. If only...damn it, that was the difference between life and death. A thousand feet above them there was sunlight, clouds, and sky. He settled back against the packs and closed his eyes.

"Ellie!"

Ken's eyes snapped open and he stumbled to his feet. In his condition, he couldn't be sure of much except that he hadn't spoken. And then her name echoed distinctly through the dark passages once more. Annie heard it this time. She stood up suddenly and bumped against Ken.

"Did you hear them? They're here somewhere!"

Ken yelled as loudly as possible. "Yes! We're here!"

'Ellie' came back to him

Annie was trying to help Ellie to her feet. "It's definitely coming from that direction."

"You can't tell, Annie. We've got to stay put. Over here!" he yelled.

"Ellie!"

"Ken, I could hardly hear them that time. They're going away."

"They won't go away. They've just entered a different passage." They yelled again and listened.

Nothing. No sound except their own shouts desperately resounding through the maze.

* * *

In the tomb-like quiet of the cave, Ken's response was heard immediately. The three young students had finally had a stroke of luck. They were not so distant from the main route that their voices were swallowed up by intervening walls.

Steve stopped in his tracks. Andy yelled again on schedule and again got a response. "Head back, Steve. We've got them!"

There were several passage entrances at Andy's location and he tried to yell down each one of them. He then paused in his excitement and didn't yell on schedule for thirty seconds, listening intently for a response so that he could determine a direction. When he yelled Ellie's name once more, there was a shouted response, a voice that was at once hopeful but afraid. He was positive of the direction and wanted desperately to yell something reassuring, but he didn't want to face Hoke if he disobeyed instructions.

In half an hour, Steve rejoined him with Hoke, Johnny, and their emergency gear. Andy waited while the rest moved forward, away from the main route.

* * *

Ken was at the same time elated and scared. Ellie's name was again sounding from somewhere ahead, but Ellie was almost comatose. She had stopped shivering and her breathing was shallow. "Hang in there, Ellie," he whispered.

Annie saw it first. A faint glow far down the passageway bobbed and moved, growing steadily brighter. "It's them, Ken! They're here!" After all the time they had prayed for rescue, Ken barely noticed. He watched as Ellie's face slowly became visible. He bent and kissed her forehead.

Hoke led his team around a corner and saw three pitiful people in the passage before him, their faces streaked with dirt. One girl was standing and trembling while a young, sandy haired boy was bent over the form of another girl. Not a word was spoken when the two groups met in the passageway, but Annie stumbled to one of the tall men who had appeared out of the darkness. Johnny took Annie into his arms, his stoic reserve yielding to his fatherly instincts. Annie sobbed as Hoke leaned over Ellie.

"Hypothermia, son?" Hoke asked. Ken nodded dumbly and then fell back against the cave wall, his face hidden in his hands. "Don't worry. We can help her right here. Steve, get some water for these folks and roll out that bag."

They stayed there for an hour while Ellie slowly responded to Hoke's ministrations.

"Here's the game plan," Hoke said. "We've got a base camp set up at the bottom of that last pit. We'll get a hot meal in you and some dry clothes. Once we've got you back at the entrance, Johnny and I will come back for your friend."

Ellie spoke weakly, but it was obvious that she was alert now. "We're sorry about all this. We just didn't know."

"There was a time when we didn't know, either. It happens to a lot of people." Hoke stroked her hair.

*   *   *

Hoke and Johnny waited at the bottom of the Great Pit while Ellie was attached to a rope and then raised by the winch. Then began the arduous trip back to the point of rescue, back to retrieve Roy's body. They had already gone a distance that might be covered by casual spelunkers in two days. Now they were starting all over again. All of which paled before the incredible task of bringing out Roy's body through obstacles like Fresh Squeezed. It would be a long night.

Returning to the passage where they had first found the students, Johnny took the lead. "They said there should be a small perlon rope about twenty feet down this way." It took only minutes to locate the rope that Roy had discovered after twenty-four hours in the passage.

"This is completely off the route," Hoke said. "I'm not sure why anybody put this rope so far into the maze."

"It sure led those kids down a primrose path. Jeez, what they've been through. You've got to duck down here, Hoke."

Suddenly they found themselves confronted with an inky well of darkness. Johnny surveyed the scene carefully. "The bolt's good. Let's head on down."

Roy's body lay crumpled at the bottom of the pit, a small room with quite a lot of broken rock material. They worked silently at their grim task, carefully placing Roy into a zippered nylon cordura bag. Johnny bent over to pick up Roy's pack and jumped back, crashing into Hoke.

"Oh shit! Shit!"

"What in the hell...?" Hoke's light swept across a partial skull and scattered bone fragments that were under the boulders on the floor of the pit.

"I don't fucking believe this." Johnny was badly shaken up. "I wonder who it is."

Hoke stood back up from his inspection of the skull. "I know who it is." Hoke handed Johnny a card that he had found, wrapped in plastic and lying next to the skeleton.

"Here are the mortal remains of Drew Cisco, husband to Meg and father to Scott and Winston, and beloved friend and caving companion of Alan Manning. 'For thou art constant as the northern star, of which there is no fellow in the firmament.'

CHAPTER NINE

Alec Martin ran the night shift for the coroner's office. No one called it the graveyard shift... just too obvious to be funny. Although Erica would relieve him for a couple of weeks once in a while, Alec really liked the late hours. He didn't have to labor through office small talk, he was a widower with no one at home, and he worked best by himself. So it was with a feeling of great satisfaction that he approached the examining room doors at ten o'clock on a chilly fall evening. Thinking better of it, Alec turned away to freshen his coffee and plowed into a tall young man of Bunyonesque proportions.

"Sorry, Doc. Didn't mean to startle you."

"No, no harm done. You're pretty quiet on your feet for such a ...a"

"Big guy. It's all right," his voice rumbled. "Are you going to examine Joshua Lowry's remains?"

Alec glanced at his clipboard. "Let's see. Joshua...Yes, I just going to start."

"Well, I'm head of the rescue crew that picked him up and some of us are sorta concerned."

"About...?"

"Radiation or maybe getting exposed to some new disease. I'd appreciate it if you'd let us know."

"Radiation?"

The rescue chief motioned toward the examining room doors. Alec opened them and stood at the entrance, transfixed. The entire room, even to its corners, was awash in a blue light which emanated from the gurney in the center of the room. There the light became intense, a few notches down from a welder's light.

Alec approached the table cautiously, while the burly EMT, who could hold his own with any four men, timidly peered through a crack between the doors.

"Not radiation," Alec called back. "Any radiation putting out this kind of light and you would have felt the effect within minutes. Disease is another story, but I've never heard of anything that would do this to a person."

"What should we do?" The deep voice had raised almost an octave.

"Some prescription antibiotics would be in order. Call me in a couple of days and I'll tell you more." This time, Alec could hear footsteps hastily running down the hallway. Without touching Joshua's remains, and wearing a biological filter mask, Alec spoke into a nearby microphone.

"Ten, Twelve, oh-Three. Ten thirty-six pm. Examination by Dr. Alec Martin of the remains of one Joshua Lowry, a Caucasian male reported to be approximately sixty-seven years of age. Cause of death not immediately known nor apparent. Remains are remarkable due to a bright blue glow that is reminiscent of bioluminescence. Remains are also remarkable in that there seems to be virtually no skeletal structure." Alec probed the mass before him, which was quickly losing all semblance to something human. The blue light seemed to pulse through the tissues and organs, throwing wild patterns of light on the walls of the room.

He swung the magnifier over Joshua's facial features, looking closely for other telltale signs of disease. With no warning, and with almost lightning speed, a mass of blue that had been Joshua's tongue shot forward and hit the magnifier. If not for the glass, it would have struck Alec squarely between the eyes.

He fell backward, tools and equipment scattered across the room. Alec adjusted his glasses and watched in fascination as the glowing mass of putrefied flesh rejoined the main body.

Alec quickly zipped the bag and rolled the gurney into the cooler. He leaned against the wall of the room, sweat beading his face and darkening his green smock. Alec quickly showered, changed clothes, and headed for the cabinet in his office where he kept a secret stash of good Scotch whiskey.

"Good morning, Erica. I just wanted to update you before I left for the day."

"*I* can always count on that, Alec. How about a cup of coffee?"

"I've lived on coffee all night. No, thank you."

"Alec, does this conversation seem at all familiar to you? Some day I'll going to offer you a scotch and soda." Erica started her morning quest for a spoon.

"I might surprise you. Besides, if I am consistently a man of procedure and rote, then you, Dr. Qwan, are consistently a woman of chaos and disorganization.

I'll have a scotch and soda with you on the morning you can keep track of your car keys for two hours. Spoon's on top of the coffee urn."

"Touché! So what do we have today?"

"We had two deceased brought in about four this morning. From what I gather, some college students had to be rescued from a cave near Croftin. Three made it out alive; we've got the two who didn't."

"What a waste," she sighed. "Where are they?"

"Still in bags, with paperwork, in the cooler."

"Okay, I'll take care of them myself. Go home and get some rest, Alec."

Alec leaned back into the room only seconds after he had left. "We had a case come in at four yesterday afternoon, just as you were leaving."

Erica gave a little grimace. "Yeah, I saw the rescue unit, but I'm afraid I kept on going."

"That's okay, but it was a strange one. Would you take a second look for me?"

"Sure! What's so strange?"

"I don't want to prejudice your observations. We can compare notes later. Oh, and wear full protection...mask, everything."

"Yeah, okay!" Erica was distracted by the sudden disappearance of her lab keys.

Alec's voice rang out from halfway down the hall. "Try your lab coat pocket."

Erica jerked the white coat off its hook and jammed her hand into the right front pocket. "Damn wiseass!" she called down the hall and started toward the examination room.

Joe Riechman, her lab technician, had prepped Roy Bergdorff per Alec Martin's schedule. Erica stood next to the stainless steel table in what she called 'full battle regalia'. In the lab, Erica shed her scatter-brained persona and proceeded with an efficiency and organization that even Alec could not match. It was as if she put all her energy and ability to focus into the examination room, with nothing left over for the remainder of her life.

"Subject is a male Caucasian in his early twenties, age to be confirmed through biographical data. A gross survey of injuries shows them to be consistent with a fall of over fifty meters as described by..." She hesitated to consult an accompanying report, "...Mr. Harold Smith of the NSS rescue team."

"Other than minor lacerations, major injuries include a compound fracture of the right tibia, massive destruction of the right carpals, metacarpals, and the left patella. However, massive trauma to the parietal region of the skull and to the underlying tissues is the most obvious cause of death." Erica turned off the recorder. "Help me turn him, Joe." An hour later, Erica was able to finish her examination. It was straightforward, the perfect rhetoric of her profession giving her a certain detachment from the human tragedy before her

When she returned to the lab after lunch, Joe Riechman was eating in his office cubical. Erica decided to start on the second victim and wheeled the cart out of the cooler. She unzipped the bag and stumbled backward at the sight of Drew's skeleton. Erica grabbed the cart edge to steady herself and then regained composure enough to scrawl 'Unarticulated skeletal remains' on the black bag's identification tag. She put on her most pleasant expression and walked purposefully to Joe's lab office.

"Um, chicken noodle soup and a ham sandwich! That looks really good, Joseph."

He looked up warily. 'Joseph' sounded like trouble brewing. "Yes, m'am. Sorry I don't have enough to share."

"Joseph, do you remember the time that your friend Mike hid in a body bag to surprise you and surprised me instead?

"Yes," Joe replied carefully. "I've always been sorry about that. Pretty childish, I guess."

Erica was leaning against the doorway. "Oh, no. In retrospect it was pretty funny. But you wouldn't be pulling another little joke on the poor, witless CME, would you?"

"Why, no! Absolutely not."

"Well, when you have a chance...don't hurry with your lunch or anything, step into the examination lab for a minute." Erica gave a little wave and walked back into the main room. As she entered the swinging double doors, Joe was at her heels.

Erica turned around in mock surprise. "Why, Joseph! You're here already." She took him by the arm. "Just come look what I found in this body bag." Erica held her arms out expansively as they approached the examination table.

"If this is the second caving victim, he took one hell of a fall."

Joe shook his head in disbelief at the bones on the table, some green with age. "I didn't have any idea. I never had to lift the body bag. I just rolled it into the cooler."

"I guess you're innocent, after all. Let's zip this back up until we can get hold of the Croftin police and find out what's going on."

Later that afternoon, Erica called Joe into her office. “Mystery solved, Joe! Our skeleton has a name.”

“What’s the story?”

“Two caving victims were brought out yesterday. They just left out the little detail that the accidents occurred fifteen years apart. So you may go now and prep the second victim. I don’t think the procedure will take too long.”

It was, after all, a perfunctory examination. Many of Drew Cisco’s lower bones were gone. Ditto the major bones of the arms, even though Hoke Smith’s report stated that they had done a very thorough job of gathering all the visible remains. Erica could see that damage to the pelvis would have caused internal bleeding. Her main function was to assure the coroner that there was no foul play involved. She was about to close out her session when she noticed some patterns on the surface of two ribs. “Joe, bring the light in close here.” Erica swung a magnifier around and looked carefully at the bone surface. “I’ve never seen anything quite like this. It’s like the surface is ...eroded? And the bones themselves are very thin, like a calcium deficiency.”

Joe came over and looked through the glass. “Doesn’t look like chewing, does it? More like it’s been dissolved. You want some sections?”

“Yes, please. Send them over to Mary.” Erica gathered up the tapes of the autopsies and headed for the office to compose her reports. It took almost half an hour to get cleaned up, grab a cup of coffee, and settle in front of the computer. She brought up a standard form and began her report on Roy Bergdorff. Three words into the report, her interoffice phone rang.There was a hesitation on the other end of the line. "It's Joe, Dr. Qwan. Sorry to bother you. Are you doing reports?"

"Yep. But you know me...any excuse to procrastinate."

"I wondered if you might come down to the microscopy lab. It would bear on your Cisco report."

"What's up, Joe? Those markings?"

"I can show you better than I can tell you, if you don't mind."

"I'm on my way."

Erica appeared at the microscopy lab fifteen minutes later. Joe waved her over to the sectioning device where he had set up the standard optical microscopes. "I was about to run the sections and had a bone sample set up and ready to go. Then I decided to look at the eroded area through the stereoscope. Here, have a seat."

Erica pulled over a rolling lab stool and adjusted the twin eyepieces of the stereoscope. While a microscope requires thin sections through which light shines from below, the stereoscope is made to illumine specimens from above and magnify its gross features. The stereoscope is perfect for viewing larger specimens such as mineral soil, insect parts, plant structures, and bone fragments.

"There seems to be a rough growth along the edges of the eroded area," Erica noted.

"Right! It reminds me of lichens on a tree trunk, but they seem to be crystalline. Now keep watching while I turn off the lights. Turn your stereoscope light off too, please."

At first Erica could see nothing, much less make out any details of the bone. But Joe's discovery became apparent as she watched.

"It's glowing! It's glowing blue!"

"10-4, Doc. Pretty neat, huh?"

"I guess it's a sort of bioluminescence, like foxfire. Only foxfire is green."

"Yeah, and so are glow worms. No, wait...glow worms and lightning bugs are the same yellow-green." Joe tapped Erica on the shoulder. "You know what I'd like to do?"

Erica looked up with a mischievous smile. "Race you to the examining room." Both Erica and Joe hurried to the darkened chamber and opened the cooler bay in which Drew's remains were stored. Joe wheeled the gurney into the center of the room and opened the black bag.

"Nothing," he exclaimed after several minutes.

"Swing the magnifier over here." Erica peered through the lens. "There! Just there on the sternum." She continued to scan the skeleton. "Yes, the glow is well distributed. Just very faint."

"I think I can see it now, without the glass. Maybe the increase in temperature has an effect."

"Well, my scientific curiosity is aroused, but I really have no reason to hold the remains. Now I've got to convince the coroner to let me keep them so that some tests could be done. That'll go over big with everybody."

Joe looked at Erica slyly. "I've got a suggestion, if you don't think that the coroner cares about glowing bacteria."

"Are they registered voters?"

"Then write up your report and include a paragraph about the bacteria. Only use enough technical terms to make it unintelligible. Knowing the coroner, he wouldn't think of asking you what it means."

Erica put a hand on Joe's shoulder. "Let me think about this." She leaned against the lab table for a moment. "Suppose we photograph the erosion pattern on the bones and then take some scrapings of the bacterial material, if that's what it is. That and one small bone sample should do us. Then I think we can release the remains tomorrow in good conscience."

"I'll get right on it."

CHAPTER TEN

"Good morning, Erica. I just wanted to let you know that nothing at all happened last night. Complete and utter boredom!"

Smiling, Erica turned from the sideboard holding a glass. "Good morning to you, Alec. Can I offer a Scotch and soda? It's a little early for me, but it's the end of your workday."

"I'm supposed to believe that you won't lose your car keys in the next two hours?" Alec took the drink warily.

"In ten minutes, I'm starting on a two hour drive to Lexington. I think I can manage to leave my keys in the ignition for all that time."

"Lexington?"

"The university, actually. I've contacted some people who are experts on bioluminescence. I'm hoping they can tell us why our client was glowing blue."

Alec sipped his drink, actually relaxing on the office sofa. "I'm glad you had a chance to look at that case. To tell the truth, I thought you'd forget."

Fully involved in a search for her briefcase, the comment whizzed by a whole foot above Erica's head. “I didn’t even see the glow at first. Joe found it under the steroscope.”

“Didn’t see the glow! I practically had to use sunglasses!”

“The source may have been dying by the time I got there. Or perhaps the refrigeration.” She held up the discovered briefcase in triumph. “I was surprised there was so little skeletal material.”

“So little! That’s an understatement. Are you taking some samples with you?”

Erica slipped on her long coat. “Yes, and I’ve released the remains. Anything else I should mention to the experts?”

Alec hesitated. “No, not really.”

“You don’t sound too sure.”

“His tongue moved.”

Erica stopped at the door and pointed to Alec’s empty glass. “Back to coffee for you, boy!”

“Here, Leo! Come out from where you are hiding at.” A small goldfish hung in the aquarium, its caudal fin neatly held by a slit cut into a wooden dowel rod. Frantically trying to swim, the goldfish merely wiggled vigorously and communicated its distress to the hidden predator. “I know you’re hungry. Such a nice goldfish...all orange and shiny with its fat little belly.”

Sue Brighton walked quietly through the open lab door. Although she could only see the back of his lab coat, the haymow of white hair and the charming Old World accent identified the man preoccupied at the aquarium. "Dr. Hinneman," she said loudly enough to be certain she was heard.

"Susan, it's very great to see you!" Alfred Hinneman turned and smiled at the young associate professor of biochemistry. Leo the lionfish chose that moment to emerge. It hovered over its hapless prey, spread its phantasm of fins, and lunged at lunch.

"Susan! It's twenty minutes I have been waiting for Leo to come out and you come waltzing in with your sexy person. And now I'm missing the show!"

Dr. Brighton, obviously flustered by Alfred's remark, shuffled some papers that didn't need shuffling.

"So I'm always afraid you'll forget you got a pretty body. It's my duty to be reminding you." Dr. Hinneman reached up and gave her a grandfatherly hug. "When is the last time you went on a date? This year?"

"Two months ago," she murmured.

"Well, of course, two months ago. You are tying your hair back in a bun..."

"It's in the way when I'm doing lab work," Sue protested.

"Which is all the time." Alfred prepared another sacrificial lamb for Leo. "Besides, you know what 'professor emeritus' means? It means I'm being seventy-two and I can say what I want to pretty girls because I'm their sweet old grandfather and I'm senile so they forgive me. Ha! Ha!"

Sue sat next to him and watched the marine drama unfold. "You know, some people would find this goldfish ritual a little ghoulish"

"Bull-hockeys," Alfred snorted. "It is being just like baiting a hook with a worm or a minnow. Leo is a predator, and predators don't like fish flakes drifting down from above."

The lionfish floated motionlessly, scores of striped fins tucked along its short body. "He is beautiful." Sue adjusted her glasses

"His adaptations are beautiful. Watch now!" Leo spread his fins outward in a stunning array just before striking. "Why is he doing that before he attacks, we must ask? The goldfish is being confused, perhaps, just for a lethal instant? How many hundred thousands of years was it taking to develop those fins and that action? I do not delight in the little goldfish's death, Susan, but in Leo's life."

Alfred suddenly was all business. "So why are you here? You come see an old man once each eon."

"We have a one o'clock meeting with Dr. Qwan from London."

"Ooh, London! How very nice!"

"You know good and well I mean London, as in Laurel County, Kentucky.

"Well, to you it's a meeting. To me, it's a diversion to what's being a boring existence. Come on, we'll have some coffee and you'll tell me what you've been doing while we wait for the good doctor." Dr. Hinneman led the way to his office. "So," he called back over his shoulder, "are you getting rid of that little boy you were dating last year?"

Alfred Hinneman, professor emeritus of evolutionary biology at the University of Kentucky, was an institution unto himself.

A few years after Hitler's invasion of Poland, the Hinneman family had fled to England. At Cambridge, Alfred had set out to explain in detail some of the most complicated symbiotic relationships between living things and how natural selection worked to bring these relationships about.

Hinneman taught and studied at several of America's more prestigious universities, but in each case the biology departments were not willing to give his evolutionary biology program the credence it deserved. It took a far-sighted dean at the University of Kentucky in Lexington to persuade Alfred Hinneman that he could build the program that he had dreamed.

So Alfred came to a university that ivory tower types considered to be in a backwater. There he built a department in evolutionary biology that gained a national reputation. "Only two hundred miles," Hinneman had observed, "from where they were trying monkeys in the courtroom. Ha! Ha!!" When Hinneman became a Nobel laureate in 1993, the University funded the Hinneman chair in evolutionary biology. From that point, research in the field had to measure up to the Hinneman yardstick.

The stature of a man like Hinneman and the influence he wielded drew some of the brightest teachers, researchers, and graduate students. One of those was a very intelligent, shy, and somewhat bookish doctoral candidate, Sue Brighton. She had come to Lexington with a Master's in microbiology and an interest in the operation of evolutionary fundamentals on a cellular level. She had done her doctoral work on the evolution of cellular organelles such as the mitochondria.

These sub-cellular structures, critical to the metabolic activities in a cell, could be traced from very simple to extremely complicated structures. Under the tutelage of Alfred Hinneman, Dr Brighton had established herself in this esoteric field. She now held an associate professorship at the university and the doting admiration of the redoubtable Dr. Hinneman.

When Erica Qwan had phoned the biology department and mentioned her interest in glowing bacteria, she was given Sue Brighton's name. For the last few years, Sue had been researching the relationship between the mitochondria and the chemical process that produces bioluminescence. When Erica walked into the Biological Sciences complex and inquired after Dr. Hinneman's office, she had little idea of the academic stature of the two people waiting for her over coffee.

Dr. Hinneman's secretary knocked on his door and peered inside. "Come in, Sarah," Alfred bellowed cheerily, "and bring the good doctor with you."

Sarah entered, but hardly blocked Erica Qwan's height. "Dr. Brighton, Dr. Hinneman, this is Dr. Erica Qwan, Chief Medical Examiner for the Laurel-Pulaski Regional Coroner's Office."

"Good job, Sarah. I am being impressed." Both professors rose to shake hands. "Ooh, brother," Alfred said, "the room is filling up with doctors. It can't be healthy. I'm Alfred, this is Susan..."

"Sue," she corrected.

Alfred looked heavenward for patience. "And may we call you Erica?"

"Please, and thank you for your time. I feel a little silly bringing this to you." Erica indicated a metal case at her feet. "But to tell the truth, I'm just curious, nothing more than that." Erica quickly reviewed the circumstances that brought her to Lexington.

"This is being strange for two reasons, Erica." Alfred was leaning back in his chair, his hands steepled, and addressing the ceiling.

"Don't be so dramatic, Alfred." Sue leaned over to Erica. "He thinks he is some sort of Darwinian Sherlock Holmes and we're to be his Watsons. What he is about to tell you is that blue is not a favored color in terrestrial bioluminescence. It is very common in marine life, where most bioluminescence occurs. In fact, 'BL', as we call it, is almost never found in fresh water and is fairly rare on land."

"We thought of lightning bugs and glow worms," Erica offered.

"Yes," continued Sue, "and a fungus known as foxfire and a rather exotic creature called a railroad worm. So your bacteria are quite probably an unknown species. The other problem..."

"Hey! Hey! So I'm a piece of liver over here? Besides, it's my point." Alfred adopted his most fatherly attitude. "Erica, my dear, creatures that are truly adapting to cave life aren't glowing in the dark like little Las Vegas signposts."

"Why not, Professor? Deep sea creatures have light and glowing parts. They live in total darkness."

"True cave creatures do not have...eyes!" In the role of professor and teacher, Alfred was out of his chair and face to face with Erica, wiggling his fingers at her eyes. Then he shrugged his shoulders. "Okay, so they're having eyes. But they're not working worth a popsicle. They're blind as bats. That in itself is a stupid phrase. You see..."

"The point that Alfred is trying to make in his own obtuse way is that if no living things in deep caves can sense light, there is no reason for light production to evolve. Deep sea creatures can sense light, even if they can't be said to see as we do."

"Well, I hope you're not disappointed in these samples. I've got some photographs and some scrapings of what seem to be a bacterium, and one small bone sample. They're not glowing nearly as much."

"Not unusual," said Sue. "Bioluminescence decreases quickly when the organism is taken from an optimal environment and starts to die."

Erica handed the metal case to Sue. "Dr. Hinneman, one more question. If true cave creatures are blind, why do they still have eyes?"

"A common misconception in evolution, Doctor. You are not going to be losing a structure just because we don't use it. Some people think that we are losing our little toe. Not a way! Humans will always have a little toe, unless its absence makes a survival difference."

"Not very likely with humans, is it?" Erica said.

"No! The operative word is 'natural' selection and humans are no longer in a natural situation."

Alfred waved a finger. "But there is being a gene...okay, okay, a genome that instructs the formation of that little, bitty, useless toe. As long as that gene is there, you are going to have a little toe."

Erica laughed. "I remember science fiction in the seventies that predicted the human evolution would lead to creatures with huge brains and big butts."

"Yes! One of my favorite fairy tales. What they are not realizing is that use and disuse cannot change the genetic makeup."

"So one of you tell me why cave creatures are blind. If there is no light, it shouldn't make a difference one way or the other from the standpoint of natural selection. I mean, sight wouldn't be selected 'for', but neither should it be selected 'against'."

"Very good! Point to Dr. Qwan," Alfred intoned.

"What you bring up is really complicated, Erica. Although there are genomes or groups of genes that dictate the structure of the eye, there are other genes that help make the eye functional. These genes help establish the neurons that carry information from the receptors in the eye to the brain. In a situation of total darkness, other senses such as tactile and olfactory are more important, and animals that have these greater senses tend to survive. It could be that as more neurons are devoted to touching and smelling, fewer would be devoted to sight. The population would tend toward blindness."

Erica held up a hand. "Slow down a minute. So the genomes that make the eyes themselves would always be there. There is no advantage or disadvantage to having 'eyeballs'.

"Right! And Sue is believing that a creature can only be having so many nerves for their senses. Those that have more smelling and touching nerves would survive better in the darkness. But I must be asking why is it that neurons driving other senses become more abundant at the expense of optical neurons? Is this a new law? Why not leave the poor optical neurons alone? Why would genetic changes that direct great neuron mass in tactile senses automatically mean a decrease in optical neuron activity?" He winked at Erica.

"I'd answer you, Alfred, but I think we need to give Erica a chance to escape. I'll take a look at your samples and give you a call as soon as we know anything."

"You have taken the coward's way out, Susan!" Alfred stood and took Erica's hand. "A great pleasure, Dr. Qwan!"

CHAPTER ELEVEN

The front doors of the geology building flew open and Jake Mitchem lunged through them and down the first flight of stairs, dodging other students like a broken field runner. Hurrying down the second flight, he sacked his Geology 301 professor. Jake began picking up assorted books and papers. “Sorry, Professor Manning. I’m running late for philosophy class.”

“It’s all right, Jake. I’ll live.” Alan stooped to pick up his briefcase. “How’s this for a philosophy...Start earlier!”

“I always mean to.” Jake started down the sidewalk that pitched steeply away from the sciences complex, but turned as Alan Manning started to enter the building. “Oh, Professor! There’s a lady looking for you. I gave her directions to your office.”

Alan waved his thanks and walked into the foyer of the brick, box-like building in which he had taught for almost twenty years. Geology and the other sciences on the campus of the University of Georgia were housed in buildings that were early functional. There was no space wasted or money spent on curves and angles, other than the ninety degree variety.

The university campus had been growing for some 250 years and like many, was bursting at the seams. The geology building was almost overhung in one place by the gigantic football stadium, nestled in a valley below. If Alan worked on a fall weekend, it was to the cacophony of bands and the endless roar of rabid fans.

Alan Manning had become one of the most popular teachers on the sprawling campus. An informal, upbeat teaching style had made his Geology 101 an elective course that filled quickly every semester. His recognized expertise in speleothems and his years on the faculty had won him tenure and an assured professorship. But fifteen years earlier, Alan had lost much of his drive. He had started his doctoral research several times, but never followed through with it. Teaching was very rewarding, starting young graduates off in geological professions, and he still enjoyed spelunking. But his desire to advance in his chosen vocation was gone. He would have made an excellent department chairman, but his lack of a doctorate had made that difficult. He had been passed over twice.

The years had treated Alan well. At forty-five, his six-foot plus frame was still spare and lean. Alan ran and exercised regularly. His hazel eyes sparkled under his close cropped graying hair. If he dropped another twenty-five pounds, Alan would have come across as downright bony. As it was, his sport coat draped on him as if he were a coat hanger. All in all, Professor Alan Manning was no model. Rather a likable and appealing academic on his way...not up. Perhaps just to where he had always been.

In the lobby, Alan navigated through groups of students, returning their greetings, and worked his way around the large sample of metamorphosed rock that was a centerpiece for the building. He had just reached the second floor landing when one of his graduate students stopped him.

"Professor, I let a Mrs. Gardino into your office. She wanted to see you and I didn't want her waiting in the hall. Hope that's all right."

"Gardino, Gardino. Doesn't ring a bell, Teresa, but that was thoughtful of you."

As he entered the office, an attractive woman about his age was peering closely at some of the framed color photographs of speleothems that covered the walls. She turned and walked toward him. Her hair was fiery red, with some gray showing, and her eyes an intense blue. She was having a little trouble keeping weight off, but she carried herself well and with great poise. Her bright blue suit and simple necklace of rough agates and amber spoke of a woman with taste and conviction. Had she dressed for this meeting, Alan wondered? She looked familiar, but...

"It's Meg, Alan."

"Meg? Meg Cisco!" Alan enveloped her in a bear hug. "I'm sorry I didn't recognize you right away. It's been...too long!"

"I've been Meg Gardino for the last eight years, Alan. A very nice guy. A dentist."

"I'm really happy for you, Meg." Alan had both of her hands in his. "Here, sit down."

Alan's office was not designed for receiving visitors. The three chairs and much of the floor were piled with textbooks, test papers, and unfiled material. A computer sat on a small desk, alone and dusty.

"You still cave, Alan?"

"Yeah. Mostly student groups...tame, predictable caves."

Meg picked up a color photo, and set it back down.

"You never went back, did you?"

"Into the Maelstrom? No, I guess..." Alan hesitated for a minute. "I guess I was bored with it. And it was more a tomb for Drew than a recreational cavern. It seemed like a desecration of sorts just to go in for fun."

"It's not Drew's tomb anymore." Meg slid a card across the desk, still wrapped in a worn plastic baggie. "That's a sweet epitaph, Alan."

Alan held the card, staring as if it were a ghost. He looked up at Meg, open mouthed. "Where did you...I mean, how...?"

"Some college students were lost in the cave last month, Alan. Tragically, one fell into the same pit that had claimed Drew. The rescue team brought out Drew's remains."

"Poor kids," Alan shook his head. "It happens more than it needs too."

Alan read over the epitaph again. "I paraphrased Shakespeare a little...thought Drew would like it." He smiled wistfully and handed the card back to Meg. "I left Drew's gear bag in the cave too. Stuck it under a boulder in a room Drew had named Moria. That was the longest two miles I had ever known, Meg. I couldn't bring Drew out so I thought I'd bring his gear to you. Finally, I couldn't even do that."

"It wasn't your fault."

"No, but I should've..."

"You should've, you could've! It was Drew that could've waited for you! It was Drew that should've remembered that he had family!" Meg leaned forward intently. "I loved Drew, but he had his faults. That kind of disregard for life was selfish."

"Drew loved adventure." Alan shifted uneasily.

"He was an addict! Like most addicts, he ended up hurting others."

"You must have had some rough years."

"I was talking about you!"

"Me?"

"Yes, you! Where's the Alan Manning who wrote this card? Where's your career, your social life, your sense of adventure? I'm the one that's been feeling guilty for the last fifteen years, guilty because of what Drew's death did to you."

"I'm fine, Meg," Alan said quietly.

"You don't sound convinced." She stood and walked to his side. "I'm having a little service at Oconee Hills cemetery next Sunday, Alan. Just a few friends and Drew's father. You could meet my husband John."

"Of course! Will Scott and Winston be there?"

Meg looked distant for a moment. 'Scott's in France, sort of a students abroad thing for his junior year. Winston is...well, I guess he's traveling too."

"You guess?"

"He dropped out of college. School wasn't for him. Then he went into the Navy for three years, and kept in touch pretty well. A few years ago he moved out to Utah and I seldom hear from him, never see him."

"I'm sorry, Meg."

"Well, you've got to let them go. Winston took Drew's death pretty hard. Scott was only five so it wasn't so bad for him. When I remarried, Winston and I just seemed to drift further apart.

Alan stood up. “I’ve got a class to teach right now, but you know I’ll be there Sunday.”

“Two o’clock. See you then.” Meg bent to kiss him on the cheek. “It’s time for you to let Drew go, too.”

* * *

Sue rushed into Alfred Hinneman’s office for the third time that day, but although it was now past midnight, her energy level was off the scale.

“Alfred, this is the third set of confirming test results. There isn’t the slightest doubt.”

“My God! We are sitting on a scientific bombshell. This will either be setting evolutionary theory back on its buttkis or we’ll be talking about the Law of Evolution. A group of scientists must go into this Maelstrom cave and I’ll find the funding, you can place a bet on that!”

“I’m going in with that group, Alfred. You can rant and rave, but I’m a microbiologist specializing in cellular development. That’s exactly what we’re dealing with here.”

“Susan, don’t be absurd! You have never set your little toe in a cave. Would you go to some Jovian moon if they were finding such a ...such a find?”

“In a heartbeat, Alfred. And so would you if you could. I’ve already contacted this Hoke Smith who led the rescue team. He says he would help as a guide, but the best man for the job is Alan Manning, a geology professor at the University of Georgia.” Sue tossed a manila folder onto Alfred’s desk.

He began to browse through the file on Alan Manning. “How is he so very qualified?”

“The man whose skeleton Erica Qwan autopsied and brought to us? Alan Manning was his best friend, caving partner, and was there when he died. Alan Manning mapped most of the Maelstrom and no one in the world knows it better!”

Alfred stood up slowly and stretched. “Here you’ve kept an old man up late again. So I’m calling a meeting for ten days from now. I’ll give you a list of attendees and Professor Manning will be on that list. All very secret, lots of cloak and daggering.” He moved slowly to his office door and Sue helped him with his overcoat. Alfred turned to face her, his old eyes alight with the enthusiasm of a college kid. “The Maelstrom! I like it.” He held Sue’s face in both hands. “That name will soon have a place in history!”

* * *

Winter in Athens, Georgia can be almost springlike, especially in November. Thanksgiving celebrations usually include playing football in short-sleeve shirts. On the second Sunday in November, a warm breeze greeted Alan as he stepped out of the geology building and started down the road that led past the stadium. He had enjoyed a nice lunch, spent an hour in his office, and now was looking forward to the short walk through Oconee Hills Cemetery.

If Alan found the proximity of his office to the stadium a bit unusual, then the permanent inhabitants of Oconee Hills must have found it damn weird. A two lane street and a set of railroad tracks were all that separated modern college football from the two hundred year old resting grounds for early nineteenth century statesmen, Civil War casualties, and a host of other historic figures.

Alan strolled through the entrance to Oconee Hills, and was immediately taken with the somber quiet of the place. Unlike modern cemeteries that are thrown up on old corn fields with an obligatory pond in the middle, Oconee Hills was bursting with character and history. Ancient oaks and cedars rose all around the gently rolling terrain. Family plots clustered on the tops, sides, and bottoms of the hills. It was an impressive collection of early American monument works. The white marble had blackened in places. Here and there angels rose from pedestals wingless, headless, or without an arm to point heavenward. Elaborate wrought iron fence works were starting to sag and missing sections, so that they grinned lop-sided and gap-toothed at Alan as he walked slowly past their headstones. Poe could not have found a more perfect collection of crumbling mausoleums, creaking iron doors, and broken locks in which to stage a moonlit tale of horror.

The older parts of Oconee Hills were in disarray, limbs down over the road and even trees fallen on some of the older plots located down in the valley near the Oconee River. The old road led Alan down past monuments meant to recreate cathedral facades, past an old Jewish section, and finally across the river and into a more modern Oconee Hills. Here the land was once pasture with islands of old trees and vistas of the countryside around the university campus. Low clouds promised rain later in the day, but it would almost be a spring shower. Alan walked toward a small knoll dotted with large pines

where a group of people had gathered, Meg's fl
hair prominent among them. She was standing ar
in arm with a short, dour-faced man. Maybe just the occasion, Alan thought.

Meg came over and gave him a brief hug. "Alan, I'd like you to meet my husband, John Gardino." John held out a delicately manicured hand that disappeared in Alan's grasp.

"It's really good to meet at last, Alan. I've heard some pretty incredible things about you now and again."

Alan decided that John Gardino was a sincere person, if not the life of the party. "I can't imagine what those stories were about, but I've got to say that I'm pleased to see Meg looking so happy and well."

"Come on! We're about to start." Meg led them both over to where a dozen people had gathered around a cloaked monument stone. Although the stone itself could not be seen, it was flanked by two large indica azaleas. Behind it rose a sizable dogwood tree, newly planted. Meg and John had evidently spared nothing to make a fitting tribute to Drew Cisco. Meg walked over and removed the light cotton cover from the monument. A single block of dark green granite was revealed. Inscribed on the front was Alan's epitaph, word for word. He was completely taken aback. "Meg, thank you. I never expected this."

"We couldn't possibly think of anything more suitable. I'm thanking you." Meg reached up and gave Alan a warm hug.

Alan looked at the small group. An elderly man, Drew's father, seemed to be particularly affected and grateful for his former daughter-in-law's thoughtfulness. Other couples, mostly from the university community, were at least vaguely familiar to Alan. One woman, however, stood apart and seemed more interested in Alan than in the memorial service that followed.

She was not dressed for a warm day. A long tan coat covered a dress of darker earth tone, hiding her figure. Gold glinted at her neck, but Alan could see no other jewelry. She wore only a light lip gloss and barely discernible coloring to highlight her cheekbones. Her tawny hair was pulled back severely and her glasses seemed much too bulky, but they framed a face that was soft and unused to much sunlight and weather. Her features were delicate, small nose and mouth and eyes that met his frankly. She wore a little pillbox a la Jackie Kennedy that Alan first thought to be a little silly. She obviously had been taught that ladies wear hats to funerals and church. But the longer Alan looked at her, the more the hat began to fit her. She wore classic heels and stood at ease with her hands clasping a small purse in front of her. A classy dame, someone would have said fifty years ago. Or today, Alan thought.

The Lutheran minister closed with a prayer and a reading from the 139th Psalm. As people began to move away, Alan went to say good-bye to Meg.

"That was a nice service and a beautiful memorial. Thanks for your part in this, John"

"Alan, who's your friend over there?" Meg indicated the woman that Alan had noticed, still standing in about the same spot. Waiting?

"I don't know her. I thought you did."

"She was watching you like a cat eyeing a saucer of cream. I thought the two of you were doing a lot of communicating."

John extended a hand once more. "If you find out who she is, bring her by for dinner some evening."

"At any rate," Meg said, "come by and visit. We're in the same city, after all." Meg and John Gardino walked down the path. As he watched them, Alan heard footsteps behind him.

"Professor Manning?" Alan turned to stand face to face with the woman who was a stranger to him. She offered a hand. "My name is Sue Brighton. Could I talk with you for a few minutes?"

CHAPTER TWELVE

Sara Okura knocked on the darkroom door. James wasn't anyplace else in the apartment, and the red light above the door was on; so where else could he be?

"James, I have your mail here. You didn't get it out of the box yet."

James Okura sighed and set the timer on his rinse. "Thanks, Mom. I've just been busy."

"You're always busy, James. No time for the family, no time for a social life; your whole life is in that darkroom or in front of that computer. You don't even read your mail."

"I've got you for that. So what's in my mail?"

"Do you know how much time we spend talking through this door? Here's something from the Marin County tax collector. You're not paying your taxes on time, are you?"

James rolled his eyes. The conversation seemed awfully familiar...every time his mother dropped by unannounced. "I can't come out right now and yes, I'm paying my taxes on what little property I own. Anything else?"

"Here's something. A light brown envelope with gold lettering from the University of Kentucky. It's really good quality paper, James. Should I read it to you?"

"Who am I to stop you? But talk louder, Mom. Water's running."

"Okay, it's an invitation," Sara yelled. "Dr. Alfred Hinneman requests that you honor him by attending a special meeting on Wednesday, December 8th, 2003, to be held in the Founder's Room of the Alumni House on the University of Kentucky campus. A startling scientific discovery of professional interest to you will be discussed at this meeting. Please RSVP Dr. Sue Brighton care of Department of Evolutionary Biology, the University of Kentucky." Sara took a deep breath. "Did you hear all that, James?"

A thoughtful 'Yes' came from the darkroom.

"James, there is a first class plane ticket from San Francisco to Lexington, Kentucky in the envelope. First class, James!"

The darkroom door opened and James stuck his head out, grabbed the envelope, and gave his mother a kiss. "If you're cooking tonight, I'll get out of this room and come to visit."

Sara's face lit up and her eyes twinkled. "Sweet and sour shrimp, and lots of it."

"That's a deal. See you and Pop later." He pulled the darkroom door shut and Sara Okura bustled off, full of good news.

The Cornell University campus is one of the most beautiful in the United States. 'Far above Cayuga's waters', its rolling campus in Ithaca, New York is bounded by steep-walled gorges, stunning waterfalls, and deep woods. Its buildings run the gamut from the old halls of its founding days to great towers of glass and steel. Alicia Marko strode into her lecture room in Rockefeller Hall, arguably the ugliest building on campus. The story goes that when old John D. pulled up in front of the building for its dedication, he took one look, made a face, and told his driver to leave.

Alicia's lecture was the final one in a series dealing with predator prey relationships on Isle Royale, where she had done extensive research on moose-timber wolf interactions. As she concluded with the last PowerPoint graphic, Alicia threw a switch and old wooden partitions rumbled down to reveal the windows and let in light. Shades of Frankenstein, she thought, and left the room for her second story office.

Two of her graduate students had been waiting to turn in student test papers. Both young men towered over her five foot five frame, but Alicia's energy swept her past them like a sprite zipping among plodding pachyderms. She grabbed the papers, plucked her mail from the office box, and motioned them to follow her in one imperious sweep.

"So I've got some field observations from Mt. McKinley that need to be coded and logged in tonight. Who volunteers?"

The two students looked at each other. "Dr. Marko, there's a huge hockey game here tonight. We're playing Harvard...first conference game of the season."

"Hockey? That's the one on the ice, right? Little black thing, lots of blood?"

"M'am, the word is that if you want to advance at Cornell you have to breathe hockey, eat hockey, and shi...well, you get the idea."

"What an interesting image. Well, you little boys run on to your game and I'll sacrifice myself to the altar of computer data entry." Alicia was going through a stack of new mail. She had come to the little brown stationary and opened it as the young men were leaving. "Whoa, whoa! Wait a minute. What's Lexington, Kentucky like this time of year? Do they play hockey there?"

"They might play some primitive form, but nothing anyone cares about"

"Gentlemen, you will have to conduct exam reviews on your own. I hope you beat the charcoal gray slacks off the "Hahvahd" boys tonight!"

"First class! Hot damn!" Sam Telliman popped another beer and threw his feet up on the table. The All-Out Armadillo Bar wasn't really open, but Sam was a regular and felt he had a right to be there anytime he was thirsty. The rest of Amarillo might not show up until five in the afternoon, but Sam wrote magazine articles for a living and for him, life was one long happy hour.

Ed George, the proprietor, barkeep, and janitor at the Armadillo, swept Sam's alligator boots off the table. "Watch the fine furniture, son! Who the hell would want you around so bad that they'd send you a plane ticket?"

"I get plane tickets all the time from admirers. This one's from a Nobel prize winner in Kentucky."

"Hell, there's no such thing in Kentucky. I sent you that ticket just to get you out of here for a while."

"Yeah? Well, Eddie, I'm going to Lexington and you and your customers can just cry in their damn watered down beer while I become more rich and more famous." Sam grabbed his oversized Stetson from the rack and started out the door. Ed followed him.

"Maybe you can pay your bar tab when you come back," he shouted from the doorway. "A hundred fifty bucks, Sam!" Sam Telliman never turned around but flipped him off anyway.

"Stupid asshole," Ed muttered as he closed the bar door behind him.

Variations of these scenes were repeated at other addresses across the United States as Drs. Hinneman and Brighton began to gather their research team. Upon arriving at the airport, the participants were met by one of Alfred's graduate students and brought to their lodgings at the Alumni house. Each person found a note on the pillow in their bedroom, thanking them for coming, and inviting them to enjoy dinner in the Alumni house. The note apologized for the absence of their hosts and asked each person to be in the Founder's room at eight o'clock for breakfast.

Hoke Smith poked his head through the door of the meeting room just before eight, with Alan Manning looking over his shoulder. Heavy curtains were drawn against a cold, rainy day. Gas flames licked ineffectually at cast logs in the fireplace, and the smell of food drifted from the laden buffet table at one end of the room. Sam Telliman had already heaped a plate with scrambled eggs, Belgian waffle, bacon, and sausage and was making his way to one of the tables set for the group. As more of the participants began to appear, Sue and Alfred circulated about the room making introductions and avoiding questions. Alfred had commandeered the

Alumni House and virtually sealed the place off to anyone else.

Alfred and Sue were the only people in the room who realized the magnitude of what they were to discuss. Alfred had used discretionary funds from his department to pay for travel and other expenses. If all went well, the meeting would form a research team and secure funding for the expedition and ongoing research.

Alfred raised himself from the breakfast table and tapped his drinking glass with a spoon. "Ladies and gentlemen, this is a time to be starting our meeting. Thank you very much for coming here like secret spies. If you will take a comfortable seat in front of the fireplace, I'm thinking you will all be happier. Bring your coffee with you."

Hoke Smith was at one side, next to Alan Manning. Both sat with their long legs stretched out full length in front of them. Erica Qwan and Joe Riechman sat together, not far from Sue Brighton. Alfred had positioned himself before the fire, warming his hands and waiting for everyone to settle in.

"My name is Dr. Alfred Hinneman and I am teaching at the University of Kentucky. Today, I will be holding class. One of my precepts is to first be gaining your attention. So allow me to say that what you hear today will change the science of biology forever. The ramifications of today's meeting and the research to follow will influence theology, philosophy, and even the search for extra-terrestrials." Alfred paused and looked at each person. "No other discovery since that of the first fossils or of nucleic acids has had the potential of what we will discuss today."

During Alfred's remarks, people had frozen in mid-motion. Alan sat up from his lounging position, his serious gray eyes staring intently at Alfred. Sam Telliman had been chewing on a Danish and suddenly stopped, setting the rest of the sweet roll down carefully. Alfred's eyebrows went up in mock astonishment. "Oh, so I am having your attention, I think?"

"I am honored," he continued, "to head up an investigative and research team concerned with this...uh, discovery. I hope that many of you will consent to be part of this team. But I will leave the announcement of this discovery, and how it came to be, to my friend and colleague, Dr. Susan Brighton."

Susan stood at her chair and walked around behind it so that she could use the back of the seat as a podium. Her appearance was stereotypical of a busy and devoted academic; her hair mostly pulled back except some wisps that had managed to escape, her heavy framed glasses, a loosely cut suit of gray and grayer. But as Alan studied her, he saw what he had seen at Drew's memorial service...a very classy dame.

"I want to add my thanks for your being here on the recommendation of a perfect stranger. Now that Dr. Hinneman has teased you, I do not want to take much more time before we make our announcement. I do want to make some introductions. Dr. Hinneman is an abundantly modest individual, as he is professor emeritus of evolutionary biology and a 1993 Nobel laureate in Biology, and in whose honor this university has established the Hinneman chair."

"Going around the room, we have Mr. Harold Smith, a spelunker and professional guide with a lifetime of experience. Next to him is Mr. Alan Manning, Professor of Geology at the University of Georgia. He has gained a national reputation for his knowledge of speleothems or cave formations. Next to him is Mr. James Okura, widely-known free-lance photographer, frequent contributor to National Geographic, and perhaps best known for his stunning photos of Lechugilla Cave. Mr. Samuel Telliman has seated himself next to Mr. Okura, for Sam's wonderful stories have accompanied James' photographs in many publications. He is also well known for his salty pro-environmental editorials in both Sierra and Audubon magazines."

Sue took a deep breath. "So far, I'm not doing too badly. Let's see if I can get through the rest of the introductions without any gaffs." She held out her hand to the next individual. "This is Mr. Robert Woods from the National Outdoor Leadership School in Lander, Wyoming. Mr. Woods' expertise is in logistical support and organization of major expeditions. Dr. Alicia Marko holds the Fuertes chair in zoology at Cornell University, and Dr. Reginald Hoven is an expert in expeditionary medicine and has advised many Himalayan ascent teams. And this is our good friend, Mr. David Lenny, Associate Curator of the Smithsonian Museum of Natural History and chairman of the Allocations and Funding committee of the Smithsonian Institute."

"Sitting next to Dr. Hinneman are Dr. Erica Qwan, Chief Medical Examiner for the Laurel-Pulaski Regional Coroner's Office, and her technical lab assistant, Mr. Joe Riechman. Is there anyone hiding under a table whom I have left out?"

Some members of the group were looking around in wonder at the credentials of the quickly assembled team. Hoke Smith was obviously uncomfortable, but Alan leaned back in his chair and nudged Hoke in the side. "Yeah, but there's only two muddy old spelunkers in the whole group." Hoke cracked a grin and leaned back also.

Sue took another sip of coffee and continued. "So here it is. In the last two weeks, Dr. Hinneman and I have confirmed the existence of the first alien life forms ever found." Sue hesitated for the bedlam that had to ensue.

Alicia's coffee cup hit the floor with a crash. Erica, knowing of the samples she had brought to Sue and Alfred, grabbed Joe's arm in excitement.

Sue motioned for quiet. "In addition, these lifeforms were not found by a remote sensing device on some other body in the solar system. The alien lifeforms were discovered from a source near Croftin, Kentucky." She looked directly at Alan and Hoke. "To be specific, gentlemen, some two thousand feet below Croftin." Alan looked at Hoke significantly and leaned forward, hands clasped between his legs, to hear more.

"Fifteen years ago a young literature professor, Drew Cisco, died in a cave called The Maelstrom. Although it is probably not familiar to you, it is an extremely difficult and dangerous cavern system. Last month, four college students were lost in the cave. One fell to his death. The rescue team, headed by Mr. Smith here, found the skeletal remains of Drew Cisco while evacuating the body of the college student. It was Dr. Qwan's job to do a routine but required autopsy on the remains of Mr. Cisco. During this process Mr. Riechman noticed a blue glow on different parts of the skeleton."

Alan Manning sat up straight at the mention of the glow. It struck a chord with him somewhere.

"The astute observation and scientific curiosity of Dr. Qwan and Mr. Riechman have led us to this point.

Dr. Qwan brought samples to Dr. Hinneman and me. While examining these samples, we realized that Drew Cisco had almost certainly been in a hitherto unknown and unexplored part of the Maelstrom. We believe that he entered a section never before seen by any human, a little world of its own cut off from the rest of Earth for perhaps millions of years...a small planet within our own planet."

Hoke and Alan exchanged glances, and Alan sat back with his arms crossed. "Dr. Brighton, how could you come up with that?"

"Are we right?"

Alan walked to the window, parting the curtains enough to watch the leaden sky. "I've never told anyone of my last words with Drew Cisco, except for his wife. It's hard even now." Alan sat back down heavily in his seat. "We, the community of spelunkers, have always considered the end of the Maelstrom to be an insurmountable obstacle...a flooded maze. Drew had evidently been in the cave several times on his own, looking for a way to bypass that obstacle. One of the last things he said to me was that he had found a passage. I had discounted it as a feverish raving."

"Why, Professor?" mused Alfred Hinneman.

Alan looked up, not responding for a moment. He was looking into the fire, but his mind was miles and years away. "Because he spoke of a soft, beautiful light. I can hear his weakened voice right now." He sat back in the upholstered Queen Anne. "Now do I get an answer to my question?"

"Of course," Sue nodded. She flicked a handheld switch and the image on a laptop computer was projected onto a screen to one side of the room. "This is a scanning electron microscope image of the bacteria found on Drew Cisco's skeleton. If you think back to your high school biology, bacteria come in several specific shapes; rods, balls, and chains. One look at these tells us that we have something new." The projection on the screen showed individual bacteria that were almost crystalline in nature, like broken grains of salt viewed under a microscope.

Alicia Marko spoke up. "Just because the bacteria is unknown doesn't make it alien, Dr. Brighton. Under those parameters, giraffes would have qualified as alien at one time. And I don't see how a new species or a new genus led you to believe that Mr. Cisco was in an unexplored region of the cave."

"This bacterium, ladies and gentlemen," Sue paused as she looked around the room, "is not carbon based."

There was complete quiet in the room. The coffee urn whistled in the background and rain drummed against the windows. Some did not realize the significance of the statement. It was the field medical expert, Dr. Hoven, who spoke in a hoarse whisper, his voice beginning to quaver. "All life on earth is carbon-based, Dr. Brighton."

"That's why we referred to this as an alien, Reginald. We commonly think of an alien lifeform as being from another planet, but location isn't critical. These bacteria are alien to all life on earth, and would have evolved in an environment virtually isolated from the rest of the world. That is why Dr. Hinneman and I were fairly sure that Drew Cisco had been in a virgin, unknown part of the cave."

The photographer, James Okura, raised his hand like a child in class. "If these are not carbon-based, what are they?"

"Silicon-based, Mr. Okura," Alfred answered from his seat. "A very close chemical relative of carbon, but not so flexible in its chemical associations and physical arrangements."

Alicia Marko was staring at the picture projected on the screen. "This is fascinating! Not a phylum or an order, but a new kingdom."

David Lenny leaned over. "Careful, Alicia. You're salivating."

"What about diatoms?" asked Alan. "They're silicacious."

"Yes, but the principle difference is that they secrete a silicon 'shell', much like mollusks secrete calcium shells. But the organism itself...its proteinacious structure, its amino acid base, its nucleic acid based DNA...are all carbon compounds. This is a completely new situation. The very being of these bacteria is silicon, not carbon."

Joe Riechman had been trying to work up courage to make a contribution. Erica could tell from his fidgeting and the several times he opened his mouth to speak and then backed down. It finally came out. "The vent creatures in the deep ocean troughs and some bacteria in hot springs. Haven't they left carbohydrates behind in favor of sulfur based compounds?"

"Same answer as before," answered Alicia. "Although they have found a different chemical process for obtaining energy, they too are carbon-based. That's why this is so truly monumental. With all its infinite variety, all living organisms have that one common denominator...carbon. Humpback whales and moss, sequoias and bats and clams, and humans...all use carbon compounds for their entire functions. If a three-headed creature from another galaxy decided to visit earth, it would probably be carbon based. That's how pervasive the element is."

"These bacteria have nothing, nothing in common with any other life. We've long wondered whether carbon-based life is as universal as Newton's laws, whether primitive life in exotic environments throughout the universe could be other than carbon-based. I suppose that in one quick stroke a daring spelunker has answered that question before any NASA probe could do so."

Sam Telliman had been uncharacteristically quiet during the entire meeting, the writer observing and listening, taking the measure of those in the room. In the brief silence that followed, he spoke directly to Dr. Hinneman. "So, Alfred, do you suppose that these bad boys have evolved from some other bacteria or..."

"Or deep within the Maelstrom," continued Alfred, "has life itself evolved? I'm thinking...I'm hoping, that the latter is true. If carbon-based genes could direct their own replacement by silicon based genes, then we should have all sorts of weird life squirming and squiggling around. But we have never seen such fantastic monsters.

"And if life has evolved in the Maelstrom, what else may be down there," finished David Lenny. "The Smithsonian Institute would like to know, as would the rest of the world. I suppose I have not been asked to this meeting because of my reputation as a bon vivant."

Alfred stood. "Wherever you are being at, David, you are such a fun person. But in addition, we are hoping that you will help secure funding for our expedition into the Maelstrom."

CHAPTER THIRTEEN

"I'd like to say something." Alan moved toward the fireplace. "This has been interesting, educational, even exciting. But Hoke Smith and I have been sitting here reading between the lines. It seems pretty obvious that we're going to be asked to lead this group into an unknown region of the Maelstrom, a cavern with a highly deserved reputation as a damn deathtrap. With the exception of Mr. Okura, not one of you has ever been in a cave, unless you paid for a trip through Luray to see Ham and Eggs or Fat Man's Squeeze."

"Alan, we've factored in the risks...," Sue began.

"Oh, no! No, you haven't! But I'm going to help you." He stood in front of Alicia Marko. "Do you know what six hundred feet is? You could sink the Bank of America building in Charlotte in the Great Pit of the Maelstrom. And you've got to go down those six hundred feet by yourself. Remember, Hoke, the climber on El Capitan who put his descender on the rope but neglected to clip it into his harness? Three thousand feet, Dr. Marko! He fell three thousand feet to the rocks below!"

"The crawlspaces are indescribable! They choke and press down on you for hours until your muscles are screaming for a different position and your mind is ready to snap. Go home and crawl under your couch if you want to approach the effect, but stay there for most of the day."

"By the way," Hoke spoke for the first time, "the crawlspace we call Fresh Squeezed will eliminate Dr. Hoven. Nothing personal, but it's just impossible. And when it comes to following Drew Cisco's passage, it makes my blood run cold. If it doesn't scare you to death, you've got no business in that cave." Hoke was admonishing a bunch of foolish children.

"I know something about that route," Alan said in a low voice. "There is a small pool at the bottom of Drew's Pit... a pit where two people have died so far. I found two twenty-minute tanks in Drew's pack, both empty. He evidently planned to go as far as he could with one tank and come back on the other. Knowing Drew, one tank ran out and he held his breath for another twenty feet, on a chance. He evidently made it, but only just."

Robert Woods shook his head. "Forty minutes in fifty degree water without a wet suit?" he asked incredulously.

"You've seen them, Mr. Woods," Alan answered. "Men and women who can endure almost anything physically. They come crawling back into high camp after a forced bivouac, walking on frozen stumps or dragging a broken leg behind them. Drew had that kind of spirit."

"At any rate," Alan said as he stood and put on his coat, "this expedition has a condition for membership. You could very well lose your lives. And I promised myself that I'd never go in the Maelstrom again." He turned at the door. "I'm not going to lead you in there," and walked out of the room.

"Professor Manning, wait!" Sue Brighton hurried after him.

Alfred Hinneman addressed the group. "Susan will be twisting the professor's arm. Let me assure you that we will have the very best equipment, and your safety will be the foremost concern. We have leased the land on which the cave entrance is located, and have hired a security firm to be keeping people out of the Maelstrom."

"That won't set well with spelunkers, Dr. Hinneman." Hoke Smith was helping himself to a cheese Danish and more coffee. "People don't like to lose their inalienable right to die horrible deaths."

"We are not wanting to repeat the tragedy of last month. We only want to make sure that lots of adventurers with equipment but no brains don't start dropping like little flies."

"That brings up the question of publicity," Sam Telliman pointed out.

"Press releases to all the major wire services will go out as soon as the team is formed and funding secured. A preliminary article is being drafted for publication in Nature. Although we are not mentioning the cave specifically, the local spelunking community will figure it out fairly soon. Expect to be flooded with requests to join this team."

"I thought you wanted a professional to report on this expedition. Seems like you've already started without me."

"It is only a press release, Mr. Telliman," Alfred said soothingly. "We are needing you for the real writing."

"And what about National Geographic? Mr. Lenny's Smithsonian Magazine doesn't have near the readership." Everyone else in the room was either excited or petrified at the prospect of an expedition into the Maelstrom. Sam was already complaining.

David Lenny spoke to the ceiling. "As long as the initial report is in the Smithsonian, you can publish anywhere else. You would have full rights to the material.

"I think it should be obvious," Alfred continued, "the contributions that could be made by each of you to the Maelstrom expedition. Dr. Qwan and Mr. Riechman, you have started us on this quest...we'd be honored if you would continue with us. Dr. Hoven, if you could still consult with Dr. Qwan, it would be appreciated." Alfred heaved himself from a deep lounge chair. "I know that we have been putting much on you. May I suggest that we break for lunch and then meet again at two o'clock? By the end of the day, it would be very wonderful to have a team committed and funding more or less secured."

Sue caught up with Alan as he walked down the hall leading to the front doors of the Alumni House. "Professor Manning, wait. Don't leave like this."

"I don't want to be talked into anything, Dr. Brighton. It's better I just get the hell out of Dodge!"

"Will you stop walking for a damn minute?" Sue got in front of Alan as if to block his way. "Just have some lunch with me. I'll leave you alone after that. I promise!"

"And you're not going to try and talk me into anything?"

"Just idle chat about the meaning of life. I know a great steak house."

Alan smiled. "Blatant bribery. All right, but I lost my appetite back in that meeting."

"You drive. I'll navigate. And thanks, ...Alan."

Sue ordered diet Italian dressing on the side; Alan dolloped chunky blue cheese all over his salad. Sue ordered a petite ground sirloin; Alan ordered the King's Prime rib, baked potato, batter-fried mushrooms, and French silk pie.

"You have me wondering about your metabolic rate."

"High! Very high. You've got me wondering why you want to risk your life in the Maelstrom."

"The thought of it scares me to death. But the thought of letting that biological treasure remain buried...that scares me too." Sue watched Alan wolfing down his steak. "I understand about Drew's death and how terrible that must have been, but fifteen years have passed. Why so adamant about returning?"

"There's a lot of baggage between that cave and me, Sue. I'll admit it's irrational." Alan set down his silverware and pushed his plate away. "Have you ever been close to death? I don't mean sudden death when a car hits someone or the death of a family member when you get a call in the early morning. I mean have you stared death in the face, eye to eye, and watched the life slowly drain from a close friend?"

"No."

"Drew left me while I was asleep, and found that passage alone. Nothing more dangerous in the world, and he knew better. When he talked to me about forcing a passage, I was tired and impatient. What if...what if I had come back with 'I bet you're right, Drew. Maybe there is a shortcut. Let's check it out tomorrow.' For fifteen years, I wondered if I drove Drew off alone into the darkness because of my stubbornness."

"He was a grown man, Alan, and made his own decisions."

Alan put his head back and closed his eyes. "Do you remember when you were a kid and scared of things that go bump in the night? Walking down a long, dark hallway, looking over your shoulder, afraid of what might be following you?" Sue nodded.

"I left my friend down there, and had to go back alone. Walking down those long corridors, ascending through the waterfall, I kept looking for Drew. I kept expecting to hear him, catching up to me. In that long crawlspace, I couldn't move fast enough. He was right at my heels; I could hear his voice. And then that last ascent out of the Great Pit, nothing to do but think. Getting closer and closer to the light and sky, farther and farther from the best friend I ever had."

"You're whipping yourself, Alan. You're reliving something terrible and beating yourself to death with it."

"And then I think of going back into that pit where Drew died, where that kid died last month. Maybe we could find some more of Drew, some little pieces that Hoke and Johnny left behind."

"I wonder what Drew would say to you now?"

" 'Get over it, cockroach!' but with a Cockney accent."

There was silence at the table for a moment. "Do you think there are things worth dying for?"

A tight smile from Alan. "I guess I want to see where you're going, so I'll bite. Yes, there are instances where you could sit down and coldly consider, 'I'll die to protect my child or my wife.' That's different from those spur of the minute sacrifices that are done without thinking. Would I die to save a stranger's life? Hard question. So I'm standing on the bank of a river, and someone I've never seen is going under. And then across the sky, in big, fiery letters... 'You may or may not save this person's life, but you will die'." Alan took a bite of chocolate pie. "Forewarned of certain death, there aren't many situations in which I'd give up my life."

"How about freedom, democracy, and the American way?"

"Bullshit! If you could guarantee me that my individual death would ensure domestic tranquility and the blessings of liberty forever, then maybe. But that's a fairy tale."

"The quest for knowledge?" Sue asked innocently.

"Total bullshit. There is a lot of knowledge I wouldn't stub my toe for."

"What would you risk death for?"

"Want some?" Alan indicated his pie. "Risk death? Well, that's a very different and sneaky question. Yes, I'd risk my life to save a drowning stranger, because it's only a risk. Nations are saved in war by legions that are willing to risk death, but aren't guaranteed of it. Police officers risk their lives every day, and sky divers do it for the adrenaline rush. Astronauts do it for knowledge. But you see, none of them really think they'll die. It always happens to someone else."

"What did Drew risk his life for?"

"An unquenchable thirst for an adrenaline rush. But then, it was his life to risk."

"I don't believe that! Look what he did to his family. He had an effect on you. That kid followed his guide rope to his death. As much as we'd like to believe otherwise, our lives are not our own. We're all tied together and you don't have the right to toss life aside!"

Alan jabbed a finger at Sue. "Do you think any of those people back at the Alumni House would go into that hole if you told them they wouldn't be coming back? I assure you that's possible, maybe even probable."

"Listen to me, Alan. Drew Cisco died tragically. It was just a caving accident, not much different than an auto accident or an airplane crash. But now, Drew's death is going to be elevated. He will have died for knowledge that could open untold doors, Alan. We can't imagine what benefits we might have lost had Drew not forced that passage."

Alan played with the last of his pie. "Last chance," he offered.

Sue stopped his fork by holding Alan's wrist. "I'm willing to risk my life for this, Professor. It's important. We're going into the Maelstrom, with or without you. I think we all stand a much better chance if you lead us. With you, we're risking our lives. Without you, it's more than a risk."

Alan looked straight into her eyes. She never wavered.

"I've got conditions," he said.

"Name them."

"I lead this team. When push comes to shove, decisions are mine. Our lives are paramount to anything else."

"And...?"

"This so-called team has got to be trained. They have to toughened and whipped into shape, and I want everyone completely at ease with all equipment and techniques. We'll need a month."

"A month," Sue started, but Alan raised his hand. "Your little alien monsters have been waiting for a million years or so...they can wait a while longer. There's more." Sue took out a notepad and pen.

"We're not going to mess up this cave. No artificial tunnels and little tracks with little cars. No underground labs with flush toilets...zero impact, even if it means considerable inconvenience and expense. Hoke will work with Robert Woods to get the desired equipment together, and it will be the best. How is Alfred going to remunerate people?"

"We'll reimburse each individual's employer for personnel to assume teaching duties. We'll pay each individual according to their current salaries."

"That works for everyone except James Okura, Sam Telliman, and Hoke Smith. James and Sam will recoup from their publications. I want Hoke to be paid a flat fee of twenty-five thousand dollars and a life insurance policy taken out on him for a million. I'll want the same policy, the beneficiary to be the NSS."

"Gee, do you want the Smithsonian to pick up the tab for lunch today?"

"No, I'm not going to be a whore about this. I just want to get everyone back alive."

"Let's head back and put these conditions to David Lenny and Alfred." Sue gave Alan a quick, awkward hug. "What would you say to my making dinner for us tonight?"

"I'd say great."

"I'll write some directions down. Maybe Alfred will come over and we can just chat some more."

As they started out the front door of the restaurant, Alan stopped suddenly. "Dr. Brighton...Sue, have you figured out the taxonomy yet?"

"Well, the Kingdom will probably be Silicacae. We can't do much with phyla and so on until we know what types of creatures may be in there."

"One last condition. I give you the genus and species of the bacteria now."

"And they are...?"

Genus Maelstromus. Species Ciscii."

Alan drove through the darkened streets of Lexington suburbia, one hand on the wheel, the other holding Sue's directions scratched out on the back of an envelope. His glasses were perched on his nose so that he could read directions and occasionally glance at the road ahead. The neighborhood was an older one, once the fashionable area in south Lexington in which to live. But now the older homes had been bought up by young professionals such as Sue. Where once the neighborhood had become quiet and deserted as children grew and moved away, now it was full of young, upwardly mobile families. Tricycles and cardboard box forts lay on the lawns of grand old houses in a happy incongruity. Alan could see little of this. The December night had settled in early and dark clouds were threatening snow.

Sue's house was a small, almost delicate Tudor hidden behind large junipers. A cement drive wound through plantings and a manicured lawn, and as Alan stepped onto the flagstone walkway, a few hesitant flakes of snow spun past him. He couldn't help but think of his brick, one-story ranch house in the yard with no trees. For a moment, Alan was a little resentful. But he had made his own choices, hadn't he?

There was no answer to the front doorbell, or none that he could hear. But on the third try, Alan thought that a faint 'Come in' had issued from somewhere inside. He entered the foyer and this time heard a distinct cry for help coming from the living room to his left. The room was tastefully but simply appointed, giving Alan the impression that Sue was saving her pennies to furnish the house. There were only a few pieces in the living room, but looming large among them was a huge sofa, easily capable of seating four people. From underneath one end appeared two delicate feet, clad in running shoes.

"What in the fires of hell..." Alan started, but in response a lower flap of the couch was lifted and the delicate, if out of place features of Sue Brighton smiled out at him.

"Hi, Alan! Everything was all ready for you and I was just sort of sitting around waiting and I thought, 'Well, hell, I might as well see if I could fit through Fresh Squeezed but there's a spring sticking down out of the couch and it's sort of got me and I've been here for about thirty minutes now so if you could give me a hand..."

Alan laughed so hard that he forgot himself and sat down on the couch. "Oh, man! This is rich. Wait until I tell Hoke Smith."

"Don't even think about it! Please just lift the couch so I can get out of here."

Alan got down on the floor, getting a better purchase on the heavy couch. He managed to lift it a scant two feet.

"Now can you find the spring? It's hooked on my jacket somewhere."

Alan shouldered the couch and reached under with one hand. "You know, this bodes ill for our expedition if I have to save your hide in your own living room."

"I am arriving at an awkward time, I guess?" Alfred stood in the door to the living room.

"Alfred! No, I was just caught on a couch spring and Alan was giving me a hand."

"Oh, well that is giving a good explanation for everything. That happens to me so often when I go out for dinner. It is so frustrating. I am spitting on couch springs. Damn them to hell!"

Sue gave Alfred a withering look. "Excuse me while I get into something a little less dusty. Dinner in about ten minutes." Dressed in a sweatsuit and wearing a towel around her head, Sue hurried from the room. Her return ten minutes later caused Alfred to sit down suddenly while Alan couldn't stand up fast enough. Sue's severe hairdo was gone, her face framed with luxurious tawny waves of hair. The drab suits and bulky sweaters had been replaced by a stunning green and gold kimono style dress.

"Oh, Susan, my dear! Don't be doing this to old men." Alfred held one hand over his heart. "They fall down and die and then you have this big mess to clean up, ambulances... "

"Alfred, you are a better scientist than you are an actor, but thanks." Sue led the men into the dining room. She wasn't sure, but Alan seemed to mutter something about a dame to Alfred.

The three sat down to a considerably lighter meal than either breakfast or lunch. Sue served broiled trout and a mesclun salad. She poured a light wine for Alan, but ginger ale for Alfred.

"I let go of alcohol twenty years ago, Alan." He took a sip of ginger ale. "Well, it certainly wasn't going to let go of me."

Alan raised his glass. "Just a little wine for me now and again. Perhaps a beer when I'm watching football."

"From what I understand," Sue said, "Sam Telliman can make up for all three of us. He doesn't strike me as much of a team player...sort of a loner."

"That's exactly why I want this month together. If there are going to be problems, I'd like to know before crunch time in the Maelstrom. And I want to have this group together someplace where they can't go running back to the motel every night. Someplace where they really have to work together."

"And where might that be?" Alfred asked.

"I've got a friend who has a ranch on the west side of the Sierras, near Visalia. He's a big wall climber from the heyday of Yosemite and really knows his stuff. But Hoke and Robert Woods will have to be excused. They'll be getting gear together. In fact, Hoke and his wife will be driving out to Wyoming for Christmas so that they can begin work right away."

Alfred and Alan had taken seats in Sue's living room while she brought in coffee, cheese, and fruit. The three new friends spent two hours getting to know one another...sharing anecdotes and finding common ground.

Alan contemplated a large chunk of Gouda and looked at the two biologists. “What exactly are you hoping to find in the Maelstrom?”

“Nothing spectacular,” Sue responded. “Perhaps clues as to how life began on earth, possible proof that it did evolve from cells, new species...”

“Alien species that are not obtaining their energy in the same way of all other life, that are not reproducing in the same way, that perhaps are using chemical compounds that other life never thought of using.” Alfred had that light in his eyes again.

“We can begin to look for alien life in other parts of the universe with a whole new set of clues. Perhaps we have already looked at such life and not even realized it.”

“I wonder why these bacteria are bioluminescent and other cave creatures aren’t,” Alan said.

“I’ve been thinking that this blue glow comes about when the little bacteria are burning fuel. It’s just a side product.” Alfred stood up and began pacing the floor. “Of course, we aren’t knowing how they get their energy. But one way is to store their energy in a chemical bond in a substance we are calling ATP.”

“But ATP is an important part of the carbon-based processes, Alfred.”

“So, who is saying that these creatures can’t be silicon based genetically but still use the same energy mechanisms?”

“At any rate, ATP is an important part of the bioluminescence formula. And calcium, as in human bones and calcium carbonate formations, is often the chemical that initiates bioluminescence. Isn’t it great?”

"You two are weird. This will never catch on as a parlor game." Alan rose and looked for his coat. "This has been one interesting day, from alien life to extricating an attractive young biologist from under her couch. And a great dinner! Alfred, tell David Lenny to get his checkbook ready. Hoke and Robert will be ordering equipment, we'll all need plane tickets to California on January 6, and everyone will have to buy clothing and gear for our month of training. I guess the Maelstrom expedition is under way."

Sue walked him to the door, and put her hand on his arm gently. "Thanks again, Alan. I know it's the right decision."

Alan shrugged. "Right or wrong, I'm in for a dollar." As he walked down the sidewalk toward his car, Alan could hear Alfred's voice booming. "So you could give him a little kiss on the cheek. This is killing you?"

CHAPTER FOURTEEN

Rolling countryside, covered with bare hardwoods and dotted with open pastures, dropped away quickly as the Boeing 747-400x rose steeply from the Louisville airport. Erica Qwan had carefully folded herself into an aisle seat. Sue was already well into a popular book on speleology that Alan had given her, while Joe Riechman was staring fixedly out of the window.

"I wonder if I could stow these legs of mine in the overhead?" A stewardess passed, and Erica refolded one long leg that she had stretched out into the aisle.

"You'd end up in San Francisco and your legs would go on to Albuquerque," Sue laughed. She laid the book down and put her head back against the seat. "I guess I don't fly enough. I still get very excited about the whole experience."

"Do you believe there are 420 people on this flight?" Erica asked. "I've flown on these big monsters plenty, but I've always wanted to go up in a little Cessna or Piper Cub...just three or four people. How about you, Joe?"

"Never." Joe turned his head cautiously as if its sudden movement might unbalance the flying behemoth. "I mean I've never flown before, at all."

Erica leaned forward and stared at him. "Joe Riechman, you're kidding. This is the third millennium and you've never been in an airplane?"

Joe resumed his vigil at the window. "Not until today. When I was a kid, we took vacations by car all over the United States. My Dad liked to see the country."

"Joe," Sue ventured, "don't take this the wrong way, but this whole Sierra-Maelstrom thing doesn't seem like your cup of tea. What's the attraction for you?"

"So why don't you think it's my cup of tea? Maybe because I'm a little pudgy and out of shape?"

"No, no! I mean, I'm out of shape. From what you've said, you spend a lot of time doing computer work.

"She's right," Erica chimed in. "This is a little out of character for you."

"So it's out of character for the two of you. What's your reason?"

Sue raised her hands. "Fair enough. I'm not your outdoor type, either. My last real outdoor experience was at summer camp, twenty years ago. As I remember, the lake water was so cold I hid my bathing suit under a rock so I wouldn't have to go swimming. But this expedition is part of my work...it's as if I've spent my life getting ready to study these bacteria."

Joe stared out the window for a minute. "I was always last to be picked for baseball, always the one to strike out, never learned to dribble a basketball. If someone invited me to go climbing or canoeing,

I guess I'd pass. But this...this is like going on the space shuttle or on a flight to Mars. It's the ultimate adventure! I've been picked first, and I'm going, damn it!" He hesitated. "Scared, but going anyway."

"Maybe some of those grade-school jocks will see your name in the papers," Erica said as she closed her eyes.

Joe grinned. "Yeah, I thought of that."

As the continent rushed beneath them, Joe continued to watch. Entranced by the sweep of the Great Plains and the Rockies, he only rested when clouds obscured the view. He was finally asleep when the plane emerged from clouds approaching the deserts of Nevada and eastern California.

Sue poked Joe awake. "There's the Sierras, Joe." Although the deserts below them were at sea level, the Sierra massif rose almost immediately to an altitude of 14,000 feet. The highest summits were wreathed in clouds, and details of the other peaks and basins were lost in deep snow, as if softened by a thick white comforter.

"The Grand Escarpment of the Sierra Nevada. There's not an elevation gain like it anywhere on the continent." Sue paused. "I've been doing a little reading on western geology."

Erica let out a whoop that startled everyone in their section. "All of a sudden, this interest in geology! I can't imagine why!"

"Because we're going to be up to our ears in geology for the next couple of months. That's all!" Sue turned to peer out over Joe's shoulder.

He looked back from the window and adjusted his glasses. "Man, it looks rough down there. And we're going to be hiking and camping in that stuff?"

"Alan says our valley is only at four thousand feet. No snow to worry about."

"Then why, Dr. Brighton, do I have this shopping list." Erica searched fruitlessly through her carry-on. "It's here somewhere. Where's my purse?" She stood to reach the overhead compartment, hitting her head sharply.

"Damn it to hell!" and smiled sweetly at the elderly lady sitting behind them. Erica dug through her purse for several minutes and finally retrieved a folded, heavily crumpled sheet of paper. "Here it is! Heavy pants and shirts, parkas, snow goggles, boots, insulated booties, ice ax...Ice axes? Is he out of his mind?"

"I guess we've got to go through snow to get there." Joe settled back, content with five hours of non-stop terrain-watching. "To paraphrase the old ads, I don't think this is my father's vacation."

An angular man, his face all cheekbones, jawbones, chin and nose, held out a sign on which was scrawled 'Maelstrom Team'. He was standing by the end of the people mover at San Francisco International, neatly dressed and sporting what looked like a brand new straw hat. Sue waved at him and pointed to Joe and Erica. The man's face cracked a grin and he came forward with an outstretched hand. "How ya doing? I'm Freddie Madrid, Rudy Metcalfe's foreman."

"I'm Sue Brighton. This is Joe Riechman and Erica Qwan." Freddie shook each offered hand. "Let's get your baggage and head out of here." He picked up the women's carry-on luggage and started down the concourse.

"I've got to get you folks checked in at the Hilton and then over to REI in Oakland where you are going to make some salesman very happy. That'll take a couple of hours. And then..."

"What's REI, Freddie?"

He looked back at Sue but never stopped walking. "Recreational Equipment Incorporated....sort of an outdoor equipment co-op. You really oughta join, what with the money you're gonna spend. Whew, doggies! Anyway, Rudy says then I've got to get you to Fisherman's Wharf for supper and back to the hotel for a good night's sleep."

Freddie helped them collect their meager baggage and escorted them to a white mini-van emblazoned with 'Visalia Citrus Products'. Driving north from the airport and across the Oakland Bay Bridge, he kept up a running dialogue on San Francisco history, illegal aliens, and the certainty that the United States should not get involved with problems in Mongolia and Kamchatka.

"Lots of folks seem to know about your expedition, Dr. Brighton. I was standing there in the terminal and several people came up to ask me about the aliens. I told them I didn't know anything about them but it was all right by me as long as they had their green card." Delighted with himself, Freddie slapped the steering wheel and shouted a laugh.

Joe leaned forward in his seat. "The tabloids have already got stuff smeared all over front pages. I've had a few calls for interviews."

"There was this one guy," Freddie continued, "...what a pain. Kept following me around asking where I was taking you, what was the team doing in California? I finally told him to buzz off."

"Reporter?" Erica asked

"Yeah! So he said!"

"Not a reporter?"

"I guess so, but he looked more like a hockey player. Built like a rock!"

"I bet it was the same guy at Alfred's press conference," Joe commented. "Remember I said something about his wrists being the same size as his upper arm?"

Sue leaned forward. "What is it you do for Mr. Metcalfe?"

"I pretty much manage a hundred and seventy acres of citrus." Freddie sat up straighter in his seat. "It was his wife's property and when she passed, he asked me to run the place for him. You know the guy doesn't even like oranges?"

An elated salesman at REI helped them make several trips to Freddie's van. Almost three thousand dollars in clothing and equipment took up most of the spare room. Sue leaned back against an open van door. "My God, I had no idea the price of this stuff."

"I'm not so worried about being in the Sierras." Joe stuffed some food items into his new pack. "At least we're well equipped."

"And I'm famished," said Erica. "Since we left Kentucky I've been thinking about Dungeness crab and beer-batter fried halibut. Where's our guide and companion?"

As if on cue, Freddie appeared at the doorway of a yogurt shop across the street and waved enthusiastically.

Sue waved back. "You know, Erica, the man has a crush on you."

"While we were shopping, he told me that you were the most beautiful woman he's ever seen." Joe gave Sue a theatrical wink.

"Oh, both of you shut up! The man spends too much time in the orange groves."

Sue prevailed on Freddie to let them find their own way back to the hotel after supper. Armed with directions from their waiter, the three of them strolled down hills and labored up them, taking in the sights and smells of a great American city.

"Makes Lexington seem a little remote, doesn't it."

Erica scoffed. "Lexington! Honey, try comparing this to London, Kentucky! Of course, I came to a small town because I was tired of big cities. Maybe I'm cured."

"You grew up in Canada, didn't you?"

"Toronto and Ottawa. Museums, art galleries, opera houses. My mother was on stage."

"Your mother sang?"

"Coloratura soprano...she came up all the way from a tenant farm in Alabama. I spent a lot of time doing my homework at rehearsals."

Joe stopped at a gallery window display. "Look at these carvings! How can they get that detail?" When the girls joined him, Joe muttered under his breath. "Keep looking in the window. You can see the other side of the street in the reflection."

"Amazing, Joe!" Erica rolled her eyes.

"No! I mean look at the man by the mailbox. It's our reporter who plays for the NHL."

"Oh, come on!"

"Don't turn around, for God's sakes! I saw him at the press conference and I just knew he was the guy Freddie met."

"Well, why don't we just walk across the street and talk to him?" Erica started to step down from the curb."

Sue grabbed her arm. "I'd rather not risk any confrontation. Let's just hail a cab and get back to the hotel."

"Okay, but I'm out of practice." Erica put two fingers to her mouth and let loose with a whistle that startled everyone for three blocks. Two cabs materialized in front of them.

"Great," Joe said as they climbed into the taxi. "You got one for Gordie, too!"

As he had warned them, the head honcho of Visalia Citrus Products was in front of the hotel at 7:00 am. He was now less a tour guide, more a ranch foreman.

"Come on, come on! Let's move it, boys and girls. I've got breakfast in the van and we've got miles to cover. Good morning, Dr. Qwan!"

Freddie quickly got them back over to Oakland and onto I-5 headed south. "Joe, if you'll open up that ice chest, I've got some breakfast for you guys." Inside the cooler was a glass jug of fresh squeezed orange juice, grapefruit pieces, tangerine slices...

"And strawberries," Sue gushed. "In January?"

Freddie laughed. "This is California, land of milk and honey."

"But evidently not the land of chocolate-covered doughnuts," Joe said, a touch of disappointment in his voice.

"I'd guess you won't be seeing any more doughnuts for a month or so." Freddie laughed and slammed the steering wheel again, weaving his way down the freeway.

The eastern rise of the Sierras is gradual, and seldom were they able to see any sign of the snowy peaks that stood to the east of Interstate 5. When they turned onto route 198 and started east toward Visalia, the foothills were immediately before them and gave no hint of the gigantic range beyond. Past Visalia, the two lane road began to wind through orchards of orange and lemon, dark green and glossy among the tawny, grass covered ridges.

Two pillars of native stone marked the entrance to Rudy Metcalfe's orchard and ranch. The blacktop wound downward to a copse of trees and then crossed a stone bridge spanning a bold stream. From there, the road climbed through neat rows of orange trees toward the ranch house. The house itself was perched on a natural bench on the side of a low hill, looking out over a valley that marked the entrance to the mountains. Built of stone and wood with wide windows, the house seemed to blend into the landscape.

Alan Manning and Alicia Marko sat in rockers, their feet on the porch railing, and watched the progress of the minivan. When Freddie pulled up in front of the house, they came down the flagstone path to the driveway.

"We were beginning to wonder about you three," Alan said as he hugged both Sue and Erica.

Freddie came around the van. "You ladies have the three bedrooms in the house. If you'll get your baggage, I'll take Joe's stuff down to the cabin. That's New West lingo for the bunkhouse." Freddie hopped in the van and headed down the road and around a sharp bend.

"Where are the others?" Sue asked.

Alan picked up some luggage and started the group toward the main house. "Sam is driving down with James. They'll be here by supper."

"And our host?"

"You probably won't see Rudy for two weeks, until we're ready to head into the mountains. He's on a Sierra Club committee that deals with climbing safety and regulations on federal lands. He also is a consultant to a couple of those companies whose gear you bought. So he has some work to do before he can spend two weeks with us."

Erica lounged on a settee that faced the views of the Sierra foothills. "So are we on our own for the next two weeks?"

"Hardly!" Alicia spoke up. "Sergeant Madrid is in charge of physical training."

"Sergeant Madrid!" Sue sat up suddenly.

"Yeah," Alan admitted casually. "Actually, Master Gunnery Sergeant Madrid, USMC, retired. His latest posting was as NCO in charge of training at Twenty-nine Palms."

"A drill instructor! Save us all," Joe muttered.

Gunny Madrid had his troops up at 5:30 the next morning. He was dressed in a crackling white T-shirt and fatigues bloused into spit-shined combat boots. The new straw hat was history. The group before him was a classic study in body language. Alan and Erica, relaxed and looking forward to the training regimen, chatted comfortably together and were already stretching out. James, as they were to find out, was never without his camera. He was hard to read. James' camera was his window on the world, but it was a one-way glass. Fear, exultation, anger, nerves...all were emotions hidden by his absorption with his work.

Sue and Alicia had spent too many years closeted with their research. Their conversation was laced with laughter...too much and too nervous.

Joe was altogether unfit. His recreational time was spent in front of a computer, talking with others from around the world and living in a very broadening but electronic world. He stood awkwardly, not knowing what to expect and dreading whatever it might be.

Sam Telliman raised a potential problem, and Alan was keeping a close eye on him. He was a gifted but egocentric writer. Sam could paint a verbal picture that would bring to life natural beauty or ecological disaster. He could also be cutting, vituperative, and opinionated. His views concerning pre-dawn physical exercise were an open book to everyone else.

He was also in lousy shape. When not on assignment, the man spent his time in whatever bars he could find. Although Joe had youth on his side in tackling the rigors of a training program, Sam had only the appearance of youth. His graying hair was tied back in a pony-tail and he sported a ring in one ear.

Neither of which gave Gunny Madrid a moment's pause. He had never trained anyone with a ponytail and earrings, but then again none of his platoons had sported three doctorates and a full professor. He gamely led them through stretching exercises and then thirty minutes of calisthenics.

"We should have seen through you right away, Gunny," Sue said during a short break.

"It was the straw hat. Pretty effective, huh?"

"It's time for breakfast!" Coming from Sam, it sounded more a demand than a statement.

"Well, first we've got a short run down to the main road and back. It's only a little more than a mile, but it'll give me an evaluation."

"What's our goal after two weeks?" Alicia asked.

"Distance isn't really so important. You'll need endurance to get to Rudy's valley, especially through deep snow. I'll make you a deal. When you can run far enough to see the Sierras, I'll call it quits."

"And that's how far?" Joe and James asked almost simultaneously.

"Three miles or thereabouts."

"You're kidding. That's nothing at all," Erica said as she stretched her legs prior to running.

Gunny Madrid smiled. "This particular three miles has a vertical quality that's really stunning." He pointed to the grassy hill rising steeply behind the house. "From the summit, you can see the Monarch Divide. It'll take you all of two weeks."

The run down to the main road wasn't hard, but the uphill stretch back to Rudy's house was too much for some, and they had to walk up to the porch where Gunny waited. "It's all right, people. By Wednesday, you'll be taking that mile in stride. Get some breakfast and I'll meet you down at the bridge at eight."

"I'm not trying to turn you into combat Marines or physical specimens," Gunny told them as they stood in the shade of old oaks bordering the stream. "But your safety in the cave is directly proportional to your physical fitness. I've devised an obstacle course that we'll go through twice a day. It's not meant to be a race, but it will increase your flexibility and toughen you up in all the right places."

Sam strolled down from the house, hands in his pockets, just in time to catch the last few words. "The obstacle course begins about 100 yards upstream. Let's head up that way and just walk through it once." James Okura, all enthusiasm, led the group off at a trot.

"Telliman, I want a word with you!" Sam, who wasn't about to trot anywhere, hung back and walked beside Gunny Madrid.

"Don't worry about apologies for being thirty minutes late, Sam. No apologies needed. But from now on, when I say be at a place at a certain time, you be there".

"I'm not one of your dumb jarhead recruits, Gunny. I'll probably be there, but I won't make you any promises."

Gunny stopped and faced Sam. "No, you are most certainly not one of my recruits, whose common sense, initiative, and courage I'll take any day over your so-called intelligence. Speaking of which, you just made a really stupid mistake." Sam started to open his mouth. "You'll do what I tell you for the next two weeks. That's because this expedition is the chance of a lifetime for a writer. If you don't get with the program, I'll tell Alan that I won't work with you. That means Rudy won't work with you and they'll find someone else to chronicle this whole affair. So when I say be there, you be there five minutes early. When I say run, you gallop." Gunny stuck his face inches from Sam's and grinned. "And when I say piss, you piss rainbow colors. Now let's trot up and join the others."

There was another quick run before lunch, and Gunny gave them an hour after their meal to relax. James walked around getting candid shots of Alan, Joe and Erica as they rocked on the porch or Sue and Alicia as they sat in the grass by the driveway. Sam was stretched out full length, a baseball cap over his eyes.

The white mini-van drove up to the front of the house, and Gunny Madrid got out, replete with his new straw hat, hiking shorts, and a 'Save the Redwoods' T-shirt.

"My God!" said James. "It's Freddie. What did you do with Gunny Madrid?"

"Ran over him with the van, I hope," Sam muttered from underneath his baseball cap.

Freddie pulled a cooler out of the van. "Rudy and Alan wanted to make a team, so I thought that every afternoon after lunch we'd take on a little project. Rudy's got another stone bridge down the creek a ways. It's about half-built and we're going to finish the job. Since no one here, including myself, knows much about stone bridges, it should be a real learning experience. I brought along a few beers and soft drinks."

Sam was immediately all enthusiasm. "Here, let me take care of the cooler."

"Fine, Sam, cause we're walking about a mile to the site."

"Why not take the van?" Joe complained.

Alan clapped a hand on his shoulder. "Joe, for the next two weeks, I don't think the Gunny plans for us to ride anywhere."

Building the bridge involved some hard physical labor... breaking rock, lifting heavy stones together, mixing mortar. It also gave everyone a chance to make decisions about the design of the bridge and placement of stones. The atmosphere was more relaxed than Gunny Madrid's exercises and run's, but the project and the time together was valuable

For two hours, they labored under the warm winter sun of southern California. When Freddie called a break, shirts and blouses were soaked with sweat. Under the bridge, a clear pool had formed about three feet deep and ten feet across. While Sue and Erica were studying the underside of the partially completed span, Alan and Joe found a pressing need to drop a large boulder into the water. The ensuing water fight ended the civil engineering session for the day, and gave even Sam some cause to smile.

Freddie stood before his sopping wet charges, his straw hat soaking, and tried to be Gunny Madrid once again. "You people are a bunch of children! Tell you what! I'll meet you in front of the house at five o'clock. You'll need your running clothes and empty day packs, which I will fill with twenty pounds of sandbags. Any questions?"

"Can you show us that technique again? The one that ends you butt first in the water?"

"No respect for an old Marine," Gunny muttered as he walked away, his wet shorts drooping and his socks past his ankles.

The team's first attempt at the hill behind the house was short-lived. They could see the summit looming, but running to the top meant a circuitous route that took them to the far side. From there, the trail began a series of switchbacks that wound toward the summit. Gunny stopped them after a half-mile, made them walk the run out for another quarter mile, and then led them slowly back down to the house.

For the next two weeks, the routine never wavered. The group became so accustomed to the schedule that even on Sunday, when Gunny disappeared for most of the day, many of the group continued some variation of their regimen. Alan and Erica took almost everyone on a bike ride east on 198 into the foothills. Sam tried to borrow a ranch van or James' car so he could ride into Visalia and spend the evening in a bar. No one cooperated, so he rode a bike twenty-five miles round trip for a few drinks.

Joe was beginning to enjoy the workouts, almost revelling in his new-found physicality. Sam had resigned himself to his fate and by the second week had even stopped complaining. Both Sue and Alicia were thrilled at the way they were feeling, and would often join Alan and Erica on hill assaults.

It was on one of these runs that they discovered the summit was a false one, the real summit hidden by the steep terrain and their proximity to the hill itself. As they crested a set of switchbacks onto a small plateau, the real peak lay far above them. The four sat down in the dry grass in disgust and promptly dubbed the mountain 'Heartbreak Hill'.

On Friday, twelve days into their training, Gunny Madrid gathered them for their last try at the mountain. Rudy was due back on Saturday, and they would start into the Sierra wilderness on Monday.

"I won't stop you this time. We're going for the top, but we've all got to make it. Those of you who can take this bad boy can either run ahead and wait for the others who are struggling, or you can try to give them some help and encouragement. See you at the top!"

It was six o'clock, later than their usual hill run. Everyone made it to the plateau, but the last third of the run began to separate the group. James, Alan, and Erica were in the best shape, and they would drop back to run beside the others. Joe was holding the front of his thighs, but was fiercely determined to make the summit. Calves burning and gasping for air, the last of the group arrived at the top, a level area of grass and rock outcroppings.

To the east lay Moro Rock and beyond that the snow-draped peaks of the Monarch Divide, glowing pink in the sun's lingering rays. Ranks of dark spruce marched up the slopes, like waves dashing against the rocks and throwing tree-spume here and there on the higher peaks.

Gunny Madrid stood looking at the Sierra massif, his hands on his hips. "And now, class, the hard work begins!"

James plopped down heavily on the ground next to Alicia, who sat with her head thrown back, breathing great gulps of air. The two of them found that they had met briefly years earlier, when James had been sent to Isle Royale to photograph the wolf population. James became the only connection that Alicia could make to the rest of the group, and was fast becoming a confidant.

"Good job, Alicia! You ready for those big boys now?" James nodded toward the towering range growing dim in the twilight.

"The mountains don't worry me, James."

"Something does?"

She stared at the distant peaks for a moment. "Do you believe in dreams?"

"What? Like telling the future?"

"My grandparents came over from Greece...Marko was a much longer name back then. Our family is full of superstitions and old stories. So I guess I believe in dreams...sometimes."

"And you've been dreaming?"

"About the Maelstrom. Night after night!"

"Big deal! So have I! It's only natural you'd have mental pictures. Stalactites, stalagmites, waterfalls..."

Alicia shook her head and looked deep into James' eyes. "...ceilings collapsing, long falls that never end, crushing weight..."

James was taken aback by Alicia's intensity. "The Maelstrom's got a bad reputation. That could be influencing your dreams."

"There's something more. I can't put my finger on it."

"Maybe our alien bugs?"

"I don't think so. I just have this sense of some malevolence, hiding and waiting."

"You can always back out."

Alicia gave a weak smile. "I'll see how things go here, but don't be surprised if I do!"

CHAPTER FIFTEEN

In the Southern Sierras, the South and Middle Forks of the Kings River crash and claw through granite walls on their way to the citrus groves that lay at the western foot of the mountains. In doing so, the Middle Fork has carved the deepest canyon in North America. The ridge of Spanish Mountain rises eight thousand feet above the canyon bottom. These great canyons and their divides comprise a wilderness ranging from low-altitude canyon lands, lush high meadows, and basins surrounded by fourteen thousand foot peaks.

The river canyons of the Sierras have been glaciated so that steep-walled gorges are formed within the borders of the deeper river canyons. These valleys are generally referred to as yosemites, like the famous park north of Kings Canyon. Deep within the heart of the rugged Kings Canyon Park lays Tehipite Valley, so secluded and difficult to reach that few people ever visit it. When the ubiquitous and tireless traveler John Muir stumbled into the valley, he declared it a rival of 'the' Yosemite.

It was in this wild and secret yosemite that Rudy Metcalfe planned to do the technical training that would be critical to the safety of the Maelstrom team. In itself, the difficult process of crossing the Monarch Divide in order to get to Tehipite was part of the whole team-building effort.

"Force yourself to go to the next switchback, Sue. You've got to set minigoals...climb the mountain two switchbacks at a time." Alan was directly behind her as Sue struggled with the rest of the team to ascend the canyon wall. It rose steeply out of the South Fork River canyon... dry, dusty and covered with manzinita and scrubby trees. They were at six thousand feet, a gain of one thousand feet from the canyon floor.

"This is a whole new story with a full pack, Alan." Sue stopped and gasped for air. "Damn it! My legs feel like lead."

"They will for a few days. Come on up here before you stop," Rudy said as he gathered the group on a level spot. "Rest standing up. It's really hard to get back on your feet and start again."

Alan stood beside Rudy as they both rested. If Drew had lived to be fifty-five, Alan thought, he would have looked like Rudy Metcalfe. He was of medium height, maybe even short, but powerfully built. His heavy wrists and hands spoke of the power to hang from insignificant handholds. Erica had noticed immediately that Rudy had extremely short, stubby fingers. She later realized that the tips of four fingers were gone. When her clinical interest finally overcame her reserve, she asked Rudy how he had lost them. "Frostbite on McKinley," Rudy had replied, but failed to elaborate.

A hat of some kind always covered Rudy's bald head, with only a short fringe of hair showing. His face, quick to smile, was weathered and lined. Any trace of age melted away when one looked into remarkable ice-blue eyes that peered from under his bushy eyebrows.

"I'm on a reward program," Erica announced as they started out again. "I make ten switchbacks and I get a sourball."

"I was thinking more a Heineken."

"Sam!" Alicia said. "That's what we call a joke. Good for you!"

"Joke, hell!" Sam muttered.

"Five hundred more feet in elevation and we'll start into Copper Creek Canyon. Then the trail will level out for a while, we'll have trees, and we'll stop for lunch." Rudy actually trotted up to the next switchback.

"That's disgusting!" Joe was resting, bent over with his hands on his knees.

"This is Rudy's backyard," said James. "You've got to expect that he'd be in great shape."

They camped that night at 7500 feet, by a rushing tributary to Copper Creek. Rudy made each group pitch and strike their tents several times, as well as practice lighting the stoves. "A blizzard is no time to learn these things."

"A blizzard?" Joe asked incredulously.

Rudy put water on to boil and sat back against his pack, lighting a pipe. "Tomorrow night you'll be in Granite Basin, in deep snow. The wind could be howling at 30 knots. That'll make the wind chill about minus twenty."

"He's just pulling your leg, Joe," Sam scoffed

"No," Alan said quietly, "he's being conservative. According to the park service, the snow pack is twenty feet deep in Granite Basin. Of course, we only have to worry about the top three or four feet."

Ten minutes out of camp the next morning, they found snow. What had been a dusting became six inches by the time they hit Upper Tent Meadows. When the snow became two feet deep at 8500 feet, Rudy called a major rest stop.

"Snowshoes! Strap on full gaiters and get out a light wind shell. You don't want to work up too much sweat over the next thousand feet." Their snowshoes were small and lightweight alloy, but sufficient to keep them from sinking more than a few inches. The nylon gaiters covered their laces and boot tops, extending up to the knees and protecting their pants from becoming wet and freezing. Alicia and Sue passed around peanut butter, honey, cheese, and summer sausage for lunch. The team could see the South Canyon rim, now far below and bathed in sunlight. Above, the sky was brooding and cheerless.

The trail was buried under six feet of snow and indicated by only a slight leveling of the slope. They wound inexorably upward, through a region of large pines and cedar. By mid-afternoon, the group had topped out on a ridge at 9500 feet. Wind-driven clouds, heavy with snow, drove past them with terrific force. Granite Basin lay five hundred feet below them, but its frozen lakes and meadows were obscured by clouds and blowing snow. As the team reached the crest and faced the full brunt of the wind, Rudy led them over to the lee side of a large rock formation, slanting up from the ledges below. Eddying winds had piled snow over twelve feet deep, but further under the outcropping there was no wind and the snow was only mid-calf.

"My God," Alicia said as the group huddled together. "What a storm!"

Rudy's face cracked into a grin. "Yeah, ain't it great?" Powdery snow glistened in his thick eyebrows and on his red knit cap. He took a small vial from his pack and passed it around. "If you're getting a headache, try a salt tablet. At any rate, drink some water and have a candy bar or something."

"Rudy, check this out!" Alan was crouching over an area of snow, well under the rock overhang. "Tracks!"

Joe overhead him. "You mean like a bear or a mountain lion?"

"I mean like size ten Vibrams!"

"The park service says no one else has registered into Granite Basin." Rudy bent to examine the prints. "He's probably a day ahead of us."

"Alone up here? That's crazy," Erica said.

"There's something to be said for solo experiences, if you're careful. He'll probably head north up LeConte Canyon. Our trail will take us downstream."

"I'm starting to get really cold," Sue said. "What's the temperature?"

Sam looked at the tiny thermometer attached to his jacket zipper. "Shit! Air temperature is twenty."

"Out there," Rudy nodded toward the wind-blasted ridge, "it'll feel like five. Take the time to put on a sweater under your wind shell. We won't have to worry about working up a sweat. It's all downhill to the basin." Rudy took four lengths of webbing from a small daypack. "Alan, help me make sure everyone's got a swami belt. We're going to rope up as we go down the steep slope into the basin. I don't want anyone wandering off in these conditions. With this visibility, getting separated could be big trouble."

They left the shelter and relative comfort of the rock, Rudy leading them over to the beginning of a steep slope that dropped off into a gulf of clouds and darker forms of spruce. Each person now had a webbing belt with a carabiner attached. Rudy and Alan began to tie loops into their 165 foot lengths of climbing rope.

"We'll wind back and forth across the face of the slope. It won't be as steep that way and an avalanche won't get all of us." Sue's laugh trailed off as she realized that Rudy wasn't joking. "Use your ice axes to help maintain balance and remember to lean back on the steep sections. I don't think anyone will be tempted to lean forward, though."

With Erica, Alicia, and James clipped into his rope, Rudy started down. Before the slack was gone so that Erica could start out, Rudy was almost invisible. Like half-perceived ghosts of a mountain legend, the eight team members wound slowly down from the ridge. Snow covered their left sides as the wind blew at them fiercely. In an hour, Rudy had led them safely to the flats along the lakes in Granite Basin. Alan asked for a halt in a thick stand of spruce that sheltered them from the wind. The Maelstrom team huddled as if it were 'third and four' to plan out their next play.

"Way to go, everybody!" Alan threw back the hood of his parka.

"I can't believe the slope we just came down," Joe said excitedly. "And the temperature doesn't seem too bad, either."

Rudy took a swig of water. "We're going to go a little further. A mile upstream there's a boulder field that will give us some shelter from the wind. It'll put us that much closer to Granite Pass."

The team was equipped with North Face VE-25 tents, one of the best expeditionary tents ever made. The dome shaped shelters could withstand any wind that Granite Basin was likely to throw at them. After each tent was pitched, Rudy and Alan staked them out with bollards...angled metal plates that anchored well in soft snow. The three women shared one of the large tents and had just changed into dry clothes when Alan 'knocked' on their door.

"Let me in! I've got supper!" Alan dove through the tent opening, pushing his day pack in front of him. Within a few minutes, his MSR GK stove was roaring, and the temperature inside the tent rose to forty degrees. Chicken stew in flexible retort pouches, bread, cheese, and hot drinks began to revive everyone.

"Rudy's fixing supper in the other tent," Alan explained. "Erica, you're not eating much."

"Headache and nausea," she answered listlessly. "Altitude sickness, according to Rudy."

"It'll pass. Try the soup and you'll feel better. It's pretty salty. At any rate, you've got to eat." A gust of wind roared down from Granite Pass and hit the tent like a fist. The fabric bowed inward for a moment, but showed no other effect.

"The temperature outside is fifteen with a lot of snow. But the snow is getting finer, it's getting colder, and the wind is getting stronger."

Sue cradled a cup of hot chocolate. "That doesn't sound good."

"Actually, it probably means that a front is coming through to clear things out. That'll make for better hiking tomorrow."

"How far?" Alicia asked.

"Not too bad. Only about seven miles to Lake of the Fallen Moon. But we've got to go over Granite Pass."

Suddenly Rudy's voice called out through the high wind. "Alan, we've got a problem!"

Alan put on his winter gear and tumbled out of the tent. He could make out Rudy's headlamp a few yards away. "What's up?"

Rudy came forward and yelled in Alan's face. "Sam left the tent fifteen minutes ago to take a leak. In this weather, he should've been back in less than a few minutes. We've been yelling, but no answer."

"Do we limit this to just you and me? Or do we pull out the others?"

"I say get them out. If he's injured or lost, every minute counts. But keep them paired up and in sight of the other headlamps."

In minutes, the area around the boulder field was dotted with bobbing headlamps. Only Alan and Rudy called out Sam's name. The others remained quiet and listened.

"We're not going to hear a response in this wind, and there's no way to see any tracks."

Alan shook his head. "I don't think he's lost. The glow from the tent is pretty distinct."

"Then he's probably close, but injured or stranded. Let's head back toward the spruce."

Their headlamps lit the snow as it blew horizontally across their field of vision. The men plowed their way toward the trees while the others continued to search the boulder field. Just as they were about to enter the small woods, a lone figure loomed out of the darkness to their left. Sam Telliman took several faltering steps and fell.

Alan turned him over so that Sam's face was out of the snow. Rudy and Alan were able to help him up and start toward the tent, Sam slumped between them. Once in the tent, James and Joe helped him out of his wet clothes. He sat shivering in his sleeping bag while Alan got hot water on the stove.

James put the clothes into a nylon bag. "Sammy, how'd these get so wet?"

"Took a swim," Sam replied weakly as he sipped a cup of tea that Rudy had laced with sugar and butter. He was silent for a minute. "I took a whiz and then saw a mule deer just a few feet away. Walked toward it a little, and then I got this big push from behind." He shuddered for a minute, but his voice was stronger when he spoke. "Another deer, I guess. Just too frisky and curious. Anyway, I went sailing down this little valley and plunged through a few feet of snow into a creek."

"Damn it," Rudy muttered. "I should have warned you. Snow tends to melt over streams so that a valley forms. You may not see the water, but it's waiting for you under the snow."

"It took me a while to get out of the creek and back up that slope. Freezing cold! And I'd lost my headlamp somewhere in the water. I feel so damn stupid."

Rudy clapped him on the shoulder. "I think you did a hell of a job getting back up that slope, Sam. You could have died out there. Real easy!"

Rudy and Alan headed back toward their own tent. The blowing snow had decreased dramatically, but the wind was still racing down from the high peaks. The two men shared a candy bar and settled in for the night.

"You're pretty quiet, Rudy. Sam's narrow escape bothering you?"

"Nah! That's what wilderness is all about. And a team is all about helping each other. But something doesn't quite ring true."

"The deer?"

"Yeah. Most of them have never seen a human and they're pretty much unafraid. When they're in rut, you better watch out. Maybe some big doe was startled and knocked against Sam when she bolted." Rudy paused. "Maybe the sun won't come up tomorrow."

"So what do you think?"

"Sam's a big blowhard. I think he just tripped and doesn't want to admit it. It's a better theory than the alternative."

"Which is?"

"Nothing, I guess. Just that if he was pushed, I hope to hell it was a deer." Rudy turned over and pulled his sleeping bag over his head. "Or he just tripped. Hell, I don't know! Good night."

Alan knew that it would be a cold morning. He had ventured out once during the night and seen the stars blazing in a deeply black sky. Before anyone else stirred, Alan had two stoves going and two pots of water on to boil. Rudy heard the stoves and was soon pounding on tents and being overly loud and cheery. James was out almost immediately, composing shots as the sun began to climb above the neighboring ridges and shine into the basin. One by one, the team members gathered by the stoves for oatmeal and a hot drink. Alicia and Erica each took a mug of coffee and sat on a boulder to watch the basin fill with sunlight. The dark spruce began to glow bright green and even the glacially polished granite seemed to brighten with pinks and blue-grays.

As they were packing their gear, Rudy gave his morning clothing instructions. “No sweaters...we’ll work up a bunch of heat climbing the pass. Just wear a wind shell. Be sure to get paint on your nose, the back of your neck, the tops of your ears, and underneath your nostrils and chin.”

“Sunblock under our chins? That seems pretty intense.” James was applying the light green oxide cream that looked like clown make-up.

“The sun will bounce right back off the snow and cook you like a lobster. Glacier glasses, too. The snow is going to be blazing.” Rudy led off, setting a good pace along the flats of the basin and across a large meadow. By ten o’clock, they arrived at the base of a steep gully leading upward toward a line of snow that marched across a brilliant blue sky.

Alan gathered the team together as Rudy worked his way to one side of the gully, climbing along the steep side wall. “Here’s the plan. We had a lot of new snow yesterday. At the top of this couloir is a mass of snow just waiting to fall.”

“I know my French, Alan. Couloir has something to do with a slide.” Sue squinted upward toward the top of the chute.

“It’s a perfect place for avalanches. And if that cornice of snow lets loose while we’re in the gully, there’s no place to run. So Rudy is stomping out a path along the side, out of the line of fire. We’ll just follow along slowly and be grateful.”

For the entire morning, they worked their way up to Granite Pass at ten thousand feet. It was past lunch time when they crossed far to the left of the cornice, which hung like a menacing tsunami over the couloir. The line of hikers singly reached the top of the pass and gasped in astonishment.

Before them lay the glory of what John Muir called 'The Range of Light'. Wave upon wave of rounded hills, broken crags, and soaring peaks rose in frozen splendor around them. In the foreground a geologic gash knifed through the mountains, as if a huge mattock had chopped a line through the mighty Sierras. "The Grand Canyon of the Middle Fork, ladies," Rudy yelled. "Arrgh, matey! In the seat of her pleasures lie lush meadows, sparkling waters, and soft breezes.

"He loves this stuff, doesn't he?" Sue whispered to Alan.

CHAPTER SIXTEEN

The sky that greeted the team on Day 3 was leaden and uninviting, although the temperature had warmed to above freezing. They left camp at Lake of the Fallen Moon and began their descent into the Grand Canyon of the Kings River Middle Fork.

The group walked for hours through gradually diminishing snow, hiking all day downhill and losing five thousand feet in elevation. The soles of their feet burning and their toes crammed into the front of their boots, eight hikers entered the lush bowers of Simpson Meadow.

"Enough, Alan!" Erica collapsed into the grass and rolled, her frame pack still on her back. "This is a perfect campsite...right here!"

It was Sam Telliman's third straight day of bitching. He had griped about the steep uphill, he had complained eloquently about the cold and deep snow, and he had been giving Rudy fits about the steep downhill into Simpson Meadows. Now he took off his boots and threw them down. "This is a bunch of crap! Three days of bad food and pure torture, and none of it has anything to do with alien life in Kentucky."

"Sammy, stuff a sock in it!" James Okura had worked with Sam on several occasions and knew him well. He sat down beside Alicia and began assembling his cameras. "He's just cranky because he hasn't had a cold brewski in more than seventy-two hours." Even after their long day coming down into the valley, James was strolling around the campsite in his bare feet, framing shots of the landscape and taking portraits of team members.

"James, this is not me at my best."

"Sorry, Alicia, but I need you as you are, and no fair turning away. I'll just get a hundred yards back and capture you anyway with my telephoto."

Rudy Metcalfe had already changed from his Danner boots to some comfortable camp shoes, but his old red cap stayed in place as it had for the last three days. Sue was sure that it had been made 'about three hundred years ago by some Native American weaver...a novice'. Rudy walked past James on his way to the river with water bottles in hand.

"What kind of camera is that, son?" Rudy asked. "Looks weird."

"It's digital, Rudy. Takes pictures electronically, so I can see the results right away. No film to develop. Then the picture is stored on this disc." James aimed the camera at Rudy and showed him the resulting screen. "I use it to compose shots, but I still use conventional film for work to be published. Man, this scenery is incredible!"

Late afternoon sun lit the snowy ridges of the Monarch and White Divides, eleven thousand foot peaks that separated the great canyons of the Kings River. Simpson Meadows, with its gigantic ponderosa pines, sugar pines, and Douglas fir, was already in deep shadow. The river rushed and chattered only a hundred yards away. Mule deer grazed serenely, seemingly oblivious to the small group of humans wallowing in the grass. A wind was beginning to stir, and gray masses of cloud were rolling in from the west.

Rudy and Sue came back from the river with full water bottles. "Let's pitch our tents and get supper going. Looks like we're in for a storm tonight." Alan smiled to himself. He felt sure that after their initial conditioning at Rudy's ranch, two weeks of rough hiking in the Sierras, and their training in Tehipite Valley, his team would have confidence, adequate skills, and a sense of working together.

It rained hard during the night, and the temperature dropped to forty-five. Heavy winds filled the canyon, bending even the larger trees before it. In the dark rain that lashed the canyon bottom, dome shaped tents glowed with the light of candle lanterns as people talked or played cards. Most were asleep by nine o'clock at the latest, for it had been an exhausting day.

Alan got up early the next morning to start hot water. Out of habit or a sense of responsibility, it had been a routine for all his adult life. He was usually alone, and enjoyed the quiet of early morning. To his surprise, Joe and Rudy were already up, sitting on some boulders by the river. Alan walked over quietly as Rudy patted a boulder and Joe put a finger to his lips.

"Rudy says it's a Sierra morning," Joe whispered. "We're just supposed to listen."

"A Sierra morning, Rudy?"

"Yeah. There's a warmth in the air, a breeze coming down off the peaks with the smell of snow. You can hear the water, a bird far off somewhere, leaves rustling. No matter where I am, this kind of morning takes me back to the Sierras. Now, you gonna talk or listen?"

"I'm going to start breakfast. You guys enjoy!"

With three stoves roaring away, there was plenty of hot water for coffee, Alan's Red Zinger tea, and Rudy's Sherpa tea, a high calorie blend of tea, butter, and sugar. The storm of the previous evening had dumped an additional eighteen inches of snow in the high country above nine thousand feet. Alan was watching the first sun touch the ridges when Sue walked up behind him.

"Share a cup of Red Zinger, sailor?" Alan put an arm around her waist. The two were becoming closer and more and more at ease with that closeness.

"Yesterday it was Simon LeGree."

"I'll probably get back to that by the end of the day. How far to the valley?"

"It's downstream about twelve miles. Two river crossings, one with ropes. But no snow."

The unmistakable whir of James' motor drive on his Canon startled them both. "Nice shot. Sue and Alan, silhouetted by the glory of the high Sierra, deer in distant foreground."

"Who gets to take your picture, James?" Sue asked.

"The photographer is the eye of the reader, and gets to remain anonymous."

"You can take pictures of the team breaking camp, because that's what's happening next. Let's get going," Alan yelled out.

Sam was in his usual dour morning mood. The beauty of the surroundings slid past him as he concentrated solely on his complaints. Sam was letting himself go, physically. Another two years and his developing beer gut would eliminate him from trips into the Maelstrom. "I still think this is too much. I just want to get into that cave, find what's there, and get the hell out." He impatiently tied his hair back and slammed on a baseball cap. "Why we have to come all the way to California..."

Alan walked over and stooped down in front of Sam. "Sue said she wanted to get the best writer she could find to record this expedition..."

"She sure has done that," Sam interrupted,

"But I'd rather have Sue or myself or my English setter write this trip up than listen to any more of your damn bitching." Sam's mouth had dropped open. "You can leave now if you want and carry your ass back up to Granite Basin, or you can stay with us and then leave when we're out of here. What I prefer is that you remain part of this team, 'cause I think you're good at what you do. Whatever you decide, keep your complaints to yourself or I'll follow James' advice and stuff a sock in it for you." Sam shrugged and began tying his boots with unfeigned anger.

Alan stood back up and addressed the group. "Look, I know you've been through a lot in the last couple of weeks...the last few days. But we're trying to build a team out of a bunch of strangers, and the best way to do that is to share some rough times. You help each other over obstacles, you cross rivers together, get cold together, get scared together, you triumph together. When we get to the Maelstrom, you'll be a group of friends who care about each other." Alan gave Sam's boot a friendly kick. "So lighten up, okay?"

"You know, I've noticed that happening," Erica said as she shouldered her pack and winked at Alicia. "Friendships developing, caring, all that stuff." Sue blushed and began fussing with her sleeping bag straps.

"Twelve miles," Rudy announced. "It's not an easy trip, but you are about to enter one of the wildest and most beautiful spots in America."

The old trail that followed the King's River downstream was actually quite easy compared to their last few days. One river crossing was achieved courtesy of a large sugar pine that had fallen across the river, providing a bridge almost three feet wide. A second crossing was required when cliffs and broken rock marched right into the river, leaving no choice but to find a path on the other side.

In winter, the moisture of the Sierras is locked up in twenty feet of snow in the high country. Thus the river levels were much lower than they would be after the spring thaw. Rudy was able to wade and swim a quiet section in order to get their rope across and set up a traverse. Their best crossing was where the river narrowed, and here the forty-two degree water roiled and churned in huge pinwheeling waves.

The packs were clipped to the traverse and pulled across with another rope. Then each person clipped into the rope with their climbing harness and two carabiners. Alan stayed on one side, checking harnesses, while Rudy helped on the other side of the river. The difficulty lay in pulling up to Rudy's side from the lowest point on the traverse. Although a safety rope was attached to each, Rudy didn't use it to pull them over. Sam and Joe each had considerable difficulty and Sue struggled for a while, but Alicia Marko was stuck in the middle.

"I can't pull up any farther," she yelled. "Pull me over!"

"A little more effort, Dr. Marko." Rudy always became formal when he was being a bastard. He puffed on his pipe, dangling his legs over the rock ledge like a schoolboy. "Use your feet to hold your position and give your arms a rest."

Alicia kept looking at the wildly surging whitewater beneath her. James and Sue were urging her on. Even Sam Telliman forgot himself for once and yelled encouragement. As Alicia came within reach, both Sue and Sam reached out to pull her in. James clicked away while everyone cheered her success.

By late afternoon they were nearing Tehipite Valley, at an elevation of only four thousand feet. As they cleared a small rise, the river rushing about one hundred feet below them, a vista of uncommon beauty presented itself. From their vantage point, the yosemite opened before them, a smaller canyon within the grand canyon. At their left, on the far side of the river, rose the black granite faces of many major walls and the polished, intricate depths of the Gorge of Despair. On the right, Tehipite Dome soared a sheer three thousand feet. The Kings River flowed placidly through the flat bottomland, bordered with forests of pine and fir. A reverential silence fell over the group as they entered the quiet valley.

"It's so beautiful it hurts." Erica was leaning against a ponderosa pine that looked more like a wall in James' viewfinder. Rudy pointed out Native American pictographs and remnants of an old prospector's cabin. The trail led them through a grove of twisted oak trees that formed a complete canopy over them. As Sam approached a clearing close to the river, he stared in surprise at a collection of equipment lying in the open.

"I thought you said we had the whole Middle Fork to ourselves, Rudy. What gives?"

"I am giving," a voice came from behind boulders close by the river. "But right now I am trying to catch some trouts."

"Alfred!" Sue yelled and ran to the riverbank where her mentor was sitting in a camp chair, waving a fly rod around ineffectually.

"Susan! Now my style is cramped. What is it being with you and fish?" By now the entire group had gathered at the beach.

"All right, professor. How did you get here?" Alan was standing with his hands on his hips in mock anger and bemusement.

"I am being a hardy individual. Would you believe I hiked over the Spanish Mountain? No? Then are you believing that I called the university president, who called the honorable United States senator from Kentucky, who is sitting on the Interior Committee, who called the Interior's secretary who is sitting in the Cabinet, who told the park rangers that it would be all right if I hired a helicopter to place me here." Alfred pointed over his shoulder. "Actually, about one hundred yards that way."

"You cheated, Alfred," Erica said. "No snow or sore feet."

Alfred was hurt. "It was a very rough one hundred yards. And I had to carry this chair and rod. The pilot would not carry everything."

"Have you caught supper yet," James asked as he loaded film.

"I have made a start." Alfred pulled a six pack of Coors out of the river. "And a Coke for us, Alicia, since I knew that you didn't indulge. But these are for supper, so as they say, 'Back down!'"

For the rest of the afternoon, with temperatures hovering near sixty-five, the team swam and bathed in the frigid pools of the river. Trout were plentiful and easily caught, so that Sam could spend most of his time dogging Alfred and begging unashamedly for a beer. In the late afternoon, as shadows in the deep canyon sent a chill across the river and woodlands, Alan, Rudy, and Alfred walked along the flats. Tucked underneath Tehipite Dome was a breakdown of gigantic boulders. These had created several rooms that had been used by Native Americans and prospectors alike. The three men walked from room to room, looking at the graffiti of more than a thousand years.

"This valley is a place of great beauty, Alan. Is everything going well?"

"Great! Rudy's foreman has done wonders and they are really getting to know one another. One of the greatest factors in keeping a group safe is that they start to look out for each other. And they do that best when they really care."

"We start their rope work tomorrow," Rudy continued. "They're going to have some real opportunities to confront their fears."

"You will be taking them up on those walls?" Alfred asked. Rudy nodded as the staggering heights of Tehipite Dome rose above them. "I think I will appreciate them from a distance."

Sam and Erica had caught quite a few sizable rainbow and Dolly Varden trout. Rudy contributed watercress that he had found in a feeder stream, and Alan cooked two cakes in special ovens designed to fit on MSR stoves. Supper that night was wild rice and broiled trout stuffed with watercress. Alan heated strawberry preserves to pour over the cake, and everyone finally got to enjoy their Coors and Cokes. A large amount of driftwood provided fuel for the first fire that Rudy had allowed on the entire trip.

The sky was still light, but the canyon was dark as the team gathered around the fire's warmth. To everyone's surprise, Joe pulled out a harmonica and played some bluegrass tunes. James began drumming on a boulder with a particularly resonant stick. Soon Sam and Alicia were trying to clog while Alfred did a passable shag with Sue. Talking, dancing, laughing, a team was born that evening.

Out of the depths of the canyon, and up to the darkening rim above the Gorge of Despair, the faint sounds of their laughter murmured with the wind and the tiny glint of their fire showed in the darkness. The team felt as if they were the only people in the entire length of the Grand Canyon of the Middle Fork.

By a much smaller fire, in the snowy pine woods that marched to the rim of the canyon, a lone figure stood far above them, watching and listening.

CHAPTER SEVENTEEN

Alan sought his morning solitude by the boulder strewn banks of the Kings River. The team's first morning in Tehipite had dawned clear and bracing, and for the first time in three days Alan gave himself the luxury of a shave and quick wash-up. He stood, enjoying the sun's warmth on his back, and realized how delighted he'd be if Sue came down to join him. It was a strange and new feeling. For almost twenty years, after his divorce and Drew's death, Alan had preferred the company of no one more than himself. What had he done with the last fifteen years? They had flown by in an unbroken chain of preparing lectures and grading papers, early morning runs and late night talk shows.

He could feel himself opening the door just a little, partly because of his close association with the Maelstrom team over the past weeks, partly because of the new challenge ahead of him, but mostly because of Sue Brighton. He was a loner; she was shy and bookish; and a certain professional detachment all made for slow progress toward a relationship. She could wake up and come down to the river, Alan thought. She would see him standing there shirtless...the warm glow of the sun would highlight his bronzed torso. He would roughly pull her to him...no, she would rush hungrily into his arms...

Oh, for Christ's sake, you idiot! Alan mentally slapped himself. You might be in good shape at forty-five, but a bronzed god you ain't. More like Abraham Lincoln forced to sunbathe at Muscle Beach! Alan hastily retrieved his shirt on the off chance that Sue might show up, and caught some movement out of the corner of his eye.

He wasn't alone after all. A hundred yards away Alicia and Alfred were moving around in the boulders at the base of Tehipite Dome. They both carried sticks and vacillated between slow, cautious movements and sudden jumps. As Alan watched, the two squatted for a few moments and then moved suddenly off to another area of the boulder field. Hands in his pockets, Alan walked casually toward them. Alfred saw him coming and hurried across the dry meadow as fast as he could.

"Good morning, Alan! Ah, I am so glad being out of that damnable lab...I feel like I'm only sixty!"

"You two are either doing some native dance or missed your monthly mental exam!"

"No, not at all! Alicia believes that the western diamondbacks in this secluded valley are darker and smaller than the standard. It could be a disjunctive sub-species restricted to Tehipite Valley!"

Alan returned Alicia's wave. "So you two are...?"

"Measuring rattlesnakes, of course! Alicia, come quickly. Alan has found another one over here!" Alan looked down to see four inches of rattlesnake peering from a small rock cavity. Alicia bounded across the river bottom like a five-foot-three sprite who had just found gold. She deftly pinned the snake's head and pulled the rest of the animal from its shelter. Alfred made a quick measurement and recorded the data in a pocket notebook.

Alan shook his head. "You kids have fun! I'm fixing pancakes for breakfast, so don't stay too long."

By the time Alan reached camp, Sue and Erica had the stoves going and hot water for breakfast. Sue approached Alan with a steaming mug of coffee. "I think this is the way you like your morning java."

"Perfect!" Alan sipped gratefully. "I can't remember when anyone's fixed me coffee out in the wilderness." He gave Sue a tentative kiss on the cheek.

"That's what we figured," Erica said. 'Course, we're looking for the pancakes you promised!"

James joined them for the first round of hotcakes. "Sam and Joe are sleeping in this morning, and Alfred left my tent way early."

"You'll never guess what he and Alicia are up to!"

"If it's romantic," Sue laughed, "I don't want to know."

Alan served seconds to James. "It's a long story, but for once I'm glad grizzlies are extinct in this area."

"Is Rudy up?" Erica asked.

"For the last two hours. He's getting things ready for our first climbing session!"

James fixed himself some coffee. "Rudy is an interesting character, Alan, but he doesn't talk much about his past."

"I'll bet he was a flower child in the sixties."

"More a child of the big walls," Alan said. "Rudy Metcalfe was a contemporary of climbers like Yvon Chounaird, Royal Robbins, and Warren Harding. Climbed the big walls in Yosemite for years and then started a climbing school much like Chounaird. But it didn't take long for liability insurance to rear its ugly head and run him out of business."

"He became disenchanted with Yosemite. Kids sitting around, drinking cheap wine from gallon jugs and dead to the world on Sunday mornings. Gawking tourists crowding double-decker buses, shopping centers, and residential neighborhoods for the park service that looked like something from suburban Atlanta."

"So he came to Tehipite," continued Rudy as he walked into Alan's little kitchen area.

"Hey, Rudy! Have your ears been burning?" Alan asked.

Rudy smiled self-consciously as he doctored his Sherpa tea. "I've thought of this place as my valley for the last twenty years. I've got a lot of first ascents and a lot of routes, but most of the climbing world doesn't know about them. Which is fine with me."

"I found Rudy when I wanted to learn big wall abseils." Alan mainly got questioning looks from the other team members. "Guess we better start lesson one, Rudy. I'll go get Sam and the snake charmers."

An hour later, the Maelstrom team members and even Alfred were trying to master knots. Rudy and Alan were patiently going over figure eights, water knots, and double fisherman knots.

"You need to know these knots, backwards and forwards," Rudy said. "I don't want to see sloppy knots. Sloppy knots aren't as efficient and weaken the rope more. More importantly, if you're sloppy about your knots, you'll be sloppy about other things. In climbing, sloppy kills!"

As the morning progressed, each person began to tie the basic knots blindfolded and behind their backs. They learned to tie simple emergency harnesses from a single piece of webbing. "And check each other's knots! Make sure those harnesses are tied correctly. It should become habit to look at the next person's setup, like a wife straightening her husband's tie. You've got to learn to take care of each other." Rudy kept hammering this point home. "It has to be second nature to look at your friends' harnesses or their knots or their carabiners. You could save a life."

After lunch, the group hiked to a rock ledge just downstream from Tehipite Dome. A large waterfall cascaded noisily off to their right. Below the ledge, a mass of polished granite sloped away at about a fifty degree angle. This was Rudy's beginner route. The ledge itself was seven feet wide and covered with short brown grass. Rudy Metcalfe's class had a spectacular view across the valley to the three thousand foot granite cliffs and the polished granite "V" that marked the opening to the Gorge of Despair.

"First, the process of going down the rope is an abseil, rhymes with pill. When you get down to the bottom, you retrieve your rope, which is called the rappel. You rarely see anyone rappelling, because most weekend rock jocks simply go down the rope and then walk back around to the top of the cliff."

Rudy brought out a single carabiner and two pieces of 7mm kevlar rope. "You'll be using some fancy-dan descenders and ascenders, but I want you to learn to abseil using the most basic equipment," holding up the carabiner, "and to ascend with even more basic gear," he said as he held up the kevlar rope. "If you only know how to use specialized equipment, you'll be stuck when someone drops your descender down a hole. It's like never learning to drive a stickshift."

For three more hours, the group learned how to abseil using a classic carabiner wrap and then using a figure eight. More importantly, they began to get in the habit of checking each other for mistakes. By the end of the afternoon, they were becoming adept and comfortable in some old and very basic techniques. "Tomorrow morning," Rudy said as he wrapped up the first session, "Alan and I will stay back at camp while you come to this same spot. It will be up to you to set up an anchor and practice your abseils."

The team was returning to camp when Alfred met them, puffing along as fast as he could.

"Look! Look across the canyon!" Everyone stared at the massive line of granite walls with its turrets and broken arches. "Here! Look through my binoculars. Just above that big dark area."

Alan looked for a minute and then saw it. "My God, there's someone abseiling the South Wall, Rudy!"

One by one the others began to see the antlike figure moving down the cliff face. The afternoon sun picked out his red coat or sweater, but on a two thousand foot cliff, the figure seemed microscopic and his progress painfully slow.

"Stay here, everybody. I'll go to camp and get some more binoculars." Alan hurried off while everyone watched the tiny figure hypnotically. When Alan returned, a clutch of binoculars in both hands, Rudy was explaining to the others.

"That's old school. He's got a three hundred foot line, but has doubled it. He descends 150 feet, places an anchor, and then clips into it. That's what he's doing now. There! That's a rappel. He's pulling the rope down from the anchor above."

Sam was watching intently. "So he'll have to do that about six more times from where is he now. Incredible!"

"He must be leaving a lot of equipment on that wall," Alan commented.

"I think he's putting his rope through slings rather than leaving carabiners."

"Using chocks?"

"Absolutely! Instead of inserting bolts," Rudy explained, "he's using metal wedges of different kinds and sizes, placing them in cracks. It's nicer to the rocks."

The tiny figure was beginning to run sideways across the cliff face, back and forth, swinging farther and farther. "What's he doing now?" James had focused in using his longest lens.

Rudy was enjoying this object lesson. "He's got to the end of that abseil, but there are no cracks for his anchor. So he's going sideways or traversing to get to another crack system."

They watched the unknown climber for another hour, but then he disappeared below the tree line of the cliff. The Maelstrom team began to walk back to camp, excited at the exhibition they had seen.

"I guess we'll see him tomorrow if he gets across the river."

"Somehow," Rudy said in grudging admiration, "I think he will, perhaps sooner than you think."

It was dusk as supper was being prepared, and the solo climber was still a subject of conversation.

Alan was standing on the riverbank with a cup of Red Zinger when a figure came running out of the woods on the far side. Alan's mouth dropped open as the man began jumping from rock to rock, splashing through shallows, and half running, half swimming, through deeper spots.

By the time he reached the shore, the entire group had gathered. He was a young man with a mop of red hair, partially covered with a gray wool cap. He wore a red sweat shirt and faded blue running pants. He still had on his woolen millar fingerless gloves. His face and arms were bruised, but his light hazel eyes sparkled and he grinned a "Hi" as if he had just walked up to a group at a fraternity party.

Rudy walked forward. "Hi, yourself! We couldn't help but notice your descent on the South Wall."

"Well, it's not the fastest way, but it's the most challenging."

"I'm Alan Manning. I once knew a guy about as crazy as you seem to be."

"I don't have my father's looks, but maybe his love of life. I'm Scott Cisco, Professor."

Alan continued to shake Scott's hand automatically while he and the rest of the group stood in shocked silence. Suddenly Alan pulled Scott toward him and wrapped the young man in a bear hug.. There was no hiding the tears that had welled in Alan's eyes. Rudy came forward and shook Scott's hand.

"You really know how to make an entrance, son. 'Course you left all sorts of chocks and slings on the South Wall."

"I figured you'd clean it the next time you do that route, Mr. Metcalfe. Will you guys hold on just a minute? I've got to change out of these wet clothes." Scott stepped behind a boulder with his pack and reemerged a few minutes later. He had put on baggy, lightweight wind pants, a knit sweater, wool socks, and river shoes.

"All right, Mr. Scott Cisco!" Alfred had walked up to him as if he were about to challenge the young man to a gunfight. "You have upstaged my own very spectacular and surprising entrance. How did you find us?"

Scott sat down on a boulder. "I don't think you realize the fuss that's being made over the Maelstrom team. It's as if the country needed heroes again and you guys are the modern day astronauts. There are articles all over about the Maelstrom aliens. Every newspaper, magazine, and tabloid in the country. I called your office, Dr. Hinneman, and told them I'd like to speak with Professor Manning. They weren't too helpful until I pulled my Drew Cisco ace. Then they gave me Mr. Metcalfe's number at his ranch. I'm a junior at Berkeley so it didn't take long to drive up to Visalia. A guy named Freddie at the ranch said you were gone for two weeks to do some training." Scott opened an energy bar. "He didn't say where, but anyone who's read anything about big walls knows where Rudy Metcalfe hangs out."

Alan was staring at him in wonder. "I'll be damned," James said. "But you didn't follow our route?"

"Up Copper Creek, over Granite Pass, and down to Simpson Meadow? No, sir! I went straight up out of the South Fork, over the divide, and straight down. Much faster."

Joe Riechman inspected Scott's internal frame pack. "Two ropes, two small ice axes, and some..."

"Crampons, Joe. What were you expecting to run up against?" Alan asked as he fingered the crampon's gleaming points.

"I just wanted to be prepared in case I hit a bad spot. Going cross-country, you can save miles if you're prepared to climb a little ice."

Sue came forward and put a hand on Scott's shoulder. "I don't think any of these lunks are going to ask you to supper. Will you join us?"

"I'd like to join you for more than that. Dr. Hinneman, Professor Manning...I want to become part of this expedition."

"Scott, we've carefully selected these people for their experience and their contributions." Alan was trying to be adamant. "We can't just add people to this group like a club."

"I want to represent my father, Professor. I feel like there's unfinished business I'd like to attend for him."

"Come on, Scott," Alan said. "Let's walk."

They strolled together in the gathering shadows of the canyon, the last light just touching the tip of the South Wall.

"Fifteen years, Scott. So you're what? Twenty?"

"Twenty-one"

"It's amazing. Talking to you is like going back in time." Alan stopped and turned to look at the young man. "Look, I don't object to your being part of the group. I suppose it would only be right. But I could never forgive myself if something happened to you in the Maelstrom."

"I'm my own responsibility, Professor Manning."

"No, you'll be mine, just like all the others are my responsibility. Does your mother know about this?"

"Yes, sir. She doesn't like it any more than my climbing, but it's not because of Dad or the Maelstrom."

"Let's go back and get some supper, Scott. On the condition that you call me Alan, you can consider yourself part of the team."

Dinner that night was country ham, rice, and applesauce. Scott worked his way through three helpings. "Sorry," he grinned sheepishly. "Guess I worked up an appetite. I had hot raspberry Jell-O for breakfast and energy bars for lunch."

"Hot raspberry Jell-O!" Rudy said. "That takes me back."

Erica and Alicia had turned in early; Alfred and James were deeply involved in a chess game; Sam was busily writing in a journal by the light of his headlamp.

"Scott," Alan said, "when we're through here in the valley, I want you to fly out with Dr. Hinneman. I know that deprives you of the opportunity of more physical abuse hiking out of here, but this is more important."

"Wait a minute, Alan," Sue protested. "Studley Doright here gets to fly out of the valley, and we have to hike back up that mountain?"

"You nailed it, Sue." Alan put an arm around her. "He doesn't need the conditioning; you do." He turned his attention again to Scott. "Dr. Hinneman will arrange for you to get to Lander, Wyoming after you drive back to Berkeley. I'll give you a letter to Hoke Smith and Bob Woods. We've decided that they'll go into the Maelstrom a week early to get the equipment set up. It all has to be taken into the

Great Pit and then shuttled through Fresh Squeezed. I think you'd be a great help."

Sue tossed a few sticks onto their small fire. "I wish I could see Hoke's face when you show up, Scott. In fact, I wonder if James caught our faces when you appeared out of nowhere." She started to laugh. "Alan, your mouth was hanging open...you looked like a fish."

There was silence for a few minutes. Using a long stick, Scott stirred the glowing coals carefully. "You know, a fire like this is pretty rare nowadays."

"Really!" Sue exclaimed. "I thought campfires and camping went together."

"Not so much anymore. Of course, there's plenty of firewood here, but usually fires are pretty rough on the environment...zero impact and everything."

"And it messes up your night vision," Alan added. "You can't see the stars and it scares away the animals."

"I think this is the first campfire I've had in two or three years. It's kind of nice." Scott stood up and stretched. "Thanks again for including me, Profes...Alan. I think I'm going to turn in."

"Nice kid," Sue commented as Scott walked over to his sleeping bag and bivvy sack.

"He's got his mother's red hair, but inside I think he's all Drew Cisco."

"You all right with his joining us?"

"Oddly enough, it seems to make things easier. I'm almost looking forward to this." Alan turned to face Sue. "Thanks for not letting a fool walk out. It's the opportunity of a lifetime."

Sue looked down, for Alan's face was close. When she looked up again, his lips brushed hers. Alan put one hand on the back of her head and gently pulled her to him. They kissed hesitantly at first, and then with passion.

"Alan, not...not now."

"I'm just putting my name on your dance card."

"You've filled it. I haven't been able to get you out of my thoughts."

"It's been so long for me...since I felt like this for someone."

Sue kissed him again, sweetly and with less urgency.

Alan held Sue close to him as the fire died, warming each other against the chill night wind that swept down slope from the Sierra ramparts.

"Rudy would be pleased. He wanted everyone to care for each other."

Tehipite Valley had been home to the Maelstrom team for ten days. It was amazing to James that the fantastic scenery had become almost mundane, like spellbinding classical music played as a background to everyday conversation. On the night before what Alan termed their 'final exam', the scenic symphony became so compelling that it could not be ignored. Glowering clouds lay low over the tops of the cliffs, so that they seemed to soar infinitely upward. James found these conditions to be visually dramatic. He fired off roll after roll of film while the setting sun blazoned the bottom of low clouds and lit the whole valley with a fiery light.

A rising wind moved the clouds out of the valley that night. The moon, almost full, lit the cliff faces with an ethereal white light. Moonlight glinted from the rapids and pools along the river course, from the polished granite faces of the big walls, and off the hard steel point of a crampon as it was shoved carefully between the weave of a climbing rope. The cut on the outer sheath was very hard to see. The damage done to the inner core was invisible...and fatal.

After breakfast, Alan stood in camp with the others and watched Rudy and Scott as they progressed up the walls of Tehipite Dome. Their goal was to fix a series of ropes up to a ledge some eight hundred feet above the river.

"Rudy is about one rope length below the ledge now. That'll give you an idea of the Maelstrom's Great Pit."

"I'm glad Scott showed up," Alicia said. "Otherwise you'd be up there and we'd be down here on our own."

Alan waved his hand to dismiss the idea. "You people would do fine. You're ready for this." He looked up wistfully. "I would like to be spending the night on the ledge with them."

"Part of me," Alfred called from his chair, "a very small and stupid part of me, is wanting to see the view from that ledge. But I know that James will be snapping away, so I will be your cheering sections."

James sat down next to Alicia, who watched pensively as the two men worked on the rock face. "You still dreaming?"

Alicia laughed. "Yes, but I'm convinced that it's just anticipating something strange and new. These two weeks in Tehipite have helped a lot."

"Good! I'm glad you're sticking with this," James said as he squeezed off more shots of Scott and Rudy.

During the night, they could see the headlamps of the two climbers as they established their camp and fixed supper. "Hope neither of them walks in their sleep," Sam commented as he made notes in his journal.

A front moved in during the night, and low clouds threatened rain in the valley. For each person to ascend the fixed rope and then descend was formidable enough, but in the mist and clouds, the granite seemed to glare at them with an almost oppressive foreboding. It would take all day for everyone in the group to take their final exam. Some chose to hang around the base of the cliff where the ascent began, while others watched the progress of their companions from the campsite.

James went first, so that he could stay on the ledge for a while and get some shots. Although at first everyone watched every move, the routine climb up the fixed ropes soon grew into an exercise in tedium for the onlookers. One after one, as the day progressed, each team member moved up the wet rock face while a fine drizzle soaked them. Rudy would have a cup of hot tea for them on the ledge, and then the descent began.

"Joe, it's either you or Erica." Alan was standing at the bottom of the cliff with the two of them.

"I guess I'll go, Erica." Joe adjusted his glasses, a nervous habit he had acquired during training at the ranch.

"It's no different than the single rope ascents we did earlier, Joe. Just more ropes and better views."

"You don't need to patronize me, Erica" Joe snapped. He busied himself with his harness and was finally ready to climb. "Sorry," he smiled weakly and began sliding the loops upward.

After a few minutes, Alan suggested that they watch Joe's ascent from camp. From that vantage point, they could see a small figure moving against the granite massif. Although jerky and unsure at first, Joe's movement seemed to smooth out after thirty minutes or so.

"He seems to be doing all right," Sue remarked.

"He's past the first rope change, so I think he'll be fine."

Each of the five fixed ropes was attached independently, requiring the climber to pass from one to another every 165 feet. Joe had worked his way to the last rope and was within talking distance of the two men on the ledge.

"How's it going down there, old Joe?" Scott's appearance in the camp bumped Joe out of the spot as youngest team member."

"No problem, punk!" Joe shouted back. He had gained a lot of confidence during the ascent and was starting to move faster in anticipation of reaching the ledge. Joe tried to slide one of the ascenders upward, but it jammed and wouldn't move any further.

"Hey, Rudy! My ascenders stuck on something."

"What do you mean by stuck?"

"Like a bulge in the rope. It won't slide past."

"Rest in your other slings and take that one off the rope." Rudy watched Joe do as he was told. "Now reattach it to the rope higher up."

Joe's frightened voice rose toward the ledge. "Rudy! Rudy, it's like there's no rope up higher. Just a nylon shell!"

"Stay where you are, Joe! Don't try to climb higher. I'm coming down with another rope.

"Hurry. The weave looks like it's coming undone! Oh God, it is!"

"It can't, Joe. I'll be there in a minute."

Suddenly a wild cry rose from the cliff face. Those below who were not watching looked up in horror as Joe's body fell through space. He never hit the smooth face of the cliff until the rope stopped him after a fall of a hundred feet. Erica screamed as his body came to a jerking halt and hung bent, like a rag doll.

Rudy had started down the rope, but it would take him twenty minutes to reach Joe and rig a pulley system by which he could lower him. Alan had started up from the bottom of the climb to help. When Rudy reached Joe, he was barely conscious and the pressure on his chest was making it difficult to breathe. An hour of excruciating work enabled them to get Joe off the cliff face and back into camp.

The harness system and the force absorption of the rope had saved Joe from serious injury. But the fall had another, more lasting effect.

"I'm sorry, but this has done it for me," Joe winced as he sat up. "I've tried my best, and I was doing pretty well, but I am not going into the Maelstrom."

"Joe, we understand, but..."

"Erica, you have to fall a hundred feet and dangle six hundred above the ground before you could understand. Not everybody is cut out for this sort of thing. That's me." Joe turned gingerly to Alfred. "Dr.

Hinneman, thanks for including me, but I'm flying out with you and Scott tomorrow."

"Whatever you wish, Joe. We are just being thankful you're all right."

"The rope broke, Rudy? Climbing ropes don't break, especially when it just has a static force like a climber hanging on it!"

"The ropes were new, Alan. But the thing broke. We're going to do some testing, but the only thing I can think of is a manufacturing defect."

"Rudy, how are we going to avoid defects while we're in the Maelstrom?"

CHAPTER EIGHTEEN

Janine Blake stood outside the bedroom door, her youngest girl perched on her hip. Trying to understand what Henry Talbot was telling her, she wiped her eyes fiercely with the heel of one hand.

"I don't know why you can't do nothin' to help him."

"Janine, I'm just stumped. I think we've got him what I call 'stabilized', but he's not getting any better. We've got to get Dennis to a specialist."

"Louisville?" Ronnie Blake had walked up behind his wife.

Henry avoided their eyes. "Chicago!"

"No! Who would go with him? And my babies here!" Janine's eyes were wide with fright.

"We haven't got any money for this, Doc." Ronnie was looking at the floor.

"Just for some tests...for a couple of days. There's some funds at the hospital that we can use."

"You'd have to go with him, Janine. I can't leave work or I'll lose my job."

"Guess my Mom could look after the little ones."

"Why don't you go call her while I talk with Doc Talbot?"

"I'll call her after supper."

Ronnie Blake turned on his wife. "Damn it! You go call her now like I tell you! Now git!"

Janine set her jaw, but marched off toward the kitchen, slamming the door behind her.

"Sorry, Doc! But I needed to talk to you alone. You remember when Dennis broke that other arm?"

"Sure do. The same night he discovered that body. It must have been pretty scary for him."

"Did you ever see that body?"

"No. I was mainly worried about the boy's arm."

"That body didn't have any bones, Doc. None at all! I was down there when the rescue squad scooped that body into a bag!"

"No skeleton? I've never heard..."

"You've never heard of a body that glows blue like a neon sign, Doc Talbot. But this one lit up the inside of that barn."

"There's no way that could happen, Ronnie. It had to be something else!"

Ronnie Blake stared at Henry for a moment. "I seen more than one body like that. You never saw the Forster kid after he died, did you?"

"No, I never had a chance." Henry Talbot was starting to feel sick to his stomach.

"They didn't want anybody to see what a mess that boy was. But I saw! We all thought maybe he was radioactive." Ronnie opened the bedroom door. "Come in her for a minute, Doc! And close that door behind you."

Dennis was asleep, a respirator over his mouth and nose due to breathing problems that had developed several days before. Ronnie turned off the room light and stood away from the bed. "Let your eyes get used to the dark, Doc."

Henry saw nothing at first, but let out a small moan as a soft, very faint glow became evident.

"This is my oldest boy, Doc Talbot, and I don't think he's got much more time. I'm not going to see him stuffed in a body bag like some piece of road kill shit! I know what happens to me if I don't do my job. I was wondering what happens to you medical boys when you screw up!"

Press releases had been sent to the wire services on December 10th, two days after the meeting in Lexington. By Christmas, word had spread worldwide. In a hundred languages, the usual headlines of the day were obliterated as people read every word they could find about alien life discovered in a Kentucky cavern. Legitimate news organizations carried interviews with Alfred Hinneman, who did his best to explain about evolutionary principles and silicon based bacteria. But one overriding factor entered all the reports. Despite its technical accuracy, the term 'alien' had caused an almost manic reaction. Most people who heard the report understood that life forms had been found in the cave, but also were convinced that the strange glowing creatures had ultimately come from outer space. Many reporters found that the word 'bacteria' did not cause nearly as much excitement as did the more general term 'creatures'.

The tabloids were having a field day. No Hollywood sex scandal, no gigantic babies, nor Nostradamean predictions sold like actual alien life. As the details became known concerning Drew's skeletal remains, the death of the college student, and finally the name of the cave, the tabloid headlines became larger and more lurid. 'Kentucky Cave Hides Alien Life' with a particularly tired looking alien being (big head, big eyes) superimposed against a background from Carlsbad Cavern. 'Team to Enter Cave of Death' with spacesuit clad researchers standing among piles of skulls.

The Maelstrom team had been announced to the wire services by the Smithsonian, which was only too glad to have beaten National Geographic to the punch. The team members, however, had disappeared into the wilds of the California mountains on what the newspapers called a 'secret training mission'. With no one authoritative to interview, the media began to carry representatives of every group world-wide that had anything to say about aliens...scientific organizations, UFO experts, members of SETI(Search for Extra-Terrestrial Intelligence), alien alarmists and alien lovers, prophets of doom and religious fanatics. All were focused on February 15, the date that the expedition would enter the Maelstrom.

Alfred Hinneman was having a wonderful time. He had resigned himself to uneventful golden years in which he would lecture and supervise graduate students. Now he was embroiled in an earth shaking discovery and wasn't going to miss out on anything. During the two months since the announcement of the Maelstrom discovery, the old Pure station at the bottom of the mountain had been renovated into an office for the expedition, a room for the security people, and an efficiency for Alfred.

Hoke, with the help of Bob Woods and Scott Cisco, had transported most of the gear up the mountain to the mouth of the Great Pit. There a gasoline powered winch had been mounted to raise and lower seven hundred feet of kernmantle rope. The equipment and supplies had arrived at the bottom of the pit via a large metal basket. All of the gear was then packed into aluminum cases that measured two feet square and six inches high. This allowed two of them to be stacked and still make it through Fresh Squeezed. Bob had ordered heavy cordura nylon bags with Velcro closures that would exactly contain two of the flat boxes. In this way, each man could take four boxes through the crawlspace, pushing two in front and dragging two behind. At twelve boxes per trip, it had still taken four grueling crawls to get all the boxes to Miami Beach. This work alone was so exhausting that in the entire week, none of the men had gone further into the cave. On the morning of the fifteenth, Hoke and his companions worked their way through the crawlspace once again and waited at the bottom of the Great Pit.

At eight in the morning, a University of Kentucky van containing the six members of the Maelstrom team pulled up at the new Maelstrom headquarters. The van was immediately besieged by three news teams. Security guards were attempting to keep about fifty onlookers from getting too close to the team members. Placards were in evidence that variously cheered the team members or defiled them for the possible destruction of 'the aliens': 'Leave The Aliens Where They Are!'; 'Don't Violate Alien Habitat'. The Maelstrom team stared open-mouthed at the furor from which they had been insulated during their training. In front of a bank of cameras and recorders, Alan was trying to defuse some of the nonsense.

"It's true that we have evidence of life from the Maelstrom that is unlike anything else on earth. But it is not from another planet, and it is not monstrous. The only organism that we know about is a glowing bacterium that probably cannot survive the ultra-violet radiation from the sun."

"But you don't know what else may be in the cave, do you?"

"No, but for some very abstruse reasons, dealing with cellular biology, we don't believe that anything much more advanced could be living in the Maelstrom."

"You don't believe, but you're not sure?"

"Well, we're about to start up that mountain to find out. We'll give you a full report when we return in ten days."

Fresh from their Sierra training, the team felt as if the snowy Kentucky mountainside was a Sunday stroll. In addition to the team, two TV reporters and their camera crew preceded them up to the cave entrance. A light snow had fallen and been crusted over with sleet. The sky was a leaden gray, entangling the dark, bare limbs of deciduous trees with mist. Except for Alan, none of the group had seen the Maelstrom's entrance. Rather than the excited chatter that might be expected from a group on the verge of a great adventure, each person was absorbed in their own thoughts.

As they crested a small rise, the Maelstrom's entrance came into view for the first time. In the snowy landscape, its black gaping maw stood out in stark relief. The air issued from the Maelstrom's depths and rose in a mist, like steam from a boiling kettle. It was the mouth of a great beast, breathing out into the frigid daylight its moist, warm breath, smelling of soil and rock and rotted leaves. The mist froze on any surface with which it came in contact so that every limb, rock, and blade of grass was covered with a hoary frost.

Sue shuddered involuntarily and touched Alan's arm. "It's not like the Sierras, Alan. We had clean, open air, with sun shining and birds singing...the whole nine yards. Somehow I don't see many harmonica hoe-downs around the campfire."

Alan put his arm around her waist and squeezed her. "Well, we have lost our harmonica player and there is a certain dearth of firewood in a cave. But no reason not to make music." He let Sue go but took her hand. "This is the first time I've stood in this spot in more than fifteen years, and I'm glad to be here. I've needed to do this for a long time." He stepped away from Sue and spoke to the entire group.

"I need everyone's attention, please. Including the media. With the snow and ice on the ground, it's important that no one step into the area that slopes toward the mouth of the pit unless you are harnessed into a safety rope. We'll be glad to help the camera operators into harnesses, but absolutely no one can be inside the bowl without a safety line. One slip and that's all she wrote." Alan pointed to one of the reporters who had taken a seat on top of the huge winch housing. "That includes the area around the winch, sir. From that location, you're only about fifteen seconds from certain death." The reporter blanched and moved carefully back up the slope.

"Now if the team members will gather here at the staging area." Alan referred to a generally level space near the top of the pit. "I have a pack for each of you, especially made for the expedition. It's very tough nylon cordura and will just contain two of these aluminum cases." Sam and Alicia began passing the metal cases around.

"When you open these," Alan continued, "you'll find that they are waterproof with seals much like a military ammo box. Inside you'll find an inflatable foam pad, a Gore-Tex bivvy sack, and an extremely lightweight sleeping bag. The whole system is only four inches thick in the box but will keep you warm to thirty degrees. The rest of the room in the boxes is for your clothing, spare batteries and bulbs, and toilet articles."

"We get to use all four inches left?" Sam asked. "Your generosity is boundless."

"No, it leaves off at four inches," Alan replied. "You can squash a lot of clothing into that much room. Let's go ahead and get these packed up so we can get ready for the descent. Alfred will send a couple of security people up later to get your duffel bags."

"Harnesses, Alan?" James asked.

"Yeah, go ahead and get into those. Same old friends you had in Tehipite Valley." As they began suiting up, Alan noticed with some pride the confidence with which they donned their harnesses. He saw Alicia eyeing the back of Sue's harness, and Sam unconsciously checking one of James' leg loops while he talked to Erica. These people are going to be all right, Alan thought. And barring a cave-in, we'll all come out again. Alan could feel himself beginning to relish the idea of the expedition. An exciting discovery, coming home to a cave he had always loved, sharing it with people new to caving. He could hardly wait to show them the Champs Elysees and Moria.

Moria! The name brought back memories of Drew, but for the first time in fifteen years they were good memories of a good friend, not the tragic phantoms that had chased him out of the cave and had continued to chase him ever since. Perhaps he had exorcised a ghost at last. Alan shook himself out of his reverie.

"Let me explain the emergency rope to you. It's seven hundred feet long and controlled by the winch. We've only used it to transport gear and we'll use it in case of an emergency. James will be on it today so that he can move up and down the rope and record the individual descents of all the team members. The winch itself is anchored by two bolts and can be started and stopped by a switch all the way at the bottom of the pit."

"That's quite an extension cord," Alicia commented.

"Mr. Lenny has spared no expense to see that we're all safe and sound. We'll be using two standard ropes for our descents, just like you did in the Sierras." Alan clapped his hands. "All right, boys and girls. Let's do it! James will head down the emergency rope. I'll go last. Do we have any volunteers for first?"

The four remaining team members looked at each other. "We already drew straws," Sue answered. "I won...or lost."

"Off you go, then. And smile for the cameras."

Sue walked over to one of the descent lines, attached her descender to the rope and to her harness, and waited for Alicia to check her out. She started to move toward the edge of the pit.

"Wait," shouted Alan. "Let me check something." He hurried over to Sue, grabbed the rope, and kissed her hard. "Okay, you can go now."

The look of serious concentration disappeared from Sue's face, and she laughed as she started down the slope. Sliding smoothly over the edge of the pit, she could hear Erica's voice.

"Hey, Professor, do I get one of those?"

CHAPTER NINETEEN

James Okura was a master of his craft. He was the consummate expedition photographer, going twice as far, working twice as hard, often risking twice the danger. As Sue cleared the edge of the pit, James was at her level on the emergency rope, about fifteen feet away. The wane, gray light of day still lit Sue and the rocks of the pit immediately below her. Exposed correctly, the picture would show the edge of shadow in deep black contrast to the line of daylight. James continued to fire away as the lower part of Sue's body crossed the line into darkness, so that she seemed to be floating in a black pool.

"Okay, Dr. Sue," James called. "Go really slow while I get set." He held the handgrip of his descender lightly and immediately dropped thirty feet, where he began composing his next shots.

The Great Pit of the Maelstrom was a doorway for each team member, open and silently waiting their entrance. Each approached that doorway with their own expectations, excitement, and fears. James was not unmindful that he was dangling six hundred feet above the bottom of the pit or that he was entering a cave known for its dangers. But as a photographer, he had the luxury of intense involvement with his equipment and the job at hand. Some moments, improperly recorded, could never be reproduced and James took this responsibility seriously. He saw the Great Pit with its striated walls and wildly eroded turrets and chutes through his viewfinder and lenses. He had been one of the early photographers of Leucugilla Cave and knew more than the others just what the team could expect to encounter. Like James, each of the other expedition members coming down the two ropes entered the Great Pit looking through their own lenses.

Sue began her descent happy and confident. She was entering Alan's world, and was determined to learn as much as she could. Sue had hopes that she would be spending more time in caves because she would be with Alan. She moved slowly down the rope, barely putting pressure on the handgrip. A Gibbs ascender was hooked on the rope above her and slid downward with her left thumb holding the catch open. Alan had told her not to expect any formations along the walls of the pit because the movement of flood water and the atmospheric conditions did not create a proper evaporative environment. Sue found the walls of the pit, nonetheless, fascinating.

On the face nearest her, she had a good view of the rock only a few feet away. Had there been a need, she could have put her feet out and walked down the rock. She tentatively pushed against the limestone and moved backward away from the wall, beginning to swing in small arcs each time she pushed away. The limestone was generally the color of cement, but had been stained by water that flowed into the pit from above during storms. These streaks, like stains moving down from the faucet of a sink, showed various hues of reddish brown and yellow. Sue was close enough to see that some bands in the rock were definitely sandy and coarse as opposed to the fine grained limestone. So, Alan had explained, we know that this limestone was close to a shore where heavier sand could be washed into the water. Intervals of deeper water and then briefer intervals of shallow. Sue could see the patterns; here a short period of shallow water followed by a four foot layer of limestone, then a six inch layer of sand, followed by...what? Twenty feet of limestone? It was like reading a book.

But the lines weren't horizontal. They must have been originally, when the layers were laid down. But some great machinations in the earth's interior had twisted and contorted the layers of sand and limestone. Sue watched the layers spiral downward until they were lost at the limits of her headlamp. She slowly spun around and looked at the opposite wall, perhaps twenty-five feet away. There were places where falling water had hit a ledge and rather than falling down the face of the ledge, the water had begun to inexorably eat into it. This began to form hollow tubes behind the face of the pit wall. Some were nearly perfect, descending the walls for unknown depths. The sides of other tubes had eaten away so that the interior was exposed for some distance. Where the erosion had been going on for a longer time, some of the older tubes had walls that had been breached in many places, so that all semblance of a tube was gone, its walls becoming weirdly shaped crenellated spires.

"Sue," James called. "Over here." James was at her level on the emergency rope. "Catch the line." He tossed a 9mm rope toward Sue with a carabiner attached to one end. Sue caught it on the second try. "Now clip the carabiner to your rope."

"Where at?"

"Between your descender and your Gibbs." Sue did as she was told. James had attached a jumar-type ascender to the small rope that connected the two of them. As James pulled on the rope, it fed through the jumar, which cammed on the rope whenever James let the rope go. In this way, he was able to pull the two ropes closer and closer, so that he and Sue met in the middle of the great chasm, only three feet apart.

"Hi, lady. I hope you don't mind some close-ups."

"Not at all. The walls of the pit are fantastic, aren't they?"

"I've never seen anything like them. I can't wait to see the pictures, although I'll have to rig lamps to get the full effect of all the vertical chambers."

Sue looked upward at the entrance, about a hundred feet above them. "Here comes someone on the other rope. I guess that's Erica."

"Then I'll let you go. Watch out now! When I release the jumar, we'll part like two negative charges."

"Oh, you can do better than that. Like jilted lovers."

"Whatever," James said and released. They swung toward their respective sides and pushed off gently with bent legs. "Sue, when you get to the bottom, tell someone to hold the emergency rope lightly. When I lift the rope a few feet, they should start the winch. They stop the winch when I drop the slack."

"Okay, I got it. Anything else?"

"Yeah! Make sure there's a big ass knot...about the size of a watermelon...on the end of this rope. I don't want to go abseiling off the end of it while I'm involved with shooting."

Sue continued her descent. The other lens through which she viewed the cave was that of a researcher. In all her experience, she had never done field work. Research on cellular organelles could pretty much be carried out in a closet, and certainly didn't require expeditions to exotic locales. Perhaps more than any other expedition member, Sue had reason to be excited at the prospect of their work in the Maelstrom, for she had both professional and private motivations.

James watched her, without his cameras, as Sue glided out of sight. In a surprisingly short time, her presence was marked only by the dim glow of her headlamp. Looking upward, he saw Erica Qwan's light as she looked down in his direction.

Dr. Qwan did not look at the Maelstrom expedition professionally. Her technical knowledge would be of little use to the team, even as a stand-in medical officer for Dr. Hoven. Erica knew that her inclusion on the team was a nod of appreciation for her professionalism and her perseverance in bringing the whole matter to the attention of people who could recognize its worth. In that respect, she was determined to enjoy the adventure, for it was her reward...her medal from academia.

Erica found that she could relate to the scene around her, despite her lack of caving and other outdoor experiences. The long fluted tubes, of different sizes and lengths and running down the inside of the pit walls, reminded her of the great cathedral in Toronto to which her mother had taken her on several occasions. On one trip, she had listened enraptured while her mother and three other soloists had taken part in a performance of Beethoven's Missas Solemnus. Erica had sat with her head back, listening to the wonderful tones of the soloists, the choir and the orchestra. Looking upward, she had been fascinated with the huge collection of pipes that was the renowned organ of that cathedral. Here, in the dreaded Maelstrom, she felt that she was descending a gigantic pipe organ. What she wouldn't have done for a cassette of Bach's Toccata and Fugue. Erica continued her descent, amazed at how smoothly she moved down the rope. By squeezing the molded handle of the descender, she moved at what seemed like free fall. But she could slow her speed gradually by lessening the pressure of her grip. James was following her down, keeping pace with her at first, but finally stopping about two hundred feet short of the bottom.

"Last picture, Erica. I promise."

"That's all right. It's a long trip when you're by yourself."

James loaded another roll of film. "You're not living up to your reputation of being a little...disorganized."

"Scatter-brained, you mean! It's pretty well-deserved, but it only extends to little things like car keys, appointments, and balancing my checkbook. Life and death situations are easy to focus on."

"Well, then I guess you won't get lost between here and the bottom of the pit. See you later, Erica." James pulled up about four feet of rope and a moment later he began to rise as the winch started turning.

"Thanks for your company." Erica watched James rising upward as if by magic. "Hey, James! Nice butt!"

By the time James had reached a point just one hundred feet from the top of the pit, he met Sam Telliman. Sam was stopped on his rope, with his back to James and his head bent downward. At first James thought that Sam was adjusting something or inspecting a knot. Little late for that, James thought. Then Sam slowly spun around and James could see that he was writing.

"What are you staring at, Okura?" Sam asked. "I've got my job too, you know."

"I just didn't think you were going to write on your way down."

"When I get a flash of brilliance, I need to write it down. Two days from now I don't want it lost among my other flashes."

"Hot flashes?" James asked innocently.

"Wiseass!" Sam put away his notebook and resumed his descent. "I just realized that this is like Alice in Wonderland. We're going down the rabbit hole, following our little glowing March Hare. I imagine there will be parts of the cave where we will feel damn small. Then again, we're going to feel like we grew twenty times when we're in the crawlspace.

"I guess that's worth making a note of," James admitted as he clicked off a few shots of Sam.

Sam suddenly stopped. "Hey, hey! Try this on for size! 'A Zoologist's Descent into Another World or Alicia in Wonderland. God, I'm so good it's scary."

James put away his gear. "No more pictures of you for a while. My wide-angle won't take care of your big head. I'm going to catch up to Alicia." With considerable effort, James lifted four feet of rope and once again the winch motor started.

Alicia was starting her walk backward down the slope that led to the edge of the pit. The ice and snow that had collected on the slope required more sure footing than usual, and Alicia looked very uncomfortable. Both James and Alan could see that she was not leaning back enough on her rope and that her feet were too close together. This gave her a pivot point rather than a wide-stanced base. Sure enough, as James was composing a shot, Alicia lost her balance and swung to one side. Instinctively, she let go with her left hand to stop her fall against the icy slope. Twenty years earlier, such a move could have had tragic consequences. But when Alicia released the rope with her left hand, she also released the Gibbs ascender. As long as there was no tension, the Gibbs slid easily down the rope. When Alicia let go of the Gibbs, its cam action grabbed the rope. Alicia could not have fallen if she had thrown herself backwards.

Alan just stood at the top of the slope and smiled. "Well, better to scare yourself here than halfway down the pit."

Alicia, more embarrassed than scared or hurt, laboriously righted herself, leaned back on the rope with her feet spread, and still went nowhere. "You're forgetting your Gibbs, Alicia," Alan explained. "You've got to reach up and take pressure off of it."

Alicia dutifully pulled herself back up the rope until she could grab the Gibbs. "I'm glad that didn't happen on the vertical," she said. "I'd have never been able to get that far up the rope." She started down the slope and went over the edge of the pit uneventfully.

In her research work as a zoologist, Alicia had specialized in mammalian predator-prey relationships, particularly in North America. She had been in the field many times to study grizzly-caribou, grizzly-elk, cougar-deer, or wolf-moose interactions. This, however, was a different story. Although the new life forms were microscopic, Alicia felt a thrill of discovery at what had been found and what might yet be found. Were there more highly developed organisms in the unknown depths of the Maelstrom? To her, the Maelstrom expedition could be the defining work of her career, and she'd known that since the November meeting in Lexington. After all of those months, she was finally here.

As he had with the others, James followed her down, but other than an encouraging wave now and again, he left her alone. Although James went to some pains to pose shots, he also knew that many of his best 'people' shots were candid. He wanted to let Alicia experience the Great Pit on her own as much as possible and to capture her in that light. Left to her own thoughts and imaginings, Alicia's biological training soon manifested itself in her own view of the Great Pit.

If she had actually been swallowed by a gargantuan prehistoric lizard, the effect could not have been much different than what she saw before her now. The dark maw of the beast continued on into the darkness below her while above her its mouth opened to the air, bellowing out some primeval voice of victory and satisfaction. The tunnel in which she found herself was lined with longitudinal musculature, possibly to aid in swallowing, she thought to herself.

The cold bracing air of the Kentucky countryside was gone. Rising toward her was the warm, heavy air of the cave, fetid and very old. As she moved farther into her imagined beast, Alicia had a clear presentiment of danger, if not doom. It had nothing to do with abseils or a cave-in or any danger inherent to a cave such as the Maelstrom. She closed her eyes and old dreams rushed back. There was something else that seemed to press her down the rope, pushing her farther into the depths.

Shake it off, she thought. This beast business is getting pretty weird. Alicia made a conscious effort to look at the pit in some other way. There was another similarity of the unusual tube formations to something zoological, but she couldn't quite remember what. A few minutes later several long tubes came into view, seemingly glued together. Mud daubers, she thought. They look just like the tubes that mud daubers stick to the sides of rocks and buildings. Absorbed in these thoughts, she was startled when Alan zipped by her and stopped about fifteen feet below on the other rope.

"Ma'am, would you like some company for the rest of the way down?"

"Yeah, thanks! My mind has been doing some pretty strange things."

"In this place? I can't imagine why."

Alan and Alicia began moving down their respective ropes at the same speed. Staring at one another, it seemed the pit walls were moving upwards. Below him, in the depths of the pit, Alan could see the blinking stars of the team's headlamps. He had his own feelings as he and Alicia came closer to the bottom.

A great adventure; Sue...his newfound friend (dare he think lover?); a homecoming for him; a justification or at least a vindication of Drew's death; Drew. How could he go through Fresh Squeezed or the Champs Elysees without thinking of Drew? How could he enter that awful, final pit?

He knew now that he would think of Drew, but with pleasure at the memory. He would hear Drew's voice chastising him, and he would smile at the thought. Alan was sure now that he could lead this group. And he was looking forward to it.

From below, the Maelstrom team saw the lights of the last two team members coming down the rope. There was a feeling among them all that this would be the start, this gathering of the whole expeditionary team at the bottom of the Great Pit of the Maelstrom. From that point, their adventure would begin.

CHAPTER TWENTY

Scott walked at the back of the group as they neared the end of the breakdown. Alicia was trying to tell him something about a bear in the Sierras, but her story was often interrupted by grunts, sighs of frustration, and occasional cursing as they negotiated the breakdown. Scott only half heard Alicia, concentrating on his footing. He stopped suddenly and looked around the long gallery.

"What's the matter, Scott?"

"I thought I saw a movement over there," Scott answered and shrugged his shoulders. "Dim light, though. Guess not."

"Ghosts," Alicia said and immediately regretted it. "Sorry for my big mouth, Scott."

"Don't worry about it, Doc. I've got to tell you though, the three of us have all felt a little strange in here for the last week."

"In what way?"

"Like we're not alone. Bob says he thought he saw someone once, but Hoke says it's just cave jitters and funny lighting on formations."

"Could be trolls, you know."

James Okura fell back with Scott and Alicia. "Dwarfs! Dwarfs live in caves and mine for precious gems. Trolls live under bridges and eat raw fish."

"Thanks, J.R.R.," Alicia said dryly. "Anyway, if someone got past security, why would they want to be down here incognito?"

"People can get some pretty wild ideas about a discovery like this," James observed. He caught himself to prevent a slide down a steep rock slab. Finally James deserted his dignity and sat down to negotiate the rock. "Imaginations run wild. Someone wants to be the first to bring alien life back to the surface. They believe there's a lot of money to be made somehow. Or they'd like to have a little expedition notoriety rub off on them. Lots of crazy reasons."

The three rejoined the rest of the research team at the end of the breakdown. Sam was lying on his back and staring at the ceiling only seven feet above. "I don't want to seem like a complainer..." A laugh erupted from Erica, and she covered her mouth. Sam glared at her. "But is the whole cave like this?"

"Nope," said Hoke. "In fact, this is unique to the whole system. Alan and I put these blocks out here one morning to separate the men from the boys. Pardon me, ladies," Hoke tipped his helmet. "But in about an hour, you folks will be making all sorts of ridiculous offers if only you can come back here and play in the breakdown."

Alan took the old register container from its niche and extracted the spiral bound notebook. "Here's where those college kids registered last fall." He shook his head sadly. Alan turned to the most recent entries and gave a startled double-take at the page in front of him. "What's this?" A sudden understanding lit his face and Alan smiled over at Scott Cisco. “Well, since everyone else has registered, I guess its time for this team to sign in! Let’s see. February 15th, 2:00 PM. Nine members of the Maelstrom Expedition...going on!”

Bob Woods spoke up, almost for the first time since the team had gathered at the bottom of the Great Pit. “Alan, keep it light! How about, ‘Our mission, to seek out new life forms, to go where one man has gone before.”

“You got it.” Alan began writing in the register. “Hoke, how do you guys want to do the Squeeze?”

“Lying down,” Hoke deadpanned. “Other than that, I hate to have nine people in there all at once. And there’s sunset to consider. We need to be out of Fresh Squeezed by six o’clock!”

“Now you’re going to have to explain that!” Sue had been tying a bandanna over her hair, but Hoke’s remark caught her attention.

Sam Telliman smiled wickedly. “Bats! Many bats on their way out for supper.” He wiggled his fingers in Sue’s face. “Many, many bats traveling through a very small tunnel already crammed full with people! Right, Hoke?”

“Yep! Bats!” Hoke replied flatly.

“Why don’t you lead off, Hoke? After four more have followed, the rest of us will wait for thirty minutes.” Alan turned and spoke to the whole group. “Going through Fresh Squeezed is mostly mental. Everyone here will physically fit through the crawlspace; there will be times when you just think you won’t make it. Talk to each other; recite all the poems you had to memorize in high school. I like to hunt for fossils.”

Hoke started down the vertical shaft like a surface diver. The novice cavers watched with fascination as his torso and legs disappeared down the opening. With a lot of nervous laughter and chattering, Erica Qwan followed him, her lean body slipping easily into the narrow opening. Sam went next, but made several false starts. On his first attempt, he let himself down only about three feet and then scrambled out backwards.

"I can't get a hold beneath me. It feels like I'll slip down and get stuck."

Scott knelt by the opening. "Use your legs to wedge yourself so that you can let go with both hands. Lower the metal cases in front of you or just let them fall. You almost have to use your feet as hands to lower yourself." Sam started in again, backed out and shook his head, at last entering a final time.

"You might think I'm crazy," Alicia Marko said as she stepped up to the opening of Fresh Squeezed, "but I've heard so much about this I'm actually looking forward to it. And you caver jocks might want to watch and learn." Alicia started immediately into the shaft, but feet-first. "This is how you cave when you're five foot-three."

. "Good for you! With that attitude, you'll make it fine. I'll be right behind you, Alicia!"

"Bob, would you mind waiting?" Alan asked. "I haven't had a chance to talk to you since the meeting in Lexington."

"Yeah, Bob," James said as he packed his cameras. "Wait with the second group and I'll go on. I want to be at Miami Beach when you folks exit."

"Fine with me." Bob put his gear down as James started into the shaft.

"Well?" James' voice came from the tunnel, his legs still visible.

"Well, what?"

"Isn't anybody going to flush?" To everyone's laughter, James disappeared down the shaft, leaving the remainder of the team to wait together. Alan leaned back against a rock shelf next to Sue.

"What's your take on everything so far, Bob?" Alan asked. "Are we running well?"

"As far as I can tell, everything's going smoothly. Of course, my end of things will tell as we use the equipment, cook the food, and so on. Having the equipment on hand is one thing; having it function properly is another." Bob stroked a Lincolnesque beard that gave him the look of an Amish elder. His face had none of the craggy weariness of a Lincoln, however. Dark, cheerful eyes peered out from beneath eyebrows that gave the beetling appearance of an eagle. His dark, curly hair framed a face that was remarkably unlined for someone who spent so much time in extreme conditions of sun and wind.

"Hoke Smith is great," he went on and then pointed to Scott, "This young powerhouse has been invaluable. I've been talking to him about working at NOLS."

"Is this your first caving expedition?" Sue leaned forward and stretched.

"Yes, and it's different and yet much the same as others I've worked on. I've done major whitewater expeditions, rain forest treks, and more technical and alpine climbing trips than I care to think about. A cave has its own special requirements, but the organization...the logistics, are much the same."

Alan was looking over the register. He turned to the page where they had just signed in and looked up at Scott. Alan mentally shrugged and then put the register back in its canister. "Time for us to get moving. Who's leading the way?"

"I weel, Pancho." Scott stood up.

Alan laughed. "Have at it, Ceesco!"

Scott entered the crawlspace and Bob followed with no hesitation. After all, the two of them had been through Fresh Squeezed five times in the last week. Sue stood up and looked downward at the opening.

"Alicia's right. I do think she's crazy. This is the one part of the trip that I've been dreading."

"I'll be right behind you. We'll talk our way through...keep your mind on other things."

"How about giving me something else to think about?"

Alan took off his helmet and then reached for Sue's. He pulled her roughly to him and held her tightly. Her mouth opened against his, their hands moving over each other.

"Alan, I want you so much," she whispered in his ear.

"Our time will come, Sue. Really soon." He let her go reluctantly, his hands lingering on her breasts. "Now down you go."

"Beg pardon?" she asked innocently and climbed headfirst into the shaft before he could respond.

Surprisingly enough, it was James Okura who panicked in Fresh Squeezed. All of the Maelstrom team new to caving were having a rough time of it. Two and a half hours under those conditions could stress out anyone. It would be hard to say just what in James' particular history and psyche affected him so differently than the others, but the breathtaking closeness of Fresh Squeezed was pressing in on James Okura with unbearable weight. He pushed along close at Alicia's heels, as if he might climb right over everyone in order to get out. He was sweating profusely and was constantly scraping his back on the crawlspace roof in a vain effort to assume a more upright crawling position. Alicia could not help but notice his frequent collisions, grunts of pain, and labored breathing.

"James, are you all right back there?"

No reply.

"James, say something! Are you all right?"

"Yes! I'm okay! Just keep moving!"

"Look, I'm coming to the part they talked about, where it gets really close. I'll do my best, but it's going to get harder and slower."

"Oh, God! I've got to change position, Doc. Roll over, hands and knees...something!"

"James, listen to me. Just lie there quietly. Fold your hands and lay your head on them. Think about the challenge of getting pictures in here."

"I'll try. I just want to get out."

Alicia turned her head sideways and extended her arms straight in front of her, as she'd been told. She began to barely inch along as James watched her from behind. Then James entered the fabled squeeze that lasted some forty feet. I can do this, he thought. And if I make it for another forty feet, the rest will seem a lot easier.

It was at this crucial time that Hoke found the bat, lying dead in the crawlspace ahead of him. He had moved past the most difficult part of the crawlspace, but his sudden stop caused a chain reaction that moved down the line to James Okura, like traffic backing up on the interstate.

"What's up, Hoke?" Erica Qwan asked.

"A dead bat! Sort of strange." Erica heard a gasp of surprise.

"Hoke?" Erica could tell that something wasn't right.

"Uh...yeah. Pass the word back that it'll be just a minute before we can get moving. I'll put the bat in my pack. Nobody wants to squirm over a dead animal."

The word traveled back to James Okura, who was on the brink. Calling a halt would be bad enough for anyone in a tight crawlspace, but in James' condition it was devastating. There was nothing that either he or Alicia could do but lie under seven hundred feet of rock, heads to the side and arms stretched in front of them. James could feel the weight of the limestone above him. It was crushing him, making it hard to breathe. In his mind's eye, he could see the mass of the earth above and below him. He could see the tiny thread of a crack from a distance, and his own minuscule body trapped there, unable to move.

He broke. James broke as quickly and suddenly as if his body had snapped under the strain. He tried to turn on his side and immediately wedged himself between the ceiling and floor.

"Help me, please. I've got to move." His shouts rang through the narrow tunnel, echoed and amplified. "I'm stuck! Help me!" His voice rose into a high yell.

"James! James, calm down! Stop yelling, damn it!" Alicia shouted and then caught herself. "Sam," she called ahead, "tell Hoke that James is having a major panic attack!"

"Got to move!" James heaved his body to one side and scraped his shoulder on the ceiling. Now he was on his back, which terrified him. The rock was only six inches from his face. James screamed and began to sob, his hands pressing against the rock immediately above him as if to hold up the roof.

"James! Just be quiet and listen." Alicia's voice had a calming effect. She could still hear his labored, short breaths. "James, we're ready to go now. You've just got to turn back over and we'll be able to move forward. Come on, we're all in here together."

James voice was shaky and racked with emotion. "I can't turn over and get stuck again, Alicia."

"You weren't stuck before, James. It just felt like it. Come on and give it a try."

His success at turning back over calmed James. He looked ahead and could see Alicia watching him. "Let's get moving, Okura. I'm ready to stand up and stretch for awhile."

"Yeah, okay," James replied weakly. I'm doing better now." He inched forward and tapped the bottom of Alicia's boot. "Sorry for the outburst. And thanks."

"It's what all of us were feeling. You just let it out."

An hour later, when Alicia and then James collapsed into Miami Beach, both of them stood, hugged, and then toppled into the sand. James rolled over and over, finally lying on his back and making 'sand angels'. "This is the best, just the best!"

"Jeez, Hoke, what was that about a bat?" Sam asked.

"A dead one. I took time to put it in my pack. Sorry about the delay, James. I take it you weren't happy with the stop."

James was fully recovered, for he had his digital camera out and was composing pictures of the crawlspace exit into Miami Beach. "I'm fine now. Sorry about the panic. I don't know what I would have done without Alicia."

Erica walked over to Hoke and spoke quietly. "That bat wasn't there this morning when you came out of Miami Beach, was it? Any idea why it died, Hoke?"

"I don't know, Doc."

"Maybe the same thing that killed this one." She held up a tiny brown bat by one wing. "It was on top of the aluminum cases."

"Could be some sort of disease," Hoke ventured. "We may find more."

Erica gave him a frank look and then turned to the gear, checking out her first aid kits while Hoke and Sam lit lanterns.

In another hour, the crawlspace opening spat forth the remainder of the team, led by Scott and followed by Bob Woods and a shaken Sue Brighton. Alan popped out a minute later and looked around him. His team had come through a major obstacle. It was hard to imagine the unknown before them, but this was the Maelstrom team. No doubt about it.

"Fifteen years since Drew Cisco and I were in this room, and it hasn't changed a bit. Except this time it's like Grand Central Station. How about supper?"

Two or three bats flew through the room and headed out the crawlspace opening. "That's the great bat exodus?" James scoffed.

Hoke looked at his watch. "You know better! Let's all gather at this end of the room!" Even as Hoke spoke, a dozen more bats entered Miami

Beach, followed by several dozen more. In the space of two minutes, the air was full of beating wings and high squeals. They flowed in a dark stream into the crawlspace, until Miami Beach was finally empty and their squeals could be heard echoing down Fresh Squeezed.

Alicia stared at the gaping crawlspace entrance. “God, I’m glad we didn’t take thirty minutes longer. I think I would have died, and that’s not an exaggeration.”

Sam and Scott fired up the stoves and with Alicia’s help, began to fix their first real meal of the expedition. As they were working and others were laying out their sleeping gear, Hoke drew Alan aside.

“Maybe we’ve got a problem, Alan.”

“I heard about James, but I think he’ll...”

“Not James. When we were coming through the crawlspace, I found a dead bat right in the middle of the tunnel.”

“So?”

Erica walked up behind the two men. “He’s about to tell you what was strange about the bat. Sorry to eavesdrop on you.” Sue waved from her sleeping pad and Erica waved back while she spoke. “And what was strange about the other two bats we’ve found.”

Hoke scratched his head briefly. “The bats didn’t die naturally, Alan.”

“I can be more specific.” Erica lowered her voice. “Some puerile monster put their thumb and forefinger on either side of the bats’ head and squeezed. Squeezed until the skull crushed.” Erica’s voiced hissed. “Now you tell me, Alan, what kind of person catches bats and does that to them?”

CHAPTER TWENTY-ONE

At Hoke's suggestion, everyone stayed in their sleeping bags until hordes of bats swept through the room and announced the beginning of a new day. During a quick, simple breakfast, Alan told everyone about the dead bats and asked for input.

"So we don't know who this guy is or what he's trying to do?" Sue asked.

"Or even if he's still in the cave," Alan responded.

"Now there's a titillating thought," Sam spoke up from his sleeping mat. If Sam wasn't hiking through the cave, he was in a prone position. "Since the bat wasn't in the crawlspace when you left in the morning to meet us, he must have come into Fresh Squeezed from this side, left his little gift, and then proceeded toward the pit himself, where he watched us until everyone was down. Then he went up one of our ropes."

Bob Woods was working on breakfast for the group. "The other possibility is that he waited near the entrance to Fresh Squeezed and entered after we headed for the Great Pit yesterday. In which case,"

Bob waved casually over his shoulder with a spoon, "he's back in there someplace right now."

"I think Sam may be right," Scott said. "I thought I saw some movement while we were in the breakdown."

"Either scenario is a little weird," Alan replied. "He's either in the cave now or he was in the cave for the entire week that you were here getting ready."

"What's the significance of the bat?" Scott Cisco poured himself a cup of hot Tang and leaned against the stacks of metal cases. "Or is there any?"

"Nothing more than a kid who pulls wings off of flies or tortures cats. Same mentality."

"Same lack of mentality," Erica muttered.

"Any chance he signed in on the register?"

"No," Alan said, "I looked it over while we were waiting to go into Fresh Squeezed. Nothing other than the advance team. And Scott

"Hot water," Alicia sang out. "Last call for hot water!"

James sat down next to Alan. "So what's his purpose?"

"A practical jokester with a bad sense of humor, in which case I'm betting he's out of the cave and we won't see him again. Or someone who wants to make a name for themselves in the tabloids. 'Phantom of the Maelstrom' or some thing."

"In which case," Sam said, "we'll probably see something of him later on. This is gonna spice up my own story a little.

"I don't think he's a threat. Just a nuisance to watch out for."

"Jokester or not, I don't like the idea of being spied on." Sue got up and dusted sand from her overalls.

"Alan and I have been waiting a long time for today," Hoke spoke up. "We're going to take you through sections of the cave called the Champs Elysees and Moria..."

"Champ Elysees," Sue offered in her best French.

Hoke glared at her. "I can't help it if the French don't use all of their letters. Seems to me if they don't want them, they should hand them over to a language that'll make good use of them. Like West Virginian. So like I was saying, the Champs and Moria are some of the most beautiful you'll ever see. It will make Fresh Squeezed seem well worth it. We'll take several trips back and forth ferrying the cases from here down to Moria, where we'll have Camp 2. This will give everyone plenty of time to enjoy the formations and for James to do his work. You need to take two cases each trip. We ought to be able to move everything by the end of the day, but we need to get going. So saddle up!"

The group took only a few minutes to repack their personal boxes and to select another box to go into their specially designed packs. They began to follow the easy path out of Miami Beach along the stream, negotiated the downclimb, and in an hour were on the brink of entering the Champs.

It was all that Alan remembered it to be; all that he wanted it to be for the sake of the team members, especially for Sue. If any area of a cavern could charm a newcomer into a lifelong love of speleology, it was the Champs Elysees. For the entire length of the gallery, the team was awestruck by the fluted columns, the ceilings forested with formations, the terraced pools of clear water. Hoke and Alan were like patient parents, commenting enthusiastically on each pebble found in a stream by their children. The Maelstrom expedition stumbled and tripped its way to Moria, their eyes on the beauty around them rather than the cave floor.

James was using his digital camera, surmounted with a bright halogen lamp.

"I can't believe you're not taking more pictures, James," Bob commented. "This is utterly fantastic."

"I'm just doing some composing right now... trying to decide what pictures to take when we come back through. Then I'll set up some halogen lamps for better effect."

Walking in an enchanted forest, the team found their way in twos and threes to the room that Drew Cisco had named Moria. It could have passed for the ancient mines of the dwarfs, long in disuse and littered with huge fallen blocks. Sam Telliman and Alicia Marko stood near the center of the room, looking upward and turning in small circles.

"Magical mushrooms," muttered Sam as they tried to take in the scope of the room.

"What?"

"Don't mind me. Just thinking about Alice in Wonderland."

Moria was big enough to contain several areas the size of Miami Beach, but there was only one place free of fallen boulders and suitable to establish Camp 2. After a quick lunch, everyone started back to Miami Beach for one of three return trips to retrieve all the cases.

James caught up to Alan on the 'trail'. "Can I use Scott to help me position some lights for pictures of the Champs?"

"Sure! I think he'd be glad to help. I'm pretty anxious myself to see this gallery with some real light on it."

"Okay, I'll speak to Scott and we'll hang back getting the lights set. Then on your return trip I can start to catch some of the team members near the formations."

"Okay, but you watch out about hanging back from the group too much. And remember, we may not be alone in here." Alan and the others moved on to Miami Beach, leaving James and Scott to work with the halogen lamps on their collapsible tripods.

On the second return trip from Miami Beach, the team members were becoming exhausted and Alan promised that the last trip to get cases would be postponed until the next day. Alan was leading, only about a hundred yards out of Moria, when Scott's voice rang out.

"Hit it, James!"

Immediately, one after another halogen lamp sprang to life as James turned them on by remote control. Alan caught his breath while the others crowded behind him. No one could have anticipated the stunning scene before them. James had positioned lamps to backlight certain formations while shining brightly on others. Some lights picked out the series of terraced travertine pools, reflecting off of them like mirrors or strung jewels. Translucent curtains hung from the ceiling and columns that glowed and sparkled in massive robes of white and tan. In all the years of its existence, no one had ever seen the

Champs Elysees lit in such a manner. James walked up beside Alan, who clapped him on the shoulder.

"You are a damned genius."

Alan and Hoke led the way through an area that was now new to them. The lights revealed formations that the men had never seen, and it was their turn to stare and point at every detail. The exhaustion of the day's work fell from the group. They were so involved with their sightseeing that James was able to get great candid shots as they walked slowly back to Moria.

Sue found the bat.

"Look, another one," she exclaimed. In the brightly lit passage, it was lying on a stalagmite in full view.

Sam came up behind her. "I don't think so. Look again!" He reached forward and turned the bat carefully.

"My God!" Alicia caught her breath. "It's been eviscerated!"

Erica stood apart, hands on butt. "No," she whispered, "more than that, Alicia. It's a ventral incision and a complete evacuation of the body cavity... a damn autopsy."

The team resumed their trek back to Miami Beach, the practical jokester a subject of debate. Alan and Hoke worked their way ahead of the others, so that they stood alone at the top of the short vertical climb.

"This has gone beyond joking. He's pointing a finger directly at Erica. But I'll tell you what really bothers me, Alan. The bat wasn't there the first couple of times we passed that point."

"Hoke, it's just the bright light. We didn't see it at first."

"Nope! Sorry, but I've got an eye for detail. If something breaks a visual pattern or seems out of place, I notice it. That bat wasn't there."

"So he's in here, watching us?"

"Yeah, and for whatever reason, he wants to show he knows us individually. Our only choice is to do the work and watch our step."

Twenty thousand years before Drew Cisco had dubbed the room Moria, its ceiling groaned under the weight of a thousand stalactites. Some individual specimens weighed several tons. The arched ceiling, with a huge unsupported span, strained to hold hundreds of tons until finally the inherent strength of the layers was surpassed.

With a force and fury unmatched in eons, limestone blocks the size of boxcars fell by the dozens, littering the floor of the room and creating a new higher ceiling. For centuries, smaller blocks would fall as the room tried to achieve some stability. Finally only a few blocks were left... those whose weight were generally supported by the walls of the room.

On the surface, geologic features like mountains and canyons are subject to wind and rain, but seem almost eternal and unchanging. Compared to the 'loose' blocks in Moria, surface features are as insubstantial and fleeting as a cloud. In Moria, there was no wind. There was no running water that affected the blocks. There was no freezing or thawing, for the cave was an almost constant fifty-two degrees. The large limestone slab that practically overhung Camp 2 had been in the same position for twenty thousand years.

Very close to the campsite, it was ten feet thick and had separated from the ceiling by as much as two feet. As the gigantic pie-shaped wedge approached the wall, this separation grew less and less. No forces had acted upon this slab, not to move it so much as an inch in millennia.

But as the Maelstrom team began to lay out their campsite and go about the routines of expedition life in a cave, forces were being applied to the slab completely foreign to any in geology. An irresistible perpendicular force had widened the gap at the end of the slab by almost an inch. Five feet further along the crack, another scissors-type car jack was applying pressure. First one and then another jack continued to separate the rock from its ceiling.

James Okura had stepped to one side to compose some shots of Camp 2, hoping to capture the team members at mundane tasks against the fabulous backdrop of the Moria formations. Erica stood next to him, holding equipment and being as helpful as she knew how. They had positioned themselves almost directly beneath nine tons of limestone block that would plunge to the floor in moments

It was excruciatingly difficult work, operating the two floor jacks from a vantage point that would hide his actions. The rock was beginning to strain and groan along the crack line. There was an imperceptible movement of the slab. Both of the jacks and the operator were attached to a safety line bolted to the ceiling.When the block finally fell, they would swing free safe and out of sight.

"I'll have Moria lit up tomorrow," James said. "It should be every bit as awesome as the Champs. "We'll get some great pictures while Alan and Hoke move forward into the cave."

"I guess most of us will need to start ferrying gear to the next camp." Erica paused at an odd creaking sound from somewhere in the room. "Maybe Scott can help you again."

Another creak and Erica moved her light upward. James put his camera back in its case. "I think you'll need Scott to..."

A loud 'pop' rang out in the cavern, and Erica saw with horror the ceiling above her start to move. She dove at James and they both rolled forward onto the rough floor of Moria. A thunderous crash sounded throughout the chamber as the slab fell to the ground. The air was filled with limestone dust as tons of smaller rock were pulverized. Smaller chunks of limestone sprayed them, lacerating their hands and faces.

Erica sat up slowly, but could not move her right foot. Funny, she thought, no pain. She reached down and felt for her boot. Inches away, the juggernaut of rock had caught the laces in a firm grip.

CHAPTER TWENTY-TWO

"Joe! There you are!" Alec Martin walked into the supply room where Joe was doing inventory. "You're a hard man to find!"

Joe glanced up from his clipboard. "Not on purpose, Dr. Martin. I've just got to get this inventory done by Friday." He quickly finished a page and set down his stack of forms. "You've been trying to find me?"

"I wanted to say I'm sorry things didn't work out for you...going into the cave and all. I know it must have meant a lot to you."

"Thanks! But believe me, I'm glad to be above ground." They walked out of the tiny store room and into the expanse of the main lab. "I was the only person on that team who wasn't really needed."

"Well, you're needed here. With Erica gone, these twelve hour days are about to do me in." Alec hesitated. "I wanted to prod your memory a little, Joe."

"Prod away."

"I know you remember the day those two caving victims were brought here."

"Sure. That's what started the whole expedition."

"On that day, I did an autopsy that Erica was supposed to double check for me... Joshua Lowery."

"I don't remember...we do so many. But we can always get the report."

"That's just it. I can't find Erica's report, but I know she looked at Mr. Lowery. We talked about the blue glow before she left for Lexington."

Joe looked up quickly. "Sure, we did that autopsy. But that was Drew Cisco, the second caving victim."

"The man I'm talking about was found dead and glowing by a kid up north of Woods Lake. No cave, just a barn. According to the kid's doctor, the boy has two broken arms and is starting to phosphoresce!"

"Where the hell have you been for the last two months, Dr. Martin? The alien creatures in the Maelstrom glow blue. Haven't you seen a paper?"

"I've been cooped up in here night and day while you and Dr. Qwan run around the country playing Indiana Jones. If Erica had been paying attention to me instead of looking for her head, we wouldn't be having this discussion." Alec threw down his daily report in exasperation. "How could your damn aliens get out of a cave where they're supposed to have been isolated for the last few million years?"

"It would have to be water supplies, I guess. I don't know! I haven't got a clue!" Joe shouted

"Have you got a clue why two people have ended up a mass of boneless flesh and this kid is heading the same way?" Alec strode out of the lab.

"Dr. Martin, wait!" Joe hurried to catch up. "It's calcium! Dr. Hinneman said that the blue light is probably produced when calcium compounds are broken down by the bacteria. There's plenty of calcium in cave formations...and in bones."

"So we've got two problems. Dr. Talbot said the kid isn't responding to antibiotics."

"Antibiotics won't work! These bacteria are silicon based. You've got to start radiation therapy on that boy right away. I'm betting you'll get an immediate effect."

"And what do we do for Erica and the others? They're in danger!"

"Their lives have been on the line since they started down the Great Pit." Joe shrugged helplessly. "We've got no way to contact them."

Joe Riechman sat in his darkened living room, his face lit by the glow of an omnipresent, omni-booted computer. A cold beer and two empty companions were nearby and a bowl of popcorn within easy reach. The drapes were drawn against the headlights and rumbling of trucks that were part of life next to the major highway through London.

He spoke into a microphone, giving a set of numbers that corresponded to a starting point, a direction, a distance, and beginning and ending elevations. The computer hesitated fractionally, and then generated a bright blue line, one of many hundreds of connected line segments.

He had undertaken the painstakingly difficult job of transferring Alan Manning's map of the Maelstrom to the computer. In combination with Joe's voice recognition program, an advanced CAD system developed especially for mining was generating a complex map of the entire Maelstrom system. Any designated segment could be rendered in either a plan or elevation view.

It was to be a gift to Alan and the Maelstrom team. Joe hoped to maintain a website that would link the photographic work of James Okura with the map itself, so that people could take a virtual tour of the cavern system. The project had become his participation in the Maelstrom expedition.

In the light of day and of cold reasoning, Joe knew that he should of stuck it out. He longed to be with the team, sharing their experiences and even the difficulties of the cave. He had thrown away the chance to break out of a hum-drum existence. When was an opportunity like this ever going to present itself again, to be involved at the edge of scientific discovery with people he liked and respected? Never! he answered himself. Joe grabbed at the beer and finished it off. Damn it! He could be there now to warn them of the danger posed by the bacteria, instead of sharing a social life with his computer.

But at night, Joe would dream of Tehipite. Once again, he was working his way up the fixed rope. From a distance, Joe could see himself. A tiny, insignificant piece of fly dirt on the face of a black, unforgiving granite wall. Once again, the mist wrapped around him and clouded his glasses. He could see the rope beginning to bunch within its sheath and could feel, night after night, the cold fear knot his stomach.

Each night, Rudy's face looked down on him from the ledge and then began to rapidly recede. The dark rock would move past him and Joe could see, in slow motion, his fingers shredding as he tried desperately to save himself. The valley floor rushed at him through the mist, but in his dreams the safety rope did not hold. Joe's own scream would awaken him. Sweating and unable to sleep, he would spend the rest of the night in front of his computer.

On those nights, Joe was sure that he had done the right thing. He had talents and abilities, and like Alfred Hinneman, Joe could contribute without risking his life in the Maelstrom. He was not ready to meet death somewhere in the dark bowels of the earth.

As for his friends, he would see that radiation treatments began as soon as the team came out...the bacteria didn't seem to act that fast.

The computer blinked a warning that he had an incoming call. Joe spoke into his microphone. "Connect."

A familiar voice came over the dual speakers. "Hello! I'd like to speak to Joe Riechman."

"This is Joe. Is that you, Rudy?"

"In the flesh, at least on this end. How are you doing?"

"I'm fine, thanks. Fingers and hands are still a little torn up, but just an inconvenience. I'm in front of my computer now working on a map of the Maelstrom. I figure I know it just about as well as Alan."

"Joe, I want to talk to you about your fall."

"It's all right, Rudy. It really is. Things like that can happen..."

"It wasn't an accident, Joe."

For a moment, there was a stunned silence. "Go on," Joe said quietly.

"Think back to how a climbing rope is made. There's an inner core of nylon...that's the real strength of the rope. Then there's a woven outer sheath or mantle to protect the core."

"Sure, I remember. Kernmantle."

"The inner core on your rope was cut almost in two, although the outer core was virtually intact. There was no way to see it."

"How can that happen?"

"In normal climbing, only one way. It's why climbers are so obsessed about people stepping on their ropes. A sharp point can penetrate the woven sheath without doing much damage, and yet ruin the nylon core."

"A sharp point, like...?"

"Like crampons. If Scott had ever worn his, I would never have let him near the rope. Scott never wore those crampons, so it wasn't an accident. What's more, it would take some real work to cut that inner core. One accidental step wouldn't do it."

"I got to know Scott pretty well, Rudy. He wouldn't do anything like that. Why would he?"

"There's more. I don't think Sam's fall in Granite Basin was caused by a startled deer and now I don't think he stumbled, either. There was someone else in the area...we saw his tracks. I wouldn't have considered the possibility until this rope thing, but he could have been pushed."

"Then the whole team is in more danger than I thought. Listen, Rudy. I appreciate your call. I'll talk to Dr. Hinneman and see what he wants to do." Joe reactivated his microphone. "Disconnect," he said flatly, adjusted his glasses, and sat back to think.

An hour later, Joe still sat in front of his computer, which had put itself to sleep. In the darkness, he sat with his hands clasped in his lap. He suddenly pushed himself out of the chair and went to the closet where he had stowed his climbing gear from Tehipite Valley. Joe carefully laid out his harnesses, jumars, Kong descender, Gibbs, and assorted nylon webbing. He fingered these for a few minutes, and then headed for the bathroom, where he violently lost an evening's worth of beer and popcorn.

"This is the fourth and last time I'm telling you, Shepard. Get back in that pen or I'm gonna lose my patience with you."

Shepard, a three-hundred pound sow, was out of her pen and having a wonderful time. There was no good reason that she could see to leave the delights of Johnny Smith's garbage bags for the slop that she had to share with fifteen other pigs and shoats. Johnny had given up nudging and kicking Shepard, and was looking for a good two by four when a late model Honda Civic pulled up at the main house. He gave Shepard one more good kick and then headed across the little pasture that surrounded his pens.

A young man left the driver's seat and came around the car, walking over the short grass to meet him. Not watching where he walks, thought Johnny.

"Are you Johnny Smith, Hoke's brother?" The man was shorter than Johnny by six inches, and pushed his glasses up the bridge of his nose three times before he came within handshake distance.

"I'm Johnny. How do you know Hoke?" He wiped his hands on his trousers before shaking hands.

"Joe Riechman. I know him from the Maelstrom team. I'm part of it...I mean, I'm supposed to be down there now."

Johnny closed the pasture gate and secured it with a loop of barb wire. "How'd you find me, anyway? I'm not listed in the phone books."

"I knew the general area," Joe said. "When I told folks that I was looking for you because Hoke needed your help, I got lots of good directions."

The taller man stopped and fixed Joe with a stare that had lost some friendliness. "You just tell them that Hoke needed me, or does he?"

"He does, Johnny!" The two men sat on the porch in the chilly February sun while Joe brought Johnny Smith up to speed. After Joe had finished, Johnny sat forward and absently picked some peeling paint from the porch railing.

"Thanks for finding me. I wouldn't want some kamikaze law enforcement types going in there and getting people hurt or killed. I can get in there quick-like and warn the team."

"I've got my gear in the car," Joe said. "I can leave now."

"That's exactly what you're doing." Johnny turned his back and started into the house. "I'm leaving for the Maelstrom. You're leaving for...wherever you came from."

Joe straightened his back, fixed his glasses, and followed Johnny through the door. "I walked out on this team before. Not this time."

"You're in my house," Johnny said as a matter of fact. "I didn't ask you in!" He started down the wooden stairs to the basement, but Joe was at his heels.

"Yessir, well pretty soon I'm going to be in your car and then I'm going to be in your big, bad cave and...Man, these stairs are about to fall apart."

"Here, hold these now that you're in my basement." Johnny handed Joe two large duffel bags. "You're worried about stairs, Mr. Maelstrom

Team? Look, I can't have anyone slowing me down. People could be dying in there!"

Joe was following up the stairs with his load. "I know the techniques! I trained with the best. I'm half your age and I know that cave foot by foot."

"Now that's a trick, seeing as how you've never been in the cave."

"Computer." Joe shrugged. "I've mapped the whole cave!"

"You may be half my age, but you've never been in a cave and you're scared shitless."

Joe grabbed his arm and stopped Johnny in mid-stride. "Yes, I am. But I'm going in that cave and try to help those folks. They're friends, damn it!"

Johnny looked at him for a moment. "Throw your gear in that pickup." He walked around to the driver's door as Joe ran to his car. "Computer caves!" he muttered.

CHAPTER TWENTY-THREE

The room was filled with thick dust that choked the light from their headlamps. Ghostly forms moved around in the thick half-light as people realized the cave-in was over. Sam and Alan had been cooking supper; food and cooking equipment were scattered everywhere.

"Quiet!" Alan shouted. "Call out your name and let me know you're all right." One by one, he heard the name of each person, until finally all had reported except for Hoke and Scott.

"Scott! Hoke!" Alan cried out. "Hoke!"

"Speechless!" He crawled from under a rock outcrop and dusted himself off. The air was clearing, and they all congregated by the slab that now rested only yards from their campsite.

"Spread out by two's and look for Scott," Alan directed. At that moment he appeared, scrambling over broken rocks with a look of wild alarm on his face.

"Is everyone all right? I was over that way about a hundred feet taking a whiz. Man, I thought we were all goners."

Hoke stood looking at the rock slab and shaking his head. "Thirty years caving and this is something I thought I'd never see. Caves just don't cave-in. Mines, yes. But not caves." He turned and sat on the convenient seat that had not been there five minutes before. "I mean, of course they do cave-in. But it's so rare. This...this is like winning the lottery."

"I feel lucky enough," James spoke up. "I was about to lose my ass when Erica shoved me. There's a Nikon somewhere under that pile, and I would have been with it."

Alicia cleared her throat. "Is it such a rare event? Are we in danger here?"

Alan considered his reply carefully. "It is rare, extremely rare. I have a good memory for things geological, and that slab was trying to peel off the roof years ago. Drew Cisco and I saw evidence of a recent cave-in at that time. And of course, it was the fall of a massive formation that killed Drew."

"That's three times in fifteen years," Bob said.

Alicia sat on the rock, her knees pulled up under her chin. She looked almost tiny and frail in the huge space of Moria. "I've had a lot of dreams about the Maelstrom, most of which I've ignored like a good little scientist. This," she said patting the fallen block, "is way close to a dream come true."

"If Hoke and I thought we were in any real danger from further cave-ins, we'd lead you out of here tonight. Remember, the last time Moria collapsed was twenty thousand years ago!"

"And you don't think Batman had anything to do with it?"

Hoke laughed. "No sir! Gutting a little bat is one thing; causing a cave-in and possibly killing somebody is another matter entirely."

"Hoke's right." Alan raised one hand. "I promise you, if there was someone capable of pulling that down on our heads, it would be a class one psychopath, and that just doesn't make sense. Come on, I think we deserve a great meal tonight!"

Sam walked past Alan and spoke in a low voice. "The Champs has never caved in, has it?"

"No sign of it."

"Ripe for the picking, I'd say."

"Do me a favor. Just don't say it to Alicia!"

An hour later, order had been restored in the camp and supper was served. True to Alan's philosophy, and in light of the near tragedy that weighed on everyone's mind, the meal was one of their best. Deep within the earth, dwarfed by the massive proportions of Moria, nine people sat on foam pads and feasted on country ham, rice and red-eye gravy, applesauce, and no-bake cheesecake. Their confidence and good humor returned, and a little of the light-heartedness of that night in Tehipite Valley.

"...so this whole cave system turned out to be one big mudhole. Everything was covered with slimy, sticky, smelly clay. Three of us had fought through that stuff for a day, and now we were following this little stream and the passage was getting smaller and smaller. I knew we were close to the surface...there were tree roots and even small plant roots and animals holes. I could feel fresh air."

"Did you find an opening, Hoke?" James clicked off a picture.

"Dead end! I told the guy's I'd be shitted on before I turned around and slimed my way back through the cave. We started kicking and clawing at the loose rocks and roots, and in five minutes we poked out through the ground like three babies being born."

Sue started laughing. "Poor Mother Earth! What a disappointment!"

"Course we didn't know it was night time. We also didn't know that when we popped out at Cloud Canyon Campground, there were two Scout Masters and eleven boys sitting around the fire not ten feet away." Hoke hesitated for effect. "Tellin' ghost stories! I actually heard one of the leaders yell 'Friggin' monsters'. Of course, we ran after them to let them know it was all right, but that just made matters worse!"

The cavern echoed with whoops of laughter. Erica wiped tears away with the back of her hand. "This is great! All we need is Joe and his harmonica."

"All we need is some stars overhead and a river running nearby," Sam observed. The group fell silent for a minute as they thought of the world above them, operating in a normal manner and on a normal schedule.

Alan stood up and stretched. "Let's talk about tomorrow. Hoke and I will move as fast as possible to Drew's Pit, and try to force a passage. The rest of you will establish Camp 3 at the bottom of the waterfall, or what Hoke tells me is no longer a waterfall. Leave the spare gear and enough for one more night at Camp 2, but bring everything else down. Hoke and I may not be back until late, so don't worry about us right away. There's just no room for all of us to sleep at Camp 3, so we'll come back here. Any questions?"

"And if you do get through?" asked Bob.

"No explorations. We'll take time to set up a safety rope as a guide. When the team goes through, you each clip into the rope so that no one wanders off course. Drew's passage probably connects to a flooded maze, and there's nothing in the Maelstrom that scares me more!"

Scott came up as Alan was laying out his sleeping bag. "I was sort of hoping I could go with you and Hoke."

"I know you were, Scott. I need your climbing skills when the cases are taken down to the bottom of the falls. With Hoke and I gone, you're the most experienced climber we've got. In fact, you're the most experienced climber, period."

Scott looked more than disappointed. "You wouldn't be trying to protect me, would you?"

Alan turned and looked at the former ceiling that lay at their feet. "I'm not sure that staying back here is all that safe."

Joe found Alfred Hinneman at the Pure station office, busily making arrangements for the storage and research of whatever specimens came out of the Maelstrom.

"You need to be getting them out right away, Joe. To hell with everything else!" Alfred was clearly ready to go himself if it would have helped.

Joe shook his head as he and Johnny started to leave. "I still can't understand why Scott would do something like this."

"If you are putting together the death of his father, this glory that is coming to Alan Manning, and a psychotic mental state, you are asking for trouble" Alfred herded them out the door. "Go! Hurry! And be safe!"

Johnny watched critically as Joe arranged his equipment and attached his harness to one of the two descent ropes. Satisfied, Johnny started to descend the other rope, leaving the emergency winch rope dangling unused. Joe removed his glasses and started down the slope toward the entrance to the Great Pit. He wasn't planning to look around very much. In fact, the less detail he saw, the safer he felt. Straight down the rope, he thought. Just keep to business.

In counterpoint to Joe's tentative and jerky progress, Johnny moved down the rope with smooth confidence. He used the same set-up...Kong descender backed up with a Gibbs that ran down the rope in his left hand. Johnny could feel the rope over his right thigh. Funny, he thought, six hundred feet ought to be heavier

He slowed to watch Joe's descent, and saved his own life as a result. Johnny was barely moving when the Kong descender went off the end of the rope. His yell came from below and hit Joe like the force of an explosion. Joe knew that yell. He had heard it almost nightly for the last two weeks. He stopped and held the rope close to him with both hands. "Johnny, are you okay? What's happened?" His own voice, weak and trembling, came back to him from the pit walls.

Johnny was dangling off of the rope, his Kong descender and its attachment to his harness completely divorced from the rope itself. The Gibbs had grabbed as soon as his thumb left the cam, but only three feet from the neatly severed end of the rope. Johnny slowly spun, suspended by the Gibbs and one piece of webbing, watching with cold fear as the Gibbs began to inch down the rope.

"Joe, listen carefully." He tried to keep his voice as calm as possible, working to get his jumars out of the pack. "The ropes end here. They've both been cut! Get your jumars out of your pack and put them on the rope!"

"What about you? Are you..."

"Shut up, damn it!" Johnny's weight on the rope had stretched it, reducing its diameter slightly. The Gibbs had slowly lost six inches. "When the jumars are on, clip into the loops with your harness, stand in the loops, and disconnect your descender. In that order, Joe!" Johnny was working feverishly, but his efforts to reach the jumar ascenders caused his legs to swing wildly in space. The Gibbs gave a heart-stopping jump and lost four inches.

"Joe!"

"Yes!"

"You may have to go it alone."

"Shut the fuck up! We're both going after them!" Joe was straining to slide his jumars up the rope, tears streaming down his face.

"If you have to, use the emergency rope. But check out the damn winch...make sure he hasn't sabotaged it!"

There were twelve inches left. Johnny made himself relax, to hang still and silent above the black depths. He carefully threaded a long nylon loop through the eye of the jumar. In a last effort, Johnny slammed the jumar onto the rope above the Gibbs and slid the device up as far as he could reach.

"Move up, Joe. I'll meet you at the top!" He was not altogether sure of that, but Johnny was close to safety.

Thirty minutes later, the two men were facing the difficult task of sliding their jumars past the ledge at the top of the Great Pit. They moved rapidly up the short slope, no longer using their foot loops, but walking gratefully on solid ground. At the top of the slope, they collapsed onto the rocks. Johnny's hands were shaking as he adjusted his harness and inspected hardware.

"I'm glad to know I'm not the only one shaking like a leaf," Joe said.

"You haven't got a corner on fear, buddy."

"I'm way past fear, Johnny. I'm mad as hell. That's twice the psychopathic bastard has almost killed me. Let's get moving!"

Both men hung grimly as the emergency rope lowered them slowly and evenly toward the bottom of the Great Pit. Johnny inspected everything as carefully as possible, and decided it was safe. They reasoned that Scott had to get out of the cave sooner or later, and that he would not have sabotaged the emergency rope.

Johnny had checked the bolts that held the winch in place, and they seemed secure. As the two men rode downward, the bolts moved slightly in the rock. They were not the original bolts. They were, in fact, slightly smaller, and would hold Johnny and Joe safely. But the two bolts would not support any greater force than two people.

Batman had seen to that.

The exit from Moria toward the waterfall and the rest of the cavern was almost like a doorway. An opening set into the massive walls of the room where one could expect a rounded door to be hung. It was here that Sue Brighton waited for Alan and

Hoke to return. She had worked with the others to move cases to the base of the former waterfall in the hundred foot pit. Moving back up the rope was their first ascent since the practice work in Tehipite Valley, and it had exhausted them all. Except for young Scott, she thought. He seemed to run on overdrive and did three times the work of the others. He had done the last two trips down the rope by himself.

With Camp 3 established, the team had retreated to Camp 2 in Moria, where they would await the arrival of Alan and Hoke. Sue and Alicia insisted on fixing supper, a way for Sue to occupy her mind. The group sat around talking for awhile, but finally even that could not settle Sue's growing fears.

It was ten o'clock, and she felt they should have returned by then. Like a captain's wife waiting for a ship on the horizon, Sue sat near the exit from Moria and watched the passageway. At times she would turn her light off and sit in darkness, better able to see the faint gleam of their headlamps. Two months earlier, her anxiety would have been due to a concern for the success of the expedition. Had they found Drew's passage? Had they found the unknown section of the Maelstrom that was the focus of so much work and preparation?

Now her concern was only for the safe return of Alan Manning. And Hoke, of course. But Alan's safety was on a different, more complicated and personal level. Sleep was about to overtake her as she sat waiting. Funny, Sue thought, two months ago she would never have imagined sitting by herself in the darkness, a thousand feet underground.

A glow showed from around the corner of the passage. Sue sat up and turned on her own headlamp. A moment later Hoke appeared and began to move toward her. There was something in the expression on his face that alarmed her, but it was simply exhaustion. Hoke was soaking wet, his face drawn and eyes lidded.

"Oh, don't worry. He's right around the corner. And yes, I'm all right too."

Sue put her hand on Hoke's arm and squeezed it. "It's good to see you boys back again."

She looked down the passage to where Alan's light was visible.

Hoke passed her and then turned back. "Oh, by the way. We made it, girl!" Hoke smiled, gave her a wink, and headed into Moria.

CHAPTER TWENTY-FOUR

Deeper and deeper the team penetrated toward the great sedimentary heart of the beast that Alicia Marko had imagined two days earlier. They had walked through its great rock-ribbed chambers and wondered at the limestone musculature that supported its structure. The previous two days had been a period of adjustment, learning to cope and operate in a cave environment. Now it was almost possible to forget that they were in a cave, and certainly easy to forget that they were two thousand feet under ground. From a scientific standpoint, Alicia was almost as comfortable as if she were doing research in a forest or an alpine cirque.

Stepping off the edge of the waterfall pit was as easy and as natural to Erica Qwan as her morning runs. Those were a world away, she thought, beginning to abseil the mere one hundred feet to the bottom of the pit. The run along Wood Creek Lake; bare winter trees against a graying sky; ducks skittering across the surface of the water as she spooked them; the long uphill pull toward her condo. And a hot bath! she screamed to herself. Erica pushed off from the overhanging ledge that had once propelled a waterfall out into the pit.

"Fifteen years ago," Alan shouted up at her, "you'd have been underwater."

"I wonder what happened to the stream?" she called back.

"Don't know for sure, but that's how crawlspaces like Fresh Squeezed are formed. A stream stops flowing before it has the chance to open the passage up further."

In the style of a major Himalayan assault, the team was gradually moving their support equipment forward. Nothing of the metal cases was left at Camp 1 in Miami Beach. Only some cases of spare food were left at Camp 2 in Moria, and everything else was gathered on the rocky 'beach' at the base of the former waterfall. Too small and too rough, Camp 3 and Camp 4 at the bottom of Drew's Pit were not sleeping camps. Instead, these were merely staging areas to gather supplies and make it easier to move them forward.

Bob began handing out cases. "Repack your personal case to include your wetsuit. You should have four minitanks, two in your personal case and two in the common case that you'll carry."

"We need to start thinking about the scientific equipment," Alicia said as she reshuffled her gear.

"I'm planning to bring those in once we've established Camp 5 on the other side." The team members had begun to refer to the unexplored region of the cave as if it were the promised land, and they were going under the river Jordan.

"What a bunch of muddy trogs!" Hoke called out. "God, but you look a lot more like spelunkers than you did two months ago at the meeting."

. Hoke led them up the small slope that marked the beginning of a Mazing Grace. “We’ve installed a small perlon rope as a guide through the maze up to the point where Drew Cisco’s rope leads off. It should be easy for anyone to get back to Camp 3 from Drew’s Pit.”

With nine people and a rope to guide them, the maze seemed only a walk through a twisted path, but nothing particularly terrifying. In an hour, they arrived at the point in the maze where Drew Cisco’s rope led off into a side tunnel. Alan turned to see Scott holding the rope and looking at it thoughtfully.

“My Dad’s rope, huh?”

“Yeah,” Alan answered. “You going to be all right going into this next pit?”

“Sure. There’s nothing...I mean, there’s no...”

Hoke put a hand on the younger man’s shoulder. “There’s nothing in the pit but rock and water, son. Alan and I checked that out yesterday.”

“You know, at some point I’d like to have this length of rope. Just something of his, I guess.”

Alan hit himself on the forehead. “Jeez, I’m an idiot. When I left the Maelstrom fifteen years ago, I ditched your Dad’s pack in Moria. I was going to get it for you, but I guess with the cave-in and all I just forgot.”

“You think it’s still there?” Scott asked.

“Absolutely! I know exactly where I left it. Nylon Cordura pack, stuff in watertight canisters. Everything should be in great shape.”

“Alan,” Hoke said quietly.

“What is it, Hoke?”

“This isn’t Drew’s rope. It looks like it, same size and everything, but it hasn’t been in here fifteen years.”

"What do you mean?" James Okura had been within listening distance.

"I mean that the rope that was in here last night was saturated with water, and had a coating of material, maybe just a microthin mineral layer."

"It was changed in the last twelve hours?"

Sue walked up with Erica. "Okay, so what's the big conference about?"

"I think," James said flatly, "the conversation is about Batman."

"But what would be the purpose?"

"I think it's a game," Erica said. "It's another little clue that tells us he's here. But are we clever enough to notice?"

"I'll admit it's pretty strange. He could have picked more obvious clues. What concerns me is that for a practical jokester, he's come a long ways into the Maelstrom, supposedly on his own." Alan adjusted the straps of his pack. "We better keep an eye out. Some people don't know where to draw the line."

Another half an hour of walking and crouching brought them to the brink of Drew's Pit...a half hour made doubly uncomfortable because everyone felt eyes watching. As the logistics of equipment and supplies became more important, so was Bob Woods' role as a leader.

"We need to change into wetsuits here. Alan says there's not much room at the bottom. Pack your clothes carefully, check your headlamp to make sure that it's sealed well, and clip two minitanks to your harness. Put fresh batteries in your lamps...I don't care how recently you changed them."

The team looked at the opening of Drew's Pit with a mixture of dread and excitement. There were completely different emotions at the opening to the Great Pit. However awe-inspiring that was, it was still known terrain...a route followed by many before them. Here they stood at the gateway to an unexplored area. Soon they would be entering an area seen by no living humans. The dark hole before them was a gateway to another world, where life operated by a different set of rules. Two men had died in the pit they were about to enter.

By habit, each person checked their gear and began to descend. But it was a more cursory check than it should have been. They were becoming comfortable. In any high-risk endeavor, comfortable can get you dead. One by one, they touched down safely at the bottom. In an area perhaps twenty by twenty feet, there was a large amount of rock and one huge block that obviously did not belong there. At the far end of the pit was a pool of crystalline water.

To everyone's surprise, it was Sam who suggested a moment of silence for Drew Cisco and the college student who had died. The nine team members stood quietly, their headlamps lighting the massive mausoleum that nature had constructed to hold, for a time, the remains of two people who had not asked to lead the way.

"Batman!" Bob Wood's voice ended the memorial moment. He showed a light on the large piece of carbonate rock that had killed Drew Cisco. A small bat had been impaled with a ball point pen refill, the point of the pen wedged into a crack in the rock. Its wings were outspread and similarly held in place with pens. Next to the tiny cadaver was a Polaroid photograph...a close-up of the bats' face.

Alicia stared and then whispered softly. "Erica Qwan, the medical examiner. Now Sam Telliman the writer and James Okura, the photographer! Why is he doing this?"

"I have a better question," Alan spoke up. "Other than this team, less than ten people in the world know about this pit, know where it might lead, or could know that we would come here. Three college students who will never enter this cave again, Johnny Smith and four other member's of Hoke's rescue team, and Joe Riechman. So who could possibly be doing this?"

"Batman could have followed you and Hoke here yesterday," James suggested.

Alan's face was set. "I'm ready to put about a thousand feet of flooded maze between us and this clown. Let's get moving!"

Alicia wasn't so sure. "We're just going to ignore him, Alan? I'm beginning to think he's dangerous."

"To the bat population. But as far as I'm concerned, he's a damn sneak who hasn't got the balls to show himself when nine people are around."

Alan was about to enter the pool at the far end of the room when Sue spoke up. "Wait just a second. I have a message from Alfred." She dug into her personal case and pulled out a small bottle. "Sparkling cider, so Alicia can participate. Alfred wanted me to offer a toast." She held up the little container. 'To each of us and to unknown worlds. May there always be things and places unknowable.'" The cider made the rounds as the team gathered at the edge of the pool.

"Remember to clip into the guide rope," Alan cautioned. "Once in a while you'll come to a ring that holds the rope in place. Unfasten your carabiner to get past, but clip back in again right away. See you on the other side!"

Johnny was moving through Fresh Squeezed with an urgency that reflected his mounting terror. He was not one to show his feelings very often, but this was a new situation to him. Without a doubt, someone had tried several times to kill. He and Joe had both escaped death by a hair.

Joe was keeping up with the veteran spelunker, showing very little concern for the tight confines of the crawlspace. After the last near miss in the Great Pit, it was as though Joe had lost much of his fear. During the worst of Fresh Squeezed, Joe chattered away about his map and how great it was to see the real thing after all. He talked almost non-stop...computers, Tehipite, how they were going to confront Scott.

"That should put us halfway through," Johnny said as they cleared the area where James had his panic attack.

"Actually, we're about sixty percent through. Fresh Squeezed is 525 feet long and the end of this really bad section is at 300 feet. Fifty percent would be 262 feet and another ten percent is 52.5 feet. That's about sixty percent."

"You can be a pain in the butt, Joe. I'm slowly finding that out."

"Sometimes that's a good thing, Johnny."

"Oh, no!" Johnny shouted. "How could I have been so stupid?" He began moving with renewed energy. "Joe, if we don't get to them before they enter Drew's underwater passage, then we're helpless. We've got no air tanks to follow them.

We're going to have to run from Miami Beach to Drew's Pit!"

Sam Telliman was going to have a hard time describing the scene before him. The rocky tunnel was filled completely with the most beautifully pure water. There was no silt or dirt whatsoever. Nothing floated in the water and the people in front of him seemed to be swimming through air. Only the resistance to his strokes gave any indication that they were not. Their lights picked out ghostly shadows and he could see far ahead to what must have been Alan's light and those of others, shining like fuzzy galaxies in the dark liquid space around them. He was not the last in line. Bob Woods and Hoke had that honor. Yet Sam kept looking behind him to make sure that he was among others and not falling behind. Time and again he checked to see that his carabiner was still attached to the guide rope.

The route seemed fairly direct, but scores of black tunnels opened to one side or the other. Sam shuddered to think of entering one of those darkened passages accidentally. How could Drew Cisco ever have found this route without dying in the attempt? He smiled grimly to himself, for indeed Drew had died in forcing the passage. He had escaped the most dangerous part, only to die in a freakish and rare accident.

It was a giddy, unnerving, and disorienting twenty minutes. Sam saw the tunnel floor rising and realized that no one was in front of him. As the water became shallower, he began to kick up some coarse sand. His head broke the surface and he saw the others standing on a small beach, removing their wetsuits.

Finally the entire group stood on the alien shore, shivering like ship-wrecked children half grateful to be saved from the sea and yet fearful of what life lie in wait beyond the trees. A team of professional adults peered into the darkness from the safety of their small beach, afraid to move forward into the unknown. They were in a small gully with a level floor. Behind them rose a wall of rock pierced only by the flooded channel. Ahead of them, blocking their view, was a small rise.

Slowly they moved forward from the beach where their channel ended. James pulled out two powerful halogen beams and played them over the landscape. As they ascended the small rise, the immensity of the room became apparent. Alan swept his lamp around him and instinctively reached for Sue's hand.

"Mother of God! Look at this room," Alan spoke breathlessly. "It's gargantuan!"

Except for the wall behind them, the chamber did seem limitless. They were evidently on a large plateau, extending perhaps fifty yards on either side of them. Ahead, after about seventy-five feet, the relatively level rock dropped away, revealing the tops of formations at almost eye level. There were scores, perhaps hundreds of columns of every size. They supported the massive ceiling like hewn timbers and gave a feeling of permanency.

Alicia Marko walked up beside Hoke Smith. "It's like a forest, Hoke. There are so many columns."

"I've never seen anything like it. And I've been in every cave in North America that's worth a lick. This is fabulous."

The columns were of infinite variety. Some were smooth and perfectly symmetrical, gleaming like marble columns that had been polished to perfection.

Others were showing the beginning of fluted layers. In the distance, their lights picked out Sequoia-like giants that were losing the rounded nature of a column and seemed to be more like walls some ten feet through. Not until they approached the ledge, however, did the chamber's full impact strike them. Every person reacted with sharp intakes of breath, murmured exclamations, and then one by one sat on the ledge itself.

Before them was a valley, thirty feet lower than their 'plateau'. It teemed with columns, graceful stalactites, and long draperies of travertine. From their position, the rock formed a series of long, wide steps that seemed to lead to some magnificent court. But the sight that held them all transfixed was the lake. It stretched past the limits of their lights, reflecting them blackly.

"Not knowing what Drew Cisco saw of this, we may be the first to see this world." Alan was cowed by the grandeur and the scope of the geological marvel before him. "And this is the first light to enter this chamber."

"I don't think so," whispered Erica. "Everyone douse your lights. Those beacons of yours too, James."

They sat in darkness for a few moments, but their eyes soon adjusted. A blue light seemed to emanate from every point of the room. Some columns seemed to have small blue spots, while others seemed draped in electric blue iridescence. Most amazingly, the surface of the lake stirred with the ghostly blue light. A universe spread before them, wispy nebulae shining in the total darkness. Finally, their eyes became so receptive of the dim light that they were able to see, almost well enough to walk around.

Bob was the first to break the spell. "This may well be the most beautiful place on or under the earth. But we've got our work cut out for us. Let's set up Camp 5."

In the space of two hours, a well-established camp was set. Areas were established for sleeping, for cooking and eating, and two areas set aside as bathrooms, with each person's own 'shitsafe' neatly stowed. On a level area not far from the ledge and with a view of what they now considered a valley, a research site was established. When they arrived with more cases, various instrumentation, microscopes, and collecting vessels would be stored at the site. Their schedule called for a week to carry out initial surveys and make some collections. Later expeditions would further the work.

"I need some help going back for the research gear," Hoke said as he began to don his wetsuit. "Any takers?"

Sam Telliman and Scott Cisco got to their feet and began to prepare for the trip. James Okura hurried over to the beach.

"Give me just a minute, guys. I've got a bunch of film back at Camp 4 that I need."

"Good," Hoke said. "With four of us, we'll get all the cases back in one trip."

"Good luck," Alan waved as they waded into the clear water of the tunnel.

CHAPTER TWENTY-FIVE

Sue and Alicia were laying out equipment on the wide ledge that overlooked Evolution Lake and Manning's Gulf, the latter name voted upon by the entire group over Alan's objections. Alicia called out to the campsite, about a hundred feet away.

"Alan, Sue and I are ready to get going. Actually, we're way past ready and moving on to frantic. We could use a professional guide."

Alan and Erica clambered over to the 'lab' area. "Are you sure you've got what you need?" The cases stacked around the two women contained basic equipment for sampling the cave environment, much like simple weather stations. With these, they could get accurate readings of air and water temperature, the pH of the lake, and humidity. There were also several small vacuum tubes that, when opened, would sample the cave's atmosphere for later analysis.

"This is enough gear to get us started, until the others return from Camp 4. What we really want," Sue said, "are pack mules."

"I guess we're all pretty anxious to look around. I think you'll have plenty of company," Erica said as she turned back toward the campsite. "I'll see if Bob wants to join us." She returned a few minutes later.

"Bob said he's going to pass. He wants to do some inventory work on food supplies, fuel, and air tanks."

The four of them walked toward the ledge. Alan held back, ready to offer advice on route and safety considerations, but letting Sue and Alicia take the lead as the expedition started its scientific research. They hesitated at the Grand Staircase that led into the valley, and sat for a moment to consider a route.

Sue pointed down to a point not far from the lake shore. "There's a huge column there that seems to have more than its fair share of bioluminescence. Let's head in that direction."

Erica Qwan turned to Alan. "Have you got any geological insights you'd like to share, Professor?'

Alan smiled. "More like geological hunches, but I'll be glad to share them. First, I don't think that this cavern is really a part of the Maelstrom system at all. I think that this room and any associated chambers are very old...much older than the Maelstrom. And this room was not formed by surface water."

"Pretty good hunches. I don't follow the surface water thing, though."

"Surface water is an important part of most cavern systems like the Maelstrom, usually in the form of a stream that goes underground. The movement of the water in response to gravity gives it the force to eat away at the limestone. Formations come from water that seeps through the limestone, but chambers, galleries, and rooms are formed by the action of moving water. I don't think there are any surface streams that flow into this system."

"How did a room like this form?" Alicia asked, "and where does the water for the lake come from?"

"The room was formed by some tectonic event, I suppose."

"An earthquake?"

"No, nothing that drastic. I mean slow rising and falling of rock masses over long periods of time. The same forces that build mountains in response to something called isostacy. That or mini-plate movements. The fact that those processes are very slow and that we haven't had any such action in this region for a very long time tells me that this room...this system, is very, very old."

"What about the lake?" Sue asked.

"The water probably comes from the aquifer in the rock beneath us, moving upward into this room rather than falling from surface streams.

Sue stood up. "Which means that our lake, however large it is, probably has no outlet or inlet. And that's perfect as an isolated test tube in which new life forms could evolve. Shall we go see," she said sweetly, "or do I have to kick butt to get this group on the move?"

The four clambered down one small ledge after another, finally finding them on a level rocky plain that stretched out of sight to their right and left and toward the lake in front of them. The floor of Manning's Gulf was filled with a forest of columns in varying ages, indicating an active and ongoing process of formation.

"But notice that the lake has no columns in it," Alan pointed out. "That means that the lake and this room may have predated the beginning of calcium carbonate deposits."

"What does that mean?" Alicia asked.

"It means that it is just possible that this room and its lake were formed before the limestone was formed above us."

"But, Alan," Sue protested, "the limestone was laid down by ancient seas. That would date this room at hundreds of millions of years."

"In one form or another, yes it does. And this valley we're in gives some more credence to the fact that this is not a solution cave. If you look carefully, you can see that it appears as if a whole section of the floor simply dropped thirty feet. That's typical of tectonic action."

Erica was beginning to understand the implications of Alan's theory. "So we are walking into an evolutionary 'planet' that has been isolated from the world for a few hundred million years? But this is a limestone cave, isn't it?"

"The columns and formations are calcium carbonate," Alan answered," and that material is dissolved from limestone and carried by seepage through the ceiling. But the ceiling itself and the floor you are walking on is mostly igneous granite and metamorphic gneiss. This is a fault cave, not a solution cave."

"If you ask me, Alan, this room has doctoral thesis written all over it." Sue put one arm around his waist and leaned on him..

"I've got to admit, it's the most amazing field study I've ever seen."

"Sue! Alan! Come look at this." Alicia had been inspecting the large column that they had noticed from the ledge. Much of it was covered with a coating of clear, Jell-O like material. It was glowing, almost pulsing, with an intense blue light. Alicia had excitedly scraped some of the material into a series of collecting jars.

"I didn't think that all of this light could come just from Maelstromus ciscii," she said.

Sue looked carefully at the column. "Alan, remember when I mentioned calcium as a part of the bioluminescence process? Look at this section where Alicia took her sample." Underneath the glowing Jell-O, the column was riddled with holes and pockmarks, like the surface of an English muffin."

"It's eating the formation?"

"I guess," Sue shrugged. "Somehow it's getting energy from the calcium compounds."

"That's what it was doing on Drew's skeleton," Erica suggested. "But why didn't it consume the whole skeleton?"

"Exposure to different conditions in the other part of the cave...different humidity, maybe. Once the skeleton was exposed, the bacteria no longer had optimal conditions."

"Makes you wonder what these bacteria could do inside a living person," Alan observed.

Alicia approached a large stalactite, burning with such an intense blue light that she could see to make some notes in her field journal. "This looks something like a slime mold." She noticed the blank looks from Erica and Alan. "It's a cross-over life form on earth." She caught herself quickly. "I mean...up there. It's a fungus that can move some distance over damp logs and rocks. This is very much like it, but a microscope is going to tell us more. Definitely another new phyla!"

Alicia donned a surgical glove and reached toward the formation. As her finger came into contact, blue lightning flowed over her hand and up her unprotected arm. She gave a cry of surprise and quickly brushed gobs of jelly away as it moved toward her shoulder. Alan used their water bottles to remove the remaining material.

"Jeez! No slime mold ever moved like that!"

"Are you okay?" Alan pulled a spare shirt from his pack. "Here, put this on."

"Thanks! I'm fine, but I guess we've learned out first rule. Look, don't touch."

From their standpoint on the shore...a commercial cave developer would have called it a "sea"...the lake seemed to be limitless. The water was completely clear and pristine, but the rocky bottom was covered with a slimy layer. With no wind or tidal forces to cause waves or ripples, the surface was mirror smooth. Alicia threw a pebble into the water and immediately set off concentric ripples of blue.

A short distance along the lake shore was a large area of perfectly flat gneiss rock. Here very few columns had formed, like a clearing in the woods by the shore of a northern lake. The shore of the 'clearing' fell about five feet directly into the crystalline water. But there were no waves, not the faintest lift or sloshing, not a ripple to disturb the glassy surface. Alan the geologist walked around the site, marveling at the contorted twists and folds of the gneiss.

"Next expedition, there will have to be inflatables," Sue said. "And this will make a perfect base camp." Suddenly, about a hundred feet offshore, there was a brilliant flash of blue, followed by another and another. Sue stared, in awe of the implications. "There was movement that caused those flashes in the water...maybe something bigger and more active than slime mold?"

Erica was spellbound. "There's a lifetime of work in here, that's for sure. Like the Leakeys in Olduvai Gorge."

"Rocks falling from the ceiling," Alan said. "Don't let your imagination carry you away. If it's all right with you biologist types, I'd like to suggest an hour more and then head back to camp."

"Yeah," Erica agreed. "By the time we get back we're going to be bone-tired and starving."

"Geologists are really whimps. Alicia and I were just saying we could go all night on pure adrenaline. Come on! Let's see how much territory we can cover in an hour and a half." The two of them started off away from the clearing

"I think I said an hour," Alan mumbled to himself. "I'm pretty sure I said an hour."

Sue and Alicia headed around a small cove, well in front of the others. Alan was about to say something about staying together when he heard Sue's scream. He rushed ahead, tripping and scrambling around columns until he found the two women kneeling by the shore.

"Sue, are you all right? We heard you and thought..."

"Alan, I'm sorry." Sue turned toward him holding several crystalline structures about the size of golf balls. "I shouldn't have screamed, but we thought we saw crystals in the shallow water of the shore. When we realized what they were..."

"Diatoms," whispered Alicia Marko reverentially. "The silicone shells of huge diatom-like creatures". The beautifully clear and intricately designed shells littered the shore at that particular spot. Like diatoms in the oceans above ground, the cases were vastly different from each other. Unlike diatoms, these cases were on an order of a billion times larger.

"But they're not unicellular?" Alan asked.

"Oh no, definitely not. A cell can only get so big before its surface area can no longer absorb and emit enough materials for the mass of protoplasm contained in the cell. Then it must divide. When these creatures were living, they were made up of millions of cells, and there had to be some specialization."

"I guess it's exciting, then," Alan said doubtfully.

"Alan, we're just now beginning to understand how DNA works. All the functioning of all your cells are based on the direction of four carbon-based acids and how they are arranged." Sue grabbed Alan's sleeve and looked into his eyes. "Evolution is based on the mutation of how those four compounds are arranged. Life on earth in all its amazing and infinite variety...on just those four compounds. What we're seeing here, each time that we find a new creature, is proof that evolution is going on within the Maelstrom, with silicon based compounds."

Alan smiled. "You're right. It is exciting."

Alicia looked out onto the lake's glass-like surface. "This proves the universality of evolution, nothing less. But theologians are going to love it. What are the chances of the same incredibly complex process of gene reproduction occurring twice? Many people are going to see a divine hand in the design of DNA and...whatever carries the traits of these creatures."

Erica was staring down the lake shore and began walking in that direction. "Alan," she said, "there's a very bright blue light down this way and I hear something too."

They were like children running from one new toy to another on Christmas morning. One species held their interest only until a new one was found, and the cave system seemed to have one surprise after another. In about thirty minutes, with Erica leading the way, they came to an outlet for the lake, with a small waterfall cascading into another pool. The resulting movement of water over the falls caused a noon-day glow of bioluminescence. Their headlamps weren't even needed in order to see each other and to see some of the room."

"Well," Alan mused, "that takes a lot of thunder out of my theory. The lake does have an outlet."

He looked around for a few minutes and then inspected the rock of the outfall closely. "Nope, I think I was right in the first place. For millions of years, this lake has been fed by the aquifer below it, and the total leakage through all the cracks in the granite led water back to the aquifer and just equaled the inflow. This waterfall hasn't been here for very long." He pointed to the pool below them. "See, there are columns in the pool itself. The room down there has been flooded very recently. So somewhere surface water has started flowing into the lake."

"How recently?" asked Sue, concerned for the inviolate virginity of Lake Evolution.

"Ten years," answered Alan, "maybe thirty. It's hard to tell exactly. I'll know more when I inspect those flooded columns down there. But we need to get started back."

Sue looked thoughtful. "Alan, if Evolution Lake has no outlet, then where is all this new water going?"

Alan was walking back toward the campsite. "I imagine, Sue, that this chamber is slowly filling up... approaching the surface in some places."

Half-way up the Grand Staircase, Erica spotted a small pile of clothing a few feet off their route. "Sue, who would have thrown their coveralls down here?"

Alan joined them. "Well, so much for zero-impact. We haven't been in Earth's most pristine environment for two hours, and we've got a dump! Damn!"

Sue knelt to pick up the clothing, but it came apart in her hands. "Alan, these coveralls have been here for a long time...years!"

"So Drew made it into the main chamber. He got to see all of this."

"He left this too." Alicia picked up an old Timex, its metal parts badly corroded. She began instinctively to wipe it clean with her shirt sleeve. "Wait a minute. It's not Drew Cisco. I think it says..."

"Roger Stickley," Alan said quietly. "Drew couldn't be bothered with a watch when he was climbing or caving." He sat down heavily. "For all these years, I thought Roger had drowned in the flooded maze. Somehow, he made it here." Alan smiled ruefully. "Maybe I can stop having that particular nightmare!"

Erica stood up from her inspection of the clothing. "Alan, I think you'll just have to exchange it for another nightmare. All of his clothing is here...shirt, underwear, socks."

"What?"

"When did Roger have knee replacement surgery?"

Alan stood up. "After a skiing accident. It still made it hard for him to go caving. One of the few things he complained about. How do you know?"

Erica held up a bright shaft of metal. Alan stammered. "You mean...?"

"These are Roger Stickley's remains."

CHAPTER TWENTY-SIX

"Let's rest a while." Sam was holding his stomach. "I worked up a cramp swimming over here."

The four men were at the base of Drew's Pit, each prepared to ferry three cases of food and equipment back to Camp 5 in the new section. Hoke sat down next to Sam and looked hard into his face and eyes. "Maybe we had better wait a little before we start back. There's no real hurry anymore. We'll be at Camp 5 for another week."

"You know, James and I could start back now," Scott said as he crouched in front of Hoke. "We can tell the others that you guys are resting. Alan will worry himself to death otherwise."

"Okay, Scott. If we're not at camp in an hour, bring Erica back here. And you guys stay clipped into the rope."

"I'll just be a few minutes, Scott."

But Scott was already in the water. Holding up his carabiner, he snapped it into the guide rope with a loud clip. Scott grinned, gave a thumbs up to Sam, and submerged.

James was still putting film in one of the aluminum cases and hurrying to catch up. "Sometimes I think he's just a little too gung-ho!"

"Stick to the rope, James. You'll be fine."

"See you in a while, Jimmy," Sam said weakly. He laid down on the rocky floor of the pit.

Hoke propped himself against a rock next to Sam and almost immediately felt his eyes getting heavy. It had been a long day, nothing much to eat since breakfast, and the previous day had been no picnic. Getting too old for this, Hoke thought as he began to doze.

Johnny called a halt at the top of the waterfall pit. "Look, Joe, you've done a great job in here. I've never seen a first-timer do as well. But this has turned into a marathon. I'm running for the bottom of Drew's pit, and I don't think you can stay with me."

"I know, I know! You just go. I'll either stay with you or not."

"I'm afraid we've already missed them. And you can't go through a Mazing Grace without me."

"If I'm not right behind you, I'll wait...promise!"

Johnny stopped at the entrance to the maze long enough to see Joe laboring up the slope toward him.

"They've left a guide rope, Joe! Follow it!"

"Be careful!"

Hoke woke suddenly. Sam's hand was desperately clutching his sleeve. The white-knuckled grip showed, in startling contrast, Sam's darkened fingernails.

"Sam...," Hoke began, but stopped in horror when he saw the face looking back at him. Sam's eyes were bulging in fear, and his chest heaving desperately in an attempt to find air. His eye sockets and lips were dark, giving his face a skeletal appearance. The man was asphyxiating in front of him.

He tried to administer mouth-to-mouth, but nothing seemed able to change Sam's condition. Hoke decided to use an air tank, but Sam grabbed him with both hands and tried to speak. His back arched in a spasmodic attempt to operate his diaphragm, his mouth worked once or twice, and then Sam went limp in Hoke's arms. In the very place where Sam Telliman had shown such unusual sensitivity for two other victims, he became a third.

Holding Sam, Hoke sat for several minutes in numbed shock and disbelief. What could have happened? How could Sam have been struck down so quickly? He gently laid Sam on the rocky floor of the chamber. Almost twelve weeks ago he and Johnny had descended into the pit to find the broken body of a boy, and then the remains of Drew Cisco. He laid a small bandanna over Sam's face, patted his shoulder, and then headed back to the pool.

It would be a lonely trip back to Camp 5 where the others waited unaware of the tragedy. Hoke took one or two deep breaths on the mini-tank and submerged.

From the top, Johnny swept his light across the floor of Drew's Pit. He was sitting, his head bowed with exhaustion, when he heard Joe's scuffling in the tunnel behind him.

"We missed them," he said in response to Joe's unasked question. "They're facing two killers, and we've got no way to warn them.

"All this for nothing!"

"Not for nothing, Joe. We tried, and that's better than sitting on our ass."

Joe played his light once more across the bottom of the pit. "Johnny, there's someone down there. Just laying still."

At that moment, Hoke resurfaced in the small pool. The beam of Joe's light flashed across the pool and came to rest on Hoke.

"Wait! Down in the pit! Who's that in the water?"

Hoke had barely heard the voice, but it was unmistakable. "Johnny? It's Hoke. What are you doing here?"

"Wait for us! We'll be right down."

Moments later, Johnny Smith touched down at the bottom of Drew's Pit and surprised his older brother by embracing him. Hoke was already at an emotional edge and tears welled up in his eyes.

"Johnny, what in the hell is going on?"

"We've been bustin' ass to catch up with you, Hoke. I didn't think to bring air tanks, so we thought we'd missed you."

"I started back to Camp 5, but realized I'd forgotten my cases."

"We came to warn you..." Johnny indicated Sam Telliman's body on the rocks behind Hoke. "I guess we weren't soon enough."

Joe Riechman came down the rope so fast that he hit the rocks hard. He quickly disengaged his harness and ran, stumbling to where Hoke and Johnny stood over Sam.

"Who is it?"

"Sam Telliman, Joe. There's nothing to be done for him."

"How did you two get together, Johnny? The both of you don't seem at all surprised to find Sam dead."

"Not Sam in particular, Hoke. But it's why we came. Why don't you tell him, Joe?"

"Hoke, that fall I took in the Sierras wasn't an accident. Someone had cut the rope in such a way that it would be hard to detect. And we believe that Sam came close to dying in the snow because he was pushed. And now this!"

"Everything points to Scott Cisco, Hoke."

"There's no way! I've been in the cave and worked with him for more than two weeks. Why, for Christ's sakes?"

"Dr. Hinneman thinks that, in some warped way, Scott holds Alan Manning responsible for his father's death. He went over the edge, and now he's taking his revenge on the whole Maelstrom team...punishing Alan by killing the others.

"We've had some weird little things happen," Hoke mused. "Mostly demented practical jokes. We've been sure that the guy is still in the cave. I've got to admit that Scott wasn't around when the ceiling came down on us in Moria."

"That slab we saw?" Joe exclaimed. "That was a damn planet. Nobody could have brought that down on purpose." Joe walked slowly over to Sam's body and sat next to it.

"Hoke, there's another thing," Johnny said. "He's cut the two descent ropes in the Great Pit. I almost went off the end of one. There's only one way out of the Maelstrom and that's the emergency rope."

"What's he doing?" Hoke was watching Joe, pressing down on Sam's chest and leaning closely over his face.

"Cyanide," said Joe flatly. "It's one of the first things you learn as a lab tech. Can't miss the odor."

"Did he put it in his food?" Johnny asked.

Joe held up Sam's minitank. "Cyanide's a liquid at room temperature... certainly down in these rooms. But it doesn't take much to change it into a gas. Just body temperature or the temperature of your breath." Joe held the flexible tubing of the minitank for a few minutes and then smelled the mouthpiece. "That's it.

Hoke stood up suddenly. "Sweet Mother of God! Scott led James back to Camp 5. Just the two of them. I've got to go after them!"

"Let me check your air supply first," Joe offered. "What do we do in the meantime?" Joe handed Hoke the tank and gave him a thumbs up.

"I think you and I ought to get back to the entrance, Joe." Johnny was preparing to ascend the rope out of Drew's Pit. "It could be that getting everybody out of the Maelstrom before they die will turn into a horse race for that emergency rope."

Once again, Hoke was in the water. "We'll stop Cisco in his tracks, and I'll bring everyone out. I'll meet you at the bottom of the pit."

"Wait a minute, Hoke! Bring them out of that place fast. There's another killer we came to tell you about.

James could see Scott at least sixty feet ahead of him, swimming along with a powerful breast stroke. He could swim well enough, but he was encumbered not only with two cases but with his digital camera.

With the demise of his Nikon in Moria, the digital was the only camera left in his arsenal that was waterproof.

Leaving him behind wasn't too damn smart, James thought. He had just decided to share some choice words with Scott when the figure ahead, turned, waved, and motioned him forward. Okay, so at least he's checking to see if I'm here.

Scott rounded a corner and his light faded from view, leaving James feeling very much alone. The watery chamber extended only as far as the light from his headlamp. Beyond that, all was an inky blackness. On both sides of the passage, dark tunnels led into unknown depths. Instinctively, James began to hurry forward, hoping to catch a glimpse of Scott's light after turning the corner.

At the turn, James carefully removed his carabiner from the rope and bypassed a large ring that Alan and Hoke had set into the rock. He replaced the carabiner and started out again, but with no sign of Scott. James swam alone for another ten minutes. He felt sure that he was getting close to Camp 5. It was a twenty minute trip and each tank would last for thirty minutes. Of course, he had an extra tank. No one was allowed to travel the flooded passage without a spare. So he would be all right even...

No rope! James couldn't believe it. There was no rope running through his carabiner. The guide rope was continuous from Camp 4 to Camp 5. It was impossible to run off the rope. And yet it had happened. He had been concentrating so much on Scott that he hadn't noticed.

Now James was truly alone, and very sure that he was not in the main passage. He swung around in a panic, hoping to see the rope end lying on the passage floor. There was no sign of it. Like black, gaping mouths, a honeycomb of tunnels opened on every side. James felt the air pressure lessening and quickly switched tanks, dropping the exhausted one to the floor of the passage. He began to swim back down the corridor, trying to follow his route as carefully as he was able.

Out of the gloom ahead a light shown feebly, and James dared to hope. The light grew stronger, and he began to cry with relief. Scott had returned and found him. James waved wildly and then raised his digital camera, taking several shots as the figure came closer.

But the swimmer wasn't slowing down. He came on at full speed, knocking the camera out of James' hand and violently ripping the light from his head. A vicious kick caught James full in the stomach, so that he doubled over and lost his mouthpiece.

The attacker swam away as quickly as he had approached. James gathered himself and followed as fast as he could, but in the rapidly dimming light and confusing passages, he lost ground. The figure disappeared down a tunnel entrance and James was left alone, floating in absolute darkness.

He had perhaps twenty minutes of air left...twenty minutes in which he could bang against the walls in the blackness, desperately seeking for that which he would never find. Somehow those twenty minutes didn't appeal to James. If a physician had told him that he had months to live, James was the kind that would be most concerned with the quality of those last months. He would not spend his last minutes in mindless panic and fear.

James began to swim slowly, almost leisurely, feeling his way along the wall. He would hit the ceiling at times, or the floor. Once he entered a tunnel that ended after twenty feet and had to swim out. Slowly the air pressure began to decrease in his tank. James was oddly at peace. Certain death, death against which one could not struggle or hope to vanquish, has an almost calming effect. Wrapped in the dark confines of the Maelstrom, James took one lung full of water and sank to the rocky bottom.

CHAPTER TWENTY-SEVEN

"So now I can think of Roger slowly starving to death." Alan was squatting near the pile of old clothing that had been Roger Stickley. "That's after his batteries ran out leaving him in total darkness. I guess that's better than drowning."

Erica sat on a nearby rock ledge. "Forensically, this would be the perfect crime scene. A place where a body could lay for...?"

"Seventeen years," Alan said.

"Seventeen years, and we can be assured that nothing could possibly move or disturb the remains. That's why something's not right here."

"How do you mean?" Sue asked.

"Well, there's absolutely no skeletal remains. Nothing! And then you would expect a person to die more or less spread out or perhaps in a fetal position. But evidently Roger died in a heap."

Bob Woods appeared at the top of the natural staircase. "Have you seen anything of James?"

"No, why?" Alan asked as he scrambled up to the top.

"Scott returned from Camp 4 and I saw James come out of the water a little later. He's evidently wandered off from the campsite by himself...taking pictures, I guess."

"Damn, he knows better than that. Let's get back to camp and start a search." For thirty minutes, they crisscrossed the area in pairs, calling for James.

"Where are Hoke and Sam?" Erica asked when they returned to camp.

Scott was sitting dejectedly on a boulder near the pool that marked the passage entrance. He walked over with his hands in his pockets. "Sam wasn't feeling well, so he and Hoke decided to rest for awhile. James and I came on back here. I'm guess I took off and left James behind."

"Why in hell, Scott? You're more responsible than that." Alan was disappointed in Scott, but it came across as anger.

"I was just in a hurry to get back here and explore with you guys. I figured as long as he was clipped into the rope..." Scott's voice trailed off and he looked around the group glumly.

"But James came out a little after Scott," said Bob. "I was working with the food cases and saw him come out of the pool and put his camera down. You know, the electronic thing. Then he waved and went off toward the bathroom."

Alicia walked over to the pool and came back. "Here's the camera, and his headlamp."

"Did you actually talk to James?" Alan asked.

"No," Bob said. "I just waved back and went about my work."

When Hoke Smith surfaced a few minutes later, the surprised group turned, half expecting, half hoping to see James. Hoke strode purposely out of the water, jerking his headgear off as he approached the rest of the team.

"There are three men back in Drew's Pit right now," he began without preamble.

"Three men?" asked Sue. "Who other than Sam? Is Sam all right?"

Hoke ignored her, but was looking at Scott Cisco. "Joe Riechman and my brother Johnny are in the Maelstrom. It seems that Sam Telliman was probably pushed into that icy stream in the Sierras, and Joe's rope was cut almost in two." Hoke took a step toward Scott. "Rudy Metcalfe did some research. The rope was cut with a crampon point, Mr. Cisco! According to Joe, you were the only one in Tehipite with crampons!"

Scott started to stand up, but Alan put a hand on his shoulder. "Slow down, Hoke," he said calmly.

Hoke turned to Sue. "Sam's not all right, Sue. He died in my arms of cyanide poisoning. The stuff was placed in some of the air tanks."

There was a stunned silence.

Scott looked up at Alan. "I didn't have anything to do with this."

"Where's James Okura?" Hoke asked. A cold anger was rising in him, so that he wanted to lash out at someone.

"We don't know."

"Well, I know where the hell he is!" Hoke shouted. "The guide rope has been cut and then tied back together right at one of the clips. I'd say that some bastard has led James into the flooded maze. He's lost in there. He's gone! If that's his headlamp, then he died in the dark, scared and alone!" Hoke kicked an aluminum case across the campsite.

Scott withered at the onslaught. "But Bob saw him. His gear is here!"

"There's a lot of circumstantial evidence against you." Bob Woods tried to lay out the facts. "Somebody was in Granite Basin before the team, and then you show up in Tehipite...with your crampons. You had the opportunity to play Batman, you weren't around when the ceiling collapsed in Moria, and as Alan pointed out this morning, how could Batman know about Drew's Pit? Now two people are dead! Ball's in your court, pal."

Alan finally weighed in. "You've got the best evidence, Bob. You said you saw Scott come out of the pool?"

"Right."

"And then you saw James...or someone, come out carrying the camera and headlamp. James is either in here with us, or his killer is. But it's not Scott."

Erica suddenly jumped to her feet. "The camera. It's digital!"

Alicia grabbed the small camera and began filing through the images. "Lots of pictures of this room; here's some in the water. Wait a minute!" She looked through five or six more shots and then triumphantly handed the camera to Alan. "James photographed his murderer...the last five frames he ever took. And it's not one of us!"

Alan took the camera and watched the screen carefully as a distant figure seem to swim ever closer to the photographer with each frame. Little by little, the face of Batman became clearer, until he saw an image that embodied raw hatred and madness. Alan's face went ashen and he dropped the camera, staring at the others.

"Alan, what is it?" Sue grabbed his arm and shook him.

"It can't be, it just can't," he whispered hoarsely.

"Damn it, Alan! Spit it out!"

He closed his eyes and a shudder racked his body for a moment. Then Alan sighed. "The diver in the tunnel...the man who killed James." Alan picked up the camera. "This is a picture of Drew Cisco!"

Scott literally dove for the camera and looked at the picture in the screen. "No!" he shouted in a plaintive cry. Then he buried his head in his hands and began sobbing. Between Scott's reaction and Alan's announcement of an utter impossibility, the rest of the group was unsure how to respond. Finally Scott looked up, tears streaking his face.

"It's Winston, Alan. He's the perfect image of Dad." His voice caught and he struggled for a moment. "Why, Winston? For God's sake, why?" The group drew even more closely to each other. Sue put her arm around Scott's shoulder.

"What can you tell us, Scott?" Bob asked gently.

Scott drew a deep breath. "Winston hates you, Alan. I don't know how else to put it. He was convinced that you left Dad to die. We knew that wasn't true, but he was ten and became obsessed with the idea. For a while, all I heard when we were alone in our room at night was 'My Dad could be alive right now' or 'I wonder how he'd like it'...stuff like that."

"Then he stopped, and I never heard anymore about it. He didn't make it in college, but did really well in the Navy."

"Navy Seals, I'm guessing," Hoke said to no one in particular.

Scott nodded, sickened. “Underwater demolition specialist. He was really proud and so were we...Mom and I.”

“That kind of training can be dangerous.” Alan ran a hand through his hair. “The men have to be able to kill, one on one, and they have to be dispassionate about it. Once in a while, a person with the wrong mental make-up gets that training.”

“Mom remarried and Winston stopped calling or writing. The last I heard from him was three years ago. He’d joined a survivalist group and was living near Bozeman, Montana.”

“That explains a lot,” Bob said. “Everyone in Missoula who was in the outdoor business knew why we were buying all that gear. If he got word of it through one of his survivalist friends, he could have bought practically the same gear.”

“Hoke, how did you guys sign in at the register for Fresh Squeezed?”

“No names, Alan. Just ‘Maelstrom Advance Team’.

“Winston was here before you. And he had scrawled the name ‘Cisco’. When I saw it, I thought Scott had put it there just to have his name in the register.”

The group gathered tightly around Alan and Hoke Smith.

“What next?” Bob asked.

Hoke sat down next to Scott. “I’m sorry, son. I was upset about Sam and James and I jumped to conclusions. I should have known better.”

“Its okay, Hoke. We’ve got other things to worry about.”

"Winston has cut the descent ropes," Hoke said. "Joe and Johnny were going to head back to protect the emergency rope. We don't want him to strand us in the Maelstrom."

"There's only one thing that matters right now, and that's getting everyone out of the cave safely. Capturing this guy, the research...nothing matters more than each of us."

Bob Woods leaned forward as if to grant even further privacy to their discussions. "I don't think this guy is a step-up, in-your-face murderer. I mean, I think we're perfectly safe sitting around here in a group."

"And that's the way we're going to stay until we're out of the Maelstrom."

"How long to get out?" asked Erica.

"Five hours to get all of us to the bottom of the Great Pit. With the wench operating, we can have everyone out in seven hours. Less if several go up the emergency rope at one time."

"How do we keep him off our backs?" Hoke nodded into the darkness.

"We've got to get everyone out and stop Winston from doing anymore harm." Alan turned toward Scott. "I know it's hard, but this isn't your brother anymore. Slowly but surely, your brother left that body and now someone else is in it."

"I know! I'll try to...to do whatever it takes."

Sue spoke up. "Why would he risk posing as James and coming in here?"

"He doesn't know the camera is digital," Alan said. "He figures no one will ever survive to get film developed."

There was a sudden movement and a splash at the pool. Bob and Hoke ran to the water in time to see a dark form swimming rapidly down the flooded passage.

"Throw me a tank, quick," shouted Hoke. Scott started to toss one, but Erica stopped him. "Let him go, Hoke! That's just what he wants you to do...grab a tank and follow him. We've got bigger problems." Erica took the tank from Scott, turned on the air supply, and threw it down in disgust. "We've got to check all the air tanks."

"But he may be after Joe and Johnny. If he's been listening to us..."

"Bring me the tanks. All of them."

Thirty minutes later the awful truth was evident. There were no more tanks left that could be considered safe.

"That answers our question," Bob said quietly. "He came in here to bait us. No one is following him, so he knows we're trapped."

"He's stranded us, Alan," Erica said flatly. "He wants us to die a slow death together."

"And he'll go after Joe and your brother, Hoke. He knows they could bring help and save us from starving to death."

Hoke was staring at the floor, running his hands over his close-cropped hair. "We won't starve to death."

"We've got a week's provisions," Bob began. "Maybe two weeks if we're careful..."

"The bacteria are deadly!" Hoke looked up. "Joe came into the Maelstrom to warn us. Our alien friends have an insatiable appetite for calcium. Somehow, they've found their way to the surface. Two people have died horribly, and another young boy is very sick."

"What happened to them?"

Erica answered. "Weakened, thin bones that break easily and don't heal. Terrible arthritic pain in the joints as the connective tissue and muscles lose their anchors. If the bacteria aren't stopped, the body's framework collapses and you can no longer breathe. I guess a person could just crumple into a pile and die."

"Like Roger Stickley?" Alicia began looking at her forearm, so recently covered with a glowing mass of alien creatures.

"Joe thinks that standard radiation therapy will take out the bacteria. But we have to depend on Johnny and him to bring help and new air tanks."

"Incredible," Alicia said as she sat down on her foam pad. "In the space of an hour, two friends are dead and we're trapped."

They were saving batteries, and in the semi-darkness, Erica spoke softly. "What makes me angry is that we don't even have time to grieve for them. We've got to worry about saving ourselves."

"Well, we're not hopelessly trapped." Alan stood up. "Bob, how about you and Hoke doing a projection on food, fuel, and batteries. Maybe give us an estimate of how long we've got... regular use and spartan use. I'm going to head 'up' the lake and try to find the source of the water that's coming into it. It's a long shot, but better than waiting to be rescued."

"I'll come with you," said Scott. "It'll take my mind off things for a while."

"Hold on! I'm coming too." Sue gathered her gear together and joined the two men.

"I think Erica and I will stay and help Bob," Alicia said as she gave Sue an impulsive hug. "You people be careful!"

Erica watched as the three headed into the distance, parallel to and above the lake. "Come on, Alicia. Let's go look at Roger Stickley's remains again. I think he's got more to tell us."

"Like what?"

"How long he had before these bacteria took him out. Our food supplies and how long they last could be a moot point."

Roger's remains were just as Erica had left them an hour ago, just as they had been for seventeen years. She knelt over them, carefully moving the cloth with forceps from her medical kit.

"Alicia, he must have had a pack of some kind. It may not be far from here." The two women began a thorough search, walking the rough granite stairway that led to Evolution Lake. Within fifteen minutes, Alicia had found both the pack and a campsite.

Roger's pack was once blue nylon cordura, but now it sported a fuzzy growth of gray-black fungus. Leather straps and pull tabs were pretty much gone, but Erica found the contents to be in excellent condition. She popped open a sealed ammo box.

"Plenty of energy bars, some dried fruit, crackers...he didn't starve. If we presume the food box was full, and it might not have been, then I don't think Roger ate more than a couple of meals."

"There's plenty of extra batteries, still in their packs," Alicia said as she looked through another box. She looked up quickly. "Erica," holding up a metal canister, "there's a spare minitank."

"The poor bastard! He had more air, but there was no way he'd chance going back into the water." Erica tried the valve. It was stubborn at first, but slowly turned. The sound of escaping air was obvious. "Huh, the pressure's still good."

"I wonder if he was tempted. You know, to go back in that maze and find his way out of here?"

"I don't think he had much time to think about it." Erica put the tank back into Roger's pack. "Alicia, I think Roger Stickley entered this chamber and was dead by the next day, or the day after, at most."

Alicia's voice was starting to tremble. "But Hoke said that the people in London lived for weeks."

"They didn't encounter as strong a concentration as..."

"As I did! Oh, God, all my nightmares about this place are coming true." She started to sob as Erica enfolded her in an embrace.

"Alan will find a way out, Alicia. We don't know if Roger fell into a mass of the damn things or even ingested some. Who knows? They weren't on you for very long!" Erica stood and pulled Alicia with her. "Come on! Show me this campsite."

"Yeah, sure!" It was a voice devoid of much spirit or hope. Alicia led the way further down the staircase and around a buttress of rock that jutted out into space, leaving a shelter of sorts.

"Nice little place," Erica said as she looked at the overhang above her. "Good protection from rain."

Alicia smiled a little in spite of her fears. She kicked around some of the scores of empty food cans that littered the area. "It's got to be Winston's camp. Some of these were opened only a day or two ago."

"Looks like he's been in here for a couple of weeks, which means we know something he doesn't. Winston has got a serious bacterial infection. Could be an ace up our sleeve."

Alicia sounded relieved. "At least he's still alive and kicking. In a strange way, that makes me feel better. Let's take Roger's pack to camp and wait for the others."

Scott led them along the declivity that sloped downward into Manning's Gulf. Below and to the right, the trio could see the waters of Evolution Lake shimmering darkly with highlights of reflected blue light. They walked in silence, each person absorbed with their own perspective on the tragedy that had befallen the expedition. The deaths of Sam and James and the dangers ahead of them drew their attentions entirely from the chamber's mystical beauty.

After fifteen minutes of walking, the plateau on which Camp 5 had been established began to slope gently upward. Evolution Lake was consequently further below them. There was no longer a 'staircase' of rock ledges down to the lake, but rather a steep cliff of outcroppings about thirty feet high.

"Maybe we should have stuck to the lake shore," Sue offered. "We're going to start scraping our heads on the ceiling pretty soon."

"No, I think we're better off up here. It's a given that we'll have to climb to get out of this chamber. Maybe we'll have saved ourselves forty feet of hard..."

Scott grabbed Alan's arm and stopped him in mid-sentence. "Look! Over to the right. I saw a flash of blue. There! See it?"

As Alan and Sue watched, several small blue lights moved a foot along the rock. One covered the distance quickly, as if flying. Alan picked up a small pebble and tossed it toward the wall. Suddenly, a wave of intense blue seemed to gather strength and sweep across the ceiling directly above their heads.

Sue screamed as blue light rained down and she was able to feel the pricking sensation of insect feet along her arms and neck.

"Cave crickets!" Alan said. "Thousands, maybe millions of them."

Scott played his light across of writhing sea of antennae and legs a foot or two above his head. "Another new species?"

"They look like standard, run-of-the-mill cave crickets to me. Eyes that are not functioning and super long antennae to serve as feelers in the dark."

Sue's curiosity had overcome her repulsion. She looked at one of the creatures closely. "So this guy's ancestor came in here a decade or so ago and began ingesting Maelstromus ciscii. The bacteria aren't hurting the crickets, maybe even aiding in digestion." One cricket had taken up residence in the palm of Sue's hand and she held it up at her eye level. "Are you eating what other cave crickets eat? Or are those little blue guys helping you find energy in some totally different way?"

"We'd better get moving," Alan said gently. "We'll be back another day."

Sue nudged the cricket off of her hand and started after Scott. "I'll guarantee it. Anything less would be like throwing those lives away." She used the heel of her hands to wipe away tears that had started up. "Oh, damn it!"

The ceiling lowered to four feet, forcing them to move on their hands and knees. The wall of the chamber had also closed in, so that Scott now had them crawling along the edge of the cliff overlooking Manning's Gulf and the lake. As they rounded a bend, the ledge became even narrower so that Scott had to sit with his back to the wall and edge his way around the corner. When Sue and then Alan edged around the narrow ledge, Scott was standing on a wide platform of rock, transfixed by the scene before him.

A long sheet of water was sliding almost soundlessly down a high cliff face. Twenty feet above the surface of Evolution Lake, the water hit a ledge and pinwheeled out into space. The waterfall struck the lake and created a focus of electric blue, pulsing and sending out arcs of blue fire as lake water splashed into the air.

Alan, however, was concentrating on the falls and the cliff face over which it fell. "That could be our way out of here."

"Up that? You can't be serious, Alan!"

"Scott thinks I'm serious, don't you?"

"He's serious, all right." Scott played the light up the granite face, studying carefully the ledges and crack system. "Of course, we've got almost no chocks; we have no idea if there's a place for all of us to gather at the end of the first pitch; and we don't know if there's a passage at the top of the falls large enough for anything bigger than a cave cricket. Other than that, it looks like a way out." Scott turned from his study of the route. "Except for climbing on wet rock. I don't like that too much."

"Do you still think this water started coming into the chamber twenty years ago?" Sue asked Alan. "How could it have eaten through all that granite?"

"It didn't. The water just got through a relatively thin limestone cap and it was working at that for eons."

"We've only got two rope lengths at Camp 5," Scott pointed out.

Alan thought for a minute. "That should do the trick. I've got the climb figured at about 230 feet."

"That's a pretty good guess, or do you know where we're coming out." Sue didn't try to hide the skepticism in her voice.

Alan smiled. "Thirty minutes from the doorway to Moria. Let's head back to Camp 5."

Joe Riechman stretched out on a thick, wedge shaped piece of limestone. Two days earlier it had been part of the ceiling in Moria.

"We need about thirty minutes, Johnny. Let's just get something to eat and get a few minutes rest."

"I've got to admit that you've surprised me. I thought you'd back out of Fresh Squeezed like a crayfish."

"Do back-handed complements come naturally to you mountain boys? Or do you just try harder?" Joe turned off his headlamp. "Wake me if Scott shows up!"

Johnny hadn't meant to sleep. He woke with a start as a loud metallic click echoed through the silent room. A headlamp shown in his eyes, blinding him. The light also glinted on the barrel of an evil looking glock leveled at his head.

The man in front of him was hard to see, but Johnny could tell that he was short and stocky. Black hair hung down wetly over his forehead and stuck out from the back of his neck. Much of his face was covered with a heavy growth of beard. He was dirt-stained and muddy, but his eyes seemed to blaze through all the rest. They were eyes like Johnny had never seen in a human; penetrating, fiery, and full of hate. They reminded him of a mad dog that years ago he had cornered and been forced to shoot. Mean eyes, trying to find a way to strike out.

When the man spoke, it was a rough, gravelly voice. "Toss me your headlamp, and then wake up the computer freak." Johnny tried to stall. "You hesitate one more time, I'll shoot your ankle off."

Joe woke protesting, turned on his headlamp, and turned to see the apparition standing in front of them.

"Give me your headlamp. Now!" He shouted and stretched his gun arm out straight.

"You look just like Drew Cisco's picture, so I guess you're Winston. I think I've seen you in San Francisco before!"

Johnny changed position on the rock, shifting his weight slightly. "So Scott didn't..."

Winston spat. "Scott hasn't got the balls to choose his own breakfast cereal. He thinks Alan fucking Manning is his second daddy or something."

Johnny managed to get some weight on one foot, but Winston's mad eyes weren't missing anything. His gun hand lashed out suddenly, striking Johnny three times in the head. Joe made a move to stop him, but the gun was quickly turned on him. Johnny lay unconscious on the floor of Moria.

Winston threw a length of rope at Joe. "Tie him up and then sit down with your hands behind your back."

Joe's voice quavered. "You comic-book villains are all alike. You're a murderer. So why should I do what you tell me to do? You'll kill me anyway. There's no incentive."

Winston walked up close to Joe. Two weeks in the cave, and his clothes reeked with sweat and cave mud. Winston never took his eyes from Joe as he aimed downward and shot him neatly through the foot. Joe screamed in pain and rolled to the ground.

Winston reached down and jerked him back to his feet. “I’ve got a few more shots I can spare before I shoot you in the damn head. Now do what I tell you to do!”

With both men tied up, Winston relaxed for a while. He stuffed the headlamps and spare batteries into an old rucksack and lay down on the cave floor, one arm thrown over his eyes.

CHAPTER TWENTY-EIGHT

The team had left Moria fourteen hours earlier, anticipating the wonders of the Maelstrom's unexplored regions. It seemed like days... days since their last hot meal, days of physical hardship, days of loss and tragedy. Getting out of the Maelstrom was going to seem like weeks.

"What are the alternatives?" Sue asked. "Other than climbing up the waterfall."

The group was huddled around the MSR stoves, finally enjoying a hot meal...if anything could be enjoyed under their circumstances

"Which might get us nowhere!" Hoke thought aloud.

"Damn it, you tell me a better plan!" Alan tossed his plate aside. "We can sit on our butts here until Johnny comes back with help...if they make it out alive."

Erica ate the last of her stew. "I think they'll be all right. They've got a major head start."

"They've also got a couple of major handicaps. They don't know we're trapped with no air tanks, they think Scott is the murderer, and they don't know Winston is coming after them." Alan stood. "I'd say they were in real danger. Which is why I think we should try to find a passage out of here."

"What's to keep me from taking Roger's air tank and swimming out?" Hoke asked.

Alan put a finger in Hoke's face. "Absolutely not! After seventeen years, you've got no idea whether the valve mechanism is still working, or if it's going to stop working when you're halfway through the maze. Crazy talk!"

"Here's our supply situation," Bob said. "We've got food for twelve days. Water's no problem, of course. Stove fuel is pretty tight."

"That doesn't sound too bad." Scott had stayed out of the discussion. Despite everyone's assurances and support, he no longer felt part of the group.

"Batteries will be gone in three days," Bob concluded

"Three days!" Hoke said. "How come?"

"Not all of the cases made it back from Drew's Pit. Most of the battery stock was in one case...maybe James had it."

"So despite the food and fuel, we'll be in the dark in three days. Then we'll have no choices."

Erica cleared her throat. "It may be worse than that. Alicia and I did a little forensic investigating. I've got every reason to believe that your friend Roger didn't last a day in this chamber."

There was a long silence before Alan spoke softly. "You think we're doomed? We'll all be dead by tomorrow?"

"No, I think Roger must have had a very close and prolonged contact with the bacteria. What I think is that we should get the hell out of here as fast as we can."

"Then it's settled. We get a night's rest and then climb out of here first thing in the morning." Alan turned to Scott Cisco. "You're the only one that can lead climb that cliff. We're looking to you to get us out of here."

"The fastest way possible," Scott muttered, almost to himself.

Fifteen years earlier, Alan had awakened at Camp 7 to find that Drew Cisco had slipped away during the night.

Deja vu!

When the camp began to stir the next morning, there was no sign of Scott. His pack was gone; his wetsuit was gone; Roger Stickley's spare tank was gone. Alan threw one of the aluminum gear cases into the entrance pool and flew into an uncharacteristic rage.

"Goddamn it, you stupid punk! Shit! You probably just killed us all!"

"Alan! Stop it!"

"Back off, Sue. I've got every right to shout. His damn father did the same thing and got himself dead. I'm tired of it! Scott's not only got himself killed, but now we've got no one to lead climb up that waterfall!"

"Alan, listen to me." Sue leaned close to his face. "Alicia's really sick."

He immediately became quiet. "Is there anything we can do?"

"Erica and Bob are with her. There's no way to get her out...she can hardly walk, much less negotiate the cliff."

"So someone has to stay here with her?"

"No," Erica walked over to the pool. "Alicia's dying. Maybe an hour or two, and it won't be pretty. It will be painful, until her organs stop functioning and she can't breathe." She walked slowly back to other side of the camp where Alicia lay wrapped in her sleeping bag. Erica arrived just in time to see Bob removing an air tank from Alicia's face.

"She's gone, Erica." Bob didn't let his eyes meet hers.

"You gave her oxygen?"

"She was having problems breathing. It's what she asked for."

"You gave her oxygen from one of our tanks...our contaminated tanks?"

"It's specifically what she asked for."

"You didn't have the right..."

"She had the right! She had the right to leave the way she wanted to. She had the right to avoid turning into an amorphous pile in front of our eyes. She had every right to let us get on with our escape. It was her gift to us!"

"You didn't have to comply," Erica hissed.

"Yes, I did! Look, Erica, I know you don't do mercy killings in London hospital. But there are places on earth...unsearchable, unknowable places where humans venture with their lives in their outstretched hands. Sometimes an accident occurs, and death is accepted as inevitable. I've seen that inevitability bring a certain calmness, as it did with Alicia."

"We might have done something. Doctors don't give up!"

"Don't give me that. There are plenty of times when doctors know they should give up, when they want to give up." Bob's tone softened. "Rudy

Metcalfe didn't tell you much about losing those fingers on McKinley, did he?"

"Not really!"

Bob reached down and covered Alicia Marko's face. "His climbing partner fell into a crevasse. A sled fell in after him and wedged his shoulders into a crack. Rudy spent hours trying to dig him out. Finally they both knew there was nothing else to be done. Rudy stayed in the crevasse and talked with his friend until the man finally died. Sometimes, you have to know when to quit."

Sue and Alan walked over. Hoke joined them, all standing silently for a moment.

"We need to get moving," Hoke said finally

"Moving where?" Alan asked.

"Up the cliff face and out the wet passage that you're going to find for us."

"You don't seem to catch it, Hoke. I can't lead that climb. I guess Scott could have, if he hadn't gone crazy!"

"Scott must have figured that using that tank was the fastest way out, even if he had to risk his life." Bob put a hand on Alan's shoulder. "He was trying to undo some of his brother's harm."

"What do you mean, 'I guess' Scott could lead the climb?" Sue asked.

"I've never done any serious climbing. There's an overhang at the top of the climb. I'm not sure who could do it."

"I'll be on the belay, Alan. The last five people in the Maelstrom team are getting out of here."

The team stayed by the lake shore because the exploratory route taken earlier gave them no access to the granite fissure. In thirty minutes, they had gathered at the base of the falls.

A small crack afforded Alan an opening for his fingers, but no more. He ascended for twenty feet by pulling back on the crack with his outstretched arms and by pushing his feet in the opposite direction against whatever irregularities he could find on the cliff face. The strenuous layback move was taking its toll on Alan, and he was glad to find the crack widening enough to allow his foot in sideways...

"Hoke, aren't you supposed to be holding the rope...belaying him or something?" Sue was watching Alan's moves nervously, one hand constantly returning to cover her mouth.

"If he fell now, all I could do is to help to pull him down. Get some protection in, Alan!" Hoke called.

"Soon as I get into this crack." Alan wedged one leg and part of his rear end into the crack. He cautiously removed a length of nylon webbing and tied a loop around the climbing rope. Alan reached out carefully to a small crack and jammed the knot of his nylon loop into it, pulling down tightly.

"Tension!" he yelled, and Hoke jammed the rope into a belay device so that the rope could not run out. "Belay on!" Hoke shouted back. Alan let himself hang from the nylon loop in order to set the knot tightly into the crack.

"Now, Sue, if he falls I'll hold him and he'll dangle from the nylon sling."

The climbing was easier in the crack, and the cliff face sloped back ten or fifteen degrees from the vertical. At the same time, the crack system veered further into the path of the waterfall. There were times when looking upward at the route meant facing the full force of the falls. In those cases, Alan felt above him for holds and kept his head ducked to absorb the force of the water.

After another fifteen minutes, Alan called down to Hoke. "Slack!" Hoke slowly let the rope slide through the belay device, until he had paid out about fifteen feet of rope.

"He's coming back down?" asked Bob.

"Nope. I think he's put in an anchor and now he's lowered himself. That way he can swing back and forth until he finds a better route. One that's out of the falls."

The better route that Alan found was dry, but extremely difficult. He levered himself up to a three inch ledge, using knifelike handholds that sloped away from the rock face.

"How's it going, Alan?" Erica called.

Alan caught his breath. "Just barely making it! I'm on a nice little ledge. I need to take a rest. Somewhere in the next thirty feet I'm going to have to find a place for all of you."

Good as his word, Alan found a sheltered platform two feet wide, far enough from the falls to be almost dry. He pulled the entire length of the climbing rope up to the ledge, thus releasing it from the various slings that he had placed as protection points. Alan then attached the rope to an anchor well above his head and lowered the rope.

"Bob, how about you going up first. We'll watch your progress and you can let us know about any rough spots."

"No problem, Hoke." Bob attached his harness to the jumars and began his ascent, standing in loops and using a third loop to support his torso. After a few minutes, he looked down. "Remember, Alan's done the hard part. This is a piece of cake for us."

Every thirty minutes, another member of the team began their ascent to the top of the first pitch. When Hoke arrived last, he found the other team members securely anchored to the cliff face, each on their own rope sling.

Erica looked past her feet into the black abyss below them. Where the waterfall hit the lake, its blue light glowed faintly, now 150 feet away. "I think I'm glad I can't see where we were," Erica looked upward, "or where we're going."

Alan gave her a half-smile. "Another couple of hours and we'll be off the cliff face. Just hang in there."

"Haven't got much choice about that," Hoke remarked. "We'll be waiting right here."

With everyone tightly secured on the cliff face, Alan began his assault on the second pitch. The difficulty of the route was marked by Hoke's having to hold Alan twice on short falls. There was very little conversation other than the terse communications between climber and belayer.

Erica leaned toward Sue, both standing on the narrow ledge. "I'm exhausted already. I can't imagine how Alan is holding up!"

"I think he'd say that what he's doing is only a risk, not a certainty. My legs feel like rubber. I wish I could change positions." She was silent for another minute. "And then I think about Sam and James and Alicia...maybe Scott. I can't believe that friends could die so miserably and that two hours later I'm worried about my damn legs."

"How's he doing, Hoke?" Erica asked.

"It must be pretty tough. I'll go for five minutes and never pay out any rope. That's not a good sign."

Above them, Alan was trying to find a way around an overhanging projection of rock that he had seen from the bottom. He felt sure that he was close to the top, if he could just get past the five feet of rock that pushed out into space above him. With his hand jammed into a crack beneath the overhang, Alan felt quickly for a good hold. There was nothing. He was thirty feet above his last belay point and a fall would mean sixty feet before Hoke could stop him. He stood on a small flake, his legs beginning to shake. A hundred feet below, several headlamps shone at him while another 150 feet further down, he could see a faint blue light.

A figure came to mind, an unbidden image from years ago. Drew Cisco perched on a precarious sloping ledge over an unfathomable pit. The image gave a devilish grin, and leaped for the little flake that no one else would consider as a handhold. Alan summoned his last reserves of strength and swung his arm once more over the rock projection. His hand met a perfect nubbin of rock, cupped almost to fit his grip.

Alan swung one leg over the projection so that he was now supported by his hand hold and one foot. He quickly moved his other hand over the ledge and was finally able to pull himself up. Sitting on the ledge of the overhang, he could see behind him that a gentle slope rose another fifty feet to an opening from which the stream issued. He sat on the ledge for several minutes, his legs and arms shaking with exhaustion.

Alan raised and lowered the rope as before and Bob Woods began a long, uneventful climb up the fixed rope. After Bob's ascent, Sue reached the top without incident, but her arms were aching from the exertion. She collapsed onto the rocky slope, shaking with relief that she was off the cliff. As Erica began her climb, Sue ventured a look over the edge. The wet cliff face gleamed in the light of her headlamp, but disappeared quickly into the well of darkness.

Erica was moving fast. Her long legs and her reach made her one of the best ascenders on the team, even more so than Alan or Hoke. Perhaps only twenty feet from the top, she felt a change in the rope's tension. As Erica approached the overhang where the rope hung free away from the cliff, she realized that it hadn't been the rope but just her harness adjusting a little. She was only ten feet from the top, but more than two hundred feet from the invisible surface of Evolution Lake.

Erica grabbed the ends of her leg loops and roughly pulled them snug. Two more quick sets and she would be at the top. The rope ran directly over the rocky ledge, making it extremely difficult to slide the jumars past the ledge itself. Only by bracing herself on the rock underhang and temporarily taking her weight off the rope was Erica able to go over the top and into the helping arms of Alan and Bob.

"Jeez," Erica said as she let herself down on the rocks next to Sue, "and we've got to do 600 feet of that to get out of the Great Pit?"

Sue shook her head. "No! Winston's cut the two ascent ropes, remember? We've got to go up the emergency rope. With the winch operating, we'll have a free ride. If Winston hasn't left already and taken the emergency rope with him, we can probably all go up at once."

Johnny regained consciousness, but was greeted with darkness. He struggled briefly with the ropes that bound him and then lay back.

"Are you awake, Johnny?" Joe whispered. "How are you feeling?"

"Sore. I think the bastard busted my nose, maybe a cheekbone."

"He started off shooting me in the foot, and promised more to come. It hurts like hell, but at least it's not bleeding."

"If we work together, I think we can sit up. Let's go on three." The two managed to right themselves and lean against a large limestone block. They tried briefly to maneuver the ropes that bound them, but Winston had not been haphazard.

"He slept for a while," Joe said. "Now he's messing around behind us with something." Winston's headlamp cast some light toward Johnny and Joe, and his shadow played across the wall of the room.

"If he's killing people off and he's got a gun, then why are we still here alive?"

"Beats me. But I'm thinking that Alan and the others ought to be out of the new section and on their way here. Not much way to warn them, I guess."

The team that Alan was leading was grim and silent. The passage worn by the stream was large enough to negotiate by crawling through water, usually only a foot deep. There was one short section that was so small that the stream came close to filling the passage, forcing them to press their faces close to the ceiling. After half an hour, they broke into a much larger gallery, where they could walk in a stoop most of the time.

In a distance of only fifty feet, their passage ended in the side of a large pit. Erica played her light across the open space and groaned loudly. "It's a dead end. How are we...?"

"Wait a minute," Sue shouted. "There's a rope hanging here. Alan, is this the waterfall pit?"

"Bingo!" Alan smiled grimly. "Just a little ascent and then we walk through Moria and Champs. We're almost home."

"So this is what happened to the waterfall. But how could it eat through all that rock in fifteen years?" Hoke was examining the rope that they had put in place less than twenty-four hours earlier.

"Oh, I think the stream has been eating at a weak spot in the limestone for eons. It just broke through fifteen years ago. That was the narrow space we practically had to swim through."

Alan sat down in the old waterfall opening. "I know everyone is about to collapse and we're torn up about Alicia and the others. But now we're at war. We take care of our injured. We return later to mourn and bury our dead. And we don't take anything for granted. We're not going to lose anyone else!"

Alan started to set an anchor. "Hoke, I want you to belay me. I'm going to get on this rope and simulate a fall...put as much force on it as I can. If it holds, we should be all right to go up."

Bob walked over to Alan. "We've got to rest sometime. We're going on almost twenty-four hours with no sleep and little to eat. People will start making mistakes and we'll lose someone, Winston or not."

"You're right. Everyone try to get some rest while you wait your turn to ascend. We'll get something to eat in Moria. If Winston thinks he's stranded us to die in the new section, he may have left the cave. That would take some pressure off us."

Hoke pulled in the rope for Alan. "Unless Johnny and Joe have escaped and taken up the emergency rope to trap Winston. Then we're still in danger."

"One step at a time, I guess. You ready, Hoke?"

CHAPTER TWENTY-NINE

He could do it. There was never any doubt in his mind. Scott Cisco knew that he could reach Drew's Pit and beat Winston out of the Maelstrom. He had stranded the rest of the team at the edge of Evolution Lake, but that meant they were safe from harm. Alone, he could move faster than any of them. Scott planned to be back with reinforcements and new tanks within twelve hours.

When he quietly submerged at the pool near camp, Scott did not immediately use the air tank. He clipped into the guide rope, took several deep breaths, and began to swim forward with powerful strokes. He lasted more than a minute before resorting to the tank, but that had increased the tanks' useful life by five per cent. He planned to hold his breath once every four minutes, greatly increasing his chances of getting out.

The headlamp was a lonely beacon in the watery blackness that had claimed James Okura. He had become good friends with James, who had kindled Scott's interest in wilderness photography. Scott looked forlornly into the various tunnels as he passed them, wondering which held James' body. This swim, he thought, is for James and the others... and to absolve himself of his brother's crimes.

Occasionally Scott would rise to the roof of the flooded tunnel on a chance that there might be air pockets. Most were small, too small to hold his face above water. Scott was surprised to find one small chamber with enough space and air to allow him to stand and breathe for a moment. Another deep breath and Scott continued his long swim.

It was his first deep breath from the tank after he had discovered the air pocket. Something was wrong! He had to almost suck a gulp of air out of the tank, and it was not enough. He fiddled with the regulator valve as he swam forward. His lungs were bursting, forcing him to try the tank once more. Scott thought that perhaps the air was flowing better, but this quickly changed. There was nothing left, or it wasn't going to come out.

He desperately swung the tank against the rock wall of the tunnel. The valve broke off, allowing a large bubble of air to escape and rush to the ceiling. Knowing it could be his last breath, Scott put his lips into the bubble and slowly inhaled.

How far could he swim in one minute? He kept close to the ceiling, so that he would have air the minute the tunnel opened up into Drew's Pit. Now his lungs burned. Scott could feel them trying to expel, but he forced the involuntary reaction aside. His head was pounding and the darkness became even blacker. Scott could feel the tunnel roof pressing against his back as his lungs forced him finally to gulp water.

Johnny saw them coming first, their lights bobbing up and down and glowing in the passage that led into Moria. He and Joe were swathed in darkness, so that headlamps were conspicuous even though some distance away. The team realized that they were close to Moria. In their excitement, they were shouting back and forth to each other as they approached the natural doorway that was the entrance to the huge room.

"Christ," Joe whispered, "why don't they shut up? They don't seem worried at all."

"They don't know about Winston. They think Scott's the problem. I guess they think that's under control." Joe felt Johnny shift position. "Damn! I think he's heard them too."

Suddenly they were bathed in the glow of Winston's headlamp. Joe winced at the glaring light as Winston looked into his face. The gun was just inches from Joe's head.

"Open your mouth," Winston snapped. Joe started to say something, but Winston crammed a dirty sock into his mouth. "You too, mountain ape!" Johnny set his mouth firmly. Winston flipped the gun around so that he was holding it by the barrel. "Open your damn mouth or I'm going to put out your lights again. Your choice!"

With Joe and Johnny gagged, Winston moved to one side of the doorway, extinguished his headlamp, and waited quietly. The first team member came through the opening into Moria and Winston swept his leg in a vicious sidekick that doubled Hoke over. In a continuous motion, he brought one fist down on the back of Hoke's neck and trained his gun on the rest of the group.

Bob Woods, at the rear of the line, started to move back into the passage. With no hesitation,

Winston fired and brought him to the ground, clutching his wounded leg.

"So now you know I mean business! All of you! Get in here, and drag sack-o-shit there with you."

Hoke moaned as Alan and Erica lifted him to his feet. Winston herded the group over to a spot close to Joe and Johnny. "All right," he said. "Sit!" Erica began to bind a pressure bandage over Bob's wound while Sue removed the gags from Joe and Johnny.

"I said to sit down, Dr. Qwan," Winston shouted

"Burn in hell, Winston," Erica spat. "We're taking care of these people and if you don't like it, fire away. I personally don't think you've got the guts for it."

Alan spoke quietly. "Erica, sit down when you're finished. I don't want anyone else hurt."

Winston walked over to Alan and crouched in front of him. "I don't know how the hell you got these folks out of the new section, but I don't care a whole lot either. This is going to work out just fine!"

"I can't figure out why you're doing this." Alan worked at keeping his voice level and calm.

"You can't? Alan, you really can't? I would have thought that was a no-brainer, Professor. Let's see if I can sum it up for you. You take my Dad off one weekend, lure him into the most dangerous cave you can find, and when he has an accident, you watch him die! And you fucking leave him there for the cave crickets to eat. You know how many nights I dreamed of my Dad in that pit, all alone? Dreamed about him still alive and laying there by himself?" Winston was in Alan's face, his mouth in an ugly snarl. "Dreamed about him being eaten and covered with mold like some dead bat?"

Sue spoke up. "Your dad was dying when Alan found him. You know that. With tons of rock on him,

Alan couldn't bring him out, short of dismembering him."

"That's always been Scott's story. My Dad used to come and visit me some nights, only Scott would never listen. Dad told me once how you dared him to go into that pit, how that rock was loose but you dared him anyway...said he wouldn't be a real caver. He told me how you shouted at him when he was under the rock for being so stupid." Winston yelled so that the room rang with his voice. "He told me everything, man!"

"So what's your beef with the rest of the people in here?"

"Oh, they're going to die along with you. And you'll know that you're responsible. You can all spend the rest of your days together stumbling around in the dark...sort of keep my Dad company when you finally buy it in some stinking pit."

Winston stood up and threw his old rucksack on the floor. "All the headlamps, all the spotlights, all the batteries. And hurry up about it."

Sue attempted to hide one headlamp behind a rock near the rucksack, but he grabbed her arm and pulled her roughly toward him. Alan started, but Winston leveled his gun at him.

"You think I'm really that stupid, Dr. Brighton?" He looked around theatrically. "Which reminds me, your group seems to be short one Ph.D. Did Dr. Marko choose to stay behind and do research?" He was greeted with a stony silence. "You see, Alan? You leave one dead person behind in the Maelstrom, it gets to be a habit. What about Scott?"

Alan's voice was terse and menacing. "Dead in the flooded maze."

"Stupid little shit!"

"He was your brother, for Christ's sake!" Sue said. Winston held her tightly with an arm behind her back.

"I had a brother once, but I haven't had much use for him in years. He chose sides a long time ago."

Winston shoved Sue past him and started backing up with her. "Everybody stay where you are and Dr. Brighton will be right back. I just want to put some distance between me and you." Alan threw down his climbing gear in frustration as Winston marched Sue toward the entrance to the Champs Elysees. They could see the two figures making their way over the rock strewn floor of Moria until they had gone about fifty yards.

"Go on back to your group," Winston said. "I'll even shine a light for you. I want to make sure they're all still where we left them."

Sue turned to face Winston. "No one else is going to die for you, Winston. I promise you that!"

Winston looked at her, his eyes flat and devoid of emotion. "You don't know enough about the future. And in here, Suzy, I am the future. Now get moving."

Alan watched Sue as she came back across the room, her way lit by the halogen lamp Winston had confiscated. As she neared the campsite, Alan pointedly turned away from the group and sat down. Sue was just able to get to him when the light went out and Winston disappeared.

"Alan, are you all right?" She touched him lightly on the shoulder

"Other than allowing three or four people to die who were depending on me, I'm just peachy."

"We don't know that Scott's dead."

"No, but I don't want Winston to know that. Besides, if he is alive, I may just kill him myself."

Sue couldn't see him, but she reached up with both hands and held his face. "You couldn't have foreseen this madness. But Alan, we are depending on you now. No one else can do it."

"Well, I'm going to get us out of the Maelstrom right now."

"We're going to need some help to do that. Who have you got in mind?"

"Drew Cisco," Alan answered. He spoke into the vast darkness of Moria. "Is everyone okay?" He waited until he had heard from each other team member. "Everybody stay where you are. We've got one ace that Winston doesn't know about." He spoke directly to Sue. "I'll never be more than fifty feet away.

While there was still light, Alan had sat down facing the portal leading from Moria, and he now began to work his way in that direction. On his hands and knees, he moved as close as he could to twenty feet away from Sue and began to feel for the opening. At first he had no luck, and was beginning to think of working his way back when his hand found the wall of the room. He had actually headed directly for the middle of the opening, missing its edges. Alan moved his hand upward as he stood and confirmed the strange rounded nature of the doorway.

"Everything going okay, Alan?" Sue's worried voice came from the darkness.

"Fine, honey. I'm at the doorway to Moria."

"Where I waited for you that night?" Sue changed her tone of voice slightly. "Alan, that's the first time you ever called me anything but Sue."

Alan stood at the doorway with its right side against his right arm. Now he was crawling along the wall of the room itself, away from the door. "Is 'honey' a good word? Or do you prefer something less saccharine?"

"No, no! 'Honey' is fine. But one pet name deserves another. I'll work on it. What are you doing?"

"A little exploring." By striking his forehead on it with a resounding crack, Alan had found a large block of limestone that was perched along the wall of the room. Feeling underneath, he found the sandy opening and carefully pulled his torso into it. At the furthermost reach of his arm, he felt Drew's pack and his heart jumped. Alan carefully pulled the old rucksack from its hiding place of fifteen years. Inside was the ammo box that he had been hoping for. It resisted his attempts to open it, so he finally gave the box several whacks with a piece of limestone.

"What was that?"

"I'm cracking walnuts, honey."

"Somehow I didn't like 'honey' that time. It had a different tone to it."

"Did it sound like 'Don't bother me for a few minutes 'cause I'm concentrating'?".

Erica crawled toward the sound of Sue's voice until she was sitting beside her. "What's Alan doing?"

"He says that he and Drew Cisco are getting us out of the Maelstrom."

Alan made a smooth place in the sand where he could place various pieces and materials without losing track of them. He felt carefully for the top of the brass container and pulled its cover open. Then he placed a small handful of pebbles that were in the ammo box into the container and carefully filled it with water from a small bottle in the pack. Alan knew that these would be there. He had put them in the pack fifteen years earlier for emergencies.

As soon as the water came in contact with the rocks, an unusual smell arose. Alan breathed it almost as incense and then closed the container. He waited for a moment, struck the flint sparker, and a bright flame of acetylene issued from the burner orifice. Alan gathered up the rest of the material and walked casually over to the waiting group. Sue stumbled toward him, falling into his arms.

"You can call me 'honey' like that anytime if it means you're going to work miracles," Sue said. "What's the smell?"

"Acetylene gas," Erica answered. "Small rocks of calcium carbide react with water to produce it. Fortunately, as long as both are sealed well, they'll last virtually forever." She shrugged at Alan's look of surprise. "Hey, I took lots of chemistry."

Hoke had regained consciousness and was trying to stand. "Are we heading for the Great Pit?"

"I am, Hoke. I can move faster by myself. With just one light, it would take too much time to get us all through."

"So we're back in the dark," Bob mused. "We need to set up food and water so we can find it, and then just take advantage of the time to rest." That's the silver lining for this cloud...food and rest."

Johnny walked forward, rubbing his wrists after Erica had untied him. "So what if Winston does get out first, Alan? I think he's done what he wanted... strand us in the cave with no light and little food. He'll just leave."

"And take the emergency rope with him. I want to get out without Winston knowing, so that I can bring help and supplies." He stood up and gathered his climbing gear. "Let me know when you're ready, Bob."

Sue walked with him to the entrance of the Champs Elysees. "Be careful, Alan. Come back soon!" Alan held her closely, stroked her hair and turned to leave. "Hey, give a girl a kiss?" He smiled and turned toward her, never noticing the light cotton thread stretched between the rocks.

"When we get out..." A flash of light and an accompanying roar threw them to the ground. There was an eerie echo around Moria and down the length of the Champs, like thunder in the mountains. Then there was silence, except for the shouts of the rest of the team 150 feet away. Several loud 'pops' alerted Alan and he flung Sue back into the Champs and rolled after her.

A groaning sound issued forth as if from the rock itself, a great weight that could no longer be supported. Several stalactites above Alan begin to cant at an angle toward them. "Run, Sue. Move out, move out." Alan pushed, shoved and dragged Sue down the Champs as the ceiling gave way with an astounding roar. A shock wave of air filled with particles of rock and dust rushed toward them as blocks began to rain down.

They were both thrown to the ground again, as if an earthquake had struck the cavern. Lying in the dust, cut and bleeding from thousands of high speed fragments, Alan thought that the worst was over. He looked to see that the entrance to Moria was completely blocked, if indeed the room existed anymore. Sue was in shock as Alan lifted her from the floor. He started to move forward to investigate the huge rock fall.

Now a new and louder groaning filled the long chamber, this time echoing all around them. Formations began to vibrate and water in the many travertine pools was sloshing out of its rims. Without comment, Alan grimly took Sue's hand and began walking fast, and then running, further down the Champs Elysees. Blocks the size of small houses started to fall behind them with ever increasing speed. A chain reaction was set in motion that Alan could hardly hope to outrun.

Much of the terror behind them could not be seen in the weak light of the carbide lamp. It could only be felt and heard. Alan's light picked out the massive white flowstone that marked the end of the gallery, but he could also see the ceiling above it beginning to cant and break.

"Stop, stop! We're too late, Sue!" Alan pulled her back and helped her clamber onto a slab behind them. The behemoth was still moving and adjusting from its fall seconds earlier. They were just in time as the last of the ceiling slammed into the floor.

Sue lay in Alan's arms, shivering with fear and exhaustion. Their faces were caked with dust and blood. For a brief time, a wind of almost hurricane force had swept the eternally still halls of the Champs Elysees. Alan took a spare T-shirt from his day pack and began to wipe Sue's face tenderly.

"It's over, honey. We're safe now. We've got to go back and see about the others, Sue. Winston doesn't matter anymore."

"Alan, I saw him...while we were running. I saw his light going off toward the side of the chamber."

Alan immediately lowered his voice. "Then, if he's alive, we don't want him to know we're here. He was probably waiting to see the results of his explosion."

"He couldn't have rigged all this!"

"No, but he rigged an explosion intended to trap us in Moria forever. We've known that there's some instability in the cavern. With all of the formation in the Champs he may have been caught in his own trap."

"Do you think the others are okay?"

Alan walked silently for a minute and then turned to Sue. "I'll be honest with you. I hope they're all safe, but they were in the dark and no where much to run even if they could see."

They began picking their way back toward Moria in a new breakdown. The devastation of the Champs Elysees was heartbreaking to Alan. He shook his head as they walked past huge broken stalactites and crushed masses of travertine curtain. At the same time, the geologist in him marveled at the destructive power to which he had been witness. It was a wild scene that was almost beautiful in its enormity.

The entrance to Moria was a jumble of smaller boulders, the force of the explosion having blown them to pieces. The dam of rocks was riddled with small openings, through which Alan called and showed his light with scant hope.

Suddenly his call was answered, and in a few minutes a dim light appeared through an opening in the wall.

"Alan, it's Hoke! What's it like out there?"

"The whole Champs is gone, Hoke. It looks like the Breakdown. How is everybody in there?"

"Not a scratch. We sat there wondering what was happening. We thought sure you folks were dead."

Sue sank to a rock. "Oh, thank you God. Thank you!"

"It makes sense, Hoke. Moria is stable. Everything that was going to fall has already done it. Where did you get the light?"

"Bob had a penlight in his coat pocket. And I had a couple of candles and some matches. Old habits, you know."

"This changes things, Hoke. Winston can't get to you, but if Sue and I don't get out, you won't make it. Winston's still in this chamber. I don't know if he's alive or dead."

"What if he comes here to check on us?"

"Keep quiet. If he does find out that you're alive, don't let him know that we're not with you. If he wants to talk to me, tell him I'm unconscious. Stall him any way you can."

Bob and Erica had worked their way up to the wall. It was good for everyone to hear each other's voices after the trauma of the last hour.

"Bob, I need Drew's pack again. Or at least the calcium carbide chips."

"I've got it right here. Let me find a hole we can reach through." After several false tries, Bob found a small tunnel large enough to accommodate his arm and shoulder. "How about this 5mm perlon rope? There's twenty feet or so in the pack."

"Might as well," replied Alan. "You never know what might come in handy."

As Bob passed him the coil of rope, their hands touched briefly. Bob was barely able to grasp Alan's fingers.

"God speed, Alan!"

CHAPTER THIRTY

Alan chose a route through the collapsed Champs Elysees that kept them to the far side of the room, away from the side where Sue had seen Winston's lamp. Alan was sure that if Winston had survived the cave-in, then he would go back to Moria to admire his handiwork. He wanted to get to Fresh Squeezed and out of the Maelstrom before Winston realized they were gone.

Sue and Alan arrived at Miami Beach, the entire length of the Champs Elysees and the remainder of the trip having been mindless movement. The two were entirely focused on the task ahead and on making sure that the others were rescued. At least, Winston couldn't get to the rest while they were trapped in Moria. He was counting on their starving to death or succumbing to hypothermia. Sue and Alan were counting on escaping the Maelstrom and getting help.

Alan was thinking hard the entire trip back to Miami Beach. This was going to be a horse race, he had decided. They had to get to the top of the Great Pit before Winston caught up with them. Sue was getting ready to enter Fresh Squeezed when Alan pulled her aside.

"Sue, I've been thinking hard about this situation and I only see one solution." Sue looked at him quizzically. "Someone has got to get out of this cave, and if Winston catches up with us while we're in Fresh Squeezed, we'll be helpless. If something happens to both of us, the others will die."

"So what's your plan?" Sue was sure she wasn't going to like it.

"I'm asking you to go through Fresh Squeezed and get out of the cave while I stall Winston."

"Alone? Alan, I can't go through there by myself. I barely made it with you there to goad me on!"

"There are lives at stake this time, Sue. You can do anything that needs to be done."

"Damn it, all right. When I get to the end..." Suddenly she stopped and stared wide-eyed at him. Alan looked away. "There's only the one headlamp, Alan. How are you going to be able to stop Winston?"

"I'll need the lamp, honey."

Sue stammered, looking wildly back at the beckoning entrance to Fresh Squeezed. "It's impossible, Alan. Even if I had enough guts to try, I couldn't make it. There must be some other way."

Alan held her by the shoulders. "If Winston catches up with the two of us, he can wipe us out with two shots. Try to imagine both of us in Fresh Squeezed with Winston and a gun behind us. It would be all over. If things don't go well for me and I have the headlamp, he'll never imagine that you've gone toward the entrance alone and in the dark." He pulled her to him and felt her trembling against his chest. "There is no way to get lost. There aren't any turns. It's just long and dark. You just keep going until your way is blocked, and then climb upwards fifteen feet. You're out!"

"I'm not out, Alan. How do I get back to the pit through all that fallen material...that breakdown?"

"Hands and knees, if you have to. You may wander some, but you'll make it to the bottom of the pit. There are no holes or side passages." He looked at his watch. "Five in the morning. There'll be some light as you near the bottom."

"What then?" Sue leaned against him in resignation.

"Clip into the emergency rope and start the winch. But take the switch and cord up with you, so you can't be stopped."

"I may catch up to you." He pulled her close to him and kissed her gently. "I will catch up to you."

"How do I know it's your headlamp I'll be seeing?"

"I'll call out Erica's name. If you don't hear that...if you hear your own name, then just hide and wait." Sue started to hold him more tightly to her. "Go now," he whispered hoarsely.

Sue walked to the entrance of Fresh Squeezed, looked back one more time, and began her ordeal.

Winston had been thrown to the ground by a small stalactite breaking from the ceiling. Dazed and his breath knocked out of him, he lay stunned while the world came down in the main gallery. He started to panic when he realized that the gun was gone. It had fallen out of his pack during the mad dash for safety. But the gun wasn't critical, he decided. His work was done!

He began working his way back toward Moria, amazed at the havoc he had caused. As Alan and Sue were approaching Miami Beach and Fresh Squeezed, Winston clambered up the huge slabs that led to Moria. For an instant, he glimpsed what might have been a light moving along the far wall of the ruined Champs. He turned his own light off, but could see nothing more. No way there was a light, he decided. He had Alan and friends trapped, he had the headlamps, he held the cards.

Winston saw immediately that his explosive device had been extremely effective. The entire area where the Champs met Moria was a shambles of domino blocks and chunks of limestone. The collapse of the entire Champs was just an added bonus. Approaching the barricade, Winston extinguished his headlamp and looked for the tale- tell glow of other lights through the chinks in the wall. Sure enough, there was some light and movement. He approached the wall and called through it.

"Well, hell's bells! Some of you are still alive."

On the other side of the wall, Hoke and Erica hurried to the rock barrier. "Is it Winston?" she whispered. Hoke nodded his head and hit his fist against the rock. They were hoping that Winston had been killed in the collapse

"What do you want with us, Winston?" Erica was fighting hard to keep her voice neutral.

"Well, I thought I wanted to know how many of you survived, but it really doesn't matter. Whoever's still alive won't last much longer

"We're all fine in here. We'll be found in a matter of time."

"Sure you will, like my Dad was found in a matter of fifteen years. Let me talk to Manning."

Erica hesitated. "He was knocked out, but he'll be fine."

"Good," Winston turned to leave, "I don't want any quick deaths for him."

Alan knelt at the entrance to Fresh Squeezed, shining his light in the crawlspace after Sue. She had gone about thirty feet when he heard her voice calling back to him. "Alan, just leave! I'd rather go ahead and face this than see your light getting dimmer and dimmer. I'll be all right and you're wasting time."

"Sue! I love you!" There was a reply, he was sure, but he couldn't make it out. No matter...he hoped he knew what it was.

He turned from Fresh Squeezed and stood for a minute. Now what? He had to find out if Winston were alive. If so, he had to give Sue a chance to get out...to get through Fresh Squeezed. No way could he stop Winston in a physical confrontation. The man was huge and insane to boot. Alan started back toward the Champs. All right, he decided. If he had to sink to Winston's level in order to save Sue and the rest, so be it. With a plan in mind, Alan hurried to the new breakdown in the Champs Elysees.

He waited only minutes before he saw the glow of Winston's headlamp coming toward him. The light rose and fell as Winston negotiated slabs ten feet thick. Alan turned and hurried back to the top of the thirty foot climb that he could chimney so well...the same climb that was such a struggle for Drew.

And would be for Winston.

Winston could no more do a decent chimney on the short climb than could his father. He had to span with both feet, and that meant his hands would be part of the climb. Alan could eat a sandwich going up or down the climb, his hands completely free. When Winston's head came above the top of the climb, Alan was waiting. He swung a large rock, hoping to put Winston out of commission immediately.

Instead, Winston let go of the cliff with one hand and caught Alan's wrist as he swung the rock. Winston began to topple backwards, but was strong enough to pull Alan with him. Both men fell thirty feet through the crack, bouncing off rock ledges on the way down. They stopped ten feet from the bottom and well off to the side of the chimney route itself, entangled with each other and partially held in the grip of a large crack.

Fifteen minutes later, Alan awoke in a fog. His head throbbed and blood had dried on his face from a cut above his eyebrow. Winston was still unconscious, but Alan had been protected to some extent by his body. He extricated himself with difficulty from the crack, and drug Winston roughly to the bottom of the gully. Alan studied the face of a man who had killed at least two people and was so ready to kill them all. In repose, his face seemed only dirty and sad. Alan had thought that he would have to fight an urge to kill Winston. Now that he had Winston's life in his hands, Alan's only thought was to stop him and save the others.

In the daypack, he found a length of nylon webbing with which he bound Winston's wrists behind his back. Alan removed Winston's headlamp and began the chimney climb once more, this time carrying Winston's daypack with all of the confiscated headlamps. Bound and in the dark, Alan felt confident that he had stopped Winston, short of killing him.

Sue had gone through every range of emotions since Alan's departure. The first, rather than panic or fear, was oddly enough sleep and safety. She was alone in the dark. There was no immediate danger and she was surrounded by a limestone vault. What had on her first trip seemed oppressive was now comforting. Wrapped in coverlets of rock and in total darkness, Sue Brighton slept. But after only fifteen minutes, some sense of shock and danger woke her so violently that she banged her head on the crawlspace ceiling. In that familiar feeling of waking in an unfamiliar place, Sue at first panicked when she found herself in such complete darkness. She tentatively moved forward, but could not keep her thoughts from the unknown. Could she squirm herself into some side crack without realizing it until too late? Had Winston left any other surprises on the floor of the crawlspace?

She continued to inch forward into blackness. She had nothing to mark her progress, could only feel the rough stone to each side. The scraping of her clothing on the rock floor was magnified by the impenetrable and infinite darkness that surrounded her. She tried singing, but her own voice sounded so desperate that she soon grew silent. Sue tried not to think about distances...how far she had come, how far she had to go. She tried to keep her mind on getting out. How great it was going to be when she got to the breakdown; how easy, comparatively, to find her way across the broken rocks toward the Great Pit. Once there, how wonderful to find herself riding upward toward the light, toward blue sky and trees and...

Sue bumped hard against rock and immediately panicked. She tried to go to the side, but there was no place to go. This can't be the end, she thought. And then her hands found empty space in front of her. It was the real squeeze, she realized. Where James Okura had lost it, where she had nearly broken down in tears. Sue lay perfectly flat against the rock floor; her arms stretched in front of her, her feet pushing on any purchase they could find. She turned her head sideways and felt the rock brush against her hair as she inched beneath it.

Don't think of the rock pressing down on you, she thought. Ignore the darkness and use your other senses. See with your fingers, listen for strange sounds, sense the air for all the cave's rich smells. You're not dead, girl; you're very much alive... just in the dark for awhile. What was the distance for the really tough part? Thirty feet? That's about sixty 'scouches', she figured, at six inches a scouch. The Gettysburg Address ought to see her through this.

Sue found herself thinking more about Lincoln's words than the narrow confines of the squeeze. At about 'We here solemnly resolve', the roof heightened and Sue was able to almost crouch. She began to laugh and move her elbows and knees freely. She still had two-thirds of the crawlspace to go, but she knew it could be done. It was just a matter of pressing forward and thinking of other things. Sue concentrated on the wonders of the Maelstrom's new section and Evolution Lake. There would be another expedition, she was sure. Her thoughts raced along a stream of consciousness track that took her to a deep concern for Alan, and then a fear of Winston. If Alan wasn't successful...if something happened to him. She couldn't let herself think of that. The thought came to her once more that Winston could be at this very moment in the crawlspace with her, approaching quietly from behind. He'd probably turn his headlamp off, just to scare her. But she could hear the scraping sound he would make, couldn't she?

She looked at the glowing face of her watch. It was early morning, just about light. Suddenly a movement of air stirred her hair, and her heightened senses heard a soft whirring sound. In only a few seconds, another movement and this time a slight touch, brushing lightly against her neck. Now the sound and movement were continuous, and Sue realized with a shudder that she was in the crawlspace just as legions of bats were flying through to the depths of the cavern. One lit momentarily on her coveralls, and she could feel its tiny claws grasping for a hold. Another landed on her back, its wing brushing repeatedly on her bare neck. Sue could stand it no longer, but began screaming as she tried to hurry down the passageway. But her frantic efforts actually slowed her down as she bumped ineffectually against the sides of the tunnel. At the same time, Sue tried to move herself forward and fend off bats that were coming straight for her face. Normally they could avoid her completely, but the passage was so small and the numbers of bats so great that Sue took up most of the available room. Intermittently crying and screaming, Sue finally lay flat on the floor and remained motionless. Bats filled every available inch of air in the crawlspace. Sue tucked her head, creating a small space under her arm that was free of bats. The thousands of bats came so thickly that it might as well have been one huge mass of fur and teeth. In an eternity of five minutes, they passed by and left Sue alone again in the passageway. She lay crying, but finally hit the wall two or three times with her fist and began to move forward.

There was no longer a sense of time for Sue. She stopped looking at her watch, for she was always disappointed to find that what she knew to be an hour was only fifteen minutes. It was time for a break, she decided. Sue stopped, laying her head on her arms. But the sound of her clothing scraping along the rock corridor, the sound that had accompanied her all through Fresh Squeezed, did not stop. Tentatively, she moved a few feet and heard the familiar sound of scraping.

She stopped once more, and knew with dread certainty that there was another sound in the crawlspace. She strained to look behind her. Far down the corridor, a faint glow lit the tunnel.

Alan! Alan had stopped Winston and was coming for her. Soon they would be at the top of the Great Pit, standing in the blessed chill of early morning. She maneuvered herself so that she could yell down the passageway.

"Sue!"

She froze, not daring to move. Her jubilation had turned to abject fear. Winston had gotten the better of Alan. He was in the crawlspace with her, and coming on fast. The light was brighter now, almost giving her light. She raced forward, scraping her knees and grinding the palms of her hands against the rock.

"Sue!"

Sue's hands struck solid rock in front of her. No gaps lower down, but just solid rock. Not daring to believe, she felt above her and found open space. It was still narrow, but Sue was able to carefully find an upright position. Her excitement growing, she started to clamber upward, keeping her arms well extended. Three times she hit her helmet hard on rock as she lifted herself, but it protected her and she was able to change position slightly and find a way further upwards. In just ten minutes, Sue was lifting herself out of the opening of Fresh Squeezed and into the paradise of open space that marked the home stretch through the Breakdown.

Looking down the vertical shaft, she could see Winston's headlamp growing brighter as she watched. It was up to her now. She had to stop Winston where Alan and the others had failed. There was only one chance. When Winston levered himself out of the vertical shaft, his head would be exposed and his hands holding on to the sides of the shaft. She found the largest rock she could lift and waited for him.

The helmet appeared at the shaft opening. Sue knew that she didn't have the strength to swing the rock, so she raised it above her head. To hell with him if she killed Winston, Sue thought. Right now, getting his headlamp seemed more important than his life.

Just as his head emerged, he called again down the length of the breakdown "Sue! Alan! Wait up!"

Sue was so surprised that she stumbled forward, and Scott Cisco turned his head to see a thirty pound rock land inches from his face.

"Scott!" Sue cried as he levered himself out of the shaft. She wrapped her arms around him. "We thought you were gone. I mean, we hoped, but when you never showed up..."

He hugged Sue tightly. "I almost bought it. I literally was losing my last breath when my head broke the surface at Drew's Pit. Just seconds earlier..." He shuddered involuntarily and sat down on the rocks. "And then I arrived in Moria to find Winston lording it over all of you. I sneaked around the perimeter of the room and got into the Champs." He noticed Sue's questioning look. "Sue, I had to weigh getting trapped with you guys or making it out of the Maelstrom. Anyway, I was in the Champs when the world came down. I saw you and Alan running and then lost track of you. Where the hell is Alan?"

"He went back to stop Winston. How could you miss him?"

"I haven't seen either of them. The main thing now is to get you out of the Maelstrom. I'll wait at the bottom of the Great Pit while you go for help!"

Alan's legs were rubber, and his whole body ached with fatigue. He stopped at a small pool and drank long from its clear water. Drinking water from a cave system had always been something that spelunkers avoided, but Alan was desperate.

All the way to Miami Beach, Alan walked and stumbled in a daze. He scarcely remembered any of his surroundings and was fully on automatic pilot. He entered Fresh Squeezed without hesitation, and found himself moving through it with a speed that Drew Cisco would have cheered. Alan was driven to save the lives of the survivors and to reach Sue as quickly as possible. Surely he could get to her before she started up the rope at the Great Pit. Three hours after leaving Moria, Alan levered himself out of the opening of Fresh Squeezed and began the tortuous crossing of the Breakdown.

Winston regained consciousness and worked to right himself. He struggled angrily to free his hands, and let out a prolonged yell of rage and frustration. Manning was alive...alive and escaping. Winston moved toward the rock wall, yelling once more in pain. He had broken a couple of ribs and every joint in his body ached like hell. Each breath was like being stabbed.

Winston began to catch the woven webbing on different rock projections, until the tearing force both ripped the nylon and served to loosen the knot. He had to get to the emergency rope in the Great Pit before Manning could get to the top.

From two oversized cargo pockets on the outside of his coveralls, Winston pulled a small lighter and a broken piece of candle. They weren't much, but it was all the light Winston needed to reach the Great Pit.

Alan moved forward as quickly as possible, shining his light and yelling out Erica's name. Nearing the pit, he got a response that he could have never imagined.

"Alan! It's Scott!"

"Scott?" Alan hurried forward, clambering and falling over the last of the Breakdown. "Man, it's like you're back from the dead! How did you get here? How come I never saw you?"

"It's a long story. I thought you and Sue were both ahead of me!"

"I had a tussle with Winston and was unconscious for a while at the base of the chimney climb. That's the only time you could have passed me."

Alan turned and looked up the emergency rope, being slowly raised by the winch at the top of the pit. "Erica!" he yelled and then again, separating the syllables. "ER-I-CA!"

He was awarded with a weak voice from above. "Alan! Are you all right?"

"Yes! Keep going. When you reach the top, keep the winch running! Okay?"

"Yes! What about Winston?"

"Stopped cold. We're going to make it!"

Lying in a heap at the bottom of the pit were the rope sections that Winston had cut. Alan began to sort through them, finding the ends. "Scott, help me tie these to the emergency rope. I want to go up after Sue. We'll be back within an hour with rescue people and equipment to get through that wall in Moria."

"I'll come up with you! I can help..."

"No, I want you to stay here and direct the rescue team. And that reminds me!" Alan hit Scott with a powerful right in the jaw that not only floored Scott but took Alan's last reserves. He fell to his knees next to Scott. "Don't you ever pull a stunt like that again! We make decisions together in the Maelstrom. No sneaking off in the night!"

Scott felt his jaw and fell back against the rock floor. "Man, you sure that was just for me?"

"No, that was also the punch I've been saving for your dad for the last fifteen years! Now if I can trust you to stay put, I'm going to get some rest while Sue finishes her ascent." Alan lay back on a rock slab while Scott made sure that the rope paid out smoothly.

A bright winter sun greeted Sue when the rope brought her out of the pit and into the real world again. The snowy woods reflected the cobalt blue of the sky and a breeze rattled trees newly covered with sheaths of ice. Sue lay on the ground, relishing the cold of the snow and the clean air. She had stopped the winch momentarily in order to disengage her equipment and then restarted it for Alan. Ignoring the cold on her damp clothes and skin, Sue sat down in front of the winch on a sun-soaked rock and closed her eyes. She let the warmth of the sun bake into her and begin to dry her clothes, which were steaming in the chill air.

Scott watched as Alan began to glide smoothly upwards, his harness connected to the rope. Scott had insisted that Alan load a daypack with ascenders, webbing, and the 5mm length of perlon rope. "The winch might break down and you'd be stuck," Scott pressed. His attention was fully on Alan when a melon-sized rock caught him full in the ribcage. Scott hit the floor, his breath knocked out of him. Another rock caught him in the face, blood spurting from his broken mouth.

Winston stood over him. He was holding his ribcage with a good arm while the other hung uselessly at his side.

"Picked the wrong team, you little prick!"

"You're nobody I know anymore, Winston. You've gone off the deep end, so just go to hell!"

"Oh, we're all going, buddy. And you know, I quit worrying about that a long time ago. Lights out, baby brother!" Winston hurled yet another rock at Scott's head, catching him just above the ear. Scott's last impression of his brother was a faint blue glow and fingers that could barely grasp a rock anymore.

Alan was two hundred feet above the ground when he saw the headlamp looking up from below. He could hear the unintelligible shouts and knew that it was not Scott's voice, full of hate and violence. There was really nothing that he could do except to let the winch reel him in and hope that Winston couldn't catch up with him. If forced to, Alan would start to use his gear to ascend the rope, but he was so physically exhausted that he knew he couldn't keep it up for long. Better save what strength you've got until you really need it, Alan thought as he stared down at Winston's light. What had Winston done with Scott, he wondered.

For some reason, Winston didn't seem to be coming after him. His light was getting smaller as Alan moved upward. Winston wasn't on the rope, and Alan wasn't sure why. After a few minutes, it hit him. Weight! Winston had done something, perhaps to the anchor system itself, so that the emergency rope wouldn't support two people. What if he had gotten on the rope with Sue? He shuddered at the thought. If he was right, then he had a free ride to the top. Maybe that's what Winston was yelling about. Alan looked around the pit noticing that the cut ends of the descent ropes had come into view. Two hundred feet to the top and he would cut the emergency rope system and leave Winston to wait at the bottom until they could return with help and reinforcements.

Winston was shouting, but in triumph. He knew he had Alan Manning at last. If it occurred to him that his own escape would be blocked, it didn't seem to matter. Winston took the remaining emergency rope and tried to tie it around his waist. But his fingers wouldn't function and his one good arm wasn't sufficient. He let out a scream of rage that sent him into a coughing fit. Winston looped the rope several times around him and slowly turned, until he was almost covered with coils of rope. He jammed the rope through a crack between two boulders and lay down behind them, watching quietly above him.

Alan felt the rope go taut, thinking for a minute that the winch had stopped. He could feel the strain as the elasticity of the rope was taken up by the winch, straining to pull the jammed rope from below. Alan realized what Winston had done. He was putting extra force on the rope. Alan knew that he only had minutes, possibly much less time before the anchors holding the winch gave way. He, the rope, and the winch would go crashing to the bottom of the Great Pit. If only Sue would realize what was happening and turn off the winch.

One hundred and fifty feet above, Sue lay in front of the winch. She had fallen into a deep sleep born from her exhaustion and the release of two day's of mind-numbing fear.

The cut descent ropes hung only a tantalizing fifteen feet away. A time to take chances, Alan reasoned. But be quick about it, damn it. He pulled the 5mm perlon from his daypack and attached a carabiner to one end as a weight. There was no way to get a lariat-type throw with the emergency rope in the way. He swung his body around the rope and used that momentum to aim toward the cut ropes. The first try wasn't even close, but he felt he had the range and the technique. If only he could get a second try. The emergency rope was being stretched so that its diameter was considerably less. Alan's protective Gibbs ascender began to slip.

Another try and the carabiner wrapped around one of the two descent ropes. Alan pulled it toward him gently until he was finally able to reach it. There was only about ten feet of rope to spare below him. Alan took his Gibbs off the emergency rope just as a loud popping sound came from above.

The sound awakened Sue, but at the same time five hundred pounds of winch and coiled rope swept past her, breaking her lower leg cleanly. Sue screamed in pain and terror as she was swept into the mouth of the Maelstrom.

Winston had made himself into a human chock, wedging the rope with his body. As the rope began to tighten and pull against the winch bolts, bones began to break as he was pulled painfully further into the crack. Winston was looking upward, watching and anxiously waiting in expectation of Alan's descent. Any second now! Come on! Come on! Come to papa, Alan fuckin' Manning. Winston felt the rope go slack. His last conscious vision was that of a hurtling juggernaut blocking the opening of the Great Pit.

Alan swung free of the emergency rope, held by the Gibbs ascender that he had literally slammed onto the descent rope. A second later he swung back so close that he could feel the falling winch rush by him. What most disturbed him was the scream that he had heard from above. Alan attached his other ascent gear to the rope and began a laborious climb up the remaining hundred and fifty feet to the top, calling Sue's name. The only reply was silence and the sound of wind rushing over the opening of the Maelstrom.

CHAPTER THIRTY-ONE

As he approached the top of the Great Pit Alan saw Sue hanging about ten feet below the lip. He could tell from the way her head lolled to one side that she was unconscious. But she had remembered what he had told them. Sue had chosen to sit inside the bowl of the pit opening. And she had anchored herself with a safety rope.

Alan reached the top of the pit and hurried over to the rope, where it was anchored securely to a large black locust tree. He set up a pulley and cam system that had been a staple of old-time crevasse and cliff rescues. With it, he was able to pull Sue's rope back over the edge of the pit. She regained consciousness as he was raising her, and was moaning with the pain of her leg.

"Oh, Alan! Thank God. Thank you..."

"Quiet, Sue. You saved yourself. Winston had the winch rigged to come loose. If you hadn't clipped into a safety rope, I would have lost you."

She yelled out in pain as Alan helped her over the edge. "My leg, Alan. The winch broke it. Sweet Jesus, it hurts."

"Listen, I'm going to drag you out of the bowl to level ground. It'll be better for your leg than trying to pick you up."

"What about Winston? How did you get off the rope?"

"Long story. But Winston is trapped down there and he can't do any more harm to the others in the room. I just hope Scott is all right.

They reached the top of the bowl-shaped depression that led to the pit entrance itself. Alan picked Sue up carefully and began to walk down the hill. "I wish you hadn't broken your leg. I was looking forward to rolling in the snow with you."

"We'll roll around later, even if I've got a cast." Sue kissed Alan on the neck as he picked his way down the steep trail.

Five minutes later Alan saw a small group of men climbing toward him. Some were county police and others were carrying their caving gear.

"Hey!" Alan shouted. "We need some help here."

A deputy took Sue from Alan and sat her down on a rock. An EMT began to administer to her while Alan explained what had been happening.

"Dr. Hinneman sent for us. Said there may be some trouble. Three dead," a deputy shook his head. "It's incredible."

Alan started to get up again. "I'm taking Sue down to headquarters and go with her to the hospital. She's got a lot to tell Dr. Hinneman."

"We'll head on up the mountain," the deputy said. "If we don't have any problem with this Winston character, we should have them out by late tonight." He poked one of his officers. "Joe, how about heading down with them. Arrange to get two or three small hydraulic jacks up here. We've got some rock to move. Oh yeah, and food, water, blankets...all that stuff."

The deputy was way off target. It was nine o'clock the next morning before Bob's face, pale and wane from his injury, appeared at the top of the pit in a litter basket. During the night, Alan had installed new secure anchors on a new winch. Sue had insisted that she be there, and several men had taken turns riding her up on their backs. Even Alfred Hinneman had struggled up the slope, using two ski poles to help him along. Everyone cheered at the sight of Bob and finally of Erica Qwan and Hoke. Scott had insisted on waiting until everyone, including his brother's body, was topside before he was hauled up. He looked around him at the covered litter and the injured, and walked a little distance into the woods.

Joe sat between Johnny and Erica Qwan. The shock of their experience was just setting in as the adrenaline ebbed. "All these wasted lives," Joe said. "I didn't do much good, after all!"

"Better than you think, Joe. Those folks have been waiting for you." Erica indicated a large muscular man approaching them, a young boy walking behind him.

"Mr. Riechman, my name's Ronnie Blake. This here's my son Dennis." Dennis lifted one cast in an ineffectual wave, but grinned. "We just wanted to say thanks!"

"Doc Talbot says I'll be fine now, thanks to you. My arms are really gonna heal now!"

Joe could feel his eyes getting full. "That's just great, Dennis. I bet you'll be playing ball by this spring."

Alan walked over to where Alfred Hinneman was sitting on a large boulder. "Alfred, I want to make sure that we're going back in the Maelstrom."

"After what Sue has been saying to me, there is no doubt, Professor. More than that, I am going to start a campaign to fund a research center here. It will be a fitting memorial for our friends.

"Sue and I have a lifetime of work to do here," Alan said as he held out a hand to her.

"We have a lifetime, period," she smiled as she placed Alan's arm around her waist.

The three of them looked across the Maelstrom's opening, where Scott Cisco sat alone, staring out across the Kentucky foothills.

"And young Scott?" Alfred asked. "I wonder what kind of lifetime he will be having?"

"He'll be fine. He's strong and loves life like his father did. I'm asking him to take a little time off from school and join us for the next expedition. You know, like getting back on the horse once you've fallen."

Alfred turned to start down the mountain. "We are all being thrown after hard rides, Professor. Life is about getting on board again...otherwise, you are just laying in the dust. We grieve our team mates, and then we start planning the next Maelstrom Expedition."

AUTHOR'S NOTE

The wilderness areas of the world are full of wonderful experiences for those who are prepared and willing to expend time and energy. Information on the Copper Creek trailhead, Simpson Meadows, and Tehipite Valley can be had from the Park Superintendent's Office at Kings Canyon National Park.

As for the indescribably beautiful world of caves, be sure to connect with experienced spelunkers before heading underground. Contact the NSS in Huntsville, Alabama or at caves.org for the location of a grotto near you, where you will find many wonderful people eager to share their love of caves.

ABOUT THE AUTHOR

David Cone is a native North Carolinian and graduated from Cornell University in Natural History Education. After a three-year hitch in the Marine Corps during Nam, he returned to the wilderness as a guide and teacher. For years, Mr. Cone taught mountaineering, whitewater skills, cross-country skiing, and spelunking. He led trips through the mountains of California, Washington State, and Alaska until returning to North Carolina as a museum curator and secondary school science teacher. For more than twenty years, he has written newspaper columns on outdoor and natural history topics.

David Cone's love for the wilderness can be seen in his adventure/mysteries. His novels feature varied outdoor locales which, he points out, can be visited by any interested backpacker.

Printed in the United States
55266LVS00001B/34

9 781420 81368